Happy Birthday
Doll face !!
I love you, my
mini. Sookie

All my love,
Mumma

FROM DEAD TO WORSE

FROM DEAD TO WORSE

Charlaine Harris

ACE BOOKS, NEW YORK

THE BERKLEY PUBLISHING GROUP
Published by the Penguin Group
Penguin Group (USA) Inc.
375 Hudson Street, New York, New York 10014, USA
Penguin Group (Canada), 90 Eglinton Avenue East, Suite 700, Toronto, Ontario M4P 2Y3, Canada
(a division of Pearson Penguin Canada Inc.)
Penguin Books Ltd., 80 Strand, London WC2R 0RL, England
Penguin Group Ireland, 25 St. Stephen's Green, Dublin 2, Ireland (a division of Penguin Books Ltd.)
Penguin Group (Australia), 250 Camberwell Road, Camberwell, Victoria 3124, Australia
(a division of Pearson Australia Group Pty. Ltd.)
Penguin Books India Pvt. Ltd., 11 Community Centre, Panchsheel Park, New Delhi—110 017, India
Penguin Group (NZ), 67 Apollo Drive, Rosedale, North Shore 0632, New Zealand
(a division of Pearson New Zealand Ltd.)
Penguin Books (South Africa) (Pty.) Ltd., 24 Sturdee Avenue, Rosebank, Johannesburg 2196, South Africa

Penguin Books Ltd., Registered Offices: 80 Strand, London WC2R 0RL, England

This is an original publication of The Berkley Publishing Group.

This is a work of fiction. Names, characters, places, and incidents either are the product of the author's imagination or are used fictitiously, and any resemblance to actual persons, living or dead, business establishments, events, or locales is entirely coincidental. The publisher does not have any control over and does not assume any responsibility for author or third-party websites or their content.

First edition: May 2008

Library of Congress Cataloging-in-Publication Data

Harris, Charlaine.
  From dead to worse / Charlaine Harris.—1st ed.
    p. cm.
  ISBN 978-0-441-01589-4
  1. Vampires—Fiction.   2. Supernatural—Fiction.   3. Louisiana—Fiction.   I. Title.
  PS3558.A6427F76 2008
  813'.54—dc22

                                                                    2008002396

PRINTED IN THE UNITED STATES OF AMERICA

10   9   8

Though she can't walk or see quite as well as she used to, my mother, Jean Harris, remains the most complete person I have ever met. She's been the bulwark of my existence, the foundation I was built on, and the best mother a woman could have.

ACKNOWLEDGMENTS

A tip of the hat to Anastasia Luettecke, who was a perfectionist in supplying me with Octavia's Latin. And thanks to Murv Sellars for being the go-between. As always, I owe a great debt of thanks to Toni L. P. Kelner and Dana Cameron for their valuable comments and the gift of their time. My one and only minion, Debi Murray, assisted me with her ency-clopedic knowledge of the Sookie universe. The group of enthusiastic readers known as Charlaine's Charlatans gave me moral (and morale) support, and I hope this book will serve as their reward.

If this was The Lord of the Rings *and I had a smart British* voice like Cate Blanchett, I could tell you the background of the events of that fall in a really suspenseful way. And you'd be straining to hear the rest.

But what happened in my little corner of northwest Louisiana wasn't an epic story. The vampire war was more of the nature of a small-country takeover, and the Were war was like a border skirmish. Even in the annals of supernatural America—I guess they exist somewhere—they were minor chapters...unless you were actively involved in the takeovers and skirmishes.

Then they became pretty damn major.

And everything was due to Katrina, the disaster that just kept on spreading grief, woe, and permanent change in its wake.

Before Hurricane Katrina, Louisiana had a flourishing vampire community. In fact, the vampire population of New Orleans had burgeoned, making it the place to go if you wanted to see vampires; and lots of Americans did. The undead jazz clubs, featuring musicians no one had seen playing in public in decades, were special draws. Vamp strip clubs, vamp psychics, vamp sex acts; secret and not-so-secret places where you could get bitten and have an orgasm on the spot: all this was available in southern Louisiana.

In the northern part of the state . . . not so much. I live in the northern part in a small town called Bon Temps. But even in my area, where vamps are relatively thin on the ground, the undead were making economic and social strides.

All in all, vampire business in the Pelican State was booming. But then came the death of the King of Arkansas while his wife, the Queen of Louisiana, was entertaining him soon after their wedding. Since the corpse vanished and all the witnesses—except me—were supernaturals, human law took no notice. But the other vampires did, and the queen, Sophie-Anne Leclerq, landed in a very dicey legal position. Then came Katrina, which wiped out the financial base of Sophie-Anne's empire. Still, the queen was floundering back from those disasters, when another one followed hard on their heels. Sophie-Anne and some of her strongest adherents—and me, Sookie Stackhouse, telepath and human—were caught in a terrible explosion in Rhodes, the destruction of the vampire hotel called the Pyramid of Gizeh. A splinter group of the Fellowship of the Sun claimed responsibility, and while the leaders of that anti-vampire "church" decried the hate crime, everyone knew that the Fellowship was hardly agonizing over those who were terribly wounded in the blast, much less over the (finally, absolutely) dead vampires or the humans who served them.

Sophie-Anne lost her legs, several members of her entourage, and her dearest companion. Her life was saved by her half-demon lawyer, Mr. Cataliades. But her recuperation time was going to be lengthy, and she was in a position of terrible vulnerability.

What part did I play in all this?

I'd helped save lives after the pyramid went down, and I was terrified I was now on the radar of people who might want me to spend my time in their service, using my telepathy for their purposes. Some of those purposes were good, and I wouldn't mind lending a hand in rescue services from time to time, but I wanted to keep my life to myself. I was alive; my boyfriend, Quinn, was alive; and the vampires most important to me had survived, too. As far as the troubles Sophie-Anne faced, the political consequences of the attack and the fact that supernatural groups were circling the weakened state of Louisiana like hyenas around a dying gazelle...I didn't think about it at all.

I had other stuff on my mind, personal stuff. I'm not used to thinking much further than the end of my fingertips; that's my only excuse. Not only was I not thinking about the vampire situation, there was another supernatural situation I didn't ponder that turned out to be just as crucial to my future.

Close to Bon Temps, in Shreveport, there's a Were pack whose ranks are swollen by the men and women from Barksdale Air Force Base. During the past year, this Were pack had become sharply divided between two factions. I'd learned in American History what Abraham Lincoln, quoting the Bible, had to say about houses divided.

To assume that these two situations would work themselves out, to fail to foresee that their resolution would involve me, well . . . that was where I was almost fatally blind. I'm telepathic, not psychic. Vampire minds are big relaxing blanks to me. Weres are difficult to read, though not impossible. That's my only excuse for being unaware of the trouble brewing all around me.

What was I so busy thinking about? Weddings—and my missing boyfriend.

Chapter 1

I was making a neat arrangement of liquor bottles on the folding table behind the portable bar when Halleigh Robinson rushed up, her normally sweet face flushed and tear-streaked. Since she was supposed to be getting married within an hour and was still wearing blue jeans and a T-shirt, she got my immediate attention.

"Sookie!" she said, rounding the bar to grab my arm. "You have to help me."

I'd already helped her by putting on my bartending clothes instead of the pretty dress I'd planned on wearing. "Sure," I said, imagining Halleigh wanted me to make her a special drink—though if I'd listened in to her thoughts, I'd have known differently already. However, I was trying to be on my best behavior, and I was shielding like crazy. Being telepathic is no picnic, especially at a high-tension event like a double wedding. I'd expected to be a guest instead of a bartender. But the caterer's bartender had been in a car wreck on her way over from Shreveport, and Sam, who'd been unhired when E(E)E had insisted on using their own bartender, was abruptly hired again.

I was a little disappointed to be on the working side of the bar, but you had to oblige the bride on her special day. "What can I do for you?" I asked.

"I need you to be my bridesmaid," she said.

"Ah . . . what?"

"Tiffany fainted after Mr. Cumberland took the first round of pictures. She's on her way to the hospital."

It was an hour before the wedding, and the photographer had been trying to get a number of group shots out of the way. The bridesmaids and the groomsmen were already togged out. Halleigh should have been getting into her wedding finery, but instead here she was in jeans and curlers, no makeup, and a tear-streaked face.

Who could resist that?

"You're the right size," she said. "And Tiffany is probably just about to have her appendix out. So, can you try on the dress?"

I glanced at Sam, my boss.

Sam smiled at me and nodded. "Go on, Sook. We don't officially open for business until after the wedding."

So I followed Halleigh into Belle Rive, the Bellefleur mansion, recently restored to something like its antebellum glory. The wooden floors gleamed, the harp by the stairs shone with gilt, the silverware displayed on the big sideboard in the dining room glowed with polishing. There were servers in white coats buzzing around everywhere, the E(E)E logo on their tunics done in an elaborate black script. Extreme(ly Elegant) Events had become the premier upscale caterer in the United States. I felt a stab in my heart when I noticed the logo, because my missing guy worked for the supernatural branch of E(E)E. I didn't have long to feel the ache, though, because Halleigh was dragging me up the stairs at a relentless pace.

The first bedroom at the top was full of youngish women in gold-colored dresses, all fussing around Halleigh's soon-to-be sister-in-law, Portia Bellefleur. Halleigh zoomed past that door to enter the second room on the left. It was equally full of younger women, but these were in midnight blue chiffon. The room was in chaos, with the bridesmaids' civilian clothes piled here and there. There was a makeup and hair station over by the west wall, staffed by a stoic woman in a pink smock, curling rod in her hand.

Halleigh tossed introductions through the air like paper pellets. "Gals, this is Sookie Stackhouse. Sookie, this is my sister Fay, my cousin Kelly, my best friend Sarah, my other best friend Dana. And here's the dress. It's an eight."

I was amazed that Halleigh had had the presence of mind to divest Tiffany of the bridesmaid dress before her departure for the hospital. Brides are ruthless. In a matter of minutes, I was stripped down to the essentials. I was glad I'd worn nice underwear, since there wasn't any time for modesty. How embarrassing it would have been to be in granny panties with holes! The dress was lined, so I didn't need a slip, another stroke of luck.

There was a spare pair of thigh-highs, which I pulled on, and then the dress went over my head. Sometimes I wear a ten—in fact, most of the time—so I was holding my breath while Fay zipped it up.

If I didn't breathe a lot, it would be okay.

"Super!" one of the other women (Dana?) said with great happiness. "Now the shoes."

"Oh, God," I said when I saw them. They were very high heels dyed to match the midnight blue dress, and I slid my feet into them, anticipating pain. Kelly (maybe) buckled the straps, and I stood up. All of us held our breath as I took a step, then another. They were about half a size too small. It was an important half.

"I can get through the wedding," I said, and they all clapped.

"Over here then," said Pink Smock, and I sat in her chair and had more makeup reapplied over my own and my hair redone while the real bridesmaids and Halleigh's mother assisted Halleigh into her dress. Pink Smock had a lot of hair to work with. I've only had light trims in the past three years, I guess, and it's way down past my shoulder blades now. My roommate, Amelia, had put some highlights in, and that had turned out real good. I was blonder than ever.

I examined myself in the full-length mirror, and it seemed impossible I could have been so transformed in twenty minutes. From working barmaid in a white ruffled tux shirt and black trousers to bridesmaid in a midnight blue dress—and three inches taller, to boot.

Hey, I looked *great*. The dress was a super color for me, the skirt was gently A-line, the short sleeves weren't too tight, and it wasn't low cut enough to look slutty. With my boobs, the slut factor kicks in if I'm not careful.

I was yanked out of self-admiration by the practical Dana, who said, "Listen, here's the drill." From that moment on, I listened and nodded. I examined a little diagram. I nodded some more. Dana was one organized gal. If I ever invaded a small country, this was the woman I wanted on my side.

By the time we made our way carefully down the stairs (long skirts and high heels, not a good combination), I was fully briefed and ready for my first trip down the aisle as a bridesmaid.

Most girls have done this a couple of times before they reach twenty-six, but Tara Thornton, the only friend I had close enough to ask me, had up and eloped while I was out of town.

The other wedding party was assembled downstairs when we descended. Portia's group would precede Halleigh's. The two grooms and their groomsmen were already outside if all was going smoothly, because now it was five minutes until liftoff.

Portia Bellefleur and her bridesmaids averaged seven years older than Halleigh's posse. Portia was the big sister of Andy Bellefleur, Bon Temps police detective and Halleigh's groom. Portia's dress was a little over-the-top—it was covered with pearls and so much lace and sequins I thought it could stand by itself—but then, it was Portia's big day and she could wear whatever she damn well pleased. All Portia's bridesmaids were wearing gold.

The bridesmaids' bouquets all matched—white and dark

blue and yellow. Coordinated with the dark blue of Halleigh's bridesmaid selection, the result was very pretty.

The wedding planner, a thin nervous woman with a big cloud of dark curly hair, counted heads almost audibly. When she was satisfied everyone she needed was present and accounted for, she flung open the double doors to the huge brick patio. We could see the crowd, backs to us, seated on the lawn in two sections of white folding chairs, with a strip of red carpet running between the two sides. They were facing the platform where the priest stood at an altar decked in cloth and gleaming candlesticks. To the right of the priest, Portia's groom, Glen Vick, was waiting, facing the house. And, therefore, us. He looked very, very nervous, but he was smiling. His groomsmen were already in position flanking him.

Portia's golden bridesmaids stepped out onto the patio, and one by one they began their march down the aisle through the manicured garden. The scent of wedding flowers made the night sweet. And the Belle Rive roses were blooming, even in October.

Finally, to a huge swell of music, Portia crossed the patio to the end of the carpet, the wedding coordinator (with some effort) lifting the train of Portia's dress so it wouldn't drag on the bricks.

At the priest's nod, everyone stood and faced the rear so they could see Portia's triumphal march. She'd waited years for this.

After Portia's safe arrival at the altar, it was our party's turn. Halleigh gave each one of us an air kiss on the cheek as we stepped past her out onto the patio. She even included me, which was sweet of her. The wedding coordinator sent us off one by one, to stand reflecting our designated groomsman up front. Mine was a Bellefleur cousin from Monroe who was quite startled to see me coming instead of Tiffany. I walked at the slow pace Dana had emphasized and held my bouquet in my clasped hands at the desired angle. I'd been watching the other maids like a hawk. I wanted to get this right.

All the faces were turned to me, and I was so nervous I forgot to block. The thoughts of the crowd rushed at me in a gush of unwanted communication. *Looks so pretty... What happened to Tiffany...? Wow, what a rack.... Hurry it up, I need a drink.... What the hell am I doing here? She drags me to every dog fight in the parish.... I love wedding cake.*

A photographer stepped in front of me and took a picture. It was someone I knew, a pretty werewolf named Maria-Star Cooper. She was the assistant of Al Cumberland, a well-known photographer based in Shreveport. I smiled at Maria-Star and she took another shot. I continued down the carpet, held on to my smile, and pushed away all the racket in my head.

After a moment I noticed there were blank spots in the crowd, which signaled the presence of vampires. Glen had requested a night wedding specifically so he could invite some of his more important vampire clients. I'd been sure Portia truly loved him when she agreed to that, because Portia didn't like bloodsuckers at all. In fact, they gave her the creeps.

I kind of liked vampires in general, because their brains were closed to me. Being in their company was oddly restful. Okay, a strain in other ways, but at least my brain could relax.

Finally, I arrived at my designated spot. I'd watched Portia and Glen's attendants arrange themselves in an inverted V, with a space at the front for the nuptial couple. Our group was doing the same thing. I'd nailed it, and I exhaled in relief. Since I wasn't taking the place of the maid of honor, my work was over. All I had to do was stand still and look attentive, and I thought I could do that.

The music swelled to a second crescendo, and the priest gave his signal again. The crowd rose and turned to look at the second bride. Halleigh began moving slowly toward us. She looked absolutely radiant. Halleigh had selected a much simpler dress than Portia's, and she looked very young and very sweet. She was at least five years younger than Andy, maybe more. Halleigh's dad, as tanned and fit as his wife, stepped out to take Halleigh's arm when she drew abreast; since Portia had come down the aisle alone (her father was long dead), it had been decided Halleigh would, too.

After I'd had my fill of Halleigh's smile, I looked over the crowd who'd rotated to follow the bride's progress.

There were so many familiar faces: teachers from the elementary school where Halleigh taught, members of the police department where Andy worked, the friends of old Mrs. Caroline Bellefleur who were still alive and tottering, Portia's fellow lawyers and other people who worked in the justice system, and Glen Vick's clients and other accountants. Almost every chair was occupied.

There were a few black faces to be seen, and a few brown faces, but most of the wedding guests were middle-class

Caucasians. The palest faces in the crowd were the vampires', of course. One of them I knew well. Bill Compton, my neighbor and former lover, was sitting about halfway back, wearing a tuxedo and looking very handsome. Bill managed to seem at home in whatever he chose to wear. Beside him sat his human girlfriend, Selah Pumphrey, a real estate agent from Clarice. She was wearing a burgundy gown that set off her dark hair. There were perhaps five vamps I didn't recognize. I assumed they were clients of Glen's. Though Glen didn't know it, there were several other attendees who were more (and less) than human.

My boss, Sam, was a rare true shapeshifter who could become any animal. The photographer was a werewolf like his assistant. To all the regular wedding guests, he looked like a well-rounded, rather short African-American male wearing a nice suit and carrying a big camera. But Al turned into a wolf at the full moon just like Maria-Star. There were a few other Weres in the crowd, though only one I knew—Amanda, a red-haired woman in her late thirties who owned a bar in Shreveport called the Hair of the Dog. Maybe Glen's firm handled the bar's books.

And there was one werepanther, Calvin Norris. Calvin had brought a date, I was glad to see, though I was less than thrilled after I identified her as Tanya Grissom. Blech. What was she doing back in town? And why had Calvin been on the guest list? I liked him, but I couldn't figure out the connection.

While I'd been scanning the crowd for familiar faces, Halleigh had assumed her position by Andy, and now all the bridesmaids and groomsmen had to face forward to listen to the service.

Since I didn't have a big emotional investment in this proceeding, I found myself mentally wandering while Father Kempton Littrell, the Episcopal priest who ordinarily came to the little Bon Temps church once every two weeks, conducted the service. The lights that had been set up to illuminate the garden glinted off Father Littrell's glasses and bleached some of the color out of his face. He looked almost like a vampire.

Things proceeded pretty much on the standard plan. Boy, it was lucky I was used to standing up at the bar, because this was a lot of standing, and in high heels, too. I seldom wore heels, much less three-inch ones. It felt strange being five foot nine. I tried not to shift around, possessed my soul with patience.

Now Glen was putting the ring on Portia's finger, and Portia looked almost pretty as she looked down at their clasped hands. She'd never be one of my favorite people—nor I hers—but I wished her well. Glen was bony and had darkish receding hair and major glasses. If you called central casting and ordered an "accountant type," they'd send you Glen. But I could tell directly from his brain that he loved Portia, and she loved him.

I let myself shift a bit, put my weight a little more on my right leg.

Then Father Littrell started all over again on Halleigh and Andy. I kept my smile pasted to my face (no problem there; I did it all the time at the bar) and watched Halleigh become Mrs. Andrew Bellefleur. I was lucky. Episcopalian weddings can be long, but the two couples had opted for having the shorter form of the service.

At last the music swelled to triumphant strains, and the newlyweds exited to the house. The wedding party trailed after them in reverse order. On my way down the aisle, I felt genuinely happy and a weensy bit proud. I'd helped Halleigh in her time of need . . . and very soon I was going to get to take these shoes off.

From his chair, Bill caught my eye and silently put his hand over his heart. It was a romantic and totally unexpected gesture, and for a moment I softened toward him. I very nearly smiled, though Selah was right there by his side. Just in time, I reminded myself that Bill was a no-good rat bastard, and I swept on my painful way. Sam was standing a couple of yards past the last row of chairs, wearing a white tux shirt like the one I'd had on and black dress pants. Relaxed and at ease, that was Sam. Even his tangled halo of strawberry blond hair somehow fit in.

I flashed him a genuine smile, and he grinned back. He gave me a thumbs-up, and though shifter brains are hard to read, I could tell he approved of the way I looked and the way I'd conducted myself. His bright blue eyes never left me. He's been my boss for five years, and we've gotten along great for the most part. He'd been pretty upset when I'd started dating a vampire, but he'd gotten over it.

I needed to get to work, and pronto. I caught up with Dana. "When can we change?" I asked.

"Oh, we have pictures to do yet," Dana said cheerfully. Her

husband had come up to put his arm around her. He was holding their baby, a tiny thing swaddled in sex-neutral yellow.

"Surely I won't be needed for those," I said. "You-all took a lot of pictures earlier, right? Before what's-her-name got sick."

"Tiffany. Yes, but there'll be more."

I seriously doubted the family would want me in them, though my absence would unbalance the symmetry in the group pictures. I found Al Cumberland.

"Yes," he said, snapping away at the brides and grooms as they beamed at each other. "I do need some shots. You got to stay in costume."

"Crap," I said, because my feet hurt.

"Listen, Sookie, the best I can do is to shoot your group first. Andy, Halleigh! That is . . . Mrs. Bellefleur! If you-all will come this way, let's get your pictures done."

Portia Bellefleur Vick looked a little astonished that her group wasn't going first, but she had way too many people to greet to really get riled. While Maria-Star snapped away at the touching scene, a distant relative wheeled old Miss Caroline up to Portia, and Portia bent to kiss her grandmother. Portia and Andy had lived with Miss Caroline for years, after their own parents had passed away. Miss Caroline's poor health had delayed the weddings at least twice. The original plan had been for last spring, and it had been a rush job because Miss Caroline was failing. She'd had a heart attack and then recovered. After that, she'd broken her hip. I had to say, for someone who'd survived two major health disasters, Miss Caroline looked . . . Well, to tell the truth, she looked just like a very old lady who'd had a heart attack and a broken hip. She was all dressed up in a beige silk suit. She even had on some makeup, and her snow-white hair was arranged à la Lauren Bacall. She'd been a beauty in her day, an autocrat her entire life, and a famous cook until the recent past.

Caroline Bellefleur was in her seventh heaven this night. She'd married off both her grandchildren, she was getting plenty of tribute, and Belle Rive was looking spectacular, thanks to the vampire who was staring at her with an absolutely unreadable face.

Bill Compton had discovered he was the Bellefleurs' ancestor, and he had anonymously given Miss Caroline a whacking big bunch of money. She'd enjoyed spending it so much, and she had had no idea it had come from a vampire. She'd thought it a legacy from a distant relative. I thought it was kind of ironic that the Bellefleurs would just as soon have spit on Bill as thanked him. But he was part of the family, and I was glad he'd found a way to attend.

I took a deep breath, banished Bill's dark gaze from my consciousness, and smiled at the camera. I occupied my designated space in the pictures to balance out the wedding party, dodged the googly-eyed cousin, and finally hotfooted it up the stairs to change into my bartender's rig.

There was no one up here, and it was a relief to be in the room by myself.

I shimmied out of the dress, hung it up, and sat on a stool to unbuckle the straps of the painful shoes.

There was a little sound at the door, and I looked up,

startled. Bill was standing just inside the room, his hands in his pockets, his skin glowing gently. His fangs were out.

"Trying to change here," I said tartly. No point in making a big show of modesty. He'd seen every inch of me.

"You didn't tell them," he said.

"Huh?" Then my brain caught up. Bill meant that I hadn't told the Bellefleurs that he was their ancestor. "No, of course not," I said. "You asked me not to."

"I thought, in your anger, you might give them the information."

I gave him an incredulous look. "No, some of us actually have honor," I said. He looked away for a minute. "By the way, your face healed real well."

During the Fellowship of the Sun bombing in Rhodes, Bill's face had been exposed to the sun with really stomach-churning results.

"I slept for six days," he said. "When I finally got up, it was mostly healed. And as for your dig about my failing in honor, I haven't any defense . . . except that when Sophie-Anne told me to pursue you . . . I was reluctant, Sookie. At first, I didn't want to even pretend to have a permanent relationship with a human woman. I thought it degraded me. I only came into the bar to identify you when I couldn't put it off any longer. And that evening didn't turn out like I'd planned. I went outside with the drainers, and things happened. When you were the one who came to my aid, I decided it was fate. I did what I had been told to do by my queen. In so doing, I fell into a trap I couldn't escape. I still can't."

The trap of LUUUUVVVV, I thought sarcastically. But he was too serious, too calm, to mock. I was simply defending my own heart with the weapon of bitchiness.

"You got you a girlfriend," I said. "You go on back to Selah." I looked down to make sure I'd gotten the little strap on the second sandal unlatched. I worked the shoe off. When I glanced back up, Bill's dark eyes were fixed on me.

"I would give anything to lie with you again," he said.

I froze, my hands in the act of rolling the thigh-high hose off my left leg.

Okay, that pretty much stunned me on several different levels. First, the biblical "lie with." Second, my astonishment that he considered me such a memorable bed partner.

Maybe he only remembered the virgins.

"I don't want to fool with you tonight, and Sam's waiting on me down there to help him tend bar," I said roughly. "You go on." I stood and turned my back to him while I pulled on my pants and my shirt, tucking the shirt in. Then it was time for the black running shoes. After a quick check in the mirror to make sure I still had on some lipstick, I faced the doorway.

He was gone.

I went down the wide stairs and out the patio doors into the garden, relieved to be resuming my more accustomed place behind a bar. My feet still hurt. So did the sore spot in my heart labeled Bill Compton.

Sam gave me a smiling glance as I scurried into place. Miss Caroline had vetoed our request to leave a tip jar out, but bar patrons had already stuffed a few bills into an empty highball glass, and I intended to let that stay in position.

"You looked real pretty in the dress," Sam said as he mixed a rum and Coke. I handed a beer across the bar and smiled at the older man who'd come to fetch it. He gave me a huge tip, and I glanced down to see that in my hurry to get downstairs I'd skipped a button. I was showing a little extra cleavage. I was momentarily embarrassed, but it wasn't a slutty button, just a "Hey, I've got boobs" button. So I let it be.

"Thanks," I said, hoping Sam hadn't noticed this quick evaluation. "I hope I did everything right."

"Of course you did," Sam said, as if the possibility of me blowing my new role had never crossed his mind. This is why he's the greatest boss I've ever had.

"Well, good evening," said a slightly nasal voice, and I looked up from the wine I was pouring to see that Tanya Grissom was taking up space and breathing air that could be better used by almost anyone else. Her escort, Calvin, was nowhere in sight.

"Hey, Tanya," Sam said. "How you doing? It's been a while."

"Well, I had to tie up some loose ends in Mississippi," Tanya said. "But I'm back here visiting, and I wondered if you needed any part-time help, Sam."

I pressed my mouth shut and kept my hands busy. Tanya stepped to the side nearest Sam when an elderly lady asked me for some tonic water with a wedge of lime. I handed it to her so quickly she looked astonished, and then I took care of Sam's next customer. I could hear from Sam's brain that he was pleased to see Tanya. Men can be idiots, right? To be fair, I did know some things about her that Sam didn't.

Selah Pumphrey was next in line, and I could only be amazed at my luck. However, Bill's girlfriend just asked for a rum and Coke.

"Sure," I said, trying not to sound relieved, and began putting the drink together.

"I heard him," Selah said very quietly.

"Heard who?" I asked, distracted by my effort to listen to what Tanya and Sam were saying—either with my ears or with my brain.

"I heard Bill when he was talking to you earlier." When I didn't speak, she continued, "I snuck up the stairs after him."

"Then he knows you were there," I said absently, and handed her the drink. Her eyes flared wide at me for a second—alarmed, angry? She stalked off. If wishes could kill, I would be lifeless on the ground.

Tanya began to turn away from Sam as if her body was thinking of leaving, but her head was still talking to my boss. Finally, her whole self went back to her date. I looked after her, thinking dark thoughts.

"Well, that's good news," Sam said with a smile. "Tanya's available for a while."

I bit back my urge to tell him that Tanya had made it quite clear she was available. "Oh, yeah, great," I said. There were so many people I liked. Why were two of the women I really didn't care for at this wedding tonight? Well, at least my feet were practically whimpering with pleasure at getting out of the too-small heels.

I smiled and made drinks and cleared away empty bottles and went to Sam's truck to unload more stock. I opened beers and poured wine and mopped up spills until I felt like a perpetual-motion machine.

The vampire clients arrived at the bar in a cluster. I uncorked one bottle of Royalty Blended, a premium blend of synthetic blood and the real blood of actual European royalty. It had to be refrigerated, of course, and it was a very special treat for Glen's clients, a treat he'd personally arranged. (The only vampire drink that exceeded Royalty Blended in price was the nearly pure Royalty, which contained only a trace of preservatives.) Sam lined up the wineglasses. Then he told me to pour it out. I was extraspecial careful not to spill a drop. Sam handed each glass to its recipient. The vampires, including Bill, all tipped very heavily, big smiles on their faces as they lifted their glasses in a toast to the newlyweds.

After a sip of the dark fluid in the wineglasses, their fangs ran out to prove their enjoyment. Some of the human guests looked a smidge uneasy at this expression of appreciation, but Glen was right there smiling and nodding. He knew enough about vampires not to offer to shake hands. I noticed the new Mrs. Vick was not hobnobbing with the undead guests, though she made one pass through the cluster with a strained smile fixed on her face.

When one of the vampires came back for a glass of ordinary TrueBlood, I handed him the warm drink. "Thank you," he said, tipping me yet again. While he had his billfold open, I saw a Nevada driver's license. I'm familiar with a wide variety of licenses from carding kids at the bar; he'd come far for this wedding. I really looked at him for the first time. When he knew he'd caught my attention, he put his hands together and bowed slightly. Since I'd been reading a mystery set in Thailand, I knew this was a *wai*, a courteous greeting practiced by Buddhists—or maybe just Thai people in general? Anyway, he meant to be polite. After a brief hesitation, I put down the rag in my hand and copied his movement. The vampire looked pleased.

"I call myself Jonathan," he said. "Americans can't pronounce my real name."

There might have been a touch of arrogance and contempt there, but I couldn't blame him.

"I'm Sookie Stackhouse," I said.

Jonathan was a smallish man, maybe five foot eight, with the light copper coloring and dusky black hair of his country. He was really handsome. His nose was small and broad, his lips plump. His brown eyes were topped with absolutely straight black brows. His skin was so fine I couldn't detect any pores. He had that little shine vampires have.

"This is your husband?" he asked, picking up his glass of blood and tilting his head in Sam's direction. Sam was busy mixing a piña colada for one of the bridesmaids.

"No, sir, he's my boss."

Just then, Terry Bellefleur, second cousin to Portia and Andy, lurched up to ask for another beer. I was real fond of

Terry, but he was a bad drunk, and I thought he was well on his way to achieving that condition. Though the Vietnam vet wanted to stand and talk about the president's policy on the current war, I walked him over to another family member, a distant cousin from Baton Rouge, and made sure the man was going to keep an eye on Terry and prevent him from driving off in his pickup.

The vampire Jonathan was keeping an eye on *me* while I did this, and I wasn't sure why. But I didn't observe anything aggressive or lustful in his stance or demeanor, and his fangs were in. It seemed safe to disregard him and take care of business. If there was some reason Jonathan wanted to talk to me, I'd find out about it sooner or later. Later was fine.

As I fetched a case of Cokes from Sam's truck, my attention was caught by a man standing alone in the shadows cast by the big live oak on the west side of the lawn. He was tall, slim, and impeccably dressed in a suit that was obviously very expensive. The man stepped forward a little and I could see his face, could realize he was returning my gaze. My first impression was that he was a lovely creature and not a man at all. Whatever he was, human wasn't part of it. Though he had some age on him, he was extremely handsome, and his hair, still pale gold, was as long as mine. He wore it pulled back neatly. He was slightly withered, like a delicious apple that had been in the crisper too long, but his back was absolutely straight and he wore no glasses. He did carry a cane, a very simple black one with a gold head.

When he stepped out of the shadows, the vampires turned

as a group to look. After a moment they slightly inclined their heads. He returned the acknowledgment. They kept their distance, as if he was dangerous or awesome.

This episode was very strange, but I didn't have time to think about it. Everyone wanted one last free drink. The reception was winding down, and people were filtering to the front of the house for the leave-taking of the happy couples. Halleigh and Portia had disappeared upstairs to change into their going-away outfits. The E(E)E staff had been vigilant about clearing up empty cups and the little plates that had held cake and finger food, so the garden looked relatively neat.

Now that we weren't busy, Sam let me know he had something on his mind. "Sookie, am I getting the wrong idea, or do you dislike Tanya?"

"I do have something against Tanya," I said. "I'm just not sure I should tell you about it. You clearly like her." You'd think I'd been sampling the bourbon. Or truth serum.

"If you don't like to work with her, I want to hear the reason," he said. "You're my friend. I respect your opinion."

This was very pleasant to hear.

"Tanya is pretty," I said. "She's bright and able." Those were the good things.

"And?"

"And she came here as a spy," I said. "The Pelts sent her, trying to find out if I had anything to do with the disappearance of their daughter Debbie. You remember when they came to the bar?"

"Yes," said Sam. In the illumination that had been strung

up all around the garden, he looked both brightly lit and darkly shadowed. "You did have something to do with it?"

"Everything," I said sadly. "But it was self-defense."

"I know it must have been." He'd taken my hand. My own jerked in surprise. "I know you," he said, and didn't let go.

Sam's faith made me feel a little warm glow inside. I'd worked for Sam a long time now, and his good opinion meant a lot to me. I felt almost choked up, and I had to clear my throat. "So, I wasn't happy to see Tanya," I continued. "I didn't trust her from the start, and when I found out why she'd come to Bon Temps, I got really down on her. I don't know if she still gets paid by the Pelts. Plus, tonight she's here with Calvin, and she's got no business hitting on you." My tone was a lot angrier than I'd intended.

"Oh." Sam looked disconcerted.

"But if you want to go out with her, go ahead," I said, trying to lighten up. "I mean—she can't be all bad. And I guess she thought she was doing the right thing, coming to help find information on a missing shifter." That sounded pretty good and might even be the truth. "I don't have to like who you date," I added, just to make it clear I understood I had no claim on him.

"Yeah, but I feel better if you do," he said.

"Same here," I agreed, to my own surprise.

Chapter 2

We began packing up in a quiet and unobtrusive way, since there were still lingering guests.

"As along as we're talking about dates, what happened to Quinn?" he asked as we worked. "You've been moping ever since you got back from Rhodes."

"Well, I told you he got hurt pretty bad in the bombing." Quinn's branch of E(E)E staged special events for the supe community: vampire hierarchal weddings, Were coming of age parties, packleader contests, and the like. That was why Quinn had been in the Pyramid of Gizeh when the Fellowship did its dirty deed.

The FotS people were anti-vampire, but they had no idea that vampires were just the visible, public tip of the iceberg in the supernatural world. No one knew this; or at least only a few people like me, though more and more were in on the big secret. I was sure the Fellowship fanatics would hate were-wolves or shapeshifters like Sam just as much as they hated vampires . . . if they knew they existed. That time might come soon.

"Yeah, but I would have thought . . ."

"I know, I would have thought Quinn and I were all set, too," I said, and if my voice was dreary, well, thinking about my missing weretiger made me feel that way. "I kept thinking I'd hear from him. But not a word."

"You still got his sister's car?" Frannie Quinn had loaned me her car so I could get home after the Rhodes disaster.

"No, it vanished one night when Amelia and I were both at work. I called and left a voice mail on his cell to say it had been taken, but I never heard back."

"Sookie, I'm sorry," Sam said. He knew that was inadequate, but what could he say?

"Yeah, me, too," I said, trying not to sound too depressed. It was an effort to keep from retreading tired mental ground. I knew Quinn didn't blame me in any way for his injuries. I'd seen him in the hospital in Rhodes before I'd left, and he'd been in the care of his sister, Fran, who didn't seem to hate me at that point. No blame, no hate—why no communication?

It was like the ground had opened to swallow him up. I threw up my hands and tried to think of something else. Keeping busy was the best remedy when I was worried. We began to shift some of our things to Sam's truck, parked about a block away. He carried most of the heavier stuff. Sam is not a big guy, but he's really strong, as all shifters are.

By ten thirty we were almost finished. From the cheers at the front of the house, I knew that the brides had descended the staircase in their honeymoon clothes, thrown their bouquets, and departed. Portia and Glen were going to San Francisco, and Halleigh and Andy were going to Jamaica to some resort. I couldn't help but know.

Sam told me I could leave. "I'll get Dawson to help me unload at the bar," he said. Since Dawson, who'd been standing in for Sam at Merlotte's Bar tonight, was built like a boulder, I agreed that was a good plan.

When we divided the tips, I got about three hundred dollars. It had been a lucrative evening. I tucked the money in my pants pocket. It made a big roll, since it was mostly ones. I was glad we were in Bon Temps instead of a big city, or I'd worry that someone would hit me on the head before I got to my car.

"Well, night, Sam," I said, and checked my pocket for my car keys. I hadn't bothered with bringing a purse. As I went down the slope of the backyard to the sidewalk, I patted my hair self-consciously. I'd been able to stop the pink smock lady from putting it on top of my head, so she'd done it puffy and curly and sort of Farrah Fawcett. I felt silly.

There were cars going by, most of them wedding guests taking their departure. There was some regular Saturday night traffic. The line of vehicles parked against the curb stretched for a very long way down the street, so all traffic was moving slowly.

I'd illegally parked with the driver's side against the curb, not usually a big deal in our little town.

I bent to unlock my car door, and I heard a noise behind me. In a single movement, I palmed my keys and clenched my fist, wheeled, and hit as hard as I could. The keys gave my fist quite a core, and the man behind me staggered across the sidewalk to land on his butt on the slope of the lawn.

"I mean you no harm," said Jonathan.

It isn't easy to look dignified and nonthreatening when you have blood running from one corner of your mouth and you're sitting on your ass, but the Asian vampire managed it.

"You surprised me," I said, which was a gross under-statement.

"I can see that," he said, and got easily to his feet. He brought out a handkerchief and patted his mouth.

I wasn't going to apologize. People who sneak up on me when I'm alone at night, well, they deserve what they get. But I reconsidered. Vampires move quietly. "I'm sorry I assumed the worst," I said, which was sort of a compromise. "I should have identified you."

"No, it would have been too late by then," Jonathan said. "A woman alone must defend herself."

"I appreciate your understanding," I said carefully. I glanced behind him, tried not to register anything on my face. Since I hear so many startling things from people's brains, I'm used to doing that. I looked directly at Jonathan. "Did you . . . Why were you here?"

"I'm passing through Louisiana, and I came to the wedding

as a guest of Hamilton Tharp," he said. "I'm staying in Area Five, with the permission of Eric Northman."

I had no idea who Hamilton Tharp was—presumably some buddy of the Bellefleurs'. But I knew Eric Northman quite well. (In fact, at one time I'd known him from his head to his toes, and all points in between.) Eric was the sheriff of Area Five, a large chunk of northern Louisiana. We were tied together in a complex way, which most days I resented like hell.

"Actually, what I was asking you was—why did you approach me just now?" I waited, keys still clutched in my hand. I'd go for his eyes, I decided. Even vampires are vulnerable there.

"I was curious," Jonathan said finally. His hands were folded in front of him. I was developing a strong dislike for the vamp.

"Why?"

"I heard a little at Fangtasia about the blond woman Eric values so highly. Eric has such a hard nose that it didn't seem likely any human woman could interest him."

"So how'd you know I was going to be here, at this wedding, tonight?"

His eyes flickered. He hadn't expected me to persist in questioning. He had expected to be able to calm me, maybe at this moment was trying to coerce me with his glamour. But that just didn't work on me.

"The young woman who works for Eric, his child Pam, mentioned it," he said.

Liar, liar, pants on fire, I thought. I hadn't talked to Pam in a couple of weeks, and our last conversation hadn't been girlish chatter about my social and work schedule. She'd been recovering from the wounds she'd sustained in Rhodes. Her recovery, and Eric's, and the queen's, had been the sole topic of our conversation.

"Of course," I said. "Well, good evening. I need to be leaving." I unlocked the door and carefully slid inside, trying to keep my eyes fixed on Jonathan so I'd be ready for a sudden move. He stood as still as a statue, inclining his head to me after I started the car and pulled off. At the next stop sign, I buckled my seat belt. I hadn't wanted to pin myself down while he was so close. I locked the car doors, and I looked all around me. No vampires in sight. I thought, *That was really, really weird.* In fact, I should probably call Eric and relate the incident to him.

You know what the weirdest part was? The withered man with the long blond hair had been standing in the shadows behind the vampire the whole time. Our eyes had even met once. His beautiful face had been quite unreadable. But I'd known he didn't want me to acknowledge his presence. I hadn't read his mind—I couldn't—but I'd known this nonetheless.

And weirdest of all, Jonathan hadn't known he was there. Given the acute sense of smell that all vampires possessed, Jonathan's ignorance was simply extraordinary.

I was still mulling over the strange little episode when I turned off Hummingbird Road and onto the long driveway through the woods that led back to my old house. The core of the house had been built more than a hundred and sixty years before, but of course very little of the original structure remained. It had been added to, remodeled, and reroofed a score of times over the course of the decades. A two-room farmhouse to begin with, it was now much larger, but it remained a very ordinary home.

Tonight the house looked peaceful in the glow of the outside security light that Amelia Broadway, my housemate, had left on for me. Amelia's car was parked in back, and I pulled alongside it. I kept my keys out in case she'd gone upstairs for the night. She'd left the screen door unlatched, and I latched it behind me. I unlocked the back door and relocked it. We were hell on security, Amelia and I, especially at night.

A little to my surprise, Amelia was sitting at the kitchen table, waiting for me. We'd developed a routine after weeks of living together, and generally Amelia would have retired upstairs by this time. She had her own TV, her cell phone, and her laptop up there, and she'd gotten a library card, so she had plenty to read. Plus, she had her spell work, which I didn't ask questions about. Ever. Amelia is a witch.

"How'd it go?" she asked, stirring her tea as if she had to create a tiny whirlpool.

"Well, they got married. No one pulled a Jane Eyre. Glen's vampire customers behaved themselves, and Miss Caroline was gracious all over the place. But I had to stand in for one of the bridesmaids."

"Oh, wow! Tell me."

So I did, and we shared a few laughs. I thought of telling

Amelia about the beautiful man, but I didn't. What could I say? "He looked at me"? I did tell her about Jonathan from Nevada.

"What do you think he really wanted?" Amelia said.

"I can't imagine." I shrugged.

"You need to find out. Especially since you'd never heard of the guy whose guest he said he was."

"I'm going to call Eric—if not tonight, then tomorrow night."

"Too bad you didn't buy a copy of that database Bill is peddling. I saw an ad for it on the Internet yesterday, on a vampire site." This might seem like a sudden change of subject, but Bill's database contained pictures and/or biographies of all the vampires he'd been able to locate all over the world, and a few he'd just heard about. Bill's little CD was making more money for his boss, the queen, than I could ever have imagined. But you had to be a vampire to purchase a copy, and they had ways of checking.

"Well, since Bill is charging five hundred dollars a pop, and impersonating a vampire is a dangerous risk..." I said.

Amelia waved her hand. "It'd be worth it," she said.

Amelia is a lot more sophisticated than I am...at least in some ways. She grew up in New Orleans, and she'd lived there most of her life. Now she was living with me because she'd made a giant mistake. She'd needed to leave New Orleans after her inexperience had caused a magical catastrophe. It was lucky she'd departed when she had, because Katrina followed soon after. Since the hurricane, her tenant was living in the top-floor apartment of Amelia's house. Amelia's own apartment on the bottom floor had sustained some damage. She wasn't charging the tenant rent because he was overseeing the repair of the house.

And here came the reason Amelia wasn't moving back to New Orleans any time soon. Bob padded into the kitchen to say hello, rubbing himself affectionately against my legs.

"Hey, my little honey bunny," I said, picking up the long-haired black-and-white cat. "How's my precious? I wuv him!"

"I'm gonna barf," Amelia said. But I knew that she talked just as disgustingly to Bob when I wasn't around.

"Any progress?" I said, raising my head from Bob's fur. He'd had a bath this afternoon—I could tell from his fluffy factor.

"No," she said, her voice flat with discouragement. "I worked on him for an hour today, and I only gave him a lizard tail. Took everything I had to get it changed back."

Bob was really a guy, that is, a man. A sort of nerdy-looking man with dark hair and glasses, though Amelia had confided he had some outstanding attributes that weren't apparent when he was dressed for the street. Amelia wasn't supposed to be practicing transformational magic when she turned Bob into a cat; they were having what must have been very adventurous sex. I'd never had the nerve to ask her what she'd been trying to do. It was clear that it was something pretty exotic.

"The deal is," Amelia said suddenly, and I went on the alert. The real reason she'd stayed up to see me was about to be revealed. Amelia was a very clear broadcaster, so I picked it right up from her brain. But I let her go on and speak, because people *really* don't like it if you tell them they don't have to actually speak to you, especially when the topic is something they've had to build up to. "My dad is going to be in Shreveport tomorrow, and he wants to come by Bon Temps to see me," she said in a rush. "It'll be him and his chauffeur, Marley. He wants to come for supper."

The next day would be Sunday. Merlotte's would be open only in the afternoon, but I wasn't scheduled to work anyway, I saw with a glance at my calendar. "So I'll just go out," I said. "I could go visit JB and Tara. No big."

"Please be here," she said, and her face was naked with pleading. She didn't spell out why. But I could read the reason easy enough. Amelia had a very conflicted relationship with her dad; in fact, she'd taken her mother's last name, Broadway, though in part that was because her father was so well-known. Copley Carmichael had lots of political clout and he was rich, though I didn't know how Katrina had affected his income. Carmichael owned huge lumberyards and was a builder, and Katrina might have wiped out his businesses. On the other hand, the whole area needed lumber and rebuilding.

"What time's he coming?" I asked.

"Five."

"Does the chauffeur eat at the same table as him?" I'd never dealt with employees. We just had the one table here in the kitchen. I sure wasn't going to make the man sit on the back steps.

"Oh, God," she said. This had clearly never occurred to her. "What will we do about Marley?"

"That's what I'm asking you." I may have sounded a little too patient.

"Listen," Amelia said. "You don't know my dad. You don't know how he is."

I knew from Amelia's brain that her feelings about her father were really mixed. It was very difficult to pick through the love, fear, and anxiety to get to Amelia's true basic attitude. I knew few rich people, and even fewer rich people who employed full-time chauffeurs.

This visit was going to be interesting.

I said good night to Amelia and went to bed, and though there was a lot to think about, my body was tired and I was soon asleep.

Sunday was another beautiful day. I thought of the newlyweds, safely launched on their new lives, and I thought of old Miss Caroline, who was enjoying the company of a couple of her cousins (youngsters in their sixties) by way of watchdogs and companions. When Portia and Glen returned, the cousins would go back to their more humble home, probably with some relief. Halleigh and Andy would move into their own small house.

I wondered about Jonathan and the beautiful withered man.

I reminded myself to call Eric the next night when he was up.

I thought about Bill's unexpected words.

For the millionth time, I speculated about Quinn's silence.

But before I could get too broody, I was caught up in Hurricane Amelia.

There are lots of things I've come to enjoy, even love, about Amelia. She's straightforward, enthusiastic, and talented. She knows all about the supernatural world, and my place in it. She thinks my weird "talent" is really cool. I can talk to her about anything. She's never going to react with disgust or horror. On the other hand, Amelia is impulsive and headstrong, but you have to take people like they are. I've really enjoyed having Amelia living with me.

On the practical side, she's a decent cook, she's careful about keeping our property separate, and God knows she's tidy. What Amelia really does well is *clean.* She cleans when she's bored, she cleans when she's nervous, and she cleans when she feels guilty. I am no slouch in the housekeeping department, but Amelia is world-class. The day she had a near-miss auto accident, she cleaned my living room furniture, upholstery and all. When her tenant called her to tell her the roof had to be replaced, she went down to EZ Rent and brought home a machine to polish and buff the wooden floors upstairs *and* downstairs.

When I got up at nine, Amelia was already deep in a cleaning frenzy because of her father's impending visit. By the time I left for church at about ten forty-five, Amelia was on her hands and knees in the downstairs hall bathroom, which admittedly is very old-fashioned looking with its tiny octagonal black-and-white tiles and a huge old claw-footed bathtub; but (thanks to my brother, Jason) it has a more modern toilet. This was the bathroom Amelia used, since there wasn't one upstairs. I had a small, private one off my bedroom, added in the fifties. In my house, you could see several major decorating trends over the past few decades all in one building.

"You really think it was that dirty?" I said, standing in the doorway. I was talking to Amelia's rump.

She raised her head and passed a rubber-gloved hand over her forehead to push her short hair out of the way.

"No, it wasn't bad, but I want it to be great."

"My house is just an old house, Amelia. I don't think it can look great." There was no point in my apologizing for the age and wear of the house and its furnishings. This was the best I could do, and I loved it.

"This is a wonderful old home, Sookie," Amelia said fiercely. "But I have to be busy."

"Okay," I said. "Well, I'm going to church. I'll be home by twelve thirty."

"Can you go to the store after church? The list is on the counter."

I agreed, glad to have something to do that would keep me out of the house longer.

The morning felt more like March (March in the south, that is) than October. When I got out of my car at the Methodist church, I raised my face to the slight breeze. There was a touch of winter in the air, a little taste of it. The windows in the modest church were open. When we sang, our combined voices floated out over the grass and trees. But I saw some leaves blow past as the pastor preached.

Frankly, I don't always listen to the sermon. Sometimes the

hour in church is just a time to think, a time to consider where my life is going. But at least those thoughts are in a context. And when you watch leaves falling off trees, your context gets pretty narrow.

Today I listened. Reverend Collins talked about giving God the things that were due him while giving Caesar the things due *him*. That seemed like an April fifteenth type sermon to me, and I caught myself wondering if Reverend Collins paid his taxes quarterly. But after a while, I figured he was talking about the laws we break all the time without feeling guilty—like the speed limit, or sticking a letter in with some presents in a box you're mailing at the post office, without paying the extra postage.

I smiled at Reverend Collins on my way out of the church. He always looks a little troubled when he sees me.

I said hello to Maxine Fortenberry and her husband, Ed, as I reached the parking lot. Maxine was large and formidable, and Ed was so shy and quiet he was almost invisible. Their son, Hoyt, was my brother Jason's best friend. Hoyt was standing behind his mother. He was wearing a nice suit, and his hair had been trimmed. Interesting signs.

"Sugar, you give me a hug!" Maxine said, and of course I did. Maxine had been a good friend to my grandmother, though she was more the age my dad would have been. I smiled at Ed and gave Hoyt a little wave.

"You're looking nice," I told him, and he smiled. I didn't think I'd ever seen Hoyt smile like that, and I glanced at Maxine. She was grinning.

"Hoyt, he's dating that Holly you work with," Maxine said. "She's got a little one, and that's a thing to think about, but he's always liked kids."

"I didn't know," I said. I really had been out of it lately. "That's just great, Hoyt. Holly's a real nice girl."

I wasn't sure I would have put it quite that way if I'd had time to think, so maybe it was lucky I didn't. There were some big positives about Holly (devoted to her son, Cody; loyal to her friends; a competent worker). She'd been divorced for several years, so Hoyt wasn't a rebound. I wondered if Holly had told Hoyt she was a Wiccan. Nope, she hadn't, or Maxine wouldn't be smiling so broadly.

"We're meeting her for lunch at the Sizzler," she said, referring to the steakhouse up by the interstate. "Holly's not much of a churchgoer, but we're working on getting her to come with us and bring Cody. We better get moving if we're gonna be on time."

"Way to go, Hoyt," I said, patting his arm as he went by me. He gave me a pleased look.

Everyone was getting married or falling in love. I was happy for them. Happy, happy, happy. I pasted a smile on my face and went to Piggly Wiggly. I fished Amelia's list out of my purse. It was pretty long, but I was sure there'd be additions by now. I called her on my cell phone, and she had already thought of three more items to add, so I was some little while in the store.

My arms were weighed down with plastic bags as I struggled up the steps to the back porch. Amelia shot out to the car to grab the other bags. "Where have you been?" she asked, as if she'd been standing by the door tapping her toe.

I looked at my watch. "I got out of church and went to the store," I said defensively. "It's only one."

Amelia passed me again, heavily laden. She shook her head in exasperation as she went by, making a noise that could only be described as "Urrrrrrgh."

The rest of the afternoon was like that, as though Amelia were getting ready for the date of her life.

I'm not a bad cook, but Amelia would let me do only the most menial chores in fixing the dinner. I got to chop onions and tomatoes. Oh, yeah, she let me wash the preparation dishes. I'd always wondered if she could do the dishes like the fairy godmothers in *Sleeping Beauty*, but she just snorted when I brought it up.

The house was spanky clean, and though I tried not to mind, I noticed that Amelia had even given the floor of my bedroom a once-over. As a rule, we didn't go into each other's space.

"Sorry I went in your room," Amelia said suddenly, and I jumped—me, the telepath. Amelia had beaten me at my own game. "It was one of those crazy impulses I get. I was vacuuming, and I just thought I'd get your floor, too. And before I thought about it, I was done. I put your slippers up under your bed."

"Okay," I said, trying to sound neutral.

"Hey, I *am* sorry."

I nodded and went back to drying the dishes and putting

them away. The menu, as decided by Amelia, was tossed green salad with tomatoes and slivered carrots, lasagna, hot garlic bread, and steamed fresh mixed vegetables. I don't know diddly-squat about steamed vegetables, but I had prepared all the raw materials—the zucchini, bell peppers, mushrooms, cauliflower. Late in the afternoon, I was deemed capable of tossing the salad, and I got to put the cloth and the little bouquet of flowers on the table and arrange the place settings. Four place settings.

I'd offered to take Mr. Marley into the living room with me, where we could eat on TV trays, but you would have thought I'd offered to wash his feet, Amelia was so horrified.

"No, you're sticking with me," she said.

"You gotta talk to your dad," I said. "At some point, I'm leaving the room."

She took a deep breath and let it out. "Okay, I'm a grown-up," she muttered.

"Scaredy-cat," I said.

"You haven't met him yet."

Amelia hurried upstairs at four fifteen to get ready. I was sitting in the living room reading a library book when I heard a car on the gravel driveway. I glanced at the clock on the mantel. It was four forty-eight. I yelled up the staircase and stood to look out the window. The afternoon was drawing to a close, but since we hadn't reverted to standard time yet, it was easy to see the Lincoln Town Car parked in front. A man with clipped dark hair, wearing a business suit, got out of the driver's seat. This must be Marley. He wasn't wearing a chauffeur's hat, somewhat to my disappointment. He opened a rear door. Out stepped Copley Carmichael.

Amelia's dad wasn't very tall, and he had short thick gray hair that looked like a really good carpet, dense and smooth and expertly cut. He was very tan, and his eyebrows were still dark. No glasses. No lips. Well, he did have lips, but they were really thin, so his mouth looked like a trap.

Mr. Carmichael looked around him as if he were doing a tax assessment.

I heard Amelia clattering down the stairs behind me as I watched the man in my front yard complete his survey. Marley the chauffeur was looking right at the house. He'd spotted my face at the window.

"Marley's sort of new," Amelia said. "He's been with my dad for just two years."

"Your dad's always had a driver?"

"Yeah. Marley's a bodyguard, too," Amelia said casually, as if everyone's dad had a bodyguard.

They were walking up the gravel sidewalk now, not even looking at its neat border of ilex. Up the wooden steps. Across the front porch. Knocking.

I thought of all the scary creatures that had been in my house: Weres, shifters, vampires, even a demon or two. Why should I be worried about this man? I straightened my spine, chilled my anxious brain, and went to the front door, though Amelia almost beat me to it. After all, this was my house.

I put my hand on the knob, and I got my smile ready before I opened the door.

"Please come in," I said, and Marley opened the screen door for Mr. Carmichael, who came in and hugged his daughter but not before he'd cast another comprehensive look around the living room.

He was as clear a broadcaster as his daughter.

He was thinking this looked mighty shabby for a daughter of his. . . . Pretty girl Amelia was living with . . . Wondered if Amelia was having sex with her . . . The girl was probably no better than she should be. . . . No police record, though she had dated a vampire and had a wild brother . . .

Of course a rich and powerful man like Copley Carmichael would have his daughter's new housemate investigated. Such a procedure had simply never occurred to me, like so many things the rich did.

I took a deep breath. "I'm Sookie Stackhouse," I said politely. "You must be Mr. Carmichael. And this is?" After shaking Mr. Carmichael's hand, I extended mine to Marley.

For a second, I thought I'd caught Amelia's dad off-footed. But he recovered in record time.

"This is Tyrese Marley," Mr. Carmichael said smoothly.

The chauffeur shook my hand gently, as if he didn't want to break my bones, and then he nodded to Amelia. "Miss Amelia," he said, and Amelia looked angry, as if she was going to tell him to cut the "Miss," but then she reconsidered. All these thoughts, pinging back and forth . . . It was enough to keep me distracted.

Tyrese Marley was a very, very light-skinned African-American. He was far from black; his skin was more the color of old ivory. His eyes were bright hazel. Though his hair was black, it wasn't curly, and it had a red cast. Marley was a man you'd always look at twice.

"I'll take the car back to town and get some gas," he said to his boss. "While you spend time with Miss Amelia. When you want me back?"

Mr. Carmichael looked down at his watch. "A couple of hours."

"You're welcome to stay for supper," I said, managing a very neutral tone. I wanted what made everyone feel comfortable.

"I have a few errands I need to run," Tyrese Marley said with no inflection. "Thanks for the invitation. I'll see you later." He left.

Okay, end of my attempt at democracy.

Tyrese couldn't have known how much I would have preferred going into town rather than staying in the house. I braced myself and began the social necessities. "Can I get you a glass of wine, Mr. Carmichael, or something else to drink? What about you, Amelia?"

"Call me Cope," he said, smiling. It was way too much like a shark's grin to warm my heart. "Sure, a glass of whatever's open. You, baby?"

"Some of the white," she said, and I heard her telling her dad to be seated as I went to the kitchen.

I served the wine and added it to the tray with our hors d'oeuvres: crackers, a warm Brie spread, and apricot jam mixed with hot peppers. We had some cute little knives that looked good with the tray, and Amelia had gotten cocktail napkins for the drinks.

Cope had a good appetite, and he enjoyed the Brie. He sipped the wine, which was an Arkansas label, and nodded politely. Well, at least he didn't spit it out. I seldom drink, and I'm no kind of wine connoisseur. In fact, I'm not a connoisseur of anything at all. But I enjoyed the wine, sip by sip.

"Amelia, tell me what you're doing with your time while you're waiting for your home to be repaired," Cope said, which I thought was a reasonable opening.

I started to tell him that for starters, she wasn't screwing around with me, but I thought that might be a little too direct. I tried very hard not to read his thoughts, but I swear, with him and his daughter in the same room, it was like listening to a television broadcast.

"I've done some filing for one of the local insurance agents. And I'm working part-time at Merlotte's Bar," Amelia said. "I serve drinks and the occasional chicken basket."

"Is the bar work interesting?" Cope didn't sound sarcastic, I'll give him that. But, of course, I was sure he'd had Sam researched, too.

"It's not bad," she said with a slight smile. That was a lot of restraint for Amelia, so I checked into her brain to see that she was squeezing herself into a conversational girdle. "I get good tips."

Her father nodded. "You, Miss Stackhouse?" Cope asked politely.

He knew everything about me but the shade of fingernail polish I was wearing, and I was sure he'd add that to my file if he could. "I work at Merlotte's full-time," I said, just as if he didn't know that. "I've been there for years."

"You have family in the area?"

"Oh, yes, we've been here forever," I said. "Or as close to forever as Americans get. But our family's dwindled down. It's just me and my brother now."

"Older brother? Younger?"

"Older," I said. "Married, real recently."

"So maybe there'll be other little Stackhouses," he said, trying to sound like he thought that would be a good thing.

I nodded as if the possibility pleased me, too. I didn't like my brother's wife much, and I thought it was entirely possible that any kids they had would be pretty rotten. In fact, one was on the way right now, if Crystal didn't miscarry again. My brother was a werepanther (bitten, not born), and his wife was a born . . . a pure . . . werepanther, that is. Being raised in the little werepanther community of Hotshot was not an easy thing, and would be even harder for kids who weren't pure.

"Dad, can I get you some more wine?" Amelia was out of her chair like a shot, and she sped on her way to the kitchen with the half-empty wineglass. Good, quality alone time with Amelia's dad.

"Sookie," Cope said, "you've been very kind to let my daughter live with you all this time."

"Amelia pays rent," I said. "She buys half the groceries. She pays her way."

"Nonetheless, I wish you'd let me give you something for your trouble."

"What Amelia gives me on rent is enough. After all, she's paid for some improvements to the property, too."

His face sharpened then, as if he was on the scent of something big. Did he think I'd talked Amelia into putting a pool in the backyard?

"She got a window air conditioner put in her bedroom upstairs," I said. "And she got an extra phone line for the computer. And I think she got a throw rug and some curtains for her room, too."

"She lives upstairs?"

"Yes," I said, surprised he didn't somehow know already. Perhaps there were a few things his intelligence net hadn't scooped up. "I live down here, she lives up there, and we share the kitchen and living room, though I think Amelia's got a TV upstairs, too. Hey, Amelia!" I called.

"Yeah?" Her voice floated down the hall from the kitchen.

"You still got that little TV up there?"

"Yeah, I hooked it up to the cable."

"Just wondered."

I smiled at Cope, indicating the conversational ball was in his court. He was thinking of several things to ask me, and he was thinking of the best way to approach me to get the most information. A name popped to the surface in the whirlpool of his thoughts, and it took everything I had to keep a polite expression.

"The first tenant Amelia had in the house on Chloe—she was your cousin, right?" Cope said.

"Hadley. Yes." I kept my face calm as I nodded. "Did you know her?"

"I know her husband," he said, and smiled.

Chapter 3

*I knew Amelia had returned and was standing by the wing-*back chair where her father sat, and I knew she was frozen in place. I knew I didn't breathe for a second.

"I never met him," I said. I felt as if I'd been walking in a jungle and fallen into a concealed pit. I was sure glad I was the only telepath in the house. I hadn't told anyone, anyone at all, about what I'd found in Hadley's lockbox when I'd cleaned it out that day at a bank in New Orleans. "They'd been divorced for a while before Hadley died."

"You should take the time to meet him someday. He's an interesting man," Cope said, as if he wasn't aware he was dropping a bombshell on me. Of course he was waiting for my reaction. He'd hoped I hadn't known about the marriage at all, that I'd be taken completely by surprise. "He's a skilled carpenter. I'd love to track him down and hire him again."

The chair he was sitting on had been upholstered in a cream-colored material with lots of tiny blue flowers on green arching stems embroidered on it. It was still pretty, if faded. I concentrated on the pattern of the chair so I wouldn't show Copley Carmichael how very angry I was.

"He doesn't mean anything to me, no matter how interesting he is," I said in a voice so level you could've played pool on it. "Their marriage was over and done. As I'm sure you know, Hadley had another partner at the time she died." Was murdered. But the government hadn't gotten around to taking much notice of vampire deaths unless those deaths were caused by humans. Vampires did most of their own self-policing.

"I'd think you'd want to see the baby, though," Copley said.

Thank God I picked this out of Copley's head a second or two before he actually spoke the words. Even knowing what he was going to say, I felt his oh-so-casual remark hit me like a blow to the stomach. But I didn't want to give him the satisfaction of letting him see that. "My cousin Hadley was wild. She used drugs and people. She wasn't the most stable person in the world. She was really pretty, and she had a way about her, so she always had admirers." There, I'd said everything pro and con about my cousin Hadley. And I hadn't said the word "baby." *What baby?*

"How'd your family feel when she became a vampire?" Cope said.

Hadley's change was a matter of public record. "Turned" vampires were supposed to register when they entered their altered state of being. They had to name their maker. It was a kind of governmental vampire birth control. You can bet the Bureau of Vampire Affairs would come down like a ton of bricks on a vampire who made too many other little vampires. Hadley had been turned by Sophie-Anne Leclerq herself.

Amelia had put her father's wineglass down within his reach and resumed her seat on the sofa beside me. "Dad, Hadley lived upstairs from me for two years," she said. "Of course we knew she was a vampire. For goodness sake, I thought you'd want to tell me all the hometown news."

God bless Amelia. I was having a hard time holding myself together, and only years of doing that very thing when I telepathically overheard something awful was keeping me glued.

"I need to check on the food. Excuse me," I murmured, and rose and left the room. I hoped I didn't scurry. I tried to walk normally. But once in the kitchen, I kept on going out the back door and across the back porch, out the screen door and into the yard.

If I thought I'd hear Hadley's ghostly voice telling me what to do, I was disappointed. Vampires don't leave ghosts, at least as far as I know. Some vampires believe they don't possess souls. I don't know. That's up to God. And here I was babbling to myself, because I didn't want to think about Hadley's baby, about the fact that I hadn't known about the child.

Maybe it was just Copley's way. Maybe he always wanted to demonstrate the extent of his knowledge, as a way of showing his power to the people he dealt with.

I had to go back in there for Amelia's sake. I braced myself, put my smile back on—though I knew it was a creepy, nervous smile—and back I went. I perched by Amelia and beamed at both of them. They looked at me expectantly, and I realized a conversational lull had fallen.

"Oh," said Cope suddenly. "Amelia, I forgot to tell you. Someone called the house for you last week, someone I didn't know."

"Her name?"

"Oh, let me think. Mrs. Beech wrote it down. Ophelia? Octavia? Octavia Fant. That was it. Unusual."

I thought Amelia was going to faint. She turned a funny color and she braced her hand against the arm of the couch. "You're sure?" she asked.

"Yes, I'm sure. I gave her your cell phone number, and I told her you were living in Bon Temps."

"Thanks, Dad," Amelia croaked. "Ah, I'll bet supper's done; let me go check."

"Didn't Sookie just look at the food?" He wore the broad tolerant smile a man wears when he thinks women are being silly.

"Oh, sure, but it's in the end stage," I said while Amelia shot out of the room as swiftly as I'd just done. "It would be awful if it burned. Amelia worked so hard."

"Do you know this Ms. Fant?" Cope asked.

"No, I can't say as I do."

"Amelia looked almost scared. No one's trying to hurt my girl, right?"

He was a different man when he said that, and one I could

almost like. No matter what else he was, Cope didn't want anyone hurting his daughter. Anyone except him, that is.

"I don't think so." I knew who Octavia Fant was because Amelia's brain had just told me, but she herself hadn't spoken it out loud, so it wasn't a thing I could share. Sometimes the things I hear out loud and the things I hear in my head become really tangled and confused—one of the reasons why I have a reputation for being borderline crazy. "You're a contractor, Mr. Carmichael?"

"Cope, please. Yes, among other things."

"I guess your business must be booming right now," I said.

"If my company was twice as big, we couldn't keep up with the jobs there are to do," he said. "But I hated to see New Orleans all torn up."

Oddly enough, I believed him.

Supper went smoothly enough. If Amelia's father was disconcerted at eating in the kitchen, he didn't give a sign of it. Since he was a builder, he noticed that the kitchen portion of the house was new and I had to tell him about the fire, but that could have happened to anyone, right? I left out the part about the arsonist.

Cope seemed to enjoy his food and complimented Amelia, who was mighty pleased. He had another glass of wine with his meal, but no more than that, and he ate moderately, too. He and Amelia talked about friends of the family and some relatives, and I was left alone to think. Believe me, I had a lot of thinking to do.

Hadley's marriage license and divorce decree had been in

her lockbox at her bank when I'd opened it after her death. The box had contained some family things—a few pictures, her mother's obituary, several pieces of jewelry. There'd also been a lock of fine hair, dark and wispy, with a bit of Scotch tape to keep it together. It had been placed in a little envelope. I'd wondered when I'd noticed how fine the hair was. But there hadn't been a birth certificate or any other scrap of evidence that Hadley had had a baby.

Up until now, I'd had no clearly defined reason to contact Hadley's former husband. I hadn't even known he existed until I'd opened her lockbox. He wasn't mentioned in her will. I'd never met him. He hadn't shown up while I was in New Orleans.

Why hadn't she mentioned the child in her will? Surely any parent would do that. And though she'd named Mr. Cataliades and me as the joint executors, she hadn't told either of us— well, she hadn't told me—that she had relinquished her rights to her child, either.

"Sookie, would you pass the butter?" Amelia asked, and I could tell from her tone it wasn't the first time she'd spoken to me.

"Of course," I said. "Can I get either of you any more water or another glass of wine?"

They both declined.

After supper, I volunteered to do the dishes. Amelia accepted my offer after a brief pause. She and her father had to have some time alone, even if Amelia didn't relish the prospect.

I washed and dried and put away the dishes in relative peace.

I wiped down the counters and whipped the tablecloth off the table and popped it into the washer on the enclosed back porch. I went into my room and read for a while, though I didn't take in much of what was happening on the page. Finally, I laid the book aside and got a box out of my underwear drawer. This box contained everything I'd retrieved from Hadley's lockbox. I checked the name on the marriage certificate. On impulse, I called information.

"I need a listing for a Remy Savoy," I said.

"What city?"

"New Orleans."

"That number's been disconnected."

"Try Metairie."

"No, ma'am."

"Okay, thanks."

Of course, a lot of people had moved since Katrina, and a lot of those moves were permanent. People who had fled the hurricane had no reason to come back, in many cases. There was nowhere to live and no job to go to, in all too many cases.

I wondered how to search for Hadley's ex-husband.

A very unwelcome solution crept into my head. Bill Compton was a computer whiz. Maybe he could track down this Remy Savoy, find out where he was now, discover if the child was with him.

I rolled the idea around in my head like a mouthful of doubtful wine. Given our exchange of the night before at the wedding, I could not imagine myself approaching Bill to ask for a favor, though he'd be the right man for the job.

A wave of longing for Quinn almost took me to my knees. Quinn was a smart and well-traveled man, and he would surely have a good piece of advice for me. If I ever saw him again.

I shook myself. I could just hear a car pulling into the parking area by the sidewalk at the front of the house. Tyrese Marley was returning for Cope. I straightened my back and left my room, my smile fixed firmly on my face.

The front door was open, and Tyrese was standing in it, pretty much filling it up from side to side. He was a big man. Cope was leaning over to give his daughter a peck on the cheek, which she accepted without a hint of a smile. Bob the cat came through the door and sat down beside her. The cat was looking up at Amelia's father with his wide-eyed stare.

"You have a cat, Amelia? I thought you hated cats."

Bob switched his gaze to Amelia. Nothing can stare like a cat.

"Dad! That was years ago! This is Bob. He's great." Amelia picked up the black-and-white cat and held him to her chest. Bob looked smug and began purring.

"Hmmm. Well, I'll be calling you. Please take care. I hate to think about you being up here at the other end of the state."

"It's just a few hours' ride away," Amelia said, sounding all of seventeen.

"True," he said, trying for rueful but charming. He missed by a foot or two. "Sookie, thanks for the evening," he called over his daughter's shoulder.

Marley had gone to Merlotte's to see if he could scope out any information on me, I heard clearly from his brain. He'd picked up quite a few odds and ends. He'd talked to Arlene, which was bad, and to our current cook and our busboy, which was good. Plus assorted bar patrons. He'd have a mixed report to convey.

The moment the car pulled away, Amelia collapsed onto the sofa with relief. "Thank God he's gone," she said. "Now do you see what I mean?"

"Yeah," I said. I sat beside her. "He's a mover and a shaker, isn't he?"

"Always has been," she said. "He's trying to maintain a relationship, but our ideas don't match."

"Your dad loves you."

"He does. But he loves power and control, too."

That was putting it conservatively.

"And he doesn't know you have your own form of power."

"No, he doesn't believe in it at all," Amelia said. "He'll tell you he's a devout Catholic, but that's not the truth."

"In a way, that's good," I said. "If he believed in your witch power, he'd try to make you do all kinds of things for him. You wouldn't want to do some of them, I bet." I could have bitten my tongue, but Amelia didn't take offense.

"You're right," she said. "I wouldn't want to help him advance his agenda. He's capable of doing that without my assistance. If he'd just leave me alone, I'd be content. He's always trying to improve my life, on his terms. I'm really doing okay."

"Who was that who had called you in New Orleans?" Though I knew, I had to pretend. "Fant, her name was?"

Amelia shuddered. "Octavia Fant is my mentor," she said. "She's the reason I left New Orleans. I figured my coven would do something awful to me when they found out about Bob. She's the head of my coven. Or what's left of it. If anything's left of it."

"Ooops."

"Yeah, no shit. I'm going to have to pay the price now."

"You think she'll come up here?"

"I'm only surprised she's not here already."

Despite her expressed fear, Amelia had been worried sick about the welfare of her mentor after Katrina. She had made a huge effort to track the woman, though she didn't want Octavia to find *her.*

Amelia feared being discovered, especially with Bob still in his cat form. She'd told me that her dabbling in transformational magic would be considered all the more reprehensible because she was still an intern, or something along those lines...a step above novice, anyway. Amelia didn't discuss the witch infrastructure.

"You didn't think of telling your father not to reveal your location?"

"Asking him to do that would have made him so curious he'd have torn up my entire life to find out why I'd asked. I never thought Octavia would call him, since she knows how I feel about him."

Which was, to say the least, conflicted.

"I have something to tell you that I forgot," Amelia said abruptly. "Speaking of phone calls, Eric called you."

"When?"

"Ah, last night. Before you got home. You were so full of

news when you got here, I just forgot to tell you. Plus, you'd said you were going to call him anyway. And I was really upset about my dad coming. I'm sorry, Sookie. I promise I'll write a note next time."

This was not the first time Amelia had neglected to tell me about a caller. I wasn't pleased, but it was water under the bridge, and our day had been stressful enough. I hoped Eric had found out about the money the queen owed me for my services in Rhodes. I hadn't gotten a check yet, and I hated to bug her since she'd been hurt so badly. I went to the phone in my room to call Fangtasia, which should be in full blast. The club was open every night except Monday.

"Fangtasia, the bar with a bite," Clancy said.

Oh, great. My least favorite vampire. I phrased my request carefully. "Clancy, it's Sookie. Eric asked me to return his call."

There was a moment of silence. I was willing to bet that Clancy was trying to figure out if he could block my access to Eric. He decided he couldn't. "One moment," he said. A brief pause while I listened to "Strangers in the Night." Then Eric picked up the phone.

"Hello?" he said.

"I'm sorry I didn't call you back before now. I just got your message. Did you call about my money?"

A moment of silence. "No, about something else entirely. Will you go out with me tomorrow night?"

I stared at the telephone. I couldn't manage a coherent thought. Finally I said, "Eric, I'm dating Quinn."

"And how long has it been since you've seen him?"

"Since Rhodes."

"How long has it been since you heard from him?"

"Since Rhodes." My voice was wooden. I was unwilling to talk to Eric about this, but we had shared blood often enough to have a much stronger tie than I liked. In fact, I loathed our bond, one we'd been compelled to forge. But when I heard his voice, I felt content. When I was with him, I felt beautiful and happy. And there was nothing I could do about it.

"I think you can give me one evening," Eric said. "It doesn't sound as though Quinn has you booked."

"That was mean."

"It's Quinn who's cruel, promising you he'd be here and then not keeping his word." There was a dark element in Eric's voice, an undertone of anger.

"Do you know what's happened to him?" I asked. "Do you know where he is?"

There was a significant silence. "No," Eric said very gently. "I don't know. But there is someone in town who wants to meet you. I promised I would arrange it. I'd like to take you to Shreveport myself."

So this wasn't a *date* date.

"You mean that guy Jonathan? He came to the wedding and introduced himself. I've got to say, I didn't much care for the guy. No offense, if he's a friend of yours."

"Jonathan? What Jonathan?"

"I'm talking about the Asian guy; he's maybe Thai? He was at the Bellefleur wedding last night. He said he wanted to see me because he was staying in Shreveport and he'd heard a lot about me. He said he'd checked in with you, like a good little visiting vampire."

"I don't know him," Eric said. His voice was much sharper. "I'll ask here at Fangtasia to see if anyone has seen him. And I'll prompt the queen about your money, though she is ... not herself. Now, will you please do what I'm asking you to do?"

I made a face at the telephone. "I guess," I said. "Who'm I meeting? And where?"

"I'll have to let the 'who' remain a mystery," Eric said. "As to where, we'll go to dinner at a nice restaurant. The kind you'd call casual dressy."

"You don't eat. What will you do?"

"I'll introduce you and stay as long as you need me to."

A crowded restaurant should be all right. "Okay," I said, not very graciously. "I'll get off work about six or six thirty."

"I'll be there to pick you up at seven."

"Give me till seven thirty. I need to change." I knew I sounded grumpy, and that was exactly how I felt. I hated the big mystery around this meeting.

"You'll feel better when you see me," he said. Dammit, he was absolutely right.

Chapter 4

I checked my Word of the Day calendar while I was waiting for my hair-straightening iron to heat up. "Epicene." Huh.

Since I didn't know what restaurant we were going to, and I didn't know who we'd meet there, I picked my most comfortable option and wore a sky blue silk T-shirt that Amelia had said was too big for her, and some black dress slacks with black heels. I don't wear a lot of jewelry, so a gold chain and some little gold earrings did the decorating for me. I'd had a tough day at work, but I was too curious about the evening ahead to feel tired.

Eric was on time, and I felt (surprise) a rush of pleasure when I saw him. I don't think that was entirely due to the blood bond between us. I think any heterosexual woman would feel a rush of pleasure at the sight of Eric. He was a tall man and must have been seen as a giant in his time. He was built to swing a heavy sword to hew down his enemies. Eric's golden blond hair sprang back like a lion's mane from a bold forehead. There was nothing *epicene* about Eric, nothing ethereally beautiful, either. He was all male.

Eric bent to kiss me on the cheek. I felt warm and safe. This was the effect Eric had on me now that we'd swapped blood more than three times. The blood sharing hadn't been for pleasure but a necessity—at least I'd thought so—every time, but the price I paid was steep. We were bonded now, and when he was near, I was absurdly happy. I tried to enjoy the sensation, but knowing it wasn't completely natural made that hard to do.

Since Eric had come in his Corvette, I was extra glad I'd worn pants. Getting into and out of a Corvette modestly was a very difficult procedure if you were wearing a dress. I made small talk on the way to Shreveport, but Eric was uncharacteristically silent. I tried to question him about Jonathan, the mysterious vampire at the wedding, but Eric said, "We'll talk about that later. You haven't seen him again, have you?"

"No," I said. "Should I expect to?"

Eric shook his head. There was an uncomfortable pause. From the way he was gripping the wheel, I could tell that Eric was building up to saying something he didn't want to say.

"I'm glad for your sake that it appears Andre didn't survive the bombing," he said.

The queen's dearest child, Andre, had died in the bombing in Rhodes. But it hadn't been the bomb that had killed him.

Quinn and I knew what had done the deed: a big splinter of wood that Quinn had driven into Andre's heart while the vampire lay disabled. Quinn had killed Andre for my sake, because he knew Andre had plans for me that made me sick with fear.

"I'm sure the queen will miss him," I said carefully.

Eric shot me a sharp glance. "The queen is distraught," he said. "And her healing will take months more. What I was beginning to say..." His voice trailed off.

This wasn't like Eric. "What?" I demanded.

"You saved my life," he said. I'd turned to look at him, but he was looking straight ahead at the road. "You saved my life, and Pam's, too."

I shifted uncomfortably. "Yeah, well." Miss Articulate. The silence lengthened until I felt I had to say something else. "We do have the blood tie thing going."

Eric didn't respond for a stretch of time. "That's not why you came to wake me, first of all, the day the hotel blew up," he said. "But we won't talk further about this now. You have a big evening ahead."

Yes, boss, I said snippily, but only to myself.

We were in a part of Shreveport I didn't know too well. It was definitely out of the main shopping area, with which I was fairly familiar. We were in a neighborhood where the houses were large and the lawns were groomed. The businesses were small and pricey...what retailers called "boutiques." We pulled into a group of such shops. It was arranged in an L, and the restaurant was at the rear of the L. It was called Les Deux Poissons. There were maybe eight cars parked there, and each one of them represented my yearly income. I looked down at my clothes, feeling suddenly uneasy.

"Don't worry, you're beautiful," Eric said quietly. He leaned over to unbuckle my seat belt (to my astonishment), and as he straightened he kissed me again, this time on the mouth. His bright blue eyes blazed out of his white face. He looked as if a whole story was on the tip of his tongue. But then he swallowed it back and unfolded himself from the car to walk around to my side to open the door for me. Maybe I wasn't the only one this blood bond worked on, huh?

From his tension I realized that some major event was coming at me fast, and I began to be afraid. Eric took my hand as we walked across to the restaurant, and he ran his thumb absently across my palm. I was surprised to find out there was a direct line from my palm to my, my, hootchie.

We stepped into the foyer, where there was a little fountain and a screen that blocked the view of the diners. The woman standing at the podium was beautiful and black, her hair shaved very close to her skull. She wore a draped dress of orange and brown and the highest heels I had ever seen. She might as well have been wearing toe shoes. I looked at her closely, and I sampled the signature of her brain, and I found she was human. She smiled brilliantly at Eric and had the sense to give me a share of that smile.

"A party of two?" she said.

"We're meeting someone," Eric said.

"Oh, the gentleman . . ."

"Yes."

"Right this way, please." Her smile replaced by a look almost of envy, she turned and walked gracefully into the depths of the restaurant. Eric gestured for me to follow her. The interior was fairly dark, and candles flickered on the tables, which were covered with snowy white cloths and elaborately folded napkins.

My eyes were on the hostess's back, so when she came to a halt, I didn't immediately recognize that she'd stopped at the table where we were to sit. She stepped aside. Seated facing me was the lovely man who'd been at the wedding two nights before.

The hostess spun on her high heel, touched the back of the chair to the man's right to indicate I should sit there, and told us our server would be with us. The man rose to pull out my chair and hold it for me. I glanced back at Eric. He gave me a reassuring nod. I slipped in front of the chair and the man pushed it forward with perfect timing.

Eric didn't sit. I wanted him to explain what was happening, but he didn't speak. He looked almost sad.

The beautiful man was looking at me intently. "Child," he said to get my attention. Then he pushed back his long, fine golden hair. None of the other diners were positioned to see what he was showing me.

His ear was pointed. He was a fairy.

I knew two other fairies. But they avoided vampires at all costs, because the smell of a fairy was as intoxicating to a vampire as honey is to a bear. According to a vampire who was particularly gifted in the scent sense, I had a trace of fairy blood.

"Okay," I said, to let him know the ears had registered.

"Sookie, this is Niall Brigant," Eric said. He pronounced it "Nye-all." "He's going to talk to you over supper. I'll be outside if you need me." He inclined his head stiffly to the fairy and then he was gone.

I watched Eric walk away, and I was bowled over with a rush of anxiety. Then I felt a hand on top of my own. I turned to meet the eyes of the fairy.

"As he said, my name is Niall." His voice was light, sexless, resonant. His eyes were green, the deepest green you can imagine. In the flickering candlelight, the color hardly mattered—it was the depth you noticed. His hand on mine was light as a feather but very warm.

"Who are you?" I asked, and I wasn't asking him to repeat his name.

"I'm your great-grandfather," Niall Brigant said.

"Oh, *shit*," I said, and covered my mouth with my hand. "Sorry, I just..." I shook my head. "Great-grandpa?" I said, trying out the concept. Niall Brigant winced delicately. On a real man, the gesture would have looked effeminate, but on Niall it didn't.

Lots of kids in our neck of the woods call their grandfathers "Papaw." I'd *love* to see his reaction to that. The idea helped me recover my scattered sense of self.

"Please explain," I said very politely. The waiter came to inquire after our drink orders and recite the specials of the day.

Niall ordered a bottle of wine and told him we would have the salmon. He did not consult me. High-handed.

The young man nodded vigorously. "Great choice," he said. He was a Were, and though I would have expected him to be curious about Niall (who after all was a supernatural being not often encountered), I seemed to be of more interest. I attributed that to the waiter's youth and my boobs.

See, here's the weird thing about meeting my self-proclaimed relative: I never doubted his truthfulness. This was my true great-grandfather, and the knowledge just clicked into place as if it fit into a puzzle.

"I'll tell you all about it," Niall said. Very slowly, telegraphing his intention, he leaned over to kiss my cheek. His mouth and eyes crinkled as his facial muscles moved to frame the kiss. The fine cobweb of wrinkles did not in any way detract from his beauty; he was like very old silk or a crackled painting by an ancient master.

This was a big night for getting kissed.

"When I was still young, perhaps five or six hundred years ago, I used to wander among the humans," Niall said. "And every now and then, as a male will, I'd see a human woman I found appealing."

I glanced around so I wouldn't be staring at him every second, and I noticed a strange thing: no one was looking at us but our waiter. I mean, not even a casual glance strayed our way. And no human brains in the room were even registering our presence. My great-grandfather paused while I did this, and resumed speaking when I'd finished evaluating the situation.

"I saw such a woman in the woods one day, and her name was Einin. She thought I was an angel." He was silent for a moment. "She was delicious," he said. "She was lively, and happy, and simple." Niall's eyes were fixed on my face. I wondered if he thought I was like Einin: simple. "I was young enough to be infatuated, young enough to be able to ignore the inevitable end of our connection as she aged and I did not. But Einin got pregnant, which was a shock. Fairies and humans don't cross-breed often. Einin gave birth to twins, which is quite common among the fae. Einin and both boys lived through the birthing, which in those times was far from certain. She called our older son Fintan. The second was Dermot."

The waiter brought our wine, and I was jerked out of the spell Niall's voice had laid on me. It was like we'd been sitting around a campfire in the woods listening to an ancient legend, and then snap! We were in a modern restaurant in Shreveport, Louisiana, and there were other people around who had no idea what was going on. I automatically lifted my glass and took a sip of wine. I felt I was entitled.

"Fintan the Half Fairy was your paternal grandfather, Sookie," Niall said.

"No. I know who my grandfather was." My voice was shaking a little, I noticed, but it was still very quiet. "My grandfather was Mitchell Stackhouse and he married Adele Hale. My father was Corbett Hale Stackhouse, and he and my mom died in a flash flood when I was a little girl. Then I was raised by my grandmother Adele." Though I remembered the vampire in

Mississippi who'd told me he detected a trace of fairy blood in my veins, and I believed this was my great-grandfather, I just couldn't adjust my inner picture of my family.

"What was your grandmother like?" Niall asked.

"She raised me when she didn't have to," I said. "She took me and Jason into her home, and she worked hard to raise us right. We learned everything from her. She loved us. She had two children herself and buried them both, and that must have about killed her, but still she was strong for us."

"She was beautiful when she was young," Niall said. His green eyes lingered on my face as if he were trying to find some trace of her beauty in her granddaughter.

"I guess," I said uncertainly. You don't think about your grandmother in terms of beauty, at least in the normal way of things.

"I saw her after Fintan made her pregnant," Niall said. "She was lovely. Her husband had told her he could not give her children. He'd had mumps at the wrong time. That's a disease, isn't it?" I nodded. "She met Fintan one day when she was beating a rug out on the clothesline, in back of the house where you now live. He asked her for a drink of water. He was smitten on the spot. She wanted children so badly, and he promised her he could give them to her."

"You said fairies and people weren't usually fertile when they crossbreed."

"But Fintan was only half fairy. And he already knew that he was able to give a woman a child." Niall's mouth quirked.

"The first woman he loved died in childbirth, but your grandmother and her son were more fortunate, and then two years later she was able to carry Fintan's daughter to completion."

"He raped her," I said, almost hoping it was so. My grandmother had been the most true-blue woman I'd ever met. I couldn't picture her cheating anyone out of anything, particularly since she'd promised in front of God to be faithful to my grandfather.

"No, he did not. She wanted children, though she didn't want to be unfaithful to her husband. Fintan didn't care about the feelings of others, and he wanted her desperately," Niall said. "But he was never violent. He would not have raped her. However, my son could talk a woman into anything, even into something against her moral judgment. . . . And if she was very beautiful, so was he."

I tried to see the woman she must have been, in the grandmother I'd known. And I just couldn't.

"What was your father like, my grandson?" Niall asked.

"He was a handsome guy," I said. "He was a hard worker. He was a good dad."

Niall smiled slightly. "How did your mother feel about him?"

That question cut sharply into my warm memories of my father. "She, ah, she was really devoted to him." Maybe at the expense of her children.

"She was obsessed?" Niall's voice was not judgmental but certain, as if he knew my answer.

"Real possessive," I admitted. "Though I was only seven when they died, even I could see that. I guess I thought it was normal. She really wanted to give him all her attention. Sometimes Jason and I were in the way. And she was really jealous, I remember." I tried to look amused, as if my mother being so jealous of my father was a charming quirk.

"It was the fairy in him that made her hold on so strongly," Niall said. "It takes some humans that way. She saw the supernatural in him, and it enthralled her. Tell me, was she a good mother?"

"She tried hard," I whispered.

She had tried. My mother had known how to be a good mother theoretically. She knew how a good mother acted toward her children. She'd made herself go through all the motions. But all her true love had been saved for my father, who'd been bemused by the intensity of her passion. I could see that now, as an adult. As a child, I'd been confused and hurt.

The red-haired Were brought our salad and set it down in front of us. He wanted to ask us if we needed anything else, but he was too scared. He'd picked up on the atmosphere at the table.

"Why did you decide now to come meet me?" I asked. "How long have you known about me?" I put my napkin in my lap and sat there holding the fork. I should take a bite. Wasting was not part of the way I'd been raised. By my grandmother. Who'd had sex with a half fairy (who'd wandered into the yard like a stray dog). Enough sex over enough time to produce two children.

"I've known about your family for the past sixty years, give or take. But my son Fintan forbade me seeing any of you."

He carefully put a bit of tomato into his mouth, held it there, thought about it, chewed it. He ate the way I would if I was visiting an Indian or Nicaraguan restaurant.

"What changed?" I said, but I figured it out. "So your son is dead now."

"Yes," he said, and put down the fork. "Fintan is dead. After all, he was half human. And he'd lived for seven hundred years."

Was I supposed to have an opinion about this? I felt so numb, as though Niall had shot Novocain into my emotional center. I probably should ask how my—my *grandfather* had come to die, but I couldn't bring myself to do it.

"So you decided to come tell me about this—why?" I was proud of how calm I sounded.

"I'm old, even for my kind. I would like to know you. I can't atone for the way your life has been shaped by the heritage Fintan gave you. But I will try to make your life a little easier, if you'll permit me."

"Can you take the telepathy away?" I asked. A wild hope, not unmixed with fear, flared in me like a sunspot.

"You are asking if I can remove something from the fiber of your being," Niall said. "No, I can't do that."

I slumped in my chair. "Thought I'd ask," I said, fighting away tears. "Do I get three wishes, or is that with genies?"

Niall regarded me with no humor at all. "You wouldn't want to meet a genie," he said. "And I'm not a figure of fun. I am a prince."

"Sorry," I said. "I'm having a little trouble coping with all this . . . Great-grandfather." I didn't remember my human great-grandfathers. My grandfathers—okay, I guess one of them hadn't truly been my grandfather—hadn't looked or acted a thing like this beautiful creature. My grandfather Stackhouse died sixteen years ago, and my mother's parents had died before I was into my teens. So I'd known my grandmother Adele much better than any of the others, actually much better than I'd known my true parents.

"Hey," I said. "How come Eric fetched me for you? You're fairy, after all. Vampires go nuts when they smell fairies."

In fact, most vampires lost their self-control when they were around fairies. Only a very disciplined vampire could behave when a fairy got within smelling distance. My fairy god-mother, Claudine, was terrified of being anywhere around a bloodsucker.

"I can suppress my essence," Niall said. "They can see me but not smell me. It's a convenient magic. I can keep humans from even noticing me, as you have observed."

The way he said this let me know that he was not only very old and very powerful, but he was also very proud. "Did you send Claudine to me?" I said.

"Yes. I hope she's been of use. Only people of part-fae blood can have such a relationship with a fairy. I knew you needed her."

"Oh, yes, she's saved my life," I said. "She's been wonderful." She'd even taken me shopping. "Are all fairies as nice as Claudine, or as beautiful as her brother?"

Claude, male stripper and now entrepreneur, was as hand-some as a man could get, and he had the personality of a self-absorbed turnip.

"Dear one," Niall said, "we are all beautiful to humans; but some fairies are very nasty indeed."

Okay, here came the downside. I had a strong feeling that finding out I had a great-grandfather who was a full-blooded fairy was supposed to be good news, from Niall's point of view—but that it wasn't a completely iced cupcake. Now I would get the bad news.

"You went many years without being found," Niall said, "in part because that was what Fintan wanted."

"But he watched me?" I almost felt warmth in my heart at hearing that.

"My son was remorseful that he'd condemned two children to the half-in, half-out existence he'd experienced as a fairy who wasn't truly a fairy. I'm afraid the others of our race weren't kind to him." My great-grandfather's gaze was steady. "I did my best to defend him, but it wasn't enough. Fintan also found he wasn't human enough to pass as human, at least not for more than a short time."

"You don't look like this normally?" I asked, very curious.

"No." And just for a split second, I saw an almost blinding light, with Niall in the middle of it, beautiful and perfect. No wonder Einin had thought he was an angel.

"Claudine said she was working her way up," I said. "What does that mean?" I was floundering through this conversation. I felt like I'd been knocked down to my knees by all this information, and I was struggling to get to my emotional feet. I wasn't having a very successful time doing it.

"She shouldn't have told you that," Niall said. He debated with himself for a second or two before continuing. "Shifters are humans with a genetic twist, vampires are dead humans transformed into something different, but the fae have only a basic shape in common with humans. There are many kinds of fae—from the grotesque, like goblins, to the beautiful, like us." He said this quite unself-consciously.

"Are there angels?"

"Angels are yet another form, and one which has undergone an almost complete transformation, physical and moral. It can take hundreds of years to become an angel."

Poor Claudine.

"But enough about this," Niall said. "I want to know about you. My son kept me from your father and your aunt, and then from their children. His death came too late for me to know your cousin Hadley. But now I can see you and touch you." Which, incidentally, Niall was doing in a way that wasn't exactly human: if his hand wasn't holding mine, it was placed flat against my shoulder, or my back. This wasn't exactly the way humans related, but it wasn't hurting me. I wasn't as freaked out as I might have been, since I'd noticed Claudine was very touchy-feely, too. Since I couldn't get telepathic vibes from fairies, this much contact was tolerable. With a regular human being, I'd be bombarded with thoughts, since touch increased my sensitivity to telepathic contact.

"Did Fintan have any other children or grandchildren?" I asked. It would be nice to have more family.

"We'll talk of that later," Niall said, which sent up an immediate red flag. "Now that you know me a little," he said, "please tell me what I can do for you."

"Why should you do anything for me?" I said. We'd had the genie conversation. I wasn't going to revisit that.

"I can tell that your life has been hard. Now that I am allowed to see you, let me help you in some way."

"You sent me Claudine. She's been a big help," I repeated. Without the crutch of my sixth sense, I was having trouble understanding my great-grandfather's emotional and mental set. Was he grieving for his son? What had their relationship really been? Had Fintan thought he was doing us all a good deed in keeping his dad away from the Stackhouses all these years? Was Niall evil, or did he have bad intentions toward me? He could have done something awful to me from afar without going to the trouble of meeting me and paying for an expensive dinner.

"You wouldn't want to explain any more, huh?"

Niall shook his head, his hair brushing his shoulders like strands of gold and silver spun out to incredible fineness.

I had an idea. "Can you find my boyfriend?" I asked hopefully.

"You have a man? Besides the vampire?"

"Eric is not my man, but since I've had his blood a few times, and he's had mine . . ."

"That's why I approached you through him. You have a tie to him."

"Yes."

"I have known Eric Northman for a long time. I thought you would come if he asked you to. Did I do wrong?"

I was startled at this appeal. "No, sir," I said. "I don't think I'd have come if he hadn't told me it was okay. He wouldn't have brought me if he hadn't trusted you.... At least, I don't think so."

"Do you want me to kill him? End the tie?"

"No!" I said, getting kind of excited in a bad way. "No!"

A few people actually glanced at us for the first time, hearing my agitation despite my great-grandfather's *don't-look* influence.

"The other boyfriend," Niall said, and took another bite of his salmon. "Who is he and when did he vanish?"

"Quinn the weretiger," I said. "He's been gone since the explosion in Rhodes. He was hurt, but I saw him afterward."

"I heard about the Pyramid," Niall said. "You were there?"

I told him about it, and my newly discovered great-grandfather listened with a refreshing lack of judgment. He was neither horrified nor appalled, and he didn't feel sorry for me. I really liked that.

While I talked, I had a chance to regroup my emotions. "You know what?" I said when there was a natural pause. "Don't look for Quinn. He knows where I am, and he's got my number." *In more ways than one,* I thought sourly. "He'll show up when he feels like he can, I guess. Or not."

"But that leaves me with nothing to do as a gift for you," my great-grandfather said.

"Just give me a raincheck," I said, smiling, and then had to explain the term to him. "Something'll come up. Am I . . . Can

I talk about you? To my friends?" I asked. "No, I guess not."
I couldn't imagine telling my friend Tara that I had a new
great-grandfather who was a fairy. Amelia might be more
understanding.

"I want to keep our relationship a secret," he said. "I am so
glad to know you finally, and I want to know you better." He laid
his hand against my cheek. "But I have powerful enemies, and I
wouldn't want them to think of harming you to get at me."

I nodded. I understood. But it was kind of deflating to have
a brand-new relative and be forbidden to talk about him. Niall's
hand left my cheek to drift down to my own hand.

"What about Jason?" I asked. "Are you gonna talk to
him, too?"

"Jason," he said, his face showing distaste. "Somehow the
essential spark passed Jason by. I know he is made of the same
material as you, but in him the blood has only shown itself in his
ability to attract lovers, which after all is not much recommen-
dation. He wouldn't understand or appreciate our connection."

Great-grandfather sounded pretty snotty when he said that.
I started to say something in Jason's defense, but then I closed
my mouth. I had to admit to my most secret self that Niall was
almost certainly right. Jason would be full of demands, and he
would talk.

"How often are you going to be around?" I said instead,
striving hard to sound nonchalant. I knew I was expressing
myself clumsily, but I didn't know how else to establish some
framework for this new and awkward relationship.

"I'll try to visit you like any other relative would," he said.

I tried hard to picture that. Niall and I eating at the Hamburger Palace? Sharing a pew at church on a Sunday? I didn't think so.

"I feel like there's a lot you're not telling me," I said bluntly.

"Then we'll have something to talk about next time," he said, and one sea green eye winked at me. Okay, that was unexpected. He handed me a business card, another thing I didn't anticipate. It said simply, "Niall Brigant," with a telephone number centered beneath. "You can reach me at that number any time. Someone will answer."

"Thanks," I said. "I guess you know my phone number?" He nodded. I'd thought he was ready to leave, but he lingered. He seemed as reluctant to part as I was. "So," I began, clearing my throat. "What do you do all day?" I can't tell you how strange and neat it felt to be with a family member. I only had Jason, and he wasn't exactly a close brother, the kind you told everything to. I could count on him in a pinch, but hanging out together? Not going to happen.

My great-grandfather answered my question, but when I tried to recall it afterward, I couldn't come up with anything specific. I guess he did secret fairy-prince stuff. He did tell me he had part ownership in a bank or two, a company that made lawn furniture, and—and this seemed odd to me—a company that created and tested experimental medicine.

I looked at him doubtfully. "Medicine for humans," I said, to be sure I understood.

"Yes. For the most part," he responded. "But a few of the chemists make special things for us."

"For the fae."

He nodded, fine corn-silk hair falling around his face as his head moved. "There is so much iron now," he said. "I don't know if you realize that we are very sensitive to iron? And yet if we wear gloves every moment, we're too conspicuous in today's world." I looked at his right hand as it lay over mine on the white tablecloth. I extracted my fingers, stroked his skin. It felt oddly smooth.

"It's like an invisible glove," I said.

"Exactly." He nodded. "One of their formulas. But enough about me."

Just when it was getting interesting, I thought. But I could see that my great-grandfather had no real reason to trust me with all his secrets yet.

Niall asked me about my job, and my boss, and my routine, like a real great-grandfather would. Though he clearly didn't like the idea of his great-granddaughter working, the bar part of it didn't seem to disturb him. As I've said, Niall wasn't easy to read. His thoughts were his own as far as I was concerned; but I did notice that every now and then he stopped himself from speaking.

Eventually, dinner got eaten, and I glanced at my watch, astounded at how many hours had passed. I needed to go. I had to work the next day. I excused myself, thanking my great-grandfather (it still made me shiver, thinking of him that way) for the meal and very hesitantly leaning forward to kiss his cheek as he'd kissed mine. He seemed to hold his breath while I did so, and his skin felt soft and lustrous as a silky plum under my lips. Even though he could look like a human, he didn't feel like one.

He stood when I left, but he remained at the table—to take care of the bill, I assumed. I went outside without registering anything my eyes saw along the way. Eric was waiting for me in the parking lot. He'd had some TrueBlood while he was waiting, and he'd been reading in the car, which was parked under a light.

I was exhausted.

I didn't realize how nerve-wracking my dinner with Niall had been until I was out of his presence. Though I'd been sitting in a comfortable chair the whole meal, I was as tired as if we'd been talking while we were running.

Niall had been able to mask the fairy odor from Eric in the restaurant, but I saw from the flare of Eric's nostrils that the intoxicating scent clung to me. Eric's eyes closed in ecstasy, and he actually licked his lips. I felt like a T-bone just out of reach of a hungry dog.

"Snap out of it," I said. I wasn't in the mood.

With a huge effort, Eric reined himself in. "When you smell like that," he said, "I just want to fuck you and bite you and rub myself all over you."

That was pretty comprehensive, and I won't say I didn't have a second (split evenly between lust and fear) of picturing such activity. But I had larger issues to think about.

"Hold your horses," I said. "What do you know about fairies? Aside from how they taste?"

Eric looked at me with clearer eyes. "They're lovely, male

and female both. Incredibly tough and ferocious. They aren't immortal, but they live a very long time unless something happens to them. You can kill them with iron, for example. There are other ways to kill them, but it's hard work. They like to keep to themselves for the most part. They like moderate climates. I don't know what they eat or drink when they're by themselves. They sample the food of other cultures; I've even seen a fairy try blood. They have a higher opinion of themselves than they have any right to. When they give their word, they keep it." He thought for a moment. "They have different magics. They can't all do the same things. And they are very magical. It's their essence. They have no gods but their own race, for they've often been mistaken for gods. In fact, some of them have taken on the attributes of a deity."

I gaped at him. "What do you mean?"

"Well, I don't mean they're *holy*," Eric said. "I mean that the fairies who inhabit the woods identify with the woods so strongly that to hurt one is to hurt the other. So they've suffered a great drop in numbers. Obviously, we vampires are not going to be up on fairy politics and survival issues, since we are so dangerous to them . . . simply because we find them intoxicating."

I'd never thought to ask Claudine about any of this. For one thing, she didn't seem to enjoy talking about being a fairy, and when she popped up, it was usually when I was in trouble and therefore sadly self-absorbed. For another thing, I'd imagined there were maybe a small handful of fairies left in the world, but Eric was telling me there once were as many fairies as there were vampires, though the fairy race was on the wane.

In sharp contrast, vampires—at least in America—were definitely on the increase. There were three bills wending their way through Congress dealing with vampire immigration. America had the distinction (along with Canada, Japan, Norway, Sweden, England, and Germany) of being a country that had responded to the Great Revelation with relative calm.

The night of the carefully orchestrated Great Revelation, vampires all over the world had appeared on television, radio, in person, whatever the best means of communication in the area might be, to tell the human population, "Hey! We actually exist. But we're not life threatening! The new Japanese synthetic blood satisfies our nutritional requirements."

The six years since then had been one big learning curve.

Tonight I'd added a huge amount to my store of supernatural lore.

"So the vampires have the upper hand," I said.

"We're not at war," Eric said. "We haven't been at war for centuries."

"So in the past the vampires and the fairies have fought each other? I mean, like, pitched battles?"

"Yes," Eric said. "And if it came to that again, the first one I'd take out is Niall."

"Why?"

"He's very powerful in the fairy world. He is very magical. If he's sincere in his desire to take you under his wing, you're both very lucky and very unlucky." Eric started the car and we pulled out of the parking lot. I hadn't seen Niall come out of the restaurant. Maybe he'd just poofed out of the dining room. I hoped he'd paid our bill first.

"I guess I have to ask you to explain that," I said. But I had a feeling I didn't really want to know the answer.

"There were thousands of fairies in the United States once," Eric said. "Now there are only hundreds. But the ones that are left are very determined survivors. And not all of those are friends of the prince's."

"Oh, good. I needed another supernatural group who dislikes me," I muttered.

We drove through the night in silence, wending our way back to the interstate that would carry us east to Bon Temps. Eric seemed heavily thoughtful. I also had plenty of food for thought; more than I'd eaten at supper, that was for sure.

I found that on the whole, I felt cautiously happy. It was good to have a kind of belated great-grandfather. Niall seemed genuinely anxious to establish a relationship with me. I still had a heap of questions to ask, but they could wait until we knew each other better.

Eric's Corvette could go pretty damn fast, and Eric wasn't exactly sticking to the speed limit on the interstate. I wasn't awfully surprised when I saw the blinking lights coming up behind us. I was only astonished the cop car could catch up with Eric.

"A-hum," I said, and Eric cursed in a language that probably hadn't been spoken out loud in centuries. But even the sheriff of Area Five has to obey human laws these days, or at least he has to pretend to. Eric pulled over to the shoulder.

"With a vanity plate like BLDSKR, what do you expect?" I asked, not so secretly enjoying the moment. I saw the dark shape of the trooper emerging from the car behind us, walking up with something in his hand—clipboard, flashlight?

I looked harder. I reached out. A snarled mass of aggression and fear met my inner ear.

"Were! There's something wrong," I said, and Eric's big hand shoved me down into the floorboard, which would have provided a little more concealment if the car had been anything other than a Corvette.

Then the patrolman came up to the window and tried to shoot me.

Chapter 5

Eric had turned to fill the window and block the rest of the car from the shooter's aim, and he got it in the neck. For an awful moment, Eric slumped back in the seat, his face blank and dark blood flowing sluggishly down his white skin. I screamed as if noise would protect me, and the gun pointed at me as the gunman leaned into the car to aim past Eric.

But he'd been a fool to do that. Eric's hand clamped on the man's wrist, and Eric began squeezing. The "patrolman" started doing a little shrieking of his own, flailing uselessly at Eric with his empty hand. The gun fell on top of me. I'm just lucky it didn't discharge when it fell. I don't know much about handguns, but this one was big and lethal-looking, and I scrambled to an upright position and aimed it at the shooter.

He froze in place, half in and half out of the window. Eric

had already broken his arm and had kept a tight grip. The fool should have been more afraid of the vampire who had a hold on him than the waitress who hardly knew how to fire the gun, but the gun commanded his attention.

I was sure I would have heard if the highway patrol had decided to start shooting speeders instead of ticketing them.

"Who are you?" I said, and no one could blame me if my voice wasn't too steady. "Who sent you?"

"They told me to," the Were gasped. Now that I had time to notice details, I could see he wasn't wearing a proper highway patrol uniform. It was the right color, and the hat was right, but the pants weren't uniform pants.

"They, who?" I asked.

Eric's fangs clamped into the Were's shoulder. Despite his wound, Eric was pulling the faux patrolman into the car inch by inch. It seemed only fair that Eric got some blood since he'd lost so much of his own. The assassin began crying.

"Don't let him turn me into one of them," he appealed to me.

"You should be so lucky," I said, not because I actually thought it was so darn great to be a vampire but because I was sure Eric had something much worse in mind.

I got out of the car because there was no point in trying to get Eric to release the Were. He wouldn't listen to me with the bloodlust on him so strong. My bond to Eric was the crucial factor in this decision. I was happy that he was enjoying himself, getting the blood he needed. I was furious that someone had tried to hurt him. Since both of these feelings would not normally be colors in my emotional palette, I knew what was to blame.

Plus, the inside of the Corvette had gotten unpleasantly crowded, what with me, Eric, and most of the Were.

Miraculously, no cars passed while I trotted along the shoulder to our attacker's vehicle, which (not so much to my surprise) turned out to be a plain white car with an illegal flashing attachment. I turned out the car's lights and, by punching or disconnecting every wire and button I could find, managed to kill the flashers, too. Now we were not nearly so conspicuous. Eric had shut down the Corvette's lights moments into the encounter.

I looked over the inside of the white car quickly but didn't see an envelope marked "Revelation of who hired me, in case I get caught." I needed a clue. There should at least have been a phone number on a scrap of paper, a phone number I could look up in a reverse directory. If I knew how to do such a thing. Rats. I trudged back to Eric's car, noticing in the lights of a passing semi that there weren't any legs sticking out of the driver's window anymore, which rendered the Corvette a lot less conspicuous. But we needed to get out of there.

I peered into the Corvette and found it empty. The only reminder of what had just happened was a smear of blood on Eric's seat, and I pulled a tissue out of my purse, spat on it, and rubbed the drying blood off; not a very elegant solution, but practical.

Suddenly, Eric was beside me, and I had to stifle a shriek. He was still excited by the unexpected attack, and he pinned me against the side of the car, holding my head at the correct angle for a kiss. I felt a lurch of desire and came very close to saying, "What the hell, take me now, you big Viking." It was not only the blood bond inclining me to accept his tacit offer, but my memory of how wonderful Eric was in bed. But I thought of Quinn and detached myself from Eric's mouth with a great effort.

For a second, I didn't think he was going to let go, but he did. "Let me see," I said in an unsteady voice, and pulled his shirt collar aside to look at the bullet wound. Eric had almost finished healing, but of course his shirt was still wet with blood.

"What was that about?" he asked. "Was that an enemy of yours?"

"I have no idea."

"He shot at you," Eric said, as if I was just a wee bit slow. "He wanted you first."

"But what if he did that to hurt you? What if he would have blamed my death on you?" I was so tired of being the object of plots that I suspected I was trying to *will* Eric into being the target. Another idea struck me, and I veered into it. "And how'd they find us?"

"Someone who knew we'd be driving back to Bon Temps tonight," Eric said. "Someone who knew what car I was in."

"It couldn't have been Niall," I said, and then rethought my flash of loyalty to my brand-new, self-proclaimed great-grandfather. After all, he might have been lying the whole time we were at the table. How would I know? I couldn't get in his head. The ignorance of my position felt strange to me.

But I didn't believe Niall had been lying.

"I don't think it was the fairy, either," Eric said. "But we'd better talk about it on the road. This isn't a good place for us to linger."

He was right about that. I didn't know where he'd put the body, and I realized that I didn't really care. A year ago it would have torn me up, leaving a body behind as we sped away along the interstate. Now I was just glad it was him and not me who was lying in the woods.

I was a terrible Christian and a decent survivalist.

As we drove through the dark, I pondered the chasm yawning right in front of me, waiting for me to take that extra step. I felt stranded on that brink. I found it harder and harder to stick to what was right, when what was expedient made better sense. Really, my brain told me ruthlessly, didn't I understand that Quinn had dumped me? Wouldn't he have gotten in touch if he still considered us a couple? Hadn't I always had a soft spot for Eric, who made love like a train thundering into a tunnel? Didn't I have beaucoup evidence that Eric could defend me better than anyone I knew?

I could hardly summon the energy to be shocked at myself.

If you find yourself considering who to take for a lover because of his ability to defend you, you're getting pretty close to selecting a mate because you think he has desirable traits to pass along to future generations. And if there'd been a chance I could have had Eric's child (a thought that made me shiver), he would have been at the top of the list, a list I hadn't even known I'd been compiling. I pictured myself as a female peacock looking for the male peacock with the prettiest display of tail, or a wolf waiting for the leader (strongest, smartest, bravest) of the pack to mount her.

Okay, I'd yucked myself out. I was a human woman. I tried to be a good woman. I had to find Quinn because I had committed myself to him...sort of.

No, no quibbling!

"What are you thinking about, Sookie?" Eric asked out of the darkness. "Your face has had thoughts rippling across it too fast to follow."

The fact that he could see me—not only in the dark, but while he was supposed to be watching the road—was exasperating and scary. And proof of his superiority, my inner cavewoman said.

"Eric, just get me home. I'm in emotional overload."

He didn't speak again. Maybe he was being wise, or maybe the healing was painful.

"We need to talk about this again," he said when he pulled into my driveway. He parked in front of the house, turned to me as much as he could in the little car. "Sookie, I'm hurting....Can I..." He leaned over, brushed his fingers over my neck.

At the very idea, my body betrayed me. A throbbing started down low, and that was just wrong. A person shouldn't get excited at the idea of being bitten. That's bad, right? I clenched my fists so tightly my fingernails made my palms hurt.

Now that I could see him better, now that the interior of the car was illuminated with the harsh glare of the security light, I realized that Eric was even paler than usual. As I watched, the bullet began exiting the wound, and he leaned back against his seat, his eyes shut. Millimeter by millimeter, the bullet was extruded until it dropped into my waiting hand. I remembered Eric getting me to suck out a bullet in his arm. Ha! What a fraud he'd been. The bullet would've come out on its own. My indignation made me feel more like myself.

"I think you can make it home," I said, though I felt an almost irresistible urge to lean over to him and offer my neck or my wrist. I gritted my teeth and got out of the car. "You can stop at Merlotte's and get bottled blood if you really need some."

"You're hard-hearted," Eric said, but he didn't sound truly angry or affronted.

"I am," I said, and I smiled at him. "You be careful, you hear?"

"Of course," he said. "And I'm not stopping for any policemen."

I made myself march into the house without looking back. When I was inside the front door and had shut it firmly behind me, I felt an immediate relief. Thank goodness. I'd wondered if I was going to turn around at every step I took away from him. This blood tie thing was really irritating. If I wasn't careful and vigilant, I was going to do something I'd regret.

"I am woman, hear me roar," I said.

"Gosh, what prompted that?" Amelia asked, and I jumped. She was coming down the hall from the kitchen in her nightgown and matching robe, peach with cream-colored lace trim. Everything of Amelia's was nice. She'd never sneer at anyone else's shopping habits, but she'd never wear anything from Wal-Mart, either.

"I've had a trying evening," I said. I looked down at myself. Only a little blood on the blue silk T-shirt. I'd have to soak it. "How have things gone here?"

"Octavia called me," Amelia said, and though she was trying to keep her voice steady, I could feel the anxiety coming off her in waves.

"Your mentor." I wasn't at my brightest.

"Yep, the one and only." She bent down to pick up Bob, who always seemed to be around if Amelia was upset. She held him to her chest and buried her face in his fur. "She had heard, of course. Even after Katrina and all the changes it made in her life, she has to bring up *the mistake*." (That was what Amelia called it—the mistake.)

"I wonder what Bob calls it," I said.

Amelia looked over Bob's head at me, and I knew instantly I'd said a tactless thing. "Sorry," I said. "I wasn't thinking. But maybe it's not too realistic to think you can get out of this without being called to account, huh?"

"You're right," she said. She didn't seem too happy about my rightness, but at least she said it. "I did wrong. I attempted something I shouldn't have, and Bob paid the price."

Wow, when Amelia decided to confess, she went whole hog.

"I'm going to have to take my licks," she said. "Maybe they'll take away my magic practice for a year. Maybe longer."

"Oh. That seems harsh," I said. In my fantasy, her mentor just scolded Amelia in front of a room full of magicians and sorcerers and witches or what-have-you, and then they transformed Bob back. He promptly forgave Amelia and told her he loved her. Since he forgave her, the rest of the assemblage did, too, and Amelia and Bob came back to my house and lived here together... for a good long while. (I wasn't too specific about that part.)

"That's the mildest punishment possible," Amelia said.

"Oh."

"You don't want to know the other possible sentences." She was right. I didn't. "Well, what mysterious errand did Eric take you on?" Amelia asked.

Amelia couldn't have tipped off anyone to our destination or route; she hadn't known where we were going. "Oh, ah, he just wanted to take me to a new restaurant in Shreveport. It had a French name. It was pretty nice."

"So, this was like a date?" I could tell she was wondering what place Quinn played in my relationship with Eric.

"Oh, no, not a date," I said, sounding unconvincing even to myself. "No guy-girl action going on. Just, you know, hanging out." Kissing. Getting shot.

"He sure is handsome," Amelia said.

"Yeah, no doubt about it. I've met some toothsome guys. Remember Claude?" I'd shown Amelia the poster that had arrived in the mail two weeks before, a blowup of the romance novel cover for which Claude had posed. She'd been impressed— what woman wouldn't be?

"Ah, I went to watch Claude strip last week." Amelia couldn't meet my eyes.

"And you didn't take me!" Claude was a very disagreeable person, especially when contrasted with his sister, Claudine, but he was beyond gorgeous. He was in the Brad Pitt stratosphere of male beauty. Of course, he was gay. Wouldn't you know it? "You went while I was at work?"

"I thought you wouldn't approve of my going," she said, ducking her head. "I mean, since you're friends with his sister. I went with Tara. JB was working. Are you mad?"

"Nah. I don't care." My friend Tara owned a dress shop, and her new husband, JB, worked at a women's exercise center. "I would like to see Claude trying to act like he was enjoying himself."

"I think he was having a good time," she said. "There's no one Claude loves better than Claude, right? So all these women looking at him and admiring him . . . He's not into women, but he's sure into being admired."

"True. Let's go see him together sometime."

"Okay," she said, and I could tell she was quite cheerful again. "Now, tell me what you ordered at this new fancy restaurant." So I told her. But all the while I was wishing I didn't have to keep silent about my great-grandfather. I wanted so badly to tell Amelia about Niall: how he looked, what he'd said, that I had a whole history I hadn't known. And it would take me a while to process what my grandmother had endured, to alter my picture of her in light of the facts I'd learned. And

I had to rethink my unpleasant memories of my mother, too. She'd fallen for my dad like a ton of bricks, and she'd had his kids because she loved him . . . only to find that she didn't want to share him with them, especially with me, another female. At least, this was my new insight.

"There was more stuff," I said, a yawn splitting my jaw in two. It was very late. "But I've got to get to bed. I get any phone calls or anything?"

"That Were from Shreveport called. He wanted to talk to you, and I told him you were out for the evening and he should call you on your cell. He asked if he could meet up with you, but I said I didn't know where you were."

"Alcide," I said. "I wonder what he wanted." I figured I'd call him tomorrow.

"And some girl called. Said she'd been a waitress at Merlotte's before, and she'd seen you at the wedding last night."

"Tanya?"

"Yeah, that was her name."

"What did she want?"

"Don't know. She said she'd call back tomorrow or see you at the bar."

"Crap. I hope Sam didn't hire her to fill in or something."

"I thought I was the fill-in bargirl."

"Yeah, unless someone's quit. I warn you, Sam likes her."

"You don't?"

"She's a treacherous bitch."

"Gosh, tell me what you really think."

"No kidding, Amelia, she took a job at Merlotte's so she could spy on me for the Pelts."

"Oh, *that's* the one. Well, she won't spy on you again. I'll take steps."

That was a scarier thought than working with Tanya. Amelia was a strong and skillful witch, don't get me wrong, but she was also prone to attempt things beyond her experience level. Hence Bob.

"Check with me first, please," I said, and Amelia looked surprised.

"Well, sure," she said. "Now, I'm off to bed."

She made her way up the steps with Bob in her arms, and I went to my small bathroom to remove my makeup and put on my own nightgown. Amelia hadn't noticed the speckles of blood on the shirt, and I put it in the sink to soak.

What a day it had been. I'd spent time with Eric, who always rattled my chain, and I'd found a living relative, though not a human one. I'd learned a lot of stuff about my family, most of it unpleasant. I'd eaten in a fancy restaurant, though I could hardly recall the food. And finally, I'd been shot at.

When I crawled into bed, I said my prayers, trying to put Quinn at the top of the list. I thought the excitement of discovering a great-grandfather would keep me awake that night, but sleep claimed me right when I was in the middle of asking God to help me find my way through the moral morass of being party to a killing.

Chapter 6

There was a knock on the front door the next morning about an hour before I wanted to wake up. I heard it only because Bob had come into my room and jumped on my bed, where he wasn't supposed to be, settling into the space behind my knees while I lay on my side. He purred loudly, and I reached down to scratch behind his ears. I loved cats. That didn't stop me from liking dogs, too, and only the fact that I was gone so much kept me from getting a puppy. Terry Bellefleur had offered me one, but I'd wavered until his pups were gone. I wondered if Bob would mind a kitten companion. Would Amelia get jealous if I bought a female cat? I had to smile even as I snuggled deeper into the bed.

But I wasn't truly asleep, and I did hear the knock.

I muttered a few words about the person at the door, and I slid on my slippers and threw on my thin blue cotton bathrobe.

The morning had a hint of chill, reminding me that despite the mild and sunny days, this was October. There were Halloweens when even a sweater was too warm, and there were Halloweens when you had to wear a light coat when you did your trick-or-treating.

I looked through the peephole and saw an elderly black woman with a halo of white hair. She was light-skinned and her features were narrow and sharp: nose, lips, eyes. She was wearing magenta lipstick and a yellow pantsuit. But she didn't seem armed or dangerous. This just goes to show how misleading first appearances can be. I opened the door.

"Young lady, I'm here to see Amelia Broadway," the woman informed me in very precisely pronounced English.

"Please come in," I said, because this was an older woman and I'd been brought up to revere old people. "Have a seat." I indicated the couch. "I'll go up and get Amelia."

I noticed she didn't apologize for getting me out of bed or for showing up unannounced. I climbed the stairs with a grim feeling that Amelia wasn't going to enjoy this message.

I so seldom went up to the second floor that it surprised me to see how nice Amelia had made it look. Since the upper bedrooms had only had basic furniture in them, she'd turned the one to the right, the larger one, into her bedroom. The one to the left was her sitting room. It held her television, an easy chair and ottoman, a small computer desk and her computer, and a plant or two. The bedroom, which I believed had been built for a generation of Stackhouses that had sired three boys in quick succession, had only a small closet, but Amelia had bought rolling clothes racks from somewhere on the Internet and assembled them handily. Then she'd bought a tri-fold screen at an auction and repainted it and arranged it in front of the racks to camouflage them. Her bright bedspread and the old table she'd repainted to serve as her makeup table added to the color that jumped out from the white-painted walls. Amid all this cheer was one dismal witch.

Amelia was sitting up in bed, her short hair mashed into strange shapes. "Who is that I hear downstairs?" she asked in a very hushed voice.

"Older black lady, light-skinned? Sharp way about her?"

"Omigod," Amelia breathed, and slumped back against her dozen or so pillows. "It's Octavia."

"Well, you come down and have a word with her. I can't entertain her."

Amelia snarled at me, but she accepted the inevitable. She got out of bed and pulled off her nightgown. She pulled on a bra and panties and some jeans, and she extracted a sweater from a drawer.

I went down to tell Octavia Fant that Amelia was coming. Amelia would have to walk right past her to get to the bathroom, since there was only the one staircase, but at least I could smooth the way.

"Can I get you some coffee?" I asked. The older woman was busy looking around the room with her bright brown eyes.

"If you have some tea, I'd like a cup," Octavia Fant said.

"Yes, ma'am, we have some," I said, relieved that Amelia had insisted on buying it. I had no idea what kind it was, and I hoped it was in a bag, because I'd never made hot tea in my life.

"Good," she said, and that was that.

"Amelia's on her way down," I said, trying to think of some graceful way to add, "And she's going to have to hurry through the room to pee and brush her teeth, so pretend you don't see her." I abandoned that lost cause and fled to the kitchen.

I retrieved Amelia's tea from one of her designated shelves, and while the water was getting hot, I got down two cups and saucers and put them on a tray. I added the sugar bowl and a tiny pitcher with milk and two spoons. *Napkins!* I thought, and wished I had some cloth ones instead of regular paper. (This was how Octavia Fant made me feel, without her using a bit of magic on me.) I heard the water running in the hall bathroom just as I put a handful of cookies on a plate and added that to the assemblage. I didn't have any flowers or a little vase, which was the only other thing I thought of that I could've added. I picked up the tray and made my way slowly down the hall to the living room.

I set the tray down on the coffee table in front of Ms. Fant. She looked up at me with her piercing eyes and gave me a curt nod of thanks. I realized that I could not read her mind. I'd been holding off, waiting for a moment when I could really give her her proper due, but she knew how to block me out. I'd never met a human who could do that. For a second I felt almost irritated. Then I remembered who and what she was, and I scooted off to my room to make my bed and visit my own little bathroom. I passed Amelia in the hall, and she gave me a scared look.

Sorry, Amelia, I thought, as I closed my bedroom door firmly. *You're on your own.*

I didn't have to be at work until the evening, so I put on some old jeans and a Fangtasia T-shirt ("The Bar with a Bite"). Pam had given it to me when the bar first started selling them. I slid my feet into some Crocs and went into the kitchen to fix my own beverage, coffee. I made some toast and got the local paper I'd grabbed when I'd answered the door. Rolling the rubber band off, I glanced at the front page. The school board had met, the local Wal-Mart had donated generously to the Boys and Girls Club's after-school program, and the state legislature had voted to recognize vampire-human marriages. Well, well. No one had thought that bill would ever pass.

I flipped open the paper to read the obituaries. First the local deaths—no one I knew, good. Then the area deaths—oh, *no.*

MARIA-STAR COOPER, read the heading. The item said only, "Maria-Star Cooper, 25, a resident of Shreveport, died unexpectedly at her home yesterday. Cooper, a photographer, is survived by her mother and father, Matthew and Stella Cooper of Minden, and three brothers. Arrangements are pending."

I felt suddenly out of breath and sank into the straight-back chair with a feeling of total disbelief. Maria-Star and I hadn't exactly been friends, but I'd liked her well enough, and she and Alcide Herveaux, a major figure in the Shreveport Were pack, had been going together for months. Poor Alcide! His first girlfriend had died violently, and now this.

The phone rang and I jumped. I grabbed it up with a terrible feeling of disaster. "Hello?" I said cautiously, as if the phone could spit at me.

"Sookie," said Alcide. He had a deep voice, and now it was husky with tears.

"I'm so sorry," I said. "I just read the paper." There was nothing else to say. Now I knew why he'd called the night before.

"She was murdered," Alcide said.

"Oh, my God."

"Sookie, it was only the beginning. On the off chance that Furnan is after you, too, I want you to stay alert."

"Too late," I said after a moment given to absorbing this awful news. "Someone tried to kill me last night."

Alcide held the phone away from him and howled. Hearing this, in the middle of the day, over the telephone . . . Even then, it was frightening.

Trouble within the Shreveport pack had been brewing for a while. Even I, separated from Were politics, had known that. Patrick Furnan, the leader of the Long Tooth pack, had gotten his office by killing Alcide's father in combat. The victory had been legal—well, Were legal—but there had been a few not-so-legal plays along the way. Alcide—strong, young, prosperous, and packing a grudge—had always been a threat to Furnan, at least in Furnan's mind.

This was a tense topic, since Weres were secret from the human population, not out in the open like vampires. The day was coming, and coming soon, when the shifter population would step forward. I'd heard them speak of it over and over.

But that hadn't happened yet, and it wouldn't be good if the first knowledge the humans had of the Weres was of bodies turning up all over the place.

"Someone will be over there right away," Alcide said.

"Absolutely not. I have to go to work tonight, and I'm so utterly on the edge of this thing that I'm sure they won't try again. But I do need to know how the guy knew where and when to find me."

"Tell Amanda the circumstances," Alcide said, his voice thick with anger, and then Amanda came on. Hard to believe that when I'd seen her at the wedding we'd both been so cheerful.

"Tell me," she said crisply, and I knew this was no time to argue. I told her the story as tersely as possible (leaving out Niall, and Eric's name, and most other details), and she was silent for a few seconds after I'd finished speaking.

"Since he was taken out, that's one less we have to worry about," she said, sounding simply relieved. "I wish you'd known who he was."

"Sorry," I said a bit acidly. "I was thinking about the gun, not his ID. How come you-all can have a war with as few people as you have?" The Shreveport pack couldn't number over thirty.

"Reinforcements from other territories."

"Why would anyone do that?" Why join in a war that wasn't yours? What was the point of losing your own people when it was the other pack's dispute?

"There are perks to backing the winning side," Amanda said. "Listen, you still got that witch living with you?"

"I do."

"Then there's something you can do to help."

"Okay," I said, though I didn't recall offering. "What would that be?"

"You need to ask your witch friend if she'll go to Maria-Star's apartment and get some kind of reading on what happened there. Is that possible? We want to know the Weres involved."

"It's possible, but I don't know if she'll do it."

"Ask her now, please."

"Ah...let me call you back. She's got a visitor."

Before I went out to the living room, I made a call. I didn't want to leave this message on the answering machine at Fangtasia, which wouldn't be open yet, so I called Pam's cell, something I'd never done before. As it rang, I found myself wondering if it was in the coffin with her. That was an eerie thing to picture. I didn't know if Pam actually slept in a coffin or not, but if she did...I shuddered. Of course, the phone went to voice mail, and I said, "Pam, I've found out why Eric and I were pulled over last night, or at least I think so. There's a Were war brewing, and I think I was the target. Someone sold us out to Patrick Furnan. And I didn't tell anyone where I was going." That was a problem Eric and I had been too shaken to discuss the night before. How had anyone, anyone at all, known where we'd be last night? That we'd be driving back from Shreveport.

Amelia and Octavia were in the middle of a discussion, but neither of them looked as angry or upset as I'd feared.

"I hate to intrude," I said as both pairs of eyes turned to

me. Octavia's eyes were brown, Amelia's bright blue, but at the moment they were eerily alike in expression.

"Yes?" Octavia was clearly queen of the situation.

Any witch worth her salt would know about Weres. I condensed the issues of the Were war down to a few sentences, told them about the attack the night before on the interstate, and explained Amanda's request.

"Is this something you should get involved with, Amelia?" Octavia asked, her voice making it quite clear there was only one answer she should give.

"Oh, I think so," Amelia said. She smiled. "Can't have someone shooting at my roomie. I'll help Amanda."

Octavia couldn't have been more shocked if Amelia had spat a watermelon seed on her pants. "Amelia! You're trying things beyond your ability! This will lead to terrible trouble! Look what you've already done to poor Bob Jessup."

Oh, boy, I hadn't known Amelia that long, but I already knew that was a poor way to get her to comply with your wishes. If Amelia was proud of anything, it was her witchy ability. Challenging her expertise was a sure way to rattle her. On the other hand, Bob was a major fuckup.

"Can you change him back?" I asked the older witch.

Octavia looked at me sharply. "Of course," she said.

"Then why don't you do it, and we can go from there?" I said.

Octavia looked very startled, and I knew I shouldn't have gotten up in her face like that. On the other hand, if she wanted to show Amelia that her magic was more powerful, here was her chance. Bob the cat was sitting in Amelia's lap, looking unconcerned. Octavia reached in her pocket and pulled out a pill container filled with what looked like marijuana; but I guess any dried herb pretty much looks the same, and I haven't ever actually handled marijuana, so I'm no judge. Anyway, Octavia took a pinch of this dried green stuff and reached out to let the bits drop on the cat's fur. Bob didn't seem to mind.

Amelia's face was a picture as she watched Octavia casting a spell, which seemed to consist of some Latin, a few motions, and the aforementioned herb. Finally, Octavia uttered what must have been the esoteric equivalent of "Allakazam!" and pointed at the cat.

Nothing happened.

Octavia repeated the phrase even more forcefully. Again with the finger pointing.

And again with the no results.

"You know what I think?" I said. No one seemed to want to know, but it was my house. "I wonder if Bob was always a cat, and for some reason he was temporarily human. That's why you can't change him back. Maybe he's in his true form right now."

"That's ridiculous," the older witch snapped. She was some kind of put out at her failure. Amelia was trying hard to suppress a grin.

"If you're so sure after this that Amelia's incompetent, which I happen to know she isn't, you might want to consider coming to see Maria-Star's apartment with us," I said. "Make sure Amelia doesn't get into any trouble."

Amelia looked indignant for a second, but she seemed to see my plan, and she added her entreaty to mine.

"Very well. I'll come along," Octavia said grandly.

I couldn't see into the old witch's mind, but I'd worked at a bar long enough to know a lonely person when I saw one.

I got the address from Amanda, who told me Dawson was guarding the place until we arrived. I knew him and liked him, since he'd helped me out before. He owned a local motorcycle repair shop a couple of miles out of Bon Temps, and he sometimes ran Merlotte's for Sam. Dawson didn't run with a pack, and the news that he was pitching in with Alcide's rebel faction was significant.

I can't say the drive to the outskirts of Shreveport was a bonding experience for the three of us, but I did fill Octavia in on the background of the pack troubles. And I explained my own involvement. "When the contest for packmaster was taking place," I said, "Alcide wanted me there as a human lie detector. I actually did catch the other guy cheating, which was good. But after that, it became a fight to the death, and Patrick Furnan was stronger. He killed Jackson Herveaux."

"I guess they covered up the death?" The old witch seemed neither shocked nor surprised.

"Yes, they put the body out at an isolated farm he owned, knowing no one would look there for a while. The wounds on the body weren't recognizable by the time he was found."

"Has Patrick Furnan been a good leader?"

"I really don't know," I admitted. "Alcide has always seemed to have a discontented group around him, and they're the ones I know best in the pack, so I guess I'm on Alcide's side."

"Did you ever consider that you could just step aside? Let the best Were win?"

"No," I said honestly. "I would have been just as glad if Alcide hadn't called me and told me about the pack troubles. But now that I know, I'll help him if I can. Not that I'm an angel or anything. But Patrick Furnan hates me, and it's only smart to help his enemy, point number one. And I liked Maria-Star, point number two. And someone tried to kill me last night, someone who may have been hired by Furnan, point number three."

Octavia nodded. She was sure no wussy old lady.

Maria-Star had lived in a rather dated apartment building on Highway 3 between Benton and Shreveport. It was a small complex, just two buildings side by side facing a parking lot, right there on the highway. The buildings backed onto a field, and the adjacent businesses were day businesses: an insurance agency and a dentist's office.

Each of the two red brick buildings was divided into four apartments. I noticed a familiar battered pickup truck in front of the building on the right, and I parked by it. These apartments were enclosed; you went in the common entrance into a hall, and there was a door on either side of the stairway to the second floor. Maria-Star had lived on the ground-floor left apartment. This was easy to spot, because Dawson was propped against the wall beside her door.

I introduced him to the two witches as "Dawson" because I didn't know his first name. Dawson was a supersized man. I'd bet you could crack pecans on his biceps. He had dark brown hair beginning to show just a little gray, and a neatly trimmed mustache. I'd known who he was all my life, but I'd never known him well. Dawson was probably seven or eight years older than me, and he'd married early. And divorced early, too. His son, who lived with the mother, was quite a football player for Clarice High School. Dawson looked tougher than any guy I'd ever met. I don't know if it was the very dark eyes, or the grim face, or simply the size of him.

There was crime scene tape across the apartment doorway. My eyes welled up when I saw it. Maria-Star had died violently in this space only hours before. Dawson produced a set of keys (Alcide's?) and unlocked the door, and we ducked under the tape to enter.

And we all stood frozen in silence, appalled at the state of the little living room. My way was blocked by an overturned occasional table with a big gash marring the wood. My eyes flickered over the irregular dark stains on the walls until my brain told me the stains were blood.

The smell was faint but unpleasant. I began to breathe shallowly so I wouldn't get sick.

"Now, what do you want us to do?" Octavia asked.

"I thought you'd do an ectoplasmic reconstruction, like Amelia did before," I said.

"Amelia did an ectoplasmic reconstruction?" Octavia had dropped the haughty tone and sounded genuinely surprised and admiring. "I've never seen one."

Amelia nodded modestly. "With Terry and Bob and Patsy," she said. "It worked great. We had a big area to cover."

"Then I'm sure we can do one here," Octavia said. She looked interested and excited. It was like her face had woken up. I realized that what I'd seen before had been her depressed face. And I was getting enough from her head (now that she wasn't concentrating on keeping me out) to let me know that Octavia had spent a month after Katrina wondering where her next meal would come from, where she'd lay her head from night to night. Now she lived with family, though I didn't get a clean picture.

"I brought the stuff with me," Amelia said. Her brain was radiating pride and relief. She might yet get out from under the Bob contretemps without paying a huge price.

Dawson stood leaning against the wall, listening with apparent interest. Since he was a Were, it was hard to read his thoughts, but he was definitely relaxed.

I envied him. It wasn't possible for me to be at ease in this terrible little apartment, which almost echoed with the violence done in its walls. I was scared to sit on the love seat or the armchair, both upholstered in blue and white checks. The carpet was a darker blue, and the paint was white. Everything matched. The apartment was a little dull for my taste. But it had been neat and clean and carefully arranged, and less than twenty-four hours ago it had been a home.

I could see through to the bedroom, where the covers were thrown back. This was the only sign of disorder in the bedroom or the kitchen. The living room had been the center of the violence.

For lack of a better place to park myself, I went to lean against the bare wall beside Dawson.

I didn't think the motorcycle repairman and I had ever had a long conversation, though he'd gotten shot in my defense a few months before. I'd heard that *the law* (in this case, Andy Bellefleur and his fellow detective Alcee Beck) suspected more took place at Dawson's shop than motorcycle repairs, but they'd never caught Dawson doing anything illegal. Dawson also hired out as a bodyguard from time to time, or maybe he volunteered his services. He was certainly suited to the job.

"Were you friends?" Dawson rumbled, nodding his head at the bloodiest spot on the floor, the spot where Maria-Star had died.

"We were more like friendly acquaintances," I said, not wanting to claim more grief than my due. "I saw her at a wedding a couple of nights ago." I started to say she'd been fine then, but that would have been stupid. You don't sicken before you're murdered.

"When was the last time anyone talked to Maria-Star?" Amelia asked Dawson. "I need to establish some time limits."

"Eleven last night," he said. "Phone call from Alcide. He was out of town, with witnesses. Neighbor heard a big to-do from in here about thirty minutes after that, called the police." That was a long speech for Dawson. Amelia went back to her preparations, and Octavia read a thin book that Amelia had extracted from her little backpack.

"Have you ever watched one of these before?" Dawson said to me.

"Yeah, in New Orleans. I gather this is kind of rare and hard to do. Amelia's really good."

"She's livin' with you?"

I nodded.

"That's what I heard," he said. We were quiet for a moment. Dawson was proving to be a restful companion as well as a handy hunk of muscle.

There was some gesturing, and there was some chanting, with Octavia following her onetime student. Octavia might never have done an ectoplasmic reconstruction, but the longer the ritual went on the more power reverberated in the small room, until my fingernails seemed to hum with it. Dawson didn't exactly look frightened, but he was definitely on the alert as the pressure of the magic built. He uncrossed his arms and stood up straight, and I did, too.

Though I knew what to expect, it was still startling to me when Maria-Star appeared in the room with us. Beside me, I felt Dawson jerk with surprise. Maria-Star was painting her toenails. Her long dark hair was gathered into a ponytail on top of her head. She was sitting on the carpet in front of the television, a sheet of newspaper spread carefully under her foot. The magically re-created image had the same watery look I'd seen in a previous reconstruction, when I'd observed my cousin Hadley during her last few hours on earth. Maria-Star wasn't exactly in color. She was like an image filled with glistening gel. Because the apartment was no longer in the same order it had been when she'd sat in that spot, the effect was odd. She was sitting right in the middle of the overturned coffee table.

We didn't have long to wait. Maria-Star finished her toenails and sat watching the television set (now dark and dead) while she waited for them to dry. She did a few leg exercises while she waited. Then she gathered up the polish and the little spacers she'd had between her toes and folded the paper. She rose and went into the bathroom. Since the actual bathroom door was now half-closed, the watery Maria-Star had to walk through it. From our angle, Dawson and I couldn't see inside, but Amelia, whose hands were extended in a kind of sustaining gesture, gave a little shrug as if to say Maria-Star was not doing anything important. Ectoplasmic peeing, maybe.

In a few minutes, the young woman appeared again, this time in her nightgown. She went into the bedroom and turned back the bed. Suddenly, her head turned toward the door.

It was like watching a pantomime. Clearly Maria-Star had heard a sound at her door, and the sound was unexpected. I didn't know if she was hearing the doorbell, a knocking, or someone trying to pick the lock.

Her alert posture turned to alarm, even panic. She went back into the living room and picked up her cell phone—we saw it appear when she touched it—and punched a couple of numbers. Calling someone on speed dial. But before the phone could even have rung on the other end, the door exploded inward and a man was on her, a half wolf, half man. He showed up because he was a living thing, but he was clearer when he was close to Maria-Star, the focus of the spell. He pinned

Maria-Star to the floor and bit her deeply on her shoulder. Her mouth opened wide, and you could tell she was screaming and she was fighting like a Were, but he'd caught her totally by surprise and her arms were pinned down. Gleaming lines indicated blood running down from the bite.

Dawson gripped my shoulder, a growl rising from his throat. I didn't know if he was furious at the attack on Maria-Star, excited by the action and the impression of flowing blood, or all of the above.

A second Were was right behind the first. He was in his human form. He had a knife in his right hand. He plunged it into Maria-Star's torso, withdrew it, reared back, and plunged it in again. As the knife rose and fell, it cast blood drops on the walls. We could see the blood drops, so there must be ectoplasm (or whatever it really is) in blood, too.

I hadn't known the first man. This guy, I recognized. He was Cal Myers, a henchman of Furnan's and a police detective on the Shreveport force.

The blitz attack had taken only seconds. The moment Maria-Star was clearly mortally wounded, they were out the door, closing it behind them. I was shocked by the sudden and dreadful cruelty of the murder, and I felt my breath coming faster. Maria-Star, glistening and almost clear, lay there before us for a moment in the middle of the wreckage, gleaming blood splotches on her shirt and on the floor around her, and then she just winked out of existence, because she had died in that moment.

We all stood in appalled silence. The witches were silent, their arms dropping down by their sides as if they were puppets whose strings had been cut. Octavia was crying, tears running down her creased cheeks. Amelia looked as though she were thinking of throwing up. I was shivering in reaction, and even Dawson looked nauseated.

"I didn't know the first guy since he'd only half changed," Dawson said. "The second one looked familiar. He's a cop, right? In Shreveport?"

"Cal Myers. Better call Alcide," I said when I thought my voice would work. "And Alcide needs to send these ladies something for their trouble, when he gets his own sorted out." I figured Alcide might not think of that since he was mourning for Maria-Star, but the witches had done this work with no mention of recompense. They deserved to be rewarded for their effort. It had cost them dearly: both of them had folded onto the love seat.

"If you ladies can manage," Dawson said, "we better get our asses out of here. No telling when the police'll be back. The crime lab finished just five minutes before you got here."

While the witches gathered their energy and all their paraphernalia, I talked to Dawson. "You said Alcide's got a good alibi?"

Dawson nodded. "He got a phone call from Maria-Star's neighbor. She called Alcide right after she called the police, when she heard all the ruckus. Granted, the call was to his cell phone, but he answered right away and she could hear the sounds of the hotel bar behind the conversation. Plus, he was in the bar with people he'd just met who swore he was there when he found out she'd been killed. They aren't likely to forget."

"I guess the police are trying to find a motive." That was what they did on the TV shows.

"She didn't have enemies," Dawson said.

"Now what?" Amelia said. She and Octavia were on their feet, but they were clearly drained. Dawson shepherded us out of the apartment and relocked it.

"Thanks for coming, ladies," Dawson told Amelia and Octavia. He turned to me. "Sookie, could you come with me, explain to Alcide what we just saw? Can Amelia drive Miss Fant back?"

"Ah. Sure. If she's not too tired."

Amelia said she thought she could manage. We'd come in my car, so I tossed her the keys. "You okay driving?" I asked, just to reassure myself.

She nodded. "I'll take it slow."

I was scrambling into Dawson's truck when I realized that this step dragged me even further into the Were war. Then I figured, *Patrick Furnan already tried to kill me. Can't get any worse.*

Chapter 7

*Dawson's pickup, a Dodge Ram, although battered on the out-*side, was orderly within. It wasn't a new vehicle by any means—probably five years old—but it was very well-maintained both under the hood and in the cab.

"You're not a member of the pack, Dawson, right?"

"It's Tray. Tray Dawson."

"Oh, I'm sorry."

Dawson shrugged, as if to say *No big deal.* "I never was a good pack animal," he said. "I couldn't keep in line. I couldn't follow the chain of command."

"So why are you joining in this fight?" I said.

"Patrick Furnan tried to put me out of business," Dawson said.

"Why'd he do that?"

"Aren't that many other motorcycle repair shops in the area, especially since Furnan bought the Harley-Davidson dealership in Shreveport," Tray explained. "That so-and-so's greedy. He wants it all for himself. He doesn't care who goes broke. When he realized I was sticking with my shop, he sent a couple of his guys down to see me. They beat me up, busted up the shop."

"They must have been really good," I said. It was hard to believe anyone could best Tray Dawson. "Did you call the police?"

"No. The cops in Bon Temps aren't that crazy about me anyway. But I threw in with Alcide."

Detective Cal Myers, obviously, was not above doing Furnan's dirty work. It was Myers who'd collaborated with Furnan in cheating in the packmaster contest. But I was truly shocked that he would go as far as murdering Maria-Star, whose only sin was being loved by Alcide. We'd seen it with our own eyes, though.

"What's the deal with you and the police in Bon Temps?" I asked, as long as we were talking about law enforcement.

He laughed. "I used to be a cop; did you know that?"

"No," I said, genuinely surprised. "No kidding?"

"For real," he said. "I was on the force in New Orleans. But I didn't like the politics, and my captain was a real bastard, pardon me."

I nodded gravely. It had been a long time since someone had apologized for using bad language within my hearing. "So, something happened?"

"Yeah, eventually things came to a head. The captain accused me of taking some money this scuzzbag had left lying on a table when we arrested him in his home." Tray shook his head in disgust. "I had to quit then. I liked the job."

"What did you like about it?"

"No two days were alike. Yeah, sure, we got in the cars and patrolled. That was the same. But every time we got out something different would happen."

I nodded. I could understand that. Every day at the bar was a little different, too, though probably not as different as Tray's days had been in the patrol car.

We drove in silence for a while. I could tell Tray was thinking about the odds of Alcide overcoming Furnan in the struggle for dominance. He was thinking Alcide was a lucky guy to have dated Maria-Star and me, and all the luckier since that bitch Debbie Pelt had vanished. Good riddance, Tray thought.

"Now I get to ask you a question," Tray said.

"Only fair."

"You have something to do with Debbie disappearing?"

I took a deep breath. "Yeah. Self-defense."

"Good for you. Someone needed to do it."

We were quiet again for at least ten minutes. Not to drag the past into the present too much, but Alcide had broken up with Debbie Pelt before I met him. Then he dated me a little. Debbie decided I was an enemy, and she tried to kill me. I got her first. I'd come to terms with it . . . as much as you ever do. However, it had been impossible for Alcide to ever look at me again in the same way, and who could blame him? He'd found Maria-Star, and that was a good thing.

Had been a good thing.

I felt tears well up in my eyes and looked out the window. We'd passed the racetrack and the turnoff to Pierre Bossier Mall, and we went a couple more exits before Tray turned the truck onto the off ramp.

We meandered through a modest neighborhood for a while, Tray checking his rearview mirror so often that even I realized he was watching for anyone following us. Tray suddenly turned into a driveway and pulled around to the back of one of the slightly larger homes, which was demurely clad in white siding. We parked under a porte cochere in the back, along with another pickup. There was a small Nissan parked off to the side. There were a couple of motorcycles, too, and Tray gave them a glance of professional interest.

"Whose place?" I was a little hesitant about asking yet another question, but after all, I did want to know where I was.

"Amanda's," he said. He waited for me to precede him, and I went up the three steps leading up to the back door and rang the bell.

"Who's there?" asked a muffled voice.

"Sookie and Dawson," I said.

The door opened cautiously, the entrance blocked by Amanda so we couldn't see past her. I don't know much about handguns, but she had a big revolver in her hand pointed steadily at my chest. This was the second time in two days I'd had a gun pointed at me. Suddenly, I felt very cold and a little dizzy.

"Okay," Amanda said after looking us over sharply.

Alcide was standing behind the door, a shotgun at the ready. He'd stepped out into view as we came in, and when his own senses had checked us out, he stood down. He put the shotgun on the kitchen counter and sat at the kitchen table.

"I'm sorry about Maria-Star, Alcide," I said, forcing the words through stiff lips. Having guns aimed at you is just plain terrifying, especially at close range.

"I haven't gotten it yet," he said, his voice flat and even. I decided he was saying that the impact of her death hadn't hit him. "We were thinking about moving in together. It would have saved her life."

There wasn't any point in wallowing in what-might-have-been. That was only another way to torture yourself. What had actually happened was bad enough.

"We know who did it," Dawson said, and a shiver ran through the room. There were more Weres in the house—I could sense them now—and they had all become alert at Tray Dawson's words.

"What? How?" Without my seeing the movement, Alcide was on his feet.

"She got her witch friends to do a reconstruction," Tray said, nodding in my direction. "I watched. It was two guys. One I'd never seen, so Furnan's brought in some wolves from outside. The second was Cal Myers."

Alcide's big hands were clenched in fists. He didn't seem to know where to start speaking, he had so many reactions. "Furnan's hired help," Alcide said, finally picking a jumping-in point. "So we're within our rights to kill on sight. We'll snatch one of the bastards and make him talk. We can't bring a hostage here; someone would notice. Tray, where?"

"Hair of the Dog," he answered.

Amanda wasn't too crazy about that idea. She owned that bar, and using it as an execution or torture site didn't appeal to her. She opened her mouth to protest. Alcide faced her and snarled, his face twisting into something that wasn't quite Alcide. She cowered and nodded her assent.

Alcide raised his voice even more for his next pronouncement. "Cal Myers is Kill on Sight."

"But he's a pack member, and members get trials," Amanda said, and then cowered, correctly anticipating Alcide's wordless roar of rage.

"You haven't asked me about the man who tried to kill me," I said. I wanted to defuse the situation, if that was possible.

As furious as he was, Alcide was still too decent to remind me that I'd lived and Maria-Star hadn't, or that he'd loved Maria-Star much more than he'd ever cared about me. Both thoughts crossed his mind, though.

"He was a Were," I said. "About five foot ten, in his twenties. He was clean-shaven. He had brown hair and blue eyes and a big birthmark on his neck."

"Oh," said Amanda. "That sounds like what's-his-name, the brand-new mechanic at Furnan's shop. Hired last week. Lucky Owens. Ha! Who were you with?"

"I was with Eric Northman," I said.

There was a long, not entirely friendly silence. Weres and vampires are natural rivals, if not out-and-out enemies.

"So, the guy's dead?" Tray asked practically, and I nodded.

"How'd he approach you?" Alcide asked in a voice that was more rational.

"That's an interesting question," I said. "I was on the inter-state driving home from Shreveport with Eric. We'd been to a restaurant here."

"So who would know where you were and who you were with?" Amanda said while Alcide frowned down at the floor, deep in thought.

"Or that you'd have to return home along the interstate last night." Tray was really rising in my opinion; he was right in there with the practical and pertinent ideas.

"I only told my roommate I was going out to dinner, not where," I said. "We met someone there, but we can leave him out. Eric knew, because he was acting as chauffeur. But I know Eric and the other man didn't tip anyone off."

"How can you be so sure?" Tray asked.

"Eric got shot protecting me," I said. "And the person he took me to meet was a relative."

Amanda and Tray didn't realize how small my family was, so they didn't get how momentous that statement was. But Alcide, who knew more about me, glared. "You're making this up," he said.

"No, I'm not." I stared back. I knew this was a terrible day for Alcide, but I didn't have to explain my life to him. But I had a sudden thought. "You know, the waiter—he was a Were." That would explain a lot.

"What's the name of the restaurant?"

"Les Deux Poissons." My accent wasn't good, but the Weres nodded.

"Kendall works there," Alcide said. "Kendall Kent. Long

reddish hair?" I nodded, and he looked sad. "I thought Kendall would come around to our side. We had a beer together a couple of times."

"That's Jack Kent's oldest. All he would have had to do was place a phone call," Amanda said. "Maybe he didn't know..."

"Not an excuse," Tray said. His deep voice reverberated in the little kitchen. "Kendall has to know who Sookie is, from the packmaster contest. She's a friend of the pack. Instead of telling Alcide she was in our territory and should be protected, he called Furnan and told him where Sookie was, maybe let him know when she started home. Made it easy for Lucky to lie in wait."

I wanted to protest that there was no certainty that it had happened like that, but when I thought about it, it had to have been exactly that way or in some manner very close to it. Just to be sure I was remembering correctly, I called Amelia and asked her if she'd told any callers where I was the night before.

"No," she said. "I heard from Octavia, who didn't know you. I got a call from that werepanther boy I met at your brother's wedding. Believe me, you didn't come up in that conversation. Alcide called, real upset. Tanya. I told her nothing."

"Thanks, roomie," I said. "You recovering?"

"Yeah, I'm feeling better, and Octavia left to go back to the family she's been staying with in Monroe."

"Okay, see you when I get back."

"You going to make it back in time for work?"

"Yeah, I *have* to make it to work." Since I'd spent that week in Rhodes, I have to be careful to stick to the schedule for a while, otherwise the other waitresses would get up in my face about Sam giving me all the breaks. I hung up. "She told no one," I said.

"So you—and Eric—had a leisurely dinner at an expensive restaurant, with another man."

I looked at him incredulously. This was so far off the point. I concentrated. I'd never poked a mental probe into such turmoil. Alcide was feeling grief for Maria-Star, guilt because he hadn't protected her, anger that I'd been drawn into the conflict, and above all, eagerness to knock some skulls. As the cherry on top of all that, Alcide—irrationally—hated that I'd been out with Eric.

I tried to keep my mouth shut out of respect for his loss; I was no stranger to mixed emotions myself. But I found I'd become abruptly and completely tired of him. "Okay," I said. "Fight your own battles. I came when you asked me to. I helped you when you asked me to, both at the battle for packleader and today, at expense and emotional grief to myself. Screw you, Alcide. Maybe Furnan is the better Were." I spun on my heel and caught the look Tray Dawson was giving Alcide while I marched out of the kitchen, down the steps, and into the carport. If there'd been a can, I would've kicked it.

"I'll take you home," Tray said, appearing at my side, and I marched over to the side of the truck, grateful that he was giving me the wherewithal to leave. When I'd stormed out, I hadn't been thinking about what would happen next. It's the ruin of a good exit when you have to go back and look in the phone book for a cab company.

CHARLAINE HARRIS

I'd believed Alcide truly loathed me after the Debbie debacle. Apparently the loathing was not total.

"Kind of ironic, isn't it?" I said after a silent spell. "I almost got shot last night because Patrick Furnan thought that would upset Alcide. Until ten minutes ago, I would have sworn that wasn't true."

Tray looked like he would rather be cutting up onions than dealing with this conversation. After another pause, he said, "Alcide's acting like a butthead, but he's got a lot on his plate."

"I understand that," I said, and shut my mouth before I said one more word.

As it turned out, I *was* on time to go to work that night. I was so upset while I was changing clothes that I almost split my black pants, I yanked them on so hard. I brushed my hair with such unnecessary vigor that it crackled.

"Men are incomprehensible assholes," I said to Amelia.

"No shit," she said. "When I was searching for Bob today, I found a female cat in the woods with kittens. And guess what? They were all black-and-white."

I really had no idea what to say.

"So to hell with the promise I made him, right? I'm going to have fun. He can go have sex; I can have sex. And if he vomits on my bedspread again, I'll get after him with the broom."

I was trying not to look directly at Amelia. "I don't blame you," I said, trying to keep my voice steady. It was nice to be on the verge of laughter instead of wanting to smack someone. I grabbed up my purse, checked my ponytail in the mirror in the hall bathroom, and exited out the back door to drive to Merlotte's.

I felt tired before I even walked through the employees' door, not a good way to start my shift.

I didn't see Sam when I stowed my purse in the deep desk drawer we all used. When I came out of the hall that accessed the two public bathrooms, Sam's office, the storeroom, and the kitchen (though the kitchen door was kept locked from the inside, most of the time), I found Sam behind the bar. I gave him a wave as I tied on the white apron I'd pulled from the stack of dozens. I slid my order pad and a pencil into a pocket, looked around to find Arlene, whom I'd be replacing, and scanned the tables in our section.

My heart sank. No peaceful evening for me. Some asses in Fellowship of the Sun T-shirts were sitting at one of the tables. The Fellowship was a radical organization that believed (a) vampires were sinful by nature, almost demons, and (b) they should be executed. The Fellowship "preachers" wouldn't say so publicly, but the Fellowship advocated the total eradication of the undead. I'd heard there was even a little primer to advise members of how that could be carried out. After the Rhodes bombing they'd become bolder in their hatred.

The FotS group was growing as Americans struggled to come to terms with something they couldn't understand—and as hundreds of vampires streamed into the country that had given them the most favorable reception of all the nations on earth. Since a few heavily Catholic and Muslim countries had adopted a policy of killing vampires on sight, the U.S. had begun accepting vampires as refugees from religious or political persecution, and the backlash against this policy was violent. I'd recently seen a bumper sticker that read, "I'll say vamps are alive when you pry my cold dead fingers from my ripped-out throat."

I regarded the FotS as intolerant and ignorant, and I despised those who belonged to its ranks. But I was used to keeping my mouth shut on the topic at the bar, the same way I was used to avoiding discussions on abortion or gun control or gays in the military.

Of course, the FotS guys were probably Arlene's buddies. My weak-minded ex-friend had fallen hook, line, and sinker for the pseudo religion that the FotS propagated.

Arlene curtly briefed me on the tables as she headed out the back door, her face set hard against me. As I watched her go, I wondered how her kids were. I used to babysit them a lot. They probably hated me now, if they listened to their mother.

I shook off my melancholy, because Sam didn't pay me to be moody. I made the rounds of the customers, refreshed drinks, made sure everyone had enough food, brought a clean fork for a woman who'd dropped hers, supplied extra napkins to the table where Catfish Hennessy was eating chicken strips, and exchanged cheerful words with the guys seated at the bar. I treated the FotS table just like I treated everyone else, and they didn't seem to be paying me any special attention, which was just fine with me. I had every expectation that they'd leave with no trouble . . . until Pam walked in.

Pam is white as a sheet of paper and looks just like Alice

in Wonderland would look if she'd grown up to become a vampire. In fact, this evening Pam even had a blue band restraining her straight fair hair, and she was wearing a dress instead of her usual pants set. She was lovely—even if she looked like a vampire cast in an episode of *Leave It to Beaver.* Her dress had little puff sleeves with white trim, and her collar had white trim, too. The tiny buttons down the front of her bodice were white, to match the polka dots on the skirt. No hose, I noticed, but any hose she bought would look bizarre since the rest of her skin was so pale.

"Hey, Pam," I said as she made a beeline for me.

"Sookie," she said warmly, and gave me a kiss as light as a snowflake. Her lips felt cool on my cheek.

"What's up?" I asked. Pam usually worked at Fangtasia in the evening.

"I have a date," she said. "Do you think I look good?" She spun around.

"Oh, sure," I said. "You always look good, Pam." That was only the truth. Though Pam's clothing choices were often ultra-conservative and strangely dated, that didn't mean they didn't become her. She had a kind of sweet-but-lethal charm. "Who's the lucky guy?"

She looked as arch as a vampire over two hundred years old can look. "Who says it's a guy?" she said.

"Oh, right." I glanced around. "Who's the lucky person?"

Just then my roomie walked in. Amelia was wearing a beautiful pair of black linen pants and heels with an off-white sweater and a pair of amber and tortoiseshell earrings. She looked conservative, too, but in a more modern way. Amelia strode over to us, smiled at Pam, and said, "Had a drink yet?"

Pam smiled in a way I'd never seen her smile before. It was . . . coy. "No, waiting for you."

They sat at the bar and Sam served them. Soon they were chatting away, and when their drinks were gone, they got up to leave.

When they passed me on their way out, Amelia said, "I'll see you when I see you"—her way of telling me she might not be home tonight.

"Okay, you two have fun," I said. Their departure was followed by more than one pair of male eyes. If corneas steamed up like glasses do, all the guys in the bar would be seeing blurry.

I made the round of my tables again, fetching new beers for one, leaving the bill at another, until I reached the table with the two guys wearing the FotS shirts. They were still watching the door as though they expected Pam to jump back inside and scream, "BOO!"

"Did I just see what I thought I saw?" one of the men asked me. He was in his thirties, clean-shaven, brown-haired, just another guy. The other man was someone I would have eyed with caution if we'd been in an elevator alone. He was thin, had a beard fringe along his jaw, was decorated with a few tattoos that looked like home jobs to me—jail tats—and he was carrying a knife strapped to his ankle, a thing that hadn't been too hard for me to spot once I'd heard in his mind that he was armed.

"What do you think you just saw?" I asked sweetly. Brown Hair thought I was a bit simple. But that was a good camouflage, and it meant that Arlene hadn't sunk to telling all and sundry about my little peculiarities. No one in Bon Temps (if you asked them outside of church on Sunday) would have said telepathy was possible. If you'd asked them outside of Merlotte's on a Saturday night, they might have said there was something to it.

"I think I saw a vamp come in here, just like she had a right. And I think I saw a woman acting happy to walk out with her. I swear to God, I cannot believe it." He looked at me as if I was sure to share his outrage. Jail Tat nodded vigorously.

"I'm sorry—you see two women walking out of a bar together, and that bothers you? I don't understand your problem with that." Of course I did, but you have to play it out sometimes.

"Sookie!" Sam was calling me.

"Can I get you gentlemen anything else?" I asked, since Sam was undoubtedly trying to call me back to my senses.

They were both looking at me oddly now, having correctly deduced that I was not exactly down with their program.

"I guess we're ready to leave," said Jail Tat, clearly hoping I'd be made to suffer for driving paying customers away. "You got our check ready?" I'd *had* their check ready, and I laid it down on the table in between them. They each glanced at it, slapped a ten on top, and shoved their chairs back.

"I'll be back with your change in just a second," I said, and turned.

"No change," said Brown Hair, though his tone was surly and he didn't seem genuinely thrilled with my service.

"Jerks," I muttered as I went to the cash register at the bar.

Sam said, "Sookie, you have to suck it up."

I was so surprised that I stared at Sam. We were both behind the bar, and Sam was mixing a vodka collins. Sam continued quietly, keeping his eyes on his hands, "You have to serve them like they were anybody else."

It wasn't too often that Sam treated me like an employee rather than a trusted associate. It hurt; the more so when I realized he was right. Though I'd been polite on the surface, I would have (and should have) swallowed their last remarks with no comment—if it hadn't been for the FotS T-shirts. Merlotte's wasn't my business. It was Sam's. If customers didn't come back, he'd suffer the consequences. Eventually, if he had to let barmaids go, I would, too.

"I'm sorry," I said, though it wasn't easy to manage saying it. I smiled brightly at Sam and went off to do an unnecessary round of my tables, one that probably crossed the line from attentive and into irritating. But if I went into the employees' bathroom or the public ladies' room, I'd end up crying, because it hurt to be admonished and it hurt to be wrong; but most of all, it hurt to be put in my place.

When we closed that night, I left as quickly and quietly as possible. I knew I was going to have to get over being hurt, but I preferred to do my healing in my own home. I didn't want to have any "little talks" with Sam—or anyone else, for that matter. Holly was looking at me with way too much curiosity.

So I scooted out to the parking lot with my purse, my apron still on. Tray was leaning against my car. I jumped before I could stop myself.

"You running scared?" he asked.

"No, I'm running upset," I said. "What are you doing here?"

"I'm going to follow you home," he said. "Amelia there?"

"No, she's out on a date."

"Then I'm definitely checking out the house," the big man said, and climbed into his truck to follow me out Hummingbird Road.

There wasn't any reason to object that I could see. In fact, it made me feel good to have someone with me, someone I pretty much trusted.

My house was just as I'd left it, or rather, as Amelia had left it. The outside security lights had come on automatically, and she'd left the light over the sink on in the kitchen as well as the back porch light. Keys in hand, I crossed to the kitchen door.

Tray's big hand gripped my arm when I started to twist the doorknob.

"There's no one there," I said, having checked in my own way. "And it's warded by Amelia."

"You stay here while I look around," he said gently. I nodded and let him in. After a few seconds' silence, he opened the door to tell me I could come into the kitchen. I was ready to follow him through the house for the rest of his search, but he said, "I'd sure like a glass of Coke, if you got any."

He'd deflected me perfectly from following him by appealing to my hospitality. My grandmother would have hit me with a fly swatter if I hadn't gotten Tray a Coke right then.

By the time he arrived back in the kitchen and pronounced

the house clear of intruders, the icy Coke was sitting in a glass on the table, and there was a meatloaf sandwich sitting by it. With a folded napkin.

Without a word, Tray sat down and put the napkin in his lap and ate the sandwich and drank the Coke. I sat opposite him with my own drink.

"I hear your man has vanished," Tray said when he'd patted his lips with the napkin.

I nodded.

"What do you think happened to him?"

I explained the circumstances. "So I haven't heard a word from him," I concluded. This story was sounding almost automatic, like I ought to tape it.

"That's bad" was all he said. Somehow it made me feel better, this quiet, undramatic discussion of a very touchy subject. After a minute of thoughtful silence, Tray said, "I hope you find him soon."

"Thanks. I'm real anxious to know how he's doing." That was a huge understatement.

"Well, I'd better be getting on," he said. "If you get nervous in the night, you call me. I can be here in ten minutes. It's no good, you being alone out here with the war starting."

I had a mental image of tanks coming down my driveway.

"How bad do you think it could get?" I asked.

"My dad told me in the last war, which was when his daddy was little, the pack in Shreveport got into it with the pack in Monroe. The Shreveport pack was about forty then, counting the halfies." Halfies was the common term for Weres who'd become wolves by being bitten. They could only turn into a kind of wolf-man, never achieving the perfect wolf form that born Weres thought was vastly superior. "But the Monroe pack had a bunch of college kids in it, so it come up to forty, forty-five, too. At the end of the fighting, both packs were halved."

I thought of the Weres I knew. "I hope it stops now," I said.

"It ain't gonna," Tray said practically. "They've tasted blood, and killing Alcide's girl instead of trying for Alcide was a cowardly way to open the fight. Them trying to get you, too; that only made it worse. You don't have a drop of Were blood. You're a friend of the pack. That should make you untouchable, not a target. And this afternoon, Alcide found Christine Larrabee dead."

I was shocked all over again. Christine Larrabee was—had been—the widow of one of the previous packleaders. She had a high standing in the Were community, and she'd rather reluctantly endorsed Jackson Herveaux for packleader. Now she had gotten a delayed payback.

"He's not going after any men?" I finally managed to speak.

Tray's face was dark with contempt. "Naw," the Were said. "The only way I can read it is, Furnan wants to set Alcide's temper off. He wants everyone to be on a hair trigger, while Furnan himself stays cool and collected. He's about got what he wants, too. Between grief and the personal insult, Alcide is aimed to go off like a shotgun. He needs to be more like a sniper rifle."

"Isn't Furnan's strategy real...unusual?"

"Yes," Tray said heavily. "I don't know what's gotten into

him. Apparently, he don't want to face Alcide in personal combat. He don't want to just beat Alcide. He's aiming to kill Alcide and all Alcide's people, as far as I can tell. A few of the Weres, the ones with little kids, they already repledged themselves to him. They're too scared of what he'd do to their kids, after the attacks against women." The Were stood. "Thanks for the food. I've got to go feed my dogs. You lock up good after me, you hear? And where's your cell phone?"

I handed it to him, and with surprisingly neat movements for such large hands, Tray programmed his cell phone number into my directory. Then he left with a casual wave of his hand. He had a small neat house by his repair shop, and I was really relieved to find he'd timed the journey from there to here at only ten minutes. I locked the door behind him, and I checked the kitchen windows. Sure enough, Amelia had left one open at some point during the mild afternoon. After that discovery, I felt compelled to check every window in the house, even the ones upstairs.

After that was done and I felt as secure as I was going to feel, I turned on the television and sat in front of it, not really seeing what was happening on the screen. I had a lot to think about.

Months ago, I'd gone to the packmaster contest at Alcide's request to watch for trickery. It was my bad luck that my presence had been noticed and my discovery of Furnan's treachery had been public. It griped me that I'd been drawn into this fight, which was none of my own. In fact, bottom line: knowing Alcide had brought me nothing but grief.

I was almost relieved to feel a head of anger building at this injustice, but my better self urged me to squash it in the bud. It wasn't Alcide's fault that Debbie Pelt had been such a murderous bitch, and it wasn't Alcide's fault that Patrick Furnan had decided to cheat in the contest. Likewise, Alcide wasn't responsible for Furnan's bloodthirsty and uncharacteristic approach to consolidating his pack. I wondered if this behavior was even remotely wolflike.

I figured it was just Patrick Furnan–like.

The telephone rang, and I jumped about a mile. "Hello?" I said, unhappy at how frightened I sounded.

"The Were Herveaux called me," Eric said. "He confirms that he's at war with his packmaster."

"Yeah," I said. "You needed confirmation from Alcide? My message wasn't enough?"

"I'd thought of an alternative to the theory that you were attacked in a strike against Alcide. I'm sure Niall must have mentioned that he has enemies."

"Uh-huh."

"I wondered if one of those enemies had acted very swiftly. If the Weres have spies, so may the fairies."

I pondered that. "So, in wanting to meet me, he almost caused my death."

"But he had the wisdom to ask me to escort you to and from Shreveport."

"So he saved my life, even though he risked it."

Silence.

"Actually," I said, leaping to firmer emotional ground, "you saved my life, and I'm grateful." I half expected Eric to ask me just how grateful I was, to refer to the kissing . . . but still he didn't speak.

Just as I was about to blurt out something stupid to break the silence, the vampire said, "I'll only interfere in the Were war to defend our interests. Or to defend you."

My turn for a silent spell. "All right," I said weakly.

"If you see trouble coming, if they try to draw you in further, call me immediately," Eric told me. "I believe the assassin truly was sent by the packmaster. Certainly he was a Were."

"Some of Alcide's people recognized the description. The guy, Lucky somebody, had just been taken on by Furnan as a mechanic."

"Strange that he'd entrust such an errand to someone he hardly knew."

"Since the guy turned out to be so unlucky."

Eric actually snorted. Then he said, "I won't talk to Niall of this any further. Of course, I told him what occurred."

I had a moment's ridiculous pang because Niall hadn't rushed to my side or called to ask if I was okay. I'd only met him once, and now I was sad he wasn't acting like my nursemaid.

"All right, Eric, thanks," I said, and hung up as he was saying good-bye. I should have asked him about my money again, but I was too dispirited; besides, it wasn't Eric's problem.

I was jumpy the whole time I was getting ready for bed, but nothing happened to make me more anxious. I reminded myself about fifty times that Amelia had warded the house. The wards would work whether she was in the house or not.

I had some good locks on the doors.

I was tired.

Finally, I slept, but I woke up more than once, listening for an assassin.

Chapter 8

I got up with heavy eyes the next day. I felt groggy and my head hurt. I had what amounted to an emotional hangover. Something had to change. I couldn't spend another night like this. I wondered if I should call Alcide and see if he'd, ah, gone to the mattresses with his soldiers. Maybe they'd let me have a corner? But the very idea of having to do that to feel safe made me angry.

I couldn't stop the thought from going through my head—*If Quinn were here, I could stay in my own home without fear.* And for a moment, I wasn't just worried about my missing wounded boyfriend, I was mad at him.

I was ready to be mad at *someone.* There was too much loose emotion hanging around.

Well, this was the beginning of a very special day, huh?

No Amelia. I had to assume she'd spent the night with Pam. I didn't have any problem with their having a relationship. I simply wanted Amelia to be around because I was lonely and scared. Her absence left a little blank spot in my landscape.

At least the air was cooler this morning. You could feel clearly that fall was on the way, was already in the ground waiting to leap up and claim the leaves and grass and flowers. I put on a sweater over my nightgown and went out on the front porch to drink my first cup of coffee. I listened to the birds for a while; they weren't as noisy as they were in the spring, but their songs and discussions let me know that nothing unusual was in the woods this morning. I finished my coffee and tried to plan out my day, but I kept running up against a mental roadblock. It was hard to make plans when you suspected someone might try to kill you. If I could tear myself away from the issue of my possibly impending death, I needed to vacuum the downstairs, do a load of my laundry, and go to the library. If I survived those chores, I had to go to work.

I wondered where Quinn was.

I wondered when I'd hear from my new great-grandfather again.

I wondered if any more Weres had died during the night.

I wondered when my phone would ring.

Since nothing happened on my front porch, I dragged myself inside and did my usual morning get-ready routine. When I looked at the mirror, I was sorry I'd troubled. I didn't look rested and refreshed. I looked like a worried person who hadn't gotten any sleep. I dabbed some concealer beneath my eyes and put on a little extra eye shadow and blush to give my face some color. Then I decided I looked like a clown and rubbed most of it off. After feeding Bob and scolding him for the litter of kittens, I checked all my locks again and hopped in the car to go to the library.

The Renard Parish library, Bon Temps branch, is not a large building. Our librarian graduated from Louisiana Tech in Ruston, and she is a super lady in her late thirties named Barbara Beck. Her husband, Alcee, is a detective on the Bon Temps force, and I really hope Barbara doesn't know what he's up to. Alcee Beck is a tough man who does good things . . . sometimes. He also does quite a few bad things. Alcee was lucky when he got Barbara to marry him, and he knows it.

Barbara's the only full-time employee of the branch library, and I wasn't surprised to find her by herself when I pushed open the heavy door. She was shelving books. Barbara dressed in what I thought of as comfortable chic, meaning she picked out knits in bright colors and wore matching shoes. She favored chunky, bold jewelry, too.

"Good morning, Sookie," she said, smiling her big smile.

"Barbara," I said, trying to smile back. She noticed I wasn't my usual self, but she kept her thoughts to herself. Not really, of course, since I have my little disability, but she didn't say anything out loud. I put the books I was returning on the appropriate desk, and I began looking at the shelves of new arrivals. Most of them were some permutation on self-help. Going by how popular these books were and how often they were checked out, everyone in Bon Temps should have become perfect by now.

I grabbed up two new romances and a couple of mysteries, and even a science fiction, which I rarely read. (I guess I thought my reality was crazier than anything a science fiction writer could dream up.) While I was looking at the jacket of a book by an author I'd never read, I heard a thunk in the background and knew someone had come in the back door of the library. I didn't pay attention; some people habitually used the back door.

Barbara made a little noise, and I looked up. The man behind her was huge, at least six foot six, and whip thin. He had a big knife, and he was holding it to Barbara's throat. For a second I thought he was a robber, and I wondered who would ever think of robbing a library. For the overdue-book money?

"Don't scream," he hissed through long sharp teeth. I froze. Barbara was in some space beyond fear. She was way into terror. But I could hear another active brain in the building.

Someone else was coming in the back door very quietly.

"Detective Beck will kill you for hurting his wife," I said very loudly. And I said it with absolute certainty. "Kiss your ass good-bye."

"I don't know who that is and I don't care," the tall man said.

"You better care, muthafucker," said Alcee Beck, who'd stepped up behind him silently. He put his gun to the man's head. "Now, you let go of my wife and you drop that knife."

But Sharp Teeth wasn't about to do that. He spun, pushed Barbara at Alcee, and ran right toward me, knife raised.

I threw a Nora Roberts hardback at him, whacking him

upside his head. I extended my foot. Blinded by the impact of the book, Sharp Teeth tripped over the foot, just as I'd hoped.

He fell on his own knife, which I *hadn't* planned.

The library fell abruptly silent except for Barbara's gasping breath. Alcee Beck and I stared down at the creeping pool of blood coming out from under the man.

"Ah-oh," I said.

"Wellllll...shit," said Alcee Beck. "Where'd you learn to throw like that, Sookie Stackhouse?"

"Softball," I said, which was the literal truth.

As you can imagine, I was late to work that afternoon. I was even more tired than I had been to start with, but I was thinking that I might live through the day. So far, two times in a row, fate had intervened to prevent my assassination. I had to assume that Sharp Teeth had been sent to kill me and had botched it, just as the fake highway patrolman had done. Maybe my luck wouldn't hold a third time; but there was a chance it would. What were the odds that another vampire would take a bullet for me, or that, by sheer accident, Alcee Beck would drop off his wife's lunch that she'd left at home on the kitchen counter? Slim, right? But I'd beaten those odds twice.

No matter what the police were officially assuming (since I didn't know the guy and no one could say I did—and he'd seized Barbara, not me), Alcee Beck now had me in his sights. He was really good at reading situations, and he had seen that Sharp Teeth was focused on me. Barbara had been a means to get my attention. Alcee would never forgive me for that, even if it hadn't been my fault. Plus, I'd thrown that book with suspicious force and accuracy.

In his place, I would probably feel the same way.

So now I was at Merlotte's, going through the motions in a weary way, wondering where to go and what to do and why Patrick Furnan had gone nuts. And where had all these strangers come from? I hadn't known the Were who'd broken down Maria-Star's door. Eric had been shot by a guy who'd worked at Patrick Furnan's dealership only a few days. I'd never seen Sharp Teeth before, and he was an unforgettable kind of guy.

The whole situation made no sense at all.

Suddenly I had an idea. I asked Sam if I could make a phone call since my tables were quiet, and he nodded. He'd been giving me those narrow looks all evening, looks that meant he was going to pin me down and talk to me soon, but for now I had a breather. So I went into Sam's office, looked in his Shreveport phone book to get the listing for Patrick Furnan's home, and I called him.

"Hello?"

I recognized the voice.

"Patrick Furnan?" I said, just to be sure.

"Speaking."

"Why are you trying to kill me?"

"What? Who is this?"

"Oh, come on. It's Sookie Stackhouse. Why are you doing this?"

There was a long pause.

"Are you trying to trap me?" he asked.

"How? You think I got the phone tapped? I want to know why. I never did anything to you. I'm not even dating Alcide. But you're trying to off me like I am powerful. You killed poor Maria-Star. You killed Christine Larrabee. What's with this? I'm not important."

Patrick Furnan said slowly, "You really believe it's me doing this? Killing female pack members? Trying to kill you?"

"Sure I do."

"It's not me. I read about Maria-Star. Christine Larrabee is dead?" He sounded almost frightened.

"Yes," I said, and my voice was as uncertain as his. "And someone's tried to kill me twice. I'm afraid some totally innocent person is going to get caught in the cross fire. And of course, I don't want to die."

Furnan said, "My wife disappeared yesterday." His voice was ragged with grief and fear. And anger. "Alcide's got her, and that fucker is going to pay."

"Alcide wouldn't do that," I said. (Well, I was pretty sure Alcide wouldn't do that.) "You're saying you *didn't* order the hits on Maria-Star and Christine? And me?"

"No, why would I go for the women? We never want to kill pure-blooded female Weres. Except maybe Amanda," Furnan added tactlessly. "If we're going to kill someone, it'd be the men."

"I think you and Alcide need to have a sit-down. He doesn't have your wife. He thinks you've gone crazy, attacking women."

There was a long silence. Furnan said, "I think you're right about that sit-down, unless you made up this whole thing to get me into a position where Alcide can kill me."

"I just want to live to see the next week myself."

"I'll agree to meet with Alcide if you'll be there and if you'll swear to tell each of us what the other is thinking. You're a friend of the pack, *all* the pack. You can help us now."

Patrick Furnan was so anxious to find his wife he was even willing to believe in me.

I thought of the deaths that had already taken place. I thought of the deaths that were to come, perhaps including my own. I wondered what the hell was going on. "I'll do it if you and Alcide will sit down unarmed," I said. "If what I suspect is true, you have a common enemy who's trying to get you two to kill each other off."

"If that black-haired bastard will agree to it, I'll give it a shot," said Furnan. "If Alcide has my wife, not a hair on her body better be disturbed, and he better bring her with him. Or I swear to God I'll dismember him."

"I understand. I'll make sure he understands, too. We'll be getting back with you," I promised, and I hoped with all my heart that I was telling the truth.

Chapter 9

It was the middle of the same night and I was about to walk into danger. It was my own damn fault. Through a swift series of phone calls, Alcide and Furnan had worked out where to meet. I'd envisioned them sitting down across a table, their lieutenants right behind them, and working this whole situation out. Mrs. Furnan would appear and the couple would reunite. Everyone would be content, or at least less hostile. I would be nowhere around.

Yet here I was at an abandoned office center in Shreveport, the same one where the contest for packmaster had taken place. At least Sam was with me. It was dark and cool and the wind was lifting my hair from my shoulders. I shifted from foot to foot, anxious to get this over with. Though he was not as fidgety as I was, I could tell Sam felt the same way.

It was my fault he was here. When he'd become so curious about what was brewing with the Weres, I'd had to tell him. After all, if someone came through the door of Merlotte's trying to shoot me down, Sam at least deserved to know why his bar was full of holes. I'd argued bitterly with him when he'd told me he was coming with me, but here we both were.

Maybe I'm lying to myself. Maybe I simply wanted a friend with me, someone definitely on my side. Maybe I was just scared. Actually, no "maybe" about that at all.

The night was brisk, and we were both wearing waterproof jackets with hoods. Not that we needed the hoods, but if it got any colder, we might be grateful for them. The abandoned office park stretched around us in gloomy silence. We stood in the loading bay of a firm that had accepted big shipments of something. The large metal pull-down doors where the trucks had been unloaded looked like big shiny eyes in the gleam of the remaining security lights.

Actually, there were lots of big shiny eyes around tonight. The Sharks and the Jets were negotiating. Oh, excuse me, the Furnan Weres and the Herveaux Weres. The two sides of the pack might come to an understanding, and they might not. And right smack dab in the middle stood Sam the Shapeshifter and Sookie the Telepath.

As I felt the hard red throbbing of Were brains approaching from both north and south, I turned to Sam and said from the bottom of my heart, "I should never have let you come with me. I should never have opened my mouth."

"You've gotten into the habit of not telling me things,

Sookie. I want you to tell me what's going on with you. Especially if there's danger." Sam's red gold hair blew around his head in the sharp little breeze wafting between the buildings. I felt his difference more strongly than I ever had. Sam is a rare true shapeshifter. He can change into anything. He prefers the form of a dog, because dogs are familiar and friendly and people don't shoot at them too often. I looked into his blue eyes and saw the wildness in them. "They're here," he said, raising his nose to the breeze.

Then the two groups were standing about ten feet away on either side of us, and it was time to concentrate.

I recognized the faces of a few of the Furnan wolves, who were more numerous. Cal Myers, the police detective, was among them. It took some kind of nerve for Furnan to bring Cal along when he was proclaiming his innocence. I also recognized the teenage girl Furnan had taken as part of his victory celebration after Jackson Herveaux's defeat. She looked a million years older tonight.

Alcide's group included auburn-haired Amanda, who nodded at me, her face serious, and some werewolves I'd seen at the Hair of the Dog the night Quinn and I had visited the bar. The scrawny girl who'd worn the red leather bustier that night was standing right behind Alcide, and she was both intensely excited and deeply scared. To my surprise, Dawson was there. He wasn't as much of a lone wolf as he'd painted himself to be.

Alcide and Furnan stepped away from their packs.

This was the agreed-on format for the parley, or sit-down, or whatever you wanted to call it: I would stand between Furnan and Alcide. Each Were leader would grip one of my hands. I would be the human lie detector while they talked. I had sworn to tell each one if the other lied, at least to the best of my ability. I could read minds, but minds can be deceptive and tricky or just dense. I'd never done anything exactly like this, and I prayed my ability would be extra precise tonight and that I would use it wisely, so I could help to end this life taking.

Alcide approached me stiffly, his face harsh in the hard glare of the security lighting. For the first time, I noticed that he looked thinner and older. There was a little gray in the black hair that hadn't been there when his father had been alive. Patrick Furnan, too, didn't look well. He'd always had a tendency to porkiness, and now he looked as though he'd gained a good fifteen or twenty pounds. Being packmaster hadn't been good to him. And the shock of the abduction of his wife had laid its mark on his face.

I did something that I never imagined I would do. I held out my right hand to him. He took it, and the flood of his ideas washed through me instantly. Even his twisty Were brain was easy to read because he was so focused. I held out my left hand to Alcide, and he grasped it too tightly. For a long minute, I felt inundated. Then, with a huge effort, I channeled them into a stream so I wouldn't be overwhelmed. It would be easy for them to lie out loud, but it's not so easy to lie inside your own head. Not consistently. I closed my eyes. A flip of the coin had given Alcide the first question.

"Patrick, why did you kill my woman?" The words sounded

like they were cutting up Alcide's throat. "She was pure Were, and she was as gentle as a Were can be."

"I never ordered any of my people to kill any of yours," Patrick Furnan said. He sounded so tired he could hardly stand up, and his thoughts were proceeding in much the same way: slowly, wearily, on a track he'd worn in his own brain. He was easier to read than Alcide. He meant what he said.

Alcide was listening with great attention, and he said next, "Did you tell anyone not in your pack to kill Maria-Star and Sookie and Mrs. Larrabee?"

"I never gave orders to kill any of you, ever," Furnan said.

"He believes that," I said.

Unfortunately, Furnan wouldn't shut up. "I hate you," he said, sounding just as tired as he had before. "I would be glad if a truck hit you. But I didn't kill anyone."

"He believes that, too," I said, maybe a little dryly.

Alcide demanded, "How can you claim to be innocent with Cal Myers standing with your pack? He stabbed Maria-Star to death."

Furnan looked confused. "Cal wasn't there," he said.

"He believes what he says," I told Alcide. I turned my face to Furnan. "Cal was there, and he murdered Maria-Star." Though I dared not lose focus, I heard the whispering start all around Cal Myers, saw the rest of the Furnan Weres step away from him.

It was Furnan's turn to ask a question.

"My wife," he said, and his voice cracked. "Why her?"

"I didn't take Libby," Alcide said. "I would never abduct a woman, especially a Were woman with young. I would never order anyone else to do it."

He believed that. "Alcide didn't do it himself, and he didn't order it done." But Alcide hated Patrick Furnan with a great ferocity. Furnan hadn't needed to kill Jackson Herveaux at the climax of the contest, but he had. Better to start his leadership with the elimination of his rival. Jackson would never have submitted to his rule, and would have been a thorn in his side for years. I was getting thoughts from both sides, wafts of ideas so strong it burned in my head, and I said, "Calm down, both of you." I could feel Sam behind me, his warmth, the touch of his mind, and I said, "Sam, don't touch me, okay?"

He understood, and he moved away.

"Neither of you killed any of the people who have died. And neither of you ordered it done. As far as I can tell."

Alcide said, "Give us Cal Myers to question."

"Then where is my wife?" Furnan growled.

"Dead and gone," said a clear voice. "And I'm ready to take her place. Cal is mine."

We all looked up, because the voice had come from the flat roof of the building. There were four Weres up there, and the brunette female who'd spoken was closest to the edge. She had a sense of the dramatic, I'll give her that. Female Weres have power and status but they're not packleader . . . ever. This woman was clearly large and in charge, though she was maybe five foot two. She had prepared to change; that is to say, she was naked. Or maybe she just wanted Alcide and Furnan to see what they could be getting. Which was a lot, both in quantity and in quality.

"Priscilla," said Furnan.

It seemed like such an unlikely name for the Were that I felt myself actually smile, which was a bad idea under the circumstances.

"You know her," Alcide said to Furnan. "Is this part of your plan?"

"No," I answered for him. My mind careened through the thoughts I could read and latched on to one thread in particular. "Furnan, Cal is her creature," I said. "He's betrayed you."

"I thought if I picked off a few key bitches, you two would kill each other off," Priscilla said. "Too bad it didn't work."

"Who is this?" Alcide asked Furnan again.

"She's the mate of Arthur Hebert, a packleader from St. Catherine Parish." St. Catherine was way south, just east of New Orleans. It had been hit hard by Katrina.

"Arthur is dead. We don't have a home anymore," Priscilla Hebert said. "We want yours."

Well, that was clear enough.

"Cal, why have you done this?" Furnan asked his lieutenant. Cal should have gotten up on the roof while he was able. The Furnan wolves and the Herveaux wolves had formed a circle around him.

"Cal's my brother," Priscilla called. "You better not touch a hair on his body." There was an edge of desperation to her voice that hadn't been there before. Cal looked up at his sister unhappily. He realized what a fix he was in, and I was pretty sure he wanted her to shut up. That would be his last thought.

Furnan's arm was suddenly out of its sleeve and covered with hair. With huge force, he swung at his former cohort, eviscerating the Were. Alcide's clawed hand took off the back of Cal's head as the traitor fell to the ground. Cal's blood sprayed over me in an arc. At my back, Sam was humming with the energy of his oncoming change, triggered by the tension, the smell of blood, and my involuntary yelp.

Priscilla Hebert roared in rage and anguish. With inhuman grace, she leaped from the top of the building to the parking lot, followed by her henchmen (henchwolves?).

The war had begun.

Sam and I had worked ourselves into the middle of the Shreveport wolves. As Priscilla's pack began closing in from each side, Sam said, "I'm going to change, Sookie."

I couldn't see what use a collie would be in this situation, but I said, "Okay, boss." He grinned at me in a lopsided way, stripped off his clothes, and bent over. All around us the Weres were doing the same. The chill night air was full of the gloppy sound, the sound of hard things moving through thick, sticky liquid, that characterizes the transformation from man to animal. Huge wolves straightened and shook themselves all around me; I recognized the wolf forms of Alcide and Furnan. I tried counting the wolves in our suddenly reunited pack, but they were milling around, positioning themselves for the coming battle, and there was no way to keep track of them.

I turned to Sam to give him a pat and found myself standing beside a lion.

"Sam," I said in a whisper, and he roared.

Everyone froze in place for a long moment. The Shreveport wolves were just as scared as the St. Catherine's wolves at first, but then they seemed to realize that Sam was on their side, and yips of excitement echoed between the empty buildings.

Then the fighting started.

Sam tried to surround me, which was impossible, but it was a gallant attempt. As an unarmed human, I was basically helpless in this struggle. It was a very unpleasant feeling—in fact, a terrifying feeling.

I was the frailest thing on site.

Sam was magnificent. His huge paws flashed, and when he hit a wolf square on, that wolf went *down.* I danced around like a demented elf, trying to stay out the way. I couldn't watch everything that was going on. Clusters of St. Catherine wolves made for Furnan, Alcide, and Sam, while individual battles went on around us. I realized that these clusters had been charged with taking down the leaders, and I knew that a lot of planning had gone into this. Priscilla Hebert hadn't allowed for getting her brother out quickly enough, but that wasn't slowing her down any.

No one seemed to be too concerned with me, since I posed no threat. But there was every chance I'd get knocked down by the snarling combatants and be hurt as severely as I would if I had been the target. Priscilla, now a gray wolf, targeted Sam. I guess she wanted to prove she had more balls than anyone by going for the biggest and most dangerous target. But Amanda was biting at Priscilla's hind legs as Priscilla worked her way through the melee. Priscilla responded by turning her head to bare her teeth at the smaller wolf. Amanda danced away, and then when Priscilla turned to resume her progress, Amanda darted back to bite the leg again. Since Amanda's bite was powerful enough to break bone, this was more than an annoyance, and Priscilla rounded on her in full display. Before I could even think *Oh no,* Priscilla seized Amanda in her iron jaws and broke her neck.

While I stood staring in horror, Priscilla dropped Amanda's body on the ground and wheeled to leap onto Sam's back. He shook and shook but she had sunk her fangs into his neck and she would not be dislodged.

Something in me snapped as surely as the bones in Amanda's neck. I lost any sense I might have had, and I launched myself in the air as if I were a wolf, too. To keep from sliding off the heaving mass of animals, I wound my arms in the fur around Priscilla's neck, and I wound my legs around Priscilla's middle, and I tightened my arms until I was just about hugging myself. Priscilla didn't want to let go of Sam, so she flung herself from side to side to knock me loose. But I was clinging to her like a homicidal monkey.

Finally, she had to let go of his neck to deal with me. I squeezed and squeezed harder, and she tried to bite me, but she couldn't reach around properly since I was on her back. She was able to curve enough to graze my leg with her fangs, but she couldn't hold on. The pain hardly registered. I tightened my grip even more though my arms were aching like hell. If I let go one little bit, I would join Amanda.

Though all of this took place so quickly it was hard to believe, I felt as if I'd been trying to kill this woman/wolf for eternity. I wasn't really thinking, "Die, die," in my head; I just wanted her to *stop what she was doing*, and she wouldn't, dammit. Then there was another ear-shattering roar, and huge teeth flashed an inch away from my arms. I understood I should let go, and the second my arms loosened, I tumbled off the wolf, rolling over the pavement to land in a heap a few feet away.

There was a sort of *pop!* and Claudine was standing over me. She was in a tank top and pajama bottoms and she had a case of bedhead. From between her striped legs I saw the lion bite the wolf's head nearly off, then spit her out in a fastidious way. Then he turned to survey the parking lot, evaluating the next threat.

One of the wolves leaped at Claudine. She proved she was completely awake. While the animal was in midair her hands clamped on its ears. She swung him, using his own momentum. Claudine flung the huge wolf with the ease of a frat boy tossing a beer can, and the wolf smacked against the loading dock with a sound that seemed quite final. The speed of this attack and its conclusion was absolutely incredible.

Claudine didn't move from her straddling stance, and I was smart enough to stay put. Actually, I was exhausted, frightened, and a little bloody, though only the red spatter on my leg seemed to be my own. Fighting takes such a short time, yet it uses up the body's reserves with amazing speed. At least, that's the way it works with humans. Claudine looked pretty sparky.

"Bring it on, fur-ass!" she shrieked, beckoning with both hands to a Were who was slinking up on her from behind. She'd twisted around without moving her legs, a maneuver that would be impossible for a mundane human body. The Were launched and got exactly the same treatment as its packmate. As far as I could tell, Claudine wasn't even breathing heavy. Her eyes were wider and more intent than usual, and she held her body in a loose crouch, clearly ready for action.

There was more roaring, and barking, and growling, and shrieks of pain, and rending noises that didn't bear thinking about. But after maybe five more minutes of battle, the noise died down.

Claudine had not even glanced down at me during this time because she was guarding my body. When she did, she winced. So I looked pretty bad.

"I was late," she said, shifting her feet so she was standing on one side of me. She reached down and I seized her hand. In a flash, I was on my feet. I hugged her. Not only did I want to, I needed to. Claudine always smelled so wonderful, and her body was curiously firmer to the touch than human flesh. She seemed happy to hug me back, and we clung together for a long moment while I regained my equilibrium.

Then I raised my head to look around, dreading what I would see. The fallen lay in heaps of fur around us. The dark stains on the pavement were not from oil drips. Here and there a bedraggled wolf nosed through the corpses, looking for some-one in particular. The lion was crouched a couple of yards away, panting. Blood streaked his fur. There was an open wound on his shoulder, the one caused by Priscilla. There was another bite on his back.

I didn't know what to do first. "Thanks, Claudine," I said, and kissed her cheek.

"I can't always make it," Claudine cautioned me. "Don't count on an automatic rescue."

"Am I wearing some kind of fairy Life Alert button? How'd you know to come?" I could tell she wasn't going to answer. "Anyway, I sure appreciate this rescue. Hey, I guess you know I met my great-grandfather." I was babbling. I was so glad to be alive.

She bowed her head. "The prince is my grandfather," she said.

"Oh," I said. "So, we're like cousins?"

She looked down at me, her eyes clear and dark and calm. She didn't look like a woman who'd just killed two wolves as quick as you could snap your fingers. "Yes," she said. "I guess we are."

"So what do you call him? Granddaddy? Popsy?"

"I call him 'my lord.' "

"Oh."

She stepped away to check out the wolves she'd disposed of (I was pretty sure they were still dead), so I went over to the lion. I crouched beside him and put my arm around his neck. He rumbled. Automatically, I scratched the top of his head and behind his ears, just like I did with Bob. The rumble intensified.

"Sam," I said. "Thanks so much. I owe you my life. How bad are your wounds? What can I do about them?"

Sam sighed. He laid his head on the ground.

"You're tired?"

Then the air around him got hyper, and I pulled away from him. I knew what was coming. After a few moments, the body that lay beside me was human, not animal. I ran my eyes over Sam anxiously and I saw that he still had the wounds, but they were much smaller than they'd been on his lion form. All shape-shifters are great at healing. It says a lot about the way my life had changed that it didn't seem significant to me that Sam was buck naked. I had kind of gone beyond that now—which was good, since there were bare bodies all around me. The corpses were changing back, as well as the injured wolves.

It had been easier to look at the bodies in wolf form.

Cal Myers and his sister, Priscilla, were dead, of course, as were the two Weres Claudine had dispatched. Amanda was dead. The skinny girl I'd met in the Hair of the Dog was alive, though severely wounded in the upper thigh. I recognized Amanda's bartender, too; he seemed unscathed. Tray Dawson was cradling an arm that looked broken.

Patrick Furnan lay in the middle of a ring of the dead and wounded, all of them Priscilla's wolves. With some difficulty, I picked my way through broken, bloody bodies. I could feel all the eyes, wolf and human, focus on me as I squatted by him. I put my fingers on his neck and got nothing. I checked his wrist. I even put my hand against his chest. No movement.

"Gone," I said, and those remaining in wolf form began to howl. Far more disturbing were the howls coming from the throats of the Weres in human form.

Alcide staggered over to me. He appeared to be more or less intact, though streaks of blood matted his chest hair. He passed the slain Priscilla, kicking her corpse as he went by. He knelt for a moment by Patrick Furnan, dipping his head as though he was bowing to the corpse. Then he rose to his feet. He looked dark, savage, and resolute.

"I am the leader of this pack!" he said in a voice of absolute certainty. The scene became eerily quiet as the surviving wolves absorbed that.

"You need to leave now," Claudine said very quietly right behind me. I jumped like a rabbit. I'd been mesmerized by the beauty of Alcide, by the primitive wildness rolling off him.

"What? Why?"

"They're going to celebrate their victory and the ascension of a new packmaster," she said.

The skinny girl clenched her hands together and brought them down on the skull of a fallen—but still twitching—enemy. The bones broke with a nasty crunch. All around me the defeated Weres were being executed, at least those who were severely wounded. A small cluster of three scrambled to kneel in front of Alcide, their heads tilted back. Two of them were women. One was an adolescent male. They were offering Alcide their throats in surrender. Alcide was very excited. All over. I remembered the way Patrick Furnan had celebrated when he got the packmaster job. I didn't know if Alcide was going to fuck the hostages or kill them. I took in my breath to exclaim. I don't know what I would've said, but Sam's grimy hand clapped over my mouth. I rolled my eyes to glare at him, both angry and agitated, and he shook his head vehemently. He held my gaze for a long moment to make sure I would stay silent, and then he removed his hand. He put his arm around my waist and turned me abruptly away from the scene. Claudine took the rear guard as Sam marched me rapidly away. I kept my eyes forward.

I tried not to listen to the noises.

Chapter 10

Sam had some extra clothes in his truck, and he pulled them on matter-of-factly. Claudine said, "I have to get back to bed," as if she'd been awoken to let the cat out or go to the bathroom, and then *pop!* she was gone.

"I'll drive," I offered, because Sam was wounded.

He handed me his keys.

We started out in silence. It was an effort to remember the route to get back to the interstate to return to Bon Temps because I was still shocked on several different levels.

"That's a normal reaction to battle," Sam said. "The surge of lust."

I carefully didn't look at Sam's lap to see if he was having his own surge. "Yeah, I know that. I've been in a few fights now. A few too many."

"Plus, Alcide did ascend to the packmaster position." Another reason to feel "happy."

"But he did this whole battle thing because Maria-Star died." So he should have been too depressed to think about celebrating the death of his enemy, was my point.

"He did this *whole battle thing* because he was threatened," Sam said. "It's really stupid of Alcide and Furnan that they didn't sit down and talk before it came to this point. They could have figured out what was happening much earlier. If you hadn't persuaded them, they'd still be getting picked off and they'd have started an all-out war. They'd have done most of Priscilla Hebert's work for her."

I was sick of the Weres, their aggression and stubbornness. "Sam, you went through all of this because of me. I feel terrible about that. I would have died if it wasn't for you. I owe you big-time. And I'm so sorry."

"Keeping you alive," Sam said, "is important to me." He closed his eyes and slept the rest of the way back to his trailer. He limped up the steps unaided, and his door shut firmly. Feeling a little forlorn and not a little depressed, I got in my own car and drove home, wondering how to fit what had happened that night into the rest of my life.

Amelia and Pam were sitting in the kitchen. Amelia had made some tea, and Pam was working on a piece of embroidery. Her hands flew as the needle pierced the fabric, and I didn't know what was most astonishing: her skill or her choice of pastimes.

"What have you and Sam been up to?" Amelia asked with

a big smile. "You look like you've been rode hard and put away wet."

Then she looked more closely and said, "What happened, Sookie?"

Even Pam put down her embroidery and gave me her most serious face. "You smell," she said. "You smell of blood and war."

I looked down at myself and registered what a mess I was. My clothes were bloody, torn, and dirty, and my leg ached. It was first aid time, and I couldn't have had better care from Nurse Amelia and Nurse Pam. Pam was a little excited by the wound, but she restrained herself like a good vampire. I knew she'd tell Eric everything, but I just couldn't find it in me to care. Amelia said a healing spell over my leg. Healing wasn't her strongest suit, she told me modestly, but the spell helped a bit. My leg did stop throbbing.

"Aren't you worried?" Amelia asked. "This is from a Were. What if you caught it?"

"It's harder to catch than almost any communicable disease," I said, since I'd asked almost every werecreature I'd met about the chances of their condition being transmitted by bite. After all, they have doctors, too. And researchers. "Most people have to be bitten several times, all over their body, to get it, and even then it's not for sure." It's not like the flu or the common cold. Plus, if you cleaned the wound soon afterward, your chances dropped considerably even from that. I'd poured a bottle of water over my leg before I'd gotten in the car. "So I'm not worried, but I *am* sore, and I think I might have a scar."

"Eric won't be happy," Pam said with an anticipatory smile.

"You endangered yourself because of the Weres. You know he holds them in low esteem."

"Yeah, yeah, yeah," I said, not caring one little bit. "He can go fly a kite."

Pam brightened. "I'll tell him that," she said.

"Why do you like to tease him so much?" I asked, realizing I was almost sluggish with weariness.

"I've never had this much ammunition to tease him with," she answered, and then she and Amelia were out of my room, and I was blessedly alone and in my own bed and alive, and then I was asleep.

The shower I took the next morning was a sublime experience. In the list of Great Showers I've Had, this one ranked at least number 4. (The best shower was the one I'd shared with Eric, and I couldn't even think of that one without shivering all over.) I scoured myself clean. My leg looked good, and though I was even more sore from pulling muscles I didn't use too much, I felt a disaster had been averted and that evil had been vanquished, at least in a gray sort of way.

As I stood under the pounding hot water, rinsing my hair, I thought about Priscilla Hebert. In my brief glimpse into her world, she'd been at least trying to find a place for her disenfranchised pack, and she'd done the research to find a weak area where she could establish a foothold. Maybe if she'd come to Patrick Furnan as a supplicant, he would have been glad to give a home to her pack. But he would never have surrendered leadership. He'd killed Jackson Herveaux to attain it, so he sure wouldn't have agreed to any kind of co-op arrangement with Priscilla—even if wolf society would permit that, which was doubtful, especially given her status as a rare female packleader.

Well, she wasn't one anymore.

Theoretically, I admired her attempt to reestablish her wolves in a new home. Since I'd met Priscilla in the flesh, I could only be glad she hadn't succeeded.

Clean and refreshed, I dried my hair and put on my makeup. I was working the day shift, so I had to be at Merlotte's at eleven. I pulled on the usual uniform of black pants and white shirt, decided to leave my hair loose for once, and tied my black Reeboks.

I decided I felt pretty good, all things considered.

A lot of people were dead, and a lot of grief was hanging around the events of last night, but at least the encroaching pack had been defeated and now the Shreveport area should be peaceful for a while. The war was over in a very short time. And the Weres hadn't been exposed to the rest of the world, though that was a step they'd have to take soon. The longer the vampires were public, the more likely it became that someone would out the Weres.

I added that fact to the giant box full of things that were not my problem.

The scrape on my leg, whether due to its nature or because of Amelia's ministrations, was already scabbed over. There were bruises on my arms and legs, but my uniform covered them. It was feasible to wear long sleeves today, because it was actually cool. In fact, a jacket would have been nice, and I regretted not having thrown one on as I drove to work. Amelia hadn't been stirring when I left, and I had no idea if Pam was in my secret vampire hidey-hole in the spare bedroom. Hey, not my concern!

As I drove, I was adding to the list of things I shouldn't have to worry about or consider. But I came to a dead halt when I got to work. When I saw my boss, a lot of thoughts came crowding in that I hadn't anticipated. Not that Sam looked beaten up or anything. He looked pretty much as usual when I stopped in his office to drop my purse in its usual drawer. In fact, the brawl seemed to have invigorated him. Maybe it had felt good to change into something more aggressive than a collie. Maybe he'd enjoyed kicking some werewolf butt. Ripping open some werewolf stomachs . . . breaking some werewolf spines.

Okay, well—whose life had been saved by the aforesaid ripping and breaking? My thoughts cleared up in a hurry. Impulsively, I bent to give him a kiss on the cheek. I smelled the smell that was Sam: aftershave, the woods, something wild yet familiar.

"How are you feeling?" he asked, as if I always kissed him hello.

"Better than I thought I would," I said. "You?"

"A little achy, but I'll do."

Holly stuck her head in. "Hey, Sookie, Sam." She came in to deposit her own purse.

"Holly, I hear you and Hoyt are an item," I said, and I hoped I looked smiling and pleased.

"Yeah, we're hitting it off okay," she said, trying for nonchalance. "He's really good with Cody, and his family's real nice." Despite her aggressively dyed spiky black hair and her heavy makeup, there was something wistful and vulnerable about Holly's face.

It was easy for me to say, "I hope it works out." Holly looked very pleased. She knew as well as I did that if she married Hoyt she'd be for all intents and purposes my sister-in-law, since the bond between Jason and Hoyt was so strong.

Then Sam began telling us about a problem he was having with one of his beer distributors, and Holly and I tied on our aprons, and our working day began. I stuck my head through the hatch to wave at the kitchen staff. The current cook at Merlotte's was an ex-army guy named Carson. Short-order cooks come and go. Carson was one of the better ones. He'd mastered burgers Lafayette right away (hamburgers steeped in a former cook's special sauce), and he got the chicken strips and fries done exactly right, and he didn't have tantrums or try to stab the busboy. He showed up on time and left the kitchen clean at the end of his shift, and that was such a huge thing Sam would have forgiven Carson a lot of weirdness.

We were light on customers, so Holly and I were getting the drinks and Sam was on the phone in his office when Tanya Grissom came in the front door. The short, curvy woman looked as pretty and healthy as a milkmaid. Tanya went light on the makeup and heavy on the self-assurance.

"Where's Sam?" she asked. Her little mouth curved up in a smile. I smiled back just as insincerely. Bitch.

"Office," I said, as if I always knew exactly where Sam was.

"That woman there," Holly said, pausing on her way to the serving hatch. "That gal is a deep well."

"Why do you say that?"

"She's living out at Hotshot, rooming with some of the women out there," Holly said. Of all the regular citizens of Bon Temps, Holly was one of the few who knew that there were such creatures as Weres and shifters. I didn't know if she'd discovered that the residents of Hotshot were werepanthers, but she knew they were inbred and strange, because that was a byword in Renard Parish. And she considered Tanya (a werefox) guilty by association, or at least *suspicious* by association.

I had a stab of genuine anxiety. I thought, *Tanya and Sam could change together. Sam would enjoy that. He could even change into a fox himself, if he wanted to.*

It was a huge effort to smile at my customers after I'd had that idea. I was ashamed when I realized I should be happy to see someone interested in Sam, someone who could appreciate his true nature. It didn't say much for me that I wasn't happy at all. But she wasn't good enough for him, and I'd warned him about her.

Tanya returned from the hallway leading to Sam's office and went out the front door, not looking as confident as she'd gone in. I smiled at her back. Ha! Sam came out to pull beers. He didn't seem nearly as cheerful.

That wiped the smile off my face. While I served Sheriff Bud Dearborn and Alcee Beck their lunch (Alcee glowering at me all the while), I worried about that. I decided to take a peek in Sam's head, because I was getting better at aiming my talent in certain ways. It was also easier to block it off and keep it out of my everyday activities now that I'd bonded with Eric, though I hated to admit that. It's not nice to flit around in someone else's thoughts, but I've always been able to do it, and it was just second nature.

I know that's a lame excuse. But I was used to knowing, not to wondering. Shifters are harder to read than regular people, and Sam was hard even for a shifter, but I got that he was frustrated, uncertain, and thoughtful.

Then I was horrified at my own audacity and lack of manners. Sam had risked his life for me the night before. He had *saved my life.* And here I was, rummaging around in his head like a kid in a box full of toys. Shame made my cheeks flush, and I lost the thread of what the gal at my table was saying until she asked me gently if I felt all right. I snapped out of it and focused and took her order for chili and crackers and a glass of sweet tea. Her friend, a woman in her fifties, asked for a hamburger Lafayette and a side salad. I got her choice of dressing and beer, and shot off to the hatch to turn in the order. I nodded at the tap when I stood by Sam, and he handed me the beer a second later. I was too rattled to talk to him. He shot me a curious glance.

I was glad to leave the bar when my shift was up. Holly and I turned over to Arlene and Danielle, and grabbed our purses. We emerged into near-darkness. The security lights were already on. It was going to rain later, and clouds obscured the stars. We could hear Carrie Underwood singing on the jukebox, faintly. She wanted Jesus to take the wheel. That seemed like a real good idea.

FROM DEAD TO WORSE

We stood by our cars for a moment in the parking lot. The wind was blowing, and it was downright chilly.

"I know Jason is Hoyt's best friend," Holly said. Her voice sounded uncertain, and though her face was hard to decipher, I knew she wasn't sure I'd want to hear what she was going to say. "I've always liked Hoyt. He was a good guy in high school. I guess—I hope you don't really get mad at me—I guess what stopped me from dating him earlier was his being so tight with Jason."

I didn't know how to respond. "You don't like Jason," I said finally.

"Oh, sure, I like Jason. Who doesn't? But is he good for Hoyt? Can Hoyt be happy if that cord between them is weaker? 'Cause I can't think about getting closer to Hoyt unless I believe he can stick with me the way he's always stuck with Jason. You can see what I mean."

"Yes," I said. "I love my brother. But I know Jason isn't really in the habit of thinking about the welfare of other people." And that was putting it mildly.

Holly said, "I like you. I don't want to hurt your feelings. But I figured you'd know, anyway."

"Yeah, I kinda did," I said. "I like you, too, Holly. You're a good mother. You've worked hard to take care of your kid. You're on good terms with your ex. But what about Danielle? I would've said you were as tight with her as Hoyt is with Jason." Danielle was another divorced mother, and she and Holly had been thick as thieves since they were in first grade. Danielle had more of a support system than Holly. Danielle's mother and father were still hale and were very glad to help out with her two kids. Danielle had been going with a guy for some time now, too.

"I would never have said anything could come between Danielle and me, Sookie." Holly pulled on her Windbreaker and fished for her keys in the depths of her purse. "But her and me, we've parted ways a little bit. We still see each other for lunch sometimes, and our kids still play together." Holly sighed heavily. "I don't know. When I got interested in something other than the world here in Bon Temps, the world we grew up in, Danielle started thinking there was something a little wrong with that, with my curiosity. When I decided to become a Wiccan, she hated that, still does hate it. If she knew about the Weres, if she knew what had happened to me..." A shapeshifting witch had tried to force Eric to give her a piece of his financial enterprises. She'd forced all the local witches she could round up into helping her, including an unwilling Holly. "That whole thing changed me," Holly said now.

"It does, doesn't it? Dealing with the supes."

"Yeah. But they're part of our world. Someday everyone will know that. Someday...the whole world will be different."

I blinked. This was unexpected. "What do you mean?"

"When they all come out," Holly said, surprised at my lack of insight. "When they all come out and admit their existence. Everyone, everyone in the world, will have to adjust. But some people won't want to. Maybe there'll be a backlash. Wars maybe. Maybe the Weres will fight all the other shifters, or maybe the humans will attack the Weres and the vampires.

Or the vampires—you know they don't like the wolves worth a durn—they'll wait until some fine night, and then they'll kill them all and get the humans to say thank you."

She had a touch of the poet in her, did Holly. And she was quite a visionary, in a doom-ridden way. I'd had no idea Holly was that deep, and I was again ashamed of myself. Mind readers shouldn't be taken by surprise like that. I'd tried so hard to stay out of people's minds that I was missing important cues.

"All of that, or none of that," I said. "Maybe people will just accept it. Not in every country. I mean, when you think of what happened to the vampires in eastern Europe and some of South America . . ."

"The pope never sorted that one out," Holly commented.

I nodded. "Kind of hard to know what to say, I guess." Most churches had had (excuse me) a hell of a time deciding on a scriptural and theological policy toward the undead. The Were announcement would sure add another wrinkle to that. They were definitely alive, no doubt about it. . . . But they had almost too much life, as opposed to already having died once.

I shifted my feet. I hadn't intended on standing out here and solving the world's problems and speculating on the future. I was still tired from the night before. "I'll see you, Holly. Maybe you and me and Amelia can go to the movies in Clarice some night?"

"Sure," she said, a little surprised. "That Amelia, she doesn't think much of my craft, but at least we can talk the talk a little."

Too late, I had a conviction the threesome wouldn't work out, but what the hell. We could give it a try.

I drove home wondering if anyone would be there waiting

for me. The answer came when I parked beside Pam's car at the back door. Pam drove a conservative car, of course, a Toyota with a Fangtasia bumper sticker. I was only surprised it wasn't a minivan.

Pam and Amelia were watching a DVD in the living room. They were sitting on the couch but not exactly twined around each other. Bob was curled up in my recliner. There was a bowl of popcorn on Amelia's lap and a bottle of TrueBlood in Pam's hand. I stepped around so I could see what they were watching. *Underworld.* Hmmm.

"Kate Beckinsale is hot," Amelia said. "Hey, how was work?"

"Okay," I said. "Pam, how come you have two evenings off in a row?"

"I deserve it," Pam said. "I haven't had time off in two years. Eric agreed I was due. How do you think I would look in that black outfit?"

"Oh, as good as Beckinsale," Amelia said, and turned her head to smile at Pam. They were at the ooey-gooey stage. Considering my own complete lack of ooey, I didn't want to be around.

"Did Eric find out any more about that Jonathan guy?" I asked.

"I don't know. Why don't you call him yourself?" Pam said with a complete lack of concern.

"Right, you're off duty," I muttered, and stomped back to my room, grumpy and a little ashamed of myself. I punched in the number for Fangtasia without even having to look it up. So not good. And it was on speed dial on my cell phone. Geez. Not something I wanted to ponder just at the moment.

The phone rang, and I put my dreary musing aside. You had to be on your game when you talked to Eric.

"Fangtasia, the bar with a bite. This is Lizbet." One of the fangbangers. I scrounged around my mental closet, trying to put a face with the name. Okay—tall, very round and proud of it, moon face, gorgeous brown hair.

"Lizbet, this is Sookie Stackhouse," I said.

"Oh, hi," she said, sounding startled and impressed.

"Um ... hi. Listen, could I speak to Eric, please?"

"I'll see if the master is available," Lizbet breathed, trying to sound reverent and all mysterious.

"Master," my ass.

The fangbangers were men and women who loved vampires so much they wanted to be around them every minute the vampires were awake. Jobs at places like Fangtasia were bread and butter to these people, and the opportunity to get bitten was regarded as close to sacred. The fangbanger code required them to be *honored* if some bloodsucker wanted to sample them; and if they died of it, well, that was just about an honor, too. Behind all the pathos and tangled sexuality of the typical fangbanger was the underlying hope that some vampire would think the fangbanger was "worthy" of being turned into a vampire. Like you had to pass a character test.

"Thanks, Lizbet," I said.

Lizbet set the phone down with a thud and went off looking for Eric. I couldn't have made her happier.

"Yes," said Eric after about five minutes.

"Busy, were you?"

"Ah . . . having supper."

I wrinkled my nose. "Well, hope you had enough," I said with a total lack of sincerity. "Listen, did you find out anything about that Jonathan?"

"Have you seen him again?" Eric asked sharply.

"Ah, no. I was just wondering."

"If you see him, I need to know immediately."

"Okay, got that. What have you learned?"

"He's been seen other places," Eric said. "He even came here one night when I was away. Pam's at your house, right?"

I had a sinking feeling in my gut. Maybe Pam wasn't sleeping with Amelia out of sheer attraction. Maybe she'd combined business with a great cover story, and she was staying with Amelia to keep an eye on me. *Damn vampires,* I thought angrily, because that scenario was entirely too close to an incident in my recent past that had hurt me incredibly.

I wasn't going to ask. Knowing would be worse than suspecting.

"Yes," I said between stiff lips. "She's here."

"Good," Eric said with some satisfaction. "If he appears again, I know she can take care of it. Not that that's why she's there," he added unconvincingly. The obvious afterthought was Eric's attempt at pacifying what he could tell were my upset feelings; it sure didn't arise from any feeling of guilt.

I scowled at my closet door. "Are you gonna give me any real information on why you're so jumpy about this guy?"

"You haven't seen the queen since Rhodes," Eric said.

This was not going to be a good conversation. "No," I said. "What's the deal with her legs?"

"They're growing back," Eric said after a brief hesitation.

I wondered if the feet were growing right out of her stumps, or if the legs would grow out and then the feet would appear at the end of the process. "That's good, right?" I said. Having legs had to be a good thing.

"It hurts very much," Eric said, "when you lose parts and they grow back. It'll take a while. She's very...She's incapacitated." He said the last word very slowly, as if it was a word he knew but had never said aloud.

I thought about what he was telling me, both on the surface and beneath. Conversations with Eric were seldom single-layered.

"She's not well enough to be in charge," I said in conclusion. "Then who is?"

"The sheriffs have been running things," Eric said. "Gervaise perished in the bombing, of course; that leaves me, Cleo, and Arla Yvonne. It would have been clearer if Andre had survived." I felt a twinge of panic and guilt. I could have saved Andre. I'd feared and loathed him, and I hadn't. I'd let him be killed.

Eric was silent for a minute, and I wondered if he was picking up on the fear and guilt. It would be very bad if he ever learned that Quinn had killed Andre for my sake. Eric continued, "Andre could have held the center because he was so established as the queen's right hand. If one of her minions had to die, I wish I could have picked Sigebert, who's all muscles and no brains. At least Sigebert's there to guard her body, though Andre could have done that and guarded her territory as well."

I'd never heard Eric so chatty about vampire affairs. I was beginning to have an awful creeping feeling that I knew where he was headed.

"You expect some kind of takeover," I said, and felt my heart plummet. Not again. "You think Jonathan was a scout."

"Watch out, or I'll begin to think you can read my mind." Though Eric's tone was light as a marshmallow, his meaning was a sharp blade hidden inside.

"That's impossible," I said, and if he thought I was lying, he didn't challenge me. Eric seemed to be regretting telling me so much. The rest of our talk was very brief. He told me again to call him at the first sight of Jonathan, and I assured him I'd be glad to.

After I'd hung up, I didn't feel quite as sleepy. In honor of the chilly night I pulled on my fleecy pajama bottoms, white with pink sheep, and a white T-shirt. I unearthed my map of Louisiana and found a pencil. I sketched in the areas I knew. I was piecing my knowledge together from bits of conversations that had taken place in my presence. Eric had Area Five. The queen had had Area One, which was New Orleans and vicinity. That made sense. But in between, there was a jumble. The finally deceased Gervaise had had the area including Baton Rouge, and that was where the queen had been living since Katrina damaged her New Orleans properties so heavily. So that should have been Area Two, due to its prominence. But it was called Area Four. Very lightly, I traced a line that I could erase, and would, after I'd looked at it for a bit.

I mined my head for other bits of information. Five, at the top of the state, stretched nearly all the way across. Eric was richer and more powerful than I'd thought. Below him, and fairly even in territory, were Cleo Babbitt's Area Three and Arla Yvonne's Area Two. A swoop down to the Gulf from the south-westernmost corner of Mississippi marked off the large areas formerly held by Gervaise and the queen, Four and One respectively. I could only imagine what vampiric political contortions had led to the numbering and arrangement.

I looked at the map for a few long minutes before I erased all the light lines I'd drawn. I glanced at the clock. Nearly an hour had passed since my conversation with Eric. In a melancholy mood, I brushed my teeth and washed my face. After I climbed into bed and said my prayers, I lay there awake for quite a while. I was pondering the undeniable truth that the most powerful vampire in the state of Louisiana, at this very point in time, was Eric Northman, my blood-bonded, once-upon-a-time lover. Eric had said in my hearing that he didn't want to be king, didn't want to take over new territory; and since I'd figured out the extent of his territory right now, the size of it made that assertion a little more likely.

I believed I knew Eric a little, maybe as much as a human can know a vampire, which doesn't mean my knowledge was profound. I didn't believe he wanted to take over the state, or he would have done so. I did think his power meant there was a giant target pinned to his back. I needed to try to sleep. I glanced at the clock again. An hour and a half since I'd talked to Eric.

Bill glided into my room quite silently.

"What's up?" I asked, trying to keep my voice very quiet, very calm, though every nerve in my body had started shrieking.

"I'm uneasy," he said in his cool voice, and I almost laughed. "Pam had to leave for Fangtasia. She called me to take her place here."

"Why?"

He sat in the chair in the corner. It was pretty dark in my room, but the curtains weren't drawn completely shut and I got some illumination from the yard's security light. There was a night-light in the bathroom, too, and I could make out the contours of his body and the blur of his face. Bill had a little glow, like all vampires do in my eyes.

"Pam couldn't get Cleo on the phone," he said. "Eric left the club to run an errand, and Pam couldn't raise him, either. But I got his voice mail; I'm sure he'll call back. It's Cleo not answering that's the rub."

"Pam and Cleo are friends?"

"No, not at all," he said, matter-of-factly. "But Pam should be able to talk to her at her all-night grocery. Cleo always answers."

"Why was Pam trying to reach her?" I asked.

"They call each other every night," Bill said. "Then Cleo calls Arla Yvonne. They have a chain. It should not be broken, not in these days." Bill stood up with a speed that I couldn't follow. "Listen!" he whispered, his voice as light on my ear as a moth wing. "Do you hear?"

I didn't hear jack shit. I held still under the covers, wishing passionately that this whole thing would just go away. Weres, vampires, trouble, strife...But no such luck. "What do you hear?" I asked, trying to be as quiet as Bill was being, an effort doomed in the attempt.

"Someone's coming," he said.

And then I heard a knock on the front door. It was a very quiet knock.

I threw back the covers and got up. I couldn't find my slippers because I was so rattled. I started for the bedroom door on my bare feet. The night was chilly, and I hadn't turned on the heat yet; my soles pressed coldly against the polished wood of the floor.

"I'll answer the door," Bill said, and he was ahead of me without my having seen him move.

"Jesus Christ, Shepherd of Judea," I muttered, and followed him. I wondered where Amelia was: asleep upstairs or on the living room couch? I hoped she was only asleep. I was so spooked by that time that I imagined she might be dead.

Bill glided silently through the dark house, down the hall, to the living room (which still smelled like popcorn), to the front door, and then he looked through the peephole, which for some reason I found funny. I had to slap a hand over my mouth to keep from giggling.

No one shot Bill through the peephole. No one tried to batter the door down. No one screamed.

The continuing silence was breaking me out in goose bumps. I didn't even see Bill move. His cool voice came from right beside my ear. "It is a very young woman. Her hair is dyed white or blond, and it's very short and dark at the roots. She's skinny. She's human. She's scared."

She wasn't the only one.

I tried like hell to think who my middle-of-the-night caller could be. Suddenly I thought I might know. "Frannie," I breathed. "Quinn's sister. Maybe."

"Let me in," a girl's voice said. "Oh, *please* let me in."

It was just like a ghost story I'd read once. Every hair on my arms stood up.

"I have to tell you what's happened to Quinn," Frannie said, and that decided me on the spot.

"Open the door," I said to Bill in my normal voice. "We have to let her in."

"She's human," Bill said, as if to say, "How much trouble can she be?" He unlocked the front door.

I won't say Frannie tumbled in, but she sure didn't waste any time getting through the door and slamming it behind her. I hadn't had a good first impression of Frannie, who was long on the aggression and attitude and short on the charm, but I'd come to know her a fraction better as she sat at Quinn's bedside in the hospital after the explosion. She'd had a hard life, and she loved her brother.

"What's happened?" I asked sharply as Frannie stumbled to the nearest chair and sat down.

"You *would* have a vampire here," she said. "Can I have a glass of water? Then I'll try to do what Quinn wants."

I hurried to the kitchen and got her a drink. I turned on the light in the kitchen, but even when I came back to the living room, we kept it dark.

"Where's your car?" Bill asked.

"It broke down about a mile back," she said. "But I couldn't wait with it. I called a tow truck and left the keys in the ignition. I hope to God they get it off the road and out of sight."

"Tell me *right now* what's happening," I said.

"Short or long version?"

"Short."

"Some vampires from Vegas are coming to take over Louisiana."

It was a showstopper.

Chapter 11

Bill's voice was very fierce. "Where, when, how many?"

"They've taken out some of the sheriffs already," Frannie said, and I could tell there was just a hint of enjoyment at getting to deliver this momentous news. "Smaller forces are taking out the weaker ones while a larger force gathers to surround Fangtasia to deal with Eric."

Bill was on his cell phone before the words had finished leaving Frannie's mouth, and I was left gaping at him. I had come so late to the realization of how weak Louisiana's situation was that it seemed to me for a second that I had brought this about by thinking of it.

"How did this happen?" I asked the girl. "How did Quinn get involved? How is he? Did he send you here?"

"*Of course* he sent me here," she said, as if I were the stupidest person she'd ever met. "He knows you're tied to that vampire Eric, so that makes you part of the target. The Vegas vamps sent someone to have a look at you, even."

Jonathan.

"I mean, they were evaluating Eric's assets, and you were considered part of that."

"Why was this Quinn's problem?" I asked, which may not have been the clearest way to put it, but she got my meaning.

"Our mother, our goddamned screwed-up, screw-up *mother*," Frannie said bitterly. "You know she got captured and raped by some hunters, right? In Colorado. Like a hundred years ago." Actually, it had been maybe nineteen years ago, because that was how Frannie had been conceived.

"And Quinn rescued her and killed them all, though he was just a kid, and he went in debt to the local vampires to get them to help him clean up the scene and get his mom away."

I knew Quinn's mother's sad history. I was nodding frantically by now, because I wanted to get to something I hadn't heard yet.

"Okay, well, my mom was pregnant with me after the rape," Frannie said, glaring at me defiantly. "So she had me, but she was never right in the head, and growing up with her was kinda hard, right? Quinn was working off his debt in the pits." (Think *Gladiator* with wereanimals.) "She never got right in the head," Frannie repeated. "And she's kept getting worse."

"I get that," I said, trying to keep my voice level. Bill seemed on the verge of thumping Frannie to speed up her narrative, but I shook my head.

"Okay, so she was in a nice place that Quinn was paying

for outside Las Vegas, the only assisted-living center in America where you can send people like my mom." The Deranged Weretiger Nursing Home? "But Mom got loose, and she killed some tourist and took her clothes and caught a ride into Vegas and picked up a man. She killed him, too. She robbed him and took his money and gambled until we caught up with her." Frannie paused and took a deep breath. "Quinn was still healing from Rhodes, and this about killed him."

"Oh, no." But I had a feeling I hadn't heard the bottom line on this incident yet.

"Yeah, what's worse, right? The escape, or the killing?"

Probably the tourists had had an opinion on that.

I vaguely noticed that Amelia had entered the room, and I also realized that she didn't seem startled to see Bill. So she'd been awake when Bill had taken Pam's place. Amelia hadn't met Frannie before, but she didn't interrupt the flow.

"Anyway, there's a huge vampire cartel in Vegas, because the pickings are so rich," Frannie told us. "They tracked down Mom before the police could catch her. They cleaned up after her *again*. Turns out that Whispering Palms, the place that lost her, had alerted all the supes in the area to be on the lookout. By the time I got to the casino where they'd grabbed Mom, the vamps were telling Quinn that they'd taken care of everything and now there was more debt for him to work off. He said he was coming off a bad injury and he couldn't go back in the pits. They offered to take me on as a blood donor or a whore for visiting vamps instead, and he just about took out the one who said that."

Of course. I exchanged a glance with Bill. The offer to "employ" Frannie had been designed to make anything else look better.

"Then they said they knew of a really weak kingdom that was just about up for grabs, and they meant Louisiana. Quinn told 'em they could get it for free if the King of Nevada would just marry Sophie-Anne, her being in no position to argue. But it turned out the king was right there. He said he detested cripples and no way would he marry a vampire who'd killed her previous husband, no matter how sweet her kingdom was, even with Arkansas thrown in." Sophie-Anne was the titular head of Arkansas as well as Louisiana since she'd been found innocent of her husband's (the King of Arkansas's) murder in a vampire court. Sophie-Anne hadn't had a chance to consolidate her claim, because of the bombing. But I was sure it was on her to-do list, right after her legs grew back.

Bill flipped his phone open again and began punching in numbers. Whoever he called, he didn't get an answer. His dark eyes were blazing. He was absolutely revved up. He leaned over to pick up a sword he'd left propped against the couch. Yep, he'd come fully armed. I didn't keep items like that in my toolshed.

"They'll want to take us out quietly and quickly so the human news media won't catch on. They'll concoct a story to explain why familiar vampires have been replaced with strange ones," Bill said. "You, girl—what part does your brother have to play in this?"

"They made him tell them how many people you-all had

and share what else he knew about the situation in Lousiana," Frannie said. To make matters perfect, she began to cry. "He didn't want to. He tried to bargain with them, but they had him where they wanted him." Now Frannie looked about ten years older than she was. "He tried to call Sookie a million times, but they were watching him, and he was scared he'd be leading them right to her. But they found out anyway. Once he knew what they were going to do, he took a big risk—for both of us—and sent me on ahead. I was glad I'd got a friend to get my car back from you."

"One of you should have called me, written me, something." Despite our current crisis, I couldn't stop myself from expressing my bitterness.

"He couldn't let you know how bad it was. He said he knew you'd try to get him out of it somehow, but there was no way out."

"Well, sure I would have tried to get him out of it," I said. "That's what you do when someone's in trouble."

Bill was silent but I felt his eyes on me. I'd rescued Bill when he'd been in trouble. Sometimes I was sorry I had.

"Your brother, why is he with them now?" Bill asked sharply. "He's given them information. They are vampires. What do they need with him?"

"They're bringing him with them so he can negotiate with the supe community, specifically the Weres," Frannie said, sounding suddenly like Miss Corporate Secretary. I felt sort of sorry for Frannie. As the product of a union between a human and a weretiger, she had no special powers to give her an edge or to provide her with a bargaining chip. Her face was streaked with smeared mascara and her nails were chewed down to the quick. She was a mess.

And this was no time to be worried about Frannie, because the vampires of Vegas were taking over the state.

"What had we better do?" I asked. "Amelia, have you checked the house wards? Do they include our cars?" Amelia nodded briskly. "Bill, you've called Fangtasia and all the other sheriffs?"

Bill nodded. "No answer from Cleo. Arla Yvonne answered, and she had already gotten wind of the attack. She said she was going to ground and would try to work her way up to Shreveport. She has six of her nest with her. Since Gervaise met his end, his vampires have been tending the queen, and Booth Crimmons has been their lieutenant. Booth says he was out tonight and his child, Audrey, who was left with the queen and Sigebert, doesn't answer. Even the deputy that Sophie-Anne sent to Little Rock is not responding."

We were all silent for a moment. The idea that Sophie-Anne might be finally dead was almost unimaginable.

Bill shook himself visibly. "So," he continued, "we might stay here, or we might find another place for you three. When I'm sure you're safe, I have to get to Eric as soon as I can. He'll need every pair of hands tonight if he's to survive."

Some of the other sheriffs were surely dead. Eric might die tonight. The full realization smacked me in the face with the force of a huge gloved hand. I sucked in a jagged breath and fought to stay on my feet. I just couldn't think about that.

"We'll be fine," Amelia said stoutly. "I'm sure you're a great fighter, Bill, but we aren't defenseless."

With all due respect to Amelia's witchcraft ability, we were so defenseless; at least against vampires.

Bill spun away from us and stared down the hall at the back door. He'd heard something that hadn't reached our human ears. But a second later, I heard a familiar voice.

"Bill, let me in. The sooner, the better!"

"It's Eric," Bill said with great satisfaction. Moving so fast he was a blur, he went to the rear of the house. Sure enough, Eric was outside, and something in me relaxed. He was alive. I noticed that he was hardly his usual tidy self. His T-shirt was torn, and he was barefoot.

"I was cut off from the club," he said as he and Bill came up the hall to join us. "My house was no good, not by myself. I couldn't reach anyone else. I got your message, Bill. So, Sookie, I'm here to ask for your hospitality."

"Of course," I said automatically, though I really should have thought about it. "But maybe we should go to—" I was about to suggest we cut across the graveyard and go to Bill's house, which was larger and would have more facilities for vampires, when trouble erupted from another source. We hadn't been paying any attention to Frannie since she'd finished her story, and the slump she'd experienced once her dramatic news had been delivered had allowed her to think of the potential for disaster we faced.

"I gotta get out of here," Frannie said. "Quinn told me to stay here, but you guys are..." Her voice was rising and she was on her feet and every muscle in her neck stood out in sharp relief as her head whipped around in her agitation.

"Frannie," Bill said. He put his white hands on each side of Frannie's face. He looked into the girl's eyes. Frannie fell silent. "You stay here, you stupid girl, and do what Sookie tells you to do."

"Okay," Frannie said in a calm voice.

"Thanks," I said. Amelia was looking at Bill in a shocked kind of way. I guess she'd never seen a vamp use his whammy before. "I'm going to get my shotgun," I said to no one, but before I could move, Eric turned to the closet by the front door. He reached in and extricated the Benelli. He turned to hand it to me with a bemused expression. Our eyes met.

Eric had remembered where I kept the shotgun. He'd learned that when he'd stayed with me while his memory was lost.

When I could look away, I saw Amelia was looking self-consciously thoughtful. Even in my short experience of living with Amelia, I had learned that this was not a look I liked. It meant she was about to make a point, and it was a point I wouldn't care for.

"Are we getting all excited about nothing?" she asked rhetorically. "Maybe we're panicking for no good reason."

Bill looked at Amelia as if she'd turned into a baboon. Frannie looked totally unconcerned.

"After all," Amelia said, wearing a small, superior smile, "why would anyone come after *us* at all? Or more specifically *you*, Sookie. Because I don't suppose vampires would come after *me*. But that aside, why would they come here? You're not an essential part of the vampire defense system. What would give them a good reason to want to kill or capture you?"

Eric had been making a circuit of the doors and windows. He finished as Amelia was winding up her speech. "What's happened?" he asked.

I said, "Amelia is explaining to me why there's no rational reason the vampires would come after me in their attempt to conquer the state."

"Of course they'll come," Eric said, barely glancing at Amelia. He examined Frannie for a minute, nodded in approval, and then stood to the side of a living room window to look out. "Sookie's got a blood tie to me. And now I am here."

"Yeah," Amelia said heavily. "Thanks a lot, Eric, for making a beeline for this house."

"Amelia. Are you not a witch with much power?"

"Yes, I am," she said cautiously.

"Isn't your father a wealthy man with a lot of influence in the state? Isn't your mentor a great witch?"

Who had been doing some research on the Internet? Eric and Copley Carmichael had something in common.

"Yeah," Amelia said. "Okay, they'd be happy if they could corral us. But still, if Eric hadn't come here, I don't think we'd need to worry about physical injury."

"You're wondering if we're actually in danger?" I said. "Vampires, excited, bloodlust?"

"We won't be any use if we're not alive."

"Accidents happen," I said, and Bill snorted. I'd never heard him make such an ordinary sound, and I looked at him. Bill was enjoying the prospect of a good fight. His fangs were out. Frannie was staring at him, but her expression didn't change. If

there'd been the slightest chance she'd stay calm and coopera-
tive, I might have asked Bill to bring her out of the artificial
state. I loved having Frannie still and quiet—but I hated her
loss of free will.

"Why did Pam leave?" I asked.

"She can be of more value at Fangtasia. The others have
gone to the club, and she can tell me if they are sealed in it
or not. It was stupid of me to call them all and tell them to
gather; I should have told them to scatter." From the way he
looked now, it wasn't a mistake Eric would ever make again.

Bill stood close to a window, listening to the sounds of the
night. He looked at Eric and shook his head. No one there yet.

Eric's phone rang. He listened for a minute, said, "Good
fortune to you," and hung up.

"Most of the others are in the club," he told Bill, who nodded.

"Where is Claudine?" Bill asked me.

"I have no idea." How come Claudine came sometimes
when I was in trouble and didn't come at others? Was I just
wearing her out? "But I don't think she'll come, because you
guys are here. There's no point in her showing up to defend me
if you and Eric can't keep your fangs off of her."

Bill stiffened. His sharp ears had picked up something. He
turned and exchanged a long glance with Eric. "Not the company I'd have chosen," Bill said in his cool voice. "But we'll make
a good showing. I do regret the women." And he looked at me,
his deep dark eyes full of some intense emotion. Love? Sorrow?
Without a hint or two from his silent brain, I couldn't tell.

"We're not in our graves yet," Eric said, just as coolly.

Now I too could hear the cars coming down the driveway. Amelia made an involuntary sound of fear, and Frannie's eyes got even wider, though she stayed in her chair as if paralyzed. Eric and Bill sank into themselves.

The cars stopped out front, and there were the sounds of doors opening and shutting, someone walking up to the house.

There was a brisk knock—not on the door, but on one of the porch uprights.

I moved toward it slowly. Bill gripped my arm and stepped in front of me. "Who is there?" he called, and immediately shifted us three feet away.

He'd expected someone to fire through the door.

That didn't happen.

"It is I, the vampire Victor Madden," said a cheerful voice.

Okay, unexpected. And especially to Eric, who closed his eyes briefly. Victor Madden's identity and presence had told Eric volumes, and I didn't know what he'd read in those volumes.

"Do you know him?" I whispered to Bill.

Bill said, "Yes. I've met him." But he didn't add any details and stood lost in an inner debate. I've never wanted more intensely to know what someone was thinking than I did at that moment. The silence was getting to me.

"Friend or foe?" I called.

Victor laughed. It was a real good laugh—genial, an "I'm laughing with you, not at you" kind of chortle. "That's an excellent question," he said, "and one only you can answer. Do I have the honor of talking to Sookie Stackhouse, famed telepath?"

"You have the honor of talking to Sookie Stackhouse,

barmaid," I said frostily. And I heard a sort of throaty ruffling noise, a vocalization of an animal. A large animal.

My heart sank into my bare feet.

"The wards will hold," Amelia was saying to herself in a rapid whisper. "The wards will hold; the wards will hold." Bill was gazing at me with his dark eyes, thoughts flickering across his face in rapid succession. Frannie was looking vague and detached, but her eyes were fixed on the door. She'd heard the sound, too.

"Quinn's out there with them," I whispered to Amelia, since she was the only one in the room who hadn't figured that out.

Amelia said, "He's on *their* side?"

"They've got his mom," I reminded her. But I felt sick inside.

"But we've got his sister," Amelia said.

Eric looked as thoughtful as Bill. In fact, they were looking at each other now, and I could believe they were having a whole dialogue without speaking a word.

All this thoughtfulness wasn't good. It meant they hadn't decided which way they were going to jump.

"May we come in?" asked the charming voice. "Or may we treat with one of you face-to-face? You seem to have quite a few safeguards on the house."

Amelia pumped her arm and said, "Yes!" She grinned at me.

Nothing wrong with a little deserved self-congratulation, though the timing of it might be a bit off. I smiled back at her, though I felt my cheeks would crack.

Eric seemed to gather himself, and after one long last look at each other, he and Bill relaxed. Eric turned to me, kissed me on the lips very lightly, and looked at my face for a long moment. "He'll spare you," Eric said, and I understood he wasn't really talking to me but to himself. "You're too unique to waste."

And then he opened the door.

Chapter 12

*Since the lights were still off in the living room and the secu-*rity light was on outside, from inside the house we could see pretty well. The vampire standing by himself in the front yard was not particularly tall, but he was a striking man. He was wearing a business suit. His hair was short and curly, and though the light wasn't good for making such a determination, I thought it was black. He stood with an attitude, like a *GQ* model.

Eric was pretty much blocking the doorway, so that was all I could tell. It seemed tacky to go to the window and stare.

"Eric Northman," said Victor Madden. "I haven't seen you in a few decades."

"You've been working hard in the desert," Eric said neutrally.

"Yes, business has been booming. There are some things

I want to discuss with you—rather urgent things, I'm afraid. May I come in?"

"How many are with you?" Eric asked.

"Ten," I whispered at Eric's back. "Nine vamps and Quinn." If a human brain left a buzzing hole in my inner consciousness, a vampire brain left an empty one. All I had to do was count the holes.

"Four companions are with me," Victor said, sounding absolutely truthful and frank.

"I think you've lost your counting ability," Eric said. "I believe there are nine vampires there, and one shifter."

Victor's silhouette realigned as his hand twitched. "No use trying to pull the wool over your eyes, old sport."

"Old sport?" muttered Amelia.

"Let them step out of the woods so I can see," Eric called.

Amelia and Bill and I abandoned being discreet and went to the windows to watch. One by one, the vampires of Las Vegas came out of the trees. Since they were at the edges of the darkness I couldn't see most of them very well, but I noticed a statuesque woman with lots of brown hair and a man no taller than me who sported a neat beard and an earring.

The last to emerge from the woods was the tiger. I was sure Quinn had shifted into his animal form because he didn't want to look at me face-to-face. I felt horribly sorry for him. I figured that however ripped up inside I was, his insides had to be like hamburger meat.

"I see a few familiar faces," Eric said. "Are they all under your charge?"

This had a meaning that I didn't understand.

"Yes," Victor said very firmly.

This meant something to Eric. He stood back from the doorway, and the the rest of us turned to look at him. "Sookie," Eric said, "it's not for me to invite him in. This is your house." Eric turned to Amelia. "Is your ward specific?" he asked. "Will the ward let in him only?"

"Yes," she said. I wished she sounded more certain. "He has to be invited in by someone the ward accepts, like Sookie."

Bob the cat strolled to the open doorway. He sat in the exact middle of the threshold, his tail wrapped around his paws, and surveyed the newcomer steadily. Victor laughed a little when Bob first appeared, but that died away after a second.

"This is not just a cat," Victor said.

"No," I said, loud enough for Victor to hear me. "Neither is the one out there." The tiger made a chuffing sound, which I'd read was supposed to be friendly. I guess it was as close as Quinn could come to telling me he was sorry about the whole damn thing. Or maybe not. I came to stand right behind Bob. He raised his head to look at me, and then strolled off with as much indifference as he'd arrived. Cats.

Victor Madden approached the front porch. Evidently the wards would not let him cross the boards, and he waited at the foot of the steps. Amelia flipped on the front porch lights, and Victor blinked in the sudden glare. He was a very attractive man, if not exactly handsome. His eyes were big and brown, and his jaw was decided. He had beautiful teeth displayed in a jaw-cracking smile. He looked at me very carefully.

"Reports of your attractions were not exaggerated," he said, which took me a minute to decipher. I was too scared to be at my most intelligent. I made out Jonathan the spy among the vampires in the yard.

"Uh-huh," I said, unimpressed. "You alone can come in."

"I'm delighted," he said, bowing. He took a cautious step up and looked relieved. After that he crossed the porch so smoothly that all of a sudden he was right in front of me, his pocket handkerchief—I swear to God, a snowy white pocket handkerchief—almost touching my white T-shirt. It was all I could do to keep from flinching, but I managed to hold very still. I met his eyes and felt the pressure behind them. He was trying his mind tricks to see what might work on me.

Not much would, in my experience. After I'd let him establish that, I moved back to give him room to enter.

Victor stood quite still just inside the door. He gave everyone in the room a very cautious look, though his smile never faded. When he spotted Bill, the smile actually brightened. "Ah, Compton," he said, and though I expected he'd follow up with a more illuminating remark, that didn't happen. He gave Amelia a thorough scrutiny. "The source of the magic," he muttered, and inclined his head to her. Frannie got a quicker evaluation. When Victor recognized her, he looked, for one second, severely displeased.

I should have hidden her. I simply hadn't thought about it. Now the Las Vegas group knew that Quinn had sent his sister ahead to warn us. I wondered if we'd survive this.

If we lived until daytime, we three humans could leave in

a car, and if the cars were disabled, well, we had cell phones and could call for a pickup. But there was no telling what other day-walking helpers the vampires of Las Vegas had...besides Quinn. And as far as Eric and Bill being able to fight their way through the line of vampires outside: they could try. I didn't know how far they'd get.

"Please have a seat," I said, though I sounded about as welcoming as a church lady forced to entertain an atheist. We all moved to the couch and the chairs. We left Frannie where she was. It would be better to maintain every bit of calm we could manage. The tension in the room was almost palpable as it was.

I switched on some lamps and asked the vampires if they would like a drink. They all looked surprised. Only Victor accepted. After a nod from me, Amelia went to the kitchen to heat up some TrueBlood. Eric and Bill were on the couch, Victor had taken the easy chair, and I perched on the edge of the recliner, my hands clenched in my lap. There was a long silence while Victor selected his opening line.

"Your queen is dead, Viking," he said.

Eric's head jerked. Amelia, entering, stopped in her tracks for a second before carrying the glass of TrueBlood to Victor. He accepted it with a little bow. Amelia stared down at him, and I noticed her hand was hidden in the folds of her robe. Just as I drew in breath to tell her not to be crazy, she moved away from him and came to stand by me.

Eric said, "I had guessed that was the case. How many of the sheriffs?" I had to hand it to him. You couldn't tell how he felt from his voice.

Victor made a show of consulting his memory. "Let me see. Oh, yes! All of them."

I pressed my lips together hard so no sound would escape. Amelia pulled out the straight-backed chair we keep to one side of the hearth. She set it close to me and sank down on it like she was a bag of sand. Now that she was sitting, I could see she had a knife clutched in her hand, the filleting knife from the kitchen. It was real sharp.

"What of their people?" Bill asked. Bill was doing the clean-slate imitation, too.

"There are a few alive. A dark young man named Rasul . . . a few servitors of Arla Yvonne. Cleo Babbitt's crew died with her even after an offer of surrender, and Sigebert seems to have perished with Sophie-Anne."

"Fangtasia?" Eric had saved this for last because he could hardly bear to speak of it. I wanted to go over to him and put my arms around him, but he wouldn't appreciate that at all. It would look weak.

There was a long silence while Victor took a swallow of the TrueBlood.

Then he said, "Eric, your people are all in the club. They have not surrendered. They say they won't until they hear from you. We're ready to burn it down. One of your minions escaped, and she—we think it is a female—is taking out any of my people stupid enough to get separated from the others."

Yay, *Pam*! I bent my head to hide an involuntary smile. Amelia grinned at me. Even Eric looked pleased, just for a split second. Bill's face didn't alter a bit.

"Why am I alive, of all the sheriffs?" Eric asked—the four-hundred-pound question.

"Because you're the most efficient, the most productive, and the most practical." Victor had the answer ready at his lips. "And you have one of the biggest moneymakers living in your area and working for you." He nodded toward Bill. "Our king would like to leave you in position, if you will swear loyalty to him."

"I suppose I know what will happen if I refuse."

"My people in Shreveport are ready with the torches," Victor said with his cheerful smile. "Actually, with more modern devices, but you get the point. And, of course, we can take care of your little group here. You are certainly fond of diversity, Eric. I trail you here thinking to find you with your elite vampires, and we find you in this odd company."

I didn't even think about bristling. We were an odd company, no doubt about it. I also noticed the rest of us didn't get a vote. This all rested on the question of how proud Eric was.

In the silence, I wondered how long Eric would ponder his decision. If he didn't cave, we'd all die. That would be Victor's way of "taking care" of us, despite Eric's out-loud thought about me being too valuable to kill. I didn't think Victor gave a fig for my "value," much less Amelia's. Even if we overwhelmed Victor (and between Bill and Eric that could probably be managed), the rest of the vampires outside had only to set this house on fire as they were threatening to do Fangtasia, and we'd be gone. They might not be able to come in without an invitation, but we certainly had to get out.

My eyes met Amelia's. Her brain was pinging with fear,

though she was making a supreme effort to keep her spine stiff. If she called Copley, he would bargain for her life, and he had the wherewithal to bargain effectively. If the Las Vegas crew was hungry enough to invade Louisiana, then they were hungry enough to accept a bribe for the life of the daughter of Copley Carmichael. And surely Frannie would be okay, since her brother was right outside? Surely they would spare Frannie to keep Quinn complaisant? Victor had already pointed out that Bill had skills they needed, because his computer database had proved lucrative. So Eric and I were the most expendable.

I thought about Sam, wished I could call him and talk to him for just a minute. But I wouldn't drag him into this for the world, because that would mean his sure death. I closed my eyes and said good-bye to him.

There was a sound outside the door, and it took me a moment to interpret it as a tiger's noise. Quinn wanted in.

Eric looked at me, and I shook my head. This was bad enough without throwing Quinn into the mix. Amelia whispered, "Sookie," and pressed her hand against me. It was the hand with the knife.

"Don't," I said. "It won't do any good." I hoped Victor didn't realize what her intent was.

Eric's eyes were wide and fixed on the future. They blazed blue in the long silence.

Then something unexpected happened. Frannie snapped out of the trance, and she opened her mouth and began to scream. When the first shriek ripped out of her mouth, the door began to thud. In about five seconds Quinn splintered my door by throwing his four hundred and fifty pounds against it. Frannie scrambled to her feet and ran for it, seizing the knob and yanking it open before Victor could grab her, though he missed her by half an inch.

Quinn bounded into the house so quickly he knocked his sister down. He stood over her, roaring at all of us.

To his credit Victor showed no fear. He said, "Quinn, listen to me."

After a second, Quinn shut up. It was always hard to say how much humanity was left in the animal form of a shifter. I'd had evidence the Weres understood me perfectly, and I'd communicated with Quinn before when he was a tiger; he'd definitely comprehended. But hearing Frannie scream had uncorked his rage and he didn't seem to know where to aim it. While Victor was paying attention to Quinn, I fished a card out of my pocket.

I hated the thought of using my great-grandfather's Get Out of Jail Free card so soon ("Love ya, Gramps—rescue me!"), and I hated the thought of bringing him without warning into a room full of vampires. But if ever there was a time for fairy intervention, that time would be now, and I might have left it too late. I had my cell phone in my pajama pocket. I pulled it out surreptitiously and flipped it open, wishing I'd put him on speed dial. I looked down, checking the number, and began to press the buttons. Victor was talking to Quinn, trying to persuade him that Frannie was not being hurt.

Did I not do everything right? Did I not wait until I was sure I needed him before I called? Had I not been so clever to have the card on me, to have the phone with me?

Sometimes, when you do everything right, it still turns out all wrong.

Just as the call went through, a quick hand reached around, plucked the phone from my hand, and dashed it against the wall.

"We can't bring him in," Eric said in my ear, "or a war will start that will kill all of us."

I think he meant all of *him*, because I was pretty sure I would be okay if Great-grandpa started a war to keep me that way, but there was no help for it now. I looked at Eric with something very close to hatred.

"There's no one you can call who would help you in this situation," Victor Madden said complacently. But then he looked a little less pleased with himself, as if he was having second thoughts. "Unless there is something I don't know about you," he added.

"There is much you don't know about Sookie," Bill said. It was the first time he'd spoken since Madden had entered. "Know this: I will die for her. If you harm her, I'll kill you." Bill turned his dark eyes on Eric. "Can you say the same?"

Eric plainly wouldn't, which put him behind in the "Who Loves Sookie More?" stakes. At the moment, that wasn't so relevant. "You must also know this," Eric said to Victor. "Even more pertinently, if anything happens to her, forces you can't imagine will be set into motion."

Victor looked deeply thoughtful. "Of course, that could be an idle threat," he said. "But somehow, I believe you are serious. If you're referring to this tiger, though, I don't think he'll kill us all for her, since we have his mother and his sister in our grasp. The tiger already has a lot to answer for, since I see his sister here."

Amelia had moved over to put her arm around Frannie, both to sooth her and to include herself in the tiger's circle of protection. She looked at me, thinking very clearly, *Should I try some magic? Maybe a stasis spell?*

It was very clever of Amelia to think of communicating this way with me, and I thought about her offer furiously. The stasis spell would hold everything exactly as it was. But I didn't know if her spell could encompass the vampires waiting outside, and I couldn't see the situation would be much improved if she froze only all of us in the room except for herself. Could she be specific about whom the spell affected? I wished that Amelia were telepathic, too, and I'd never wished that on anyone before. As things lay, there was just too much I didn't know. Reluctantly I shook my head.

"This is ridiculous," Victor said. His impatience was calculated. "Eric, this is the bottom line and my last offer. Do you accept my king's takeover of Louisiana and Arkansas, or do you want to fight to the death?"

There was another, shorter pause.

"I accept the sovereignty of your king," Eric said, his voice flat.

"Bill Compton?" Victor asked.

Bill looked at me, his dark eyes dwelling on my face. "I accept," he said.

And just like that, Louisiana had a new king, and the old regime was gone.

CHARLAINE HARRIS

[212]

Chapter 13

*I felt the tension whoosh out of me like the air out of a punc-*tured tire.

Eric said, "Victor, call your people off. I want to hear you tell them."

Victor, beaming harder than ever, whipped a tiny cell phone from his pocket and called someone named Delilah to give her his orders. Eric used his own cell to phone Fangtasia. Eric told Clancy about the change in leadership.

"Don't forget to tell Pam," Eric said very clearly, "lest she kill off a few more of Victor's people."

There was an awkward pause. Everyone was wondering what came next.

Now that I was pretty sure I was going to live, I hoped Quinn would change back to his human form so I could talk to him. There was a lot to talk about. I wasn't sure I had a right to feel this, but I felt betrayed.

I don't think the world is about me. I could see he'd been forced into this situation.

There was always a lot of forcing around vampires.

As I saw it, this was the second time his mother had set Quinn up, quite inadvertently, to take her fall with the vamps. I got that she wasn't responsible; truly, I did. She'd never wanted to be raped, and she hadn't chosen to become mentally ill. I'd never met the woman and probably never would, but she was surely a loose cannon. Quinn had done what he could. He'd sent his sister ahead to warn us, though I wasn't exactly sure that had ended up helping so very much.

But points for trying.

Now, as I watched the tiger nuzzle Frannie, I knew I'd made mistakes all the way down the line with Quinn. And I felt the anger of betrayal; no matter how I reasoned with myself, the image of seeing my boyfriend on the side of vampires I had to regard as enemies had lit a fire in me. I shook myself, looking around the room.

Amelia had made a dash for the bathroom as soon as she could decently let go of Frannie, who was still crying. I suspected the tension had been too much for my witchy roommate, and sounds from the hall bathroom confirmed that. Eric was still on the phone with Clancy, pretending to be busy while he absorbed the huge change in his circumstances. I couldn't read his mind, but I knew that. He walked down the hall, maybe wanting some privacy to reassess his future.

CHARLAINE HARRIS

Victor had gone outside to talk to his cohorts, and I heard one of them say, "Yeah! *Yes!*" as if his team had scored a winning goal, which I supposed was the case.

As for me, I felt a little weak in the knees, and my thoughts were in such a tumult they could scarcely be called thoughts. Bill's arm went around me, and he lowered me to the chair Eric had vacated. I felt his cool lips brush my cheek. I would have to possess a heart of stone not to be affected by his little speech to Victor—I hadn't forgotten it, no matter how terrifying the night had been—and my heart is not made of stone.

Bill knelt by my feet, his white face turned up to me. "I hope someday you'll turn to me," he said. "I'll never force myself or my company on you." And he got up and walked outside to meet his new vampire kin.

Okey-dokey.

God bless me; the night wasn't over yet.

I trudged back to my bedroom and pushed the door open, intending to wash my face or brush my teeth or make some stab at smoothing my hair, because I thought it might make me feel a little less trampled.

Eric was sitting on my bed, his face buried in his hands.

He looked up at me as I entered, and he looked shocked. Well, no wonder, what with the very thorough takeover and traumatic changing of the guard.

"Sitting here on your bed, smelling your scent," he said in a voice so low I had to strain to hear it. "Sookie...I remember everything."

"Oh, *hell*," I said, and went in the bathroom and shut the

door. I brushed my hair and my teeth and scrubbed my face, but I had to come out. I was being as cowardly as Quinn if I didn't face the vampire.

Eric started talking the minute I emerged. "I can't believe I—"

"Yeah, yeah, I know, loved a mere human, made all those promises, was as sweet as pie and wanted to stay with me forever," I muttered. Surely there was a shortcut we could take through this scene.

"I can't believe I felt something so strongly and was so happy for the first time in hundreds of years," Eric said with some dignity. "Give me some credit for that, too."

I rubbed my forehead. It was the middle of the night, I'd thought I was going to die, the man I'd been thinking of as my boyfriend had just turned my whole picture of him upside down. Though now "his" vamps were on the same side as "my" vamps, I'd emotionally aligned myself with the vampires of Louisiana, even if some of them had been terrifying in the extreme. Could Victor Madden and his crew be any less scary? I thought not. This very night they'd killed quite a few vamps I'd known and liked.

Coming on top of all these events, I didn't think I could cope with an Eric who'd just had a revelation.

"Can we talk about this some other time, if we have to talk about it?" I asked.

"Yes," he said after a long pause. "Yes. This isn't the right moment."

"I don't know that any time will be right for this conversation."

"But we're going to have it," Eric said.

"Eric...oh, okay." I made an "erase" movement with my hand. "I'm glad the new regime wants to keep you on."

"It would hurt you if I died."

"Yeah, we're blood bound, yadda yadda yadda."

"Not because of the bond."

"Okay, you're right. It would hurt me if you died. Also I would have died, too, most likely, so it wouldn't have hurt for long. Now can you please scoot?"

"Oh, yes," he said with a return of the old Eric flare. "I'll *scoot* for now, but I'm going to see you later. And rest assured, my lover, we'll come to an understanding. As for the vampires of Las Vegas, they'll be well-suited to running another state that relies heavily on tourism. The King of Nevada is a powerful man, and Victor is not one you can take lightly. Victor is ruthless, but he won't destroy something he may be able to use. He's very good at reining in his temper."

"So you're not really that unhappy with the takeover?" I couldn't keep the shock out of my voice.

"It's happened," Eric said. "There's no goal to be met in being 'unhappy' now. I can't bring anyone back to life, and I can't defeat Nevada by myself. I won't ask my people to die in a futile attempt."

I just couldn't match Eric's pragmatism. I could see his points, and in fact when I'd had some rest, I might agree with him. But not here, not now; he seemed way too cold for me. Of course, he'd had a few hundred years to get that way, and maybe he'd had to go through this process many times.

What a bleak prospect.

Eric paused on his way out the door to bend down to kiss me on the cheek. This was another evening for collecting kisses. "I'm sorry about the tiger," he said, and that was the final cap to the night as far as I was concerned. I sat slumped in the little chair in the bedroom corner until I was sure everyone was out of the house. When only one warm brain remained, Amelia's, I peered out of my room to get a visual. Yep, everyone else was gone.

"Amelia?" I called.

"Yeah," she answered, and I went to find her. She was in the living room, and she was as exhausted as I was.

"Are you going to be able to sleep?" I asked.

"I don't know. I'm going to try." She shook her head. "This changes everything."

"Which this?" Amazingly, she understood me.

"Oh, the vampire takeover. My dad had lots of dealings with the New Orleans vampires. He was going to be working for Sophie-Anne, repairing her headquarters in New Orleans. All her other properties, too. I better call him and tell him. He's going to want to get in there early with the new guy."

In her own way Amelia was being as practical as Eric. I felt out of tune with the whole world. I couldn't think of anyone I could call who would feel the least bit mournful over the loss of Sophie-Anne, Arla Yvonne, Cleo... And the list went on. It made me wonder, for the first time, if vampires might not get inured to loss. Look at all the life that passed them by and then vanished. Generation after generation went to their graves, while still the undead lived on. And on.

Well, this tired human—who would eventually pass on—needed some sleep in the worst possible way. If there was another hostile takeover tonight, it would have to proceed without me. I locked the doors all over again, called up the stairs to Amelia to tell her good night, and crawled back into my bed. I lay awake for at least thirty minutes, because my muscles twitched just when I was about to drift off. I would start up into full wakefulness, thinking someone was coming in the room to warn me about a great disaster.

But finally even the twitching couldn't keep me awake any longer. I fell into a heavy sleep. When I woke, the sun was up and shining in the window, and Quinn was sitting in the chair in the corner where I'd slumped the night before while I was trying to deal with Eric.

This was an unpleasant trend. I didn't want a lot of guys popping in and out of my bedroom. I wanted one who would stay.

"Who let you in?" I asked, propping myself up on one elbow. He looked good for someone who hadn't gotten much sleep. He was a very large man with a very smooth head and huge purple eyes. I had always loved the way he looked.

"Amelia," he said. "I know I shouldn't have come in; I should have waited until you were up. You might not want me in the house."

I went in the bathroom to give myself a minute, another

ploy that was getting all too familiar. When I came out, a little neater and more awake than when I'd entered, Quinn had a mug of coffee for me. I took a sip and instantly felt better able to cope with whatever was coming. But not in my bedroom.

"Kitchen," I said, and we went to the room that had always been the heart of the house. It had been dated when the fire had gotten it. Now I had a brand-new kitchen, but I still missed the old one. The table where my family had eaten for years had been replaced with a modern one, and the new chairs were lots more comfortable than the old ones, but regret still caught at me every now and then when I thought of what had been lost.

I had an ominous feeling that "regret" was going to be the theme of the day. During my troubled sleep, apparently I'd absorbed a dose of the practicality that had seemed so sad to me the night before. To stave off the conversation we were going to have to have, I stepped to the back door and looked to see that Amelia's car was gone. At least we were alone.

I sat down opposite the man I'd hoped to love.

"Babe, you look like someone just told you I was dead," Quinn said.

"Might as well have," I said, because I had to plow into this and look to neither the right nor the left. He flinched.

"Sookie, what could I have done?" he asked. "What could I have done?" There was an edge of anger in his voice.

"What can *I* do?" I asked in return, because I had no answer for him.

"I sent Frannie! I tried to warn you!"

"Too little, too late," I said. I second-guessed myself immediately: Was I being too hard, unfair, ungrateful? "If you'd called me weeks ago, even once, I might feel different. But I guess you were too busy trying to find your mother."

"So you're breaking up with me because of my mother," he said. He sounded bitter and I didn't blame him.

"Yes," I said after a moment's inner testing of my own resolve. "I think I am. It's not your mom as much as her whole situation. Your mother will always have to come first as long as she's alive, because she's so damaged. I've got sympathy for that, believe me. And I'm sorry that you and Frannie have a hard row to hoe. I know all about hard rows."

Quinn was looking down into his coffee mug, his face drawn with anger and weariness. This was probably the worst possible moment to be having this showdown, and yet it had to be done. I hurt too bad to let it last any longer.

"Yet, knowing all this, and knowing I care for you, you don't want to see me anymore," Quinn said, biting each word out. "You don't want to try to make it work."

"I care for you, too, and I had hoped we'd have a lot more," I said. "But last night was just too much for me. Remember, I had to find out your past from someone else? I think maybe you didn't tell me about it from the start because you knew it would be an issue. Not your pit fighting—I don't care about that. But your mom and Frannie... Well, they're your family. They're... dependent. They have to have you. They'll always come first." I stopped for a moment, biting the inside of my cheek. This was the hardest part. "I want to be first. I know that's selfish, and maybe unattainable, and maybe shallow. But

I just want to come first with someone. If that's wrong of me, so be it. I'll be wrong. But that's the way I feel."

"Then there's nothing left to talk about," Quinn said after a moment's thought. He looked at me bleakly. I couldn't disagree. His big hands flat on the table, he pushed to his feet and left.

I felt like a bad person. I felt miserable and bereft. I felt like a selfish bitch.

But I let him walk out the door.

Chapter 14

While I was getting ready for work—yes, even after a night like the one I'd had, I had to go to work—there was a knock at the front door. I'd heard something big coming down the driveway, so I'd tied my shoes hastily.

The FedEx truck was not a frequent visitor at my house, and the thin woman who hopped out was a stranger. I opened the battered front door with some difficulty. It was never going to be the same after Quinn's entrance the night before. I made a mental note to call the Lowe's in Clarice to ask about a replacement. Maybe Jason would help me hang it. The FedEx lady gave a long look at the door's splintered condition when I finally got it open.

"You want to sign for this?" she said as she held out a package, tactfully not commenting.

"Sure." I accepted the box, a little puzzled. It had come from Fangtasia. Huh. As soon as the truck had wheeled back out to Hummingbird Road, I opened the package. It was a red cell phone. It was programmed to my number. There was a note with it. "Sorry about the other one, lover," it read. Signed with a big "E." There was a charger included. And a car charger, too. And a notice that my first six months' bill had been paid.

With a kind of bemused feeling, I heard another truck coming. I didn't even bother to move from the front porch. The new arrival was from the Shreveport Home Depot. It was a new front door, very pretty, with a two-man crew to install it. All charges had been taken care of.

I wondered if Eric would clean out my dryer vent.

I got to Merlotte's early so I could have a talk with Sam. But his office door was shut, and I could hear voices inside. Though not unheard of, the closed door was rare. I was instantly concerned and curious. I could read Sam's familiar mental signature, and there was another one that I had encountered before. I heard a scrape of chair legs inside, and I hastily stepped into the storeroom before the door opened.

Tanya Grissom walked by.

I waited for a couple of beats, then decided my business was so urgent I had to risk a conversation with Sam, though he might not be in the mood for it. My boss was still in his creaky wooden rolling chair, his feet propped on the desk. His hair was even more of a mess than usual. He looked like he had a reddish halo. He also looked thoughtful and preoccupied, but when I said I needed to tell him some things, he nodded and asked me to shut the door.

"Do you know what happened last night?" I asked.

"I hear there was a hostile takeover," Sam said. He tilted back on the springs of his rolling chair, and they squeaked in an irritating way. I was definitely balancing on a thin edge today, so I had to bite my lip to keep from snapping at him.

"Yeah, you might say that." A hostile takeover was pretty much a perfect way to put it. I told him what had happened at my house.

Sam looked troubled. "I don't ever interfere in vamp business," he said. "The two-natured and vamps don't mix well. I'm really sorry you got pulled into that, Sookie. That asshole Eric." He looked like there was more he wanted to say, but he pressed his lips together.

"Do you know anything about the King of Nevada?" I asked.

"I know he has a publishing empire," Sam said promptly. "And he has at least one casino and some restaurants. He's also the ultimate owner of a management company that handles vampire entertainers. You know, the Elvis Undead Revue with all-vamp Elvis tribute artists, which is pretty funny when you think about it, and some great dance groups." We both knew that the real Elvis was still around but rarely in any shape to perform. "If there had to be a takeover of a tourist state, Felipe de Castro is the right vampire for the job. He'll make sure New Orleans gets rebuilt like it ought to be, because he'll want the revenue."

"Felipe de Castro . . . That sounds exotic," I said.

"I haven't met him, but I understand he's very, ah, charismatic," Sam said. "I wonder if he'll be coming to Louisiana to live or if this Victor Madden will be his agent here. Either way, it won't affect the bar. But there's no doubt it'll affect you, Sookie." Sam uncrossed his legs and sat up straight in his chair, which shrieked in protest. "I wish there was some way to get you out of the vampire loop."

"The night I met Bill, if I'd known what I know now, I wonder if I'd have done anything different," I said. "Maybe I would've let the Rattrays have him." I'd rescued Bill from a sleazy couple who turned out to be not only sleazy, but murderers. They were vampire drainers, people who lured vampires to spots where the vamps could be subdued with silver chains and drained of blood, which sold for big bucks on the black market. Drainers lived hazardous lives. The Rattrays had paid the full price.

"You don't mean that," Sam said. He rocked in the chair again (*squeak! squeak!*) and rose to his feet. "You would never do that."

It felt really pleasant to hear something nice about myself, especially after the morning's conversation with Quinn. I was tempted to talk to Sam about that, too, but he was edging toward the door. Time to go to work, for both of us. I got up, too. We went out and began the usual motions. My mind was hardly on it, though.

To revive my flagging spirits, I tried to think of some bright point in the future, something to look forward to. I couldn't come up with anything. For a long, bleak moment I stood by the bar, my hand on my order pad, trying not to step over the edge into the chasm of depression. Then I slapped myself on the cheek. *Idiot! I have a house, and friends, and a job. I'm luckier than millions of people on the planet. Things will look up.*

For a while, that worked. I smiled at everyone, and if that smile was brittle, by God, it was still a smile.

After an hour or two, Jason came into the bar with his wife, Crystal. Crystal was looking sullen and slightly pregnant, and Jason was looking . . . Well, he had that hard look about him, the mean look he got sometimes when he'd been disappointed.

"What's up?" I asked.

"Oh, not much," Jason said expansively. "You bring us a couple beers?"

"Sure," I said, thinking he'd never ordered for Crystal before. Crystal was a pretty woman several years younger than Jason. She was a werepanther, but she wasn't a very good one, mostly because of all the inbreeding in the Hotshot community. Crystal had a hard time changing if it wasn't the full moon, and she had miscarried at least twice that I knew of. I pitied her losses, the more so because I knew the panther community considered her weak. Now Crystal was pregnant a third time. That pregnancy had maybe been the only reason Calvin had let her marry Jason, who was bitten, not born. That is, he'd become a panther by being repeatedly bitten—by a jealous male who wanted Crystal for himself. Jason couldn't change into a real panther but into a sort of half-beast, half-man version. He enjoyed it.

I brought them their beers along with two frosted mugs

and waited to see if they were going to place a food order. I wondered about Crystal drinking, but decided it wasn't my business.

"I'd like me a cheeseburger with fries," Jason said. No surprise there.

"What about you, Crystal?" I asked, trying to sound friendly. After all, this was my sister-in-law.

"Oh, *I* don't have enough money to eat," she said.

I had no idea what to say. I looked at Jason inquiringly, and he gave me a shrug. This shrug said (to his sister), "I've done something stupid and wrong but I'm not going to back down, because I'm a stubborn shit."

"Crystal, I'll be glad to stand you lunch," I said very quietly. "What would you like?"

She glared at her husband. "I'd like the same, Sookie."

I wrote her order down on a separate slip and strode to the hatch to turn them in. I had been ready to get angry, and Jason had lit a match and thrown it on my temper. The whole story was clear in their heads, and as I came to understand what was going on, I was sick of both of them.

Crystal and Jason had settled into Jason's house, but almost every day Crystal rode out to Hotshot, her comfort zone, where she didn't have to pretend anything. She was used to being surrounded by her kin, and she especially missed her sister and her sister's babies. Tanya Grissom was renting a room from Crystal's sister, the room Crystal had lived in until she married Jason. Crystal and Tanya had become instant buddies. Since Tanya's favorite occupation was shopping, Crystal had gone along for the ride several times. In fact, she'd spent all the money Jason had given her for household expenses. She'd done this two paychecks in a row, despite multiple scenes and promises.

Now Jason refused to give her any more money. He was doing all the grocery shopping and picking up any dry cleaning, paying every bill himself. He'd told Crystal if she wanted any money of her own, she had to get a job. The unskilled and pregnant Crystal had not succeeded in finding one, so she didn't have a dime.

Jason was trying to make a point, but by humiliating his wife in public he was making the wrong point entirely. What an idiot my brother could be.

What I could do about this situation? Well...nothing. They had to work it out themselves. I was looking at two stunted people who'd never grown up, and I wasn't optimistic about their chances.

With a deep twinge of unease, I remembered their unusual wedding vows; at least, they'd seemed odd to me, though I supposed they were the Hotshot norm. As Jason's closest living relative, I'd had to promise to take the punishment if Jason misbehaved, just as her uncle Calvin had promised the same on Crystal's behalf. I'd been pretty damn rash to make that promise.

When I carried their plates to their table, I saw that the two were in the jaw-clenching, looking-anywhere-but-at-each-other stage of quarreling. I put the plates down carefully, got them a bottle of Heinz ketchup, and skedaddled. I'd interfered enough by buying Crystal lunch.

There was a person involved in this I *could* approach, and I promised myself then and there that I would. All my anger and unhappiness focused on Tanya Grissom. I really wanted to do something awful to that woman. What the hell was she hanging around for, sniffing around Sam? What was her goal in drawing Crystal into this spending spiral? (And I didn't think for a second it was by chance that Tanya's newest big buddy was my sister-in-law.) Was Tanya trying to irritate me to death? It was like having a horsefly buzzing around and lighting occasionally... but never quite close enough to swat. While I went about my job on autopilot, I pondered what I could do to get her out of my orbit. For the first time in my life, I wondered if I could forcibly pin another person down to read her mind. It wouldn't be so easy, since Tanya was a wereanimal, but I would find out what was driving her. And I had the conviction that information would save me a lot of heartache... a lot.

While I plotted and schemed and fumed, Crystal and Jason silently ate their food, and Jason pointedly paid his own bill, while I took care of Crystal's. They left, and I wondered what their evening would be like. I was glad I wasn't going to be a party to it.

From behind the bar Sam had observed all this, and he asked me in a low voice, "What's up with those two?"

"They're having the newlywed blues," I said. "Severe adjustment problems."

He looked troubled. "Don't let them drag you into it," he said, and then looked like he regretted opening his mouth. "Sorry, don't mean to give you unwanted advice," he said.

Something prickled at the corners of my eyes. Sam was giving me advice because he cared about me. In my overwrought state, that was cause for sentimental tears. "That's okay, boss," I said, trying to sound perky and carefree. I spun on my heel and went to patrol my tables. Sheriff Bud Dearborn was sitting in my section, which was unusual. Normally he'd pick a seat somewhere else if he knew I was working. Bud had a basket of onion rings in front of him, liberally doused with ketchup, and he was reading a Shreveport paper. The lead story was POLICE SEARCH FOR SIX, and I stopped to ask Bud if I could have his paper when he was through with it.

He looked at me suspiciously. His little eyes in his mashed-in face scanned me as if he suspected he'd find a bloody cleaver hanging from my belt. "Sure, Sookie," he said after a long moment. "You got any of these missing people stowed away at your house?"

I beamed at him, anxiety transforming my smile into the bright grin of someone who wasn't all there mentally. "No, Bud, I just want to find out what's going on in the world. I'm behind on the news."

Bud said, "I'll leave it on the table," and he began reading again. I think he would have pinned Jimmy Hoffa on me if he could have figured a way to make it stick. Not that he necessarily thought I was a murderer, but he thought I was fishy and maybe involved in things that he didn't want happening in his parish. Bud Dearborn and Alcee Beck had that conviction in common, especially since the death of the man in the library. Luckily for me, the man had turned out to have a record as long as my arm; and not only a record, but one for violent crimes.

FROM DEAD TO WORSE

Though Alcee knew I'd acted in self-defense, he'd never trust me . . . and neither would Bud Dearborn.

When Bud had finished his beer and his onion rings and departed to rain terror on the evildoers of Renard Parish, I took his paper over to the bar and read the story with Sam looking over my shoulder. I had deliberately stayed away from the news after the bloodbath at the empty office park. I'd been sure the Were community couldn't cover up something so big; all they could do was muddy the trail the police would surely be following. That proved to be the case.

After more than twenty-four hours, police remain baffled in their search for six missing Shreveport citizens. Hampering them is their inability to discover anyone who saw any of the missing people after ten o'clock on Wednesday night.

"We can't find anything they had in common," said Detective Willie Cromwell.

Among the missing is a Shreveport police detective, Cal Myers; Amanda Whatley, owner of a bar in the central Shreveport area; Patrick Furnan, owner of the local Harley-Davidson dealership, and his wife, Libby; Christine Larrabee, widow of John Larrabee, retired school superintendent; and Julio Martinez, an airman from Barksdale Air Force Base. Neighbors of the Furnans say they hadn't seen Libby Furnan for a day prior to Patrick Furnan's disappearance, and Christine Larrabee's cousin says she had not been able to contact Larrabee by phone for three days, so police speculate that the two women may have met with foul play prior to the disappearance of the others.

The disappearance of Detective Cal Myers has the force on edge. His partner, Detective Mike Loughlin, said, "Myers was one of the newly promoted detectives, and we hadn't had time to get to know each other well. I have no idea what could have happened to him." Myers, 29, had been with the Shreveport force for seven years. He was not married.

"If they are all dead, you would think at least one body would have turned up by now," Detective Cromwell said yesterday. "We have searched all their residences and businesses for clues, and so far we have come up with nothing."

To add to the mystery, on Monday another Shreveport area resident was murdered. Maria-Star Cooper, photographer's assistant, was slain in her apartment on Highway 3. "The apartment was like a butcher shop," said Cooper's landlord, among the first on the scene. No suspects have been reported in the slaying. "Everyone loved Maria-Star," said her mother, Anita Cooper. "She was so talented and pretty."

Police do not yet know if Cooper's death is related to the disappearances.

In other news, Don Dominica, owner of Don's RV Park, reported the absence of the owners of three RVs parked on his property for a week. "I'm not sure how many people were in each trailer," he said. "They all arrived together and rented the spaces for a month. The name on the rental is Priscilla Hebert. I think at least six people were in each RV. They all seemed pretty normal to me."

Asked if all their belongings were still in place, Dominica replied, "I don't know; I haven't been checking. I ain't got time for that. But I haven't seen hide nor hair of them for days."

Other residents of the RV park had not met the newcomers. "They kept to themselves," said a neighbor.

Police Chief Parfit Graham said, "I'm sure we'll solve these crimes. The right piece of information will surface. In the meantime, if anyone has knowledge of the whereabouts of any of these people, call the Tipster Hotline."

I considered it. I imagined the phone call. "All of these people died as a result of the werewolf war," I would say. "They were all Weres, and a displaced and hungry pack from south Louisiana decided the dissension in the ranks in Shreveport created an opening for them."

I didn't think I'd get much of a hearing.

"So they haven't found the site yet," Sam said very quietly.

"I guess that really was a good place for the meeting."

"Sooner or later, though . . ."

"Yeah. I wonder what's left?"

"Alcide's crew's had plenty of time now," Sam said. "So, not much. They probably burned the bodies somewhere out in the sticks. Or buried them on someone's land."

I shuddered. Thank God I hadn't had to be part of that; and at least I really *didn't* know where the bodies were buried. After checking my tables and serving some more drinks, I went back to the paper and flipped it open to the obituaries. Reading down the column headed "State Deaths," I got an awful shock.

> SOPHIE-ANNE LECLERQ, prominent businesswoman, residing in Baton Rouge since Katrina, died of Sino-AIDS in her home. Leclerq, a vampire, had extensive holdings in New Orleans and in many places in the state. Sources close to Leclerq say she had lived in Louisiana for a hundred years or more.

I'd never seen an obituary for a vampire. This one was a complete fabrication. Sophie-Anne had not had Sino-AIDS, the only disease that could cross from humans to vampires. Sophie-Anne had probably had an acute attack of Mr. Stake. Sino-AIDS was dreaded among vampires, of course, despite the fact that it was hard to communicate. At least it provided a palatable explanation for the human business community as to why Sophie-Anne's holdings were being managed by another vampire, and it was an explanation that no one would question too closely, especially since there was no body to refute the claim. To get it in today's paper, someone must have called it in directly after she'd been killed, perhaps even before she was dead. Ugh. I shivered.

I wondered what had really happened to Sigebert, Sophie-Anne's devoted bodyguard. Victor had implied Sigebert had perished along with the queen, but he hadn't definitely said so. I couldn't believe the bodyguard could still be alive. He would never have let anyone get close enough to kill Sophie-Anne.

Sigebert had been at her side for so many years, hundreds upon hundreds, that I didn't think he could have survived her loss.

I left the newspaper open to the obituaries and placed it on Sam's desk, figuring the bar was too busy a place to talk about it even if we had the time. We'd had an influx of customers. I was running my feet off serving them and pocketing some good tips, too. But after the week I'd had, it was not only hard to feel normally happy about the money, it was also impossible to feel normally cheerful about being at work. I just did my best to smile and respond when I was spoken to.

By the time I got off work, I didn't want to talk to anyone about anything.

But of course, I didn't get my druthers.

There were two women waiting in the front yard at my house, and they both radiated anger. One, I already knew: Frannie Quinn. The woman with her had to be Quinn's mother. In the harsh glare of the security light I had a good look at the woman whose life had been such a disaster. I realized no one had ever told me her name. She was still pretty, but in a Goth sort of way that wasn't kind to her age. She was in her forties; her face was gaunt, her eyes shadowed. She had dark hair with more than a touch of gray, and she was very tall and thin. Frannie was wearing a tank top that showed her bra, and tight jeans, and boots. Her mother was wearing pretty much the same outfit but in different colors. I guessed Frannie had charge of dressing her mother.

I parked beside them, because I had no intention of inviting them in. I got out of my car reluctantly.

"You bitch," Frannie said passionately. Her young face was rigid with anger. "How could you do that to my brother? He did so much for you!"

That was one way to look at it. "Frannie," I said, keeping my voice as calm and level as I could, "what happens between Quinn and me is really not any of your business."

The front door opened, and Amelia stepped out on the porch. "Sookie, you need me?" she asked, and I smelled magic around her.

"I'm coming in, in just a second," I said clearly, but didn't tell her to go back inside. Mrs. Quinn was a pureblood were-tiger, and Frannie was half; they were both stronger than me.

Mrs. Quinn stepped forward and looked at me quizzically. "You're the one John loved," she said. "You're the one who broke up with him."

"Yes, ma'am. It just wasn't going to work out."

"They say I have to go back to that place in the desert," she said. "Where they store all the crazy Weres."

No shit. "Oh, do they?" I said, to make it clear I had nothing to do with it.

"Yes," she said, and lapsed into silence, which was kind of a big relief.

Frannie, however, had not done with me. "I loaned you my car," she said. "I came to warn you."

"And I thank you," I said. My heart sank. I couldn't think of any magic words to lessen the pain in the air. "Believe me, I wish things had worked out different." Lame but true.

"What's wrong with my brother?" Frannie asked. "He's handsome; he loves you; he's got money. *He's a great guy.* What's wrong with you that you don't want him?"

The bald answer—that I really admired Quinn but didn't want to play second fiddle to his family's needs—was simply unspeakable for two reasons: it was unnecessarily hurtful, and I might be seriously injured as a result. Mrs. Quinn might not be compos mentis, but she was listening with growing agitation. If she changed to her tiger form, I had no idea what would happen. She might run off into the woods, or she might attack. All this zoomed through my mind in little pictures. I had to say something.

"Frannie," I said very slowly and deliberately because I had no idea what I was going to follow that up with. "There's nothing wrong with your brother at all. I think he's the greatest. But we just have too many strikes against us as a couple. I want him to have the best chance at making a match with some lucky, lucky woman. So I cut him loose. Believe me, I'm hurting, too." This was mostly true, which helped. But I hoped Amelia had her fingertips primed to deliver some good magic. And I hoped she got the spell right. Just in case, I began shifting away from Frannie and her mother.

Frannie was teetering on the brink of action, and her mother was looking increasingly restless. Amelia had eased forward to the edge of the porch. The smell of magic intensified. For a long moment, the night seemed to catch its breath.

And then Frannie turned away. "Come on, Mama," she said, and the two women got into Frannie's car. I took advantage of the moment to run up on the porch. Amelia and I stood shoulder to shoulder wordlessly until Frannie started up the car and drove away.

"Well," Amelia said. "So, you broke up with him, I'm gathering."

"Yeah." I was exhausted. "He had too much baggage." Then I winced. "Gosh, I never thought I'd catch myself saying that. Especially considering my own."

"He had his mama." Amelia was on a perceptive roll that night.

"Yeah, he had his mama. Listen, thanks for coming out of the house and risking a mauling."

"What are roommates for?" Amelia gave me a light hug and said, "You look like you need to have a bowl of soup and go to bed."

"Yeah," I said. "That sounds about right."

Chapter 15

I slept very late the next day. And I slept like a stone. I didn't dream. I didn't toss or turn. I didn't get up to pee. When I woke up, it was close to noon, so it was good I didn't have to be at Merlotte's until evening.

I could hear voices in the living room. This was the downside of having a roommate. There was someone there when you woke up, and sometimes that person had company. However, Amelia was very good about making enough coffee for me when she got up earlier. That prospect got me out of bed.

I had to get dressed since we had company; besides, the other voice sounded masculine. I did a little brisk grooming in the bathroom and threw off my nightgown. I put on a bra and a T-shirt and some khakis. Good enough. I made a beeline for the kitchen and found that Amelia had indeed made a big pot of coffee. And she'd left a mug ready for me. Oh, great. I poured, and popped some sourdough bread in the toaster. The back porch door slammed, and I turned in surprise to see Tyrese Marley enter with an armful of firewood.

"Where do you keep your wood after you bring it in?" he asked.

"I have a rack by the fireplace in the living room." He'd been splitting the wood Jason had cut and stacked by the toolshed the spring before. "That's really nice of you," I said, floundering. "Um, have you had any coffee, or some toast? Or . . ." I glanced at the clock. "What about a ham or meatloaf sandwich?"

"Food sounds good," he said, striding down the hall as though the wood weighed nothing.

So the guest in the living room was Copley Carmichael. Why Amelia's dad was here, I had no clue. I scrambled to assemble a couple of sandwiches, poured some water, and put two kinds of chips by his plate so Marley could pick what he wanted. Then I sat down at the table myself and finally got to drink my coffee and eat my toast. I still had some of my grandmother's plum jam to spread on it, and I tried not to be melancholy every time I used it. No point in letting good jam go to waste. She would have certainly looked at it that way.

Marley returned and sat down opposite me with no sign of discomfort. I relaxed myself.

"I appreciate the work," I said after he'd had a bite of his food.

"I got nothing else to do while he talks to Amelia," Marley said. "Plus, if she's still here all winter, he'll be glad if she can have a fire. Who cut that wood for you and didn't split it?"

"My brother," I said.

"Humph," Marley said, and settled into eating.

I finished my toast, poured myself a second mug of coffee, and asked Marley if he needed anything.

"I'm good, thank you," he said, and opened the bag of barbecue potato chips.

I excused myself to take a shower. It was definitely cooler today, and I got a long-sleeved T-shirt out of a drawer I hadn't opened in months. It was Halloween weather. It was past time to buy a pumpkin and some candy . . . not that I got many trick-or-treaters. For the first time in days, I felt normal: that is to say, comfortably happy with myself and my world. There was a lot to grieve about, and I would, but I wasn't walking around expecting a smack in the face.

Of course, the minute I thought that, I began to brood on bad things. I realized I hadn't heard anything from the Shreveport vampires, and then I wondered why I thought I should or would. This period of adjustment from one regime to another had to be full of tension and negotiation, and it was best to leave them to it. I hadn't heard from the Weres of Shreveport, either. Since the investigation into the disappearance of all those people was still active, that was a good thing.

And since I'd just broken up with my boyfriend, that meant (theoretically) I was footloose and fancy-free. I put on eye makeup as a gesture toward my freedom. And then I added some lipstick. It was hard to feel adventurous, actually. I hadn't wanted to be fancy-free.

As I finished making my bed, Amelia knocked at my door.

"Come on in," I said, folding my nightgown and putting it in the drawer. "What's up?"

"Well, my father has a favor to ask you," she said.

I could feel my face settle into grim lines. Of course, there had to be something Copley wanted if he'd driven up from New Orleans to talk to his daughter. And I could imagine what that request was.

"Go on," I said, crossing my arms over my chest.

"Oh, Sookie, your body language is already saying no!"

"Ignore my body and speak your piece."

She heaved a big sigh to indicate how reluctant she was to drag me into her dad's stuff. But I could tell she was tickled pink that he'd asked her to help him. "Well, since I told him about the Vegas vampire takeover, he wants to reestablish his business link with the vampires. He wants an introduction. He was hoping you could, like, broker that."

"I don't even know Felipe de Castro."

"No, but you know that Victor. And he looks like he's got his eyes on his own advancement."

"You know him as well as I do," I pointed out.

"Maybe, but what's more important is that he knows who you are, and I'm just the other woman in the room," Amelia said, and I could see her point—though I hated it. "I mean, he knows who I am, who my dad is, but he really noticed you."

"Oh, Amelia," I moaned, and for just a moment felt like kicking her.

"I know you won't like this, but he said he was ready to pay, like, a finder's fee," Amelia muttered, looking embarrassed.

I waved my hands in front of me to fan that thought away. I was not going to let my friend's father pay me money to make a phone call or whatever I had to do. At that moment I knew I'd decided I had to do this for Amelia's sake.

We went to the living room to talk face-to-face with Copley.

He greeted me with far more enthusiasm than he'd shown on his previous visit. He fixed his gaze on me, did the whole "I'm focused on you" thing. I regarded him with a skeptical eye. Since he was no fool, he picked up on that immediately.

"I'm sorry, Miss Stackhouse, for intruding here so soon after my last visit," he said, laying on the smarm. "But things in New Orleans are so desperate. We're trying to rebuild to bring the jobs back in. This connection is really important to me, and I employ a lot of people."

One, I didn't think Copley Carmichael was hurting for business even without the contracts for rebuilding the vampire properties. Two, I didn't for a minute think his sole motivation was the improvement of the damaged city; but after a moment of looking into his head, I was willing to concede that accounted for at least a fraction of his urgency.

Also, Marley had split the wood for the winter and carried a load in. That counted for more with me than any appeal based on emotion.

"I'll call Fangtasia tonight," I said. "I'll see what they say. That's the limit of my involvement."

"Miss Stackhouse, I'm indeed indebted," he said. "What can I do for you?"

"Your chauffeur already did it," I said. "If he could finish splitting that oak, that would be a great favor." I'm not a very good wood splitter, and I know because I've tried. Three or four logs done, and I'm wiped out.

"That's what he's been doing?" Copley did a good job of looking astonished. I wasn't sure if it was genuine or not. "Well, how enterprising of Marley."

Amelia was smiling and trying not to let her dad notice it. "Okay, then we're settled," she said briskly. "Dad, can I fix you a sandwich or soup? We have some chips or some potato salad."

"Sounds good," he said, since he was still trying to be just plain folks.

"Marley and I have already eaten," I said casually, and added, "I need to run to town, Amelia. You need anything?"

"I could use some stamps," she said. "You going by the post office?"

I shrugged. "It's on the way. Bye, Mr. Carmichael."

"Call me Cope, please, Sookie."

I'd just known he was going to say that. Next he was going to try being courtly. Sure enough, he smiled at me with exactly the right blend of admiration and respect.

I got my purse and headed out the back door. Marley was still working on the woodpile in his shirtsleeves. I hoped that had been his very own idea. I hoped he got a raise.

I didn't really have anything to do in town. But I had wanted to dodge any further conversation with Amelia's dad. I stopped by the store and got some more paper towels, bread, and tuna, and I stopped by the Sonic and got an Oreo Blast. Oh, I was a bad girl, no doubt about it. I was sitting in my car working on the Blast when I spied an interesting couple two cars away. They hadn't noticed me, apparently, because Tanya and Arlene were talking steadily. The two were in Tanya's Mustang. Arlene's hair was newly colored, so it was flaming red to the roots, caught up at the back in a banana clip. My former friend was wearing a tiger-print knit top, all I could see of her ensemble. Tanya was wearing a pretty lime green blouse and a dark brown sweater. And she was listening intently.

I tried to believe they were talking about something other than me. I mean, I try not to be too paranoid. But when you see your ex-buddy talking to your known enemy, you have to at least entertain the possibility that the topic of you has come up in an unflattering way.

It wasn't so much that they didn't like me. I've known people all my life who didn't like me. I've known exactly why and how much they didn't like me. That's really unpleasant, as you can well imagine. What bothered me was that I thought Arlene and Tanya were moving into the realm of actually doing something to me.

I wondered what I could find out. If I moved closer, they'd definitely notice me, but I wasn't sure I could "hear" them from where I was. I bent over like I was fiddling with my CD player, and I focused on them. I tried to mentally skip over or plow through the people in the intervening cars to reach them, which wasn't an easy task.

Finally, the familiar pattern of Arlene helped me to home in. The first impression I got was one of pleasure. Arlene was enjoying herself immensely, since she had the undivided attention of a fairly new audience and she was getting to talk about her new boyfriend's convictions about the need to kill all vampires and maybe people who collaborated with them. Arlene had no hard convictions that she'd formed for herself, but she was great at adopting other people's if they suited her emotionally.

When Tanya had an especially strong surge of exasperation, I zoomed in on her thought pattern. I was in. I remained in my half-concealed position, my hand moving every now and then over the CDs in my little car folder, while I tried to pick out everything I could.

Tanya was still in the pay of the Pelts: Sandra Pelt, specifically. And gradually I came to understand that Tanya had been sent here to do anything she could to make me miserable.

Sandra Pelt was the sister of Debbie Pelt, whom I'd shot to death in my kitchen. (After she'd tried to kill *me*. Several times. Let me point that out.)

Dammit. I was sick to death of the issue of Debbie Pelt. The woman had been a bane to me alive. She had been as malicious and vindictive as her little sister, Sandra. I'd suffered over her death, felt guilty, felt remorseful, felt like I had a huge *C* for "Cain" on my forehead. Killing a vampire is bad enough, but the corpse goes away and they're sort of . . . erased. Killing another human being changes you forever.

That's how it ought to be.

But it's possible to grow sick of that feeling, tired of that albatross around your emotional neck. And I'd grown both sick and tired of Debbie Pelt. Then her sister and her parents had begun giving me grief, had had me kidnapped. The tables had turned, and I'd held them in my power. In return for me letting them go, they'd agreed to leave me alone. Sandra had promised to stay away until her parents died. I had to wonder if the elder Pelts were still among the living.

I started up my car and began cruising around Bon Temps, waving at familiar faces in almost every vehicle I passed. I had no idea what to do. I stopped at the little town park and got out of my car. I began to stroll, my hands jammed in my pockets. My head was all in a snarl.

I remembered the night I'd confessed to my first lover, Bill, that my great-uncle had molested me when I'd been a child. Bill had taken my story so to heart that he had arranged for a visitor to drop by my great-uncle's house. Lo and behold, my uncle had died from a fall down the stairs. I'd been furious at Bill for taking over my own past. But I couldn't deny that having my great-uncle dead had felt good. That profound relief had made me feel complicit in the assassination.

When I'd been trying to find survivors in the twisted debris of the Pyramid of Gizeh, I'd found someone still living, a vampire who wanted to keep me firmly under his control for the queen's benefit. Andre had been terribly wounded, but he would have lived if an injured Quinn hadn't crawled over and snuffed Andre out. I'd walked away without stopping Quinn or saving Andre, and that had made me several degrees more guilty of Andre's death than of my great-uncle's.

I strode through the empty park, kicking at the stray leaves that came my way. I was struggling with a sick temptation. I had only to say the word to any of many members of the supernatural community, and Tanya would be dead. Or I could set my sights on the source and have Sandra taken out. And again—what a relief her departure from the world would be.

I just couldn't do it.

But I couldn't live with Tanya nipping at my heels, either. She'd done her best to ruin my brother's already shaky relationship with his wife. That was just wrong.

I finally thought of the right person to consult. And she lived with me, so that was convenient.

When I got back to my house, Amelia's dad and his obliging chauffeur had departed. Amelia was in the kitchen, washing dishes.

"Amelia," I said, and she jumped. "Sorry," I apologized. "I should've walked heavier."

"I was hoping that my dad and I understood each other a little better," she confessed. "But I don't think that's really true. He just needs me to do something for him now and then."

"Well, at least we got the firewood split."

She laughed a little and dried off her hands. "You look like you have something big to say."

"I want to clear the decks before I tell you this long story. I'm doing your dad a favor, but I'm really doing it for you," I said. "I'll call Fangtasia for your father no matter what, because you're my roommate and that'll make you happy. So that's a done deal. Now I'm going to tell you about a terrible thing I did."

Amelia sat at the table and I sat opposite her, just like Marley and I had done earlier. "This sounds interesting," she said. "I'm ready. Bring it on."

I told Amelia all about it: Debbie Pelt, Alcide, Sandra Pelt and her parents, their vow that Sandra would never bother me again while they lived. What they had on me and how I felt about it. Tanya Grissom, spy and sneak and saboteur of my brother's marriage.

"Whoa," she said when I'd finished. She thought for a minute. "Okay, first off, let's check on Mr. and Mrs. Pelt." We used the computer I'd brought back from Hadley's apartment in New Orleans. It took all of five minutes to discover that Gordon and Barbara Pelt had died two weeks before when they'd attempted to make a left turn into a gas station only to be hit broadside by a tractor trailer.

We looked at each other, our noses wrinkled. "Ewww," Amelia said. "Bad way to go."

"I wonder if she even waited till they were in the ground before she activated the Aggravate Sookie to Death plan," I said.

"This bitch isn't going to let up. You sure Debbie Pelt was adopted? Because this totally vindictive attitude seems to run in that family."

"They must have really bonded," I said. "In fact, I got the impression that Debbie was more of a sister to Sandra than she was a daughter to her parents."

Amelia nodded thoughtfully. "A little pathology going on there," she said. "Well, let me think about what I can do. I don't do death magic. And you've said you don't want Tanya and Sandra to die, so I'm taking you at your word."

"Good," I said briefly. "And, uh, I'm willing to pay for this, of course."

"Poo," Amelia said. "You were willing to take me in when I needed to get out of town. You've put up with me all this time."

"Well, you do pay rent," I pointed out.

"Yeah, enough to cover my part of the utilities. And you put up with me, and you don't seem to be all up in arms about the Bob situation. So believe me, I'm really glad to do this for you. I've just got to figure out what I'm actually going to do. Do you mind if I consult with Octavia?"

"No, not at all," I said, trying not to show that I was relieved at the idea of the older witch offering her expertise. "You got it, right? Got that she was at loose ends? Out of money?"

"Yeah," Amelia said. "And I don't know how to give her some without offering offense. This is a good way to do it. I understand that she's stuck in a random corner of the living room in the house of the niece she's staying with. She told me that—more or less—but I don't know what I can do about it."

"I'll think about it," I promised. "If she really, really needs to move out of her niece's, she could stay in my extra bedroom for a little while." That wasn't an offer that delighted me, but the old witch had seemed pretty miserable. She'd been entertained by going on the little jaunt to poor Maria-Star's apartment, which had been a ghastly sight.

"We'll try to come up with something long-term," Amelia said. "I'm going to go give her a call."

"Okay. Let me know what you-all come up with. I got to get ready for work."

There weren't too many houses between mine and Merlotte's, but all of them had ghosts hanging from trees, inflated plastic pumpkins in the yard, and a real pumpkin or two sitting on the front porch. The Prescotts had a sheaf of corn, a bale of hay, and some ornamental squash and pumpkins arranged artfully on the front lawn. I made a mental memo to tell Lorinda Prescott how attractive it was when next I saw her at Wal-Mart or the post office.

By the time I got to work, it was dark. I got out my cell phone to call Fangtasia before I went inside.

"Fangtasia, the bar with a bite. Come into Shreveport's premier vampire bar, where the undead do their drinking every single night," said a recording. "For bar hours, press one. To schedule a private party, press two. To speak to a live human or a dead vampire, press three. And know this: prank calls are not tolerated. We will find you."

I was sure the voice was Pam's. She'd sounded remarkably bored. I pressed three.

"Fangtasia, where all your undead dreams come true," said one of the fangbangers. "This is Elvira. How may I direct you?"

Elvira, my ass. "This is Sookie Stackhouse. I need to speak with Eric," I said.

"Could Clancy help you?" Elvira asked.

"No."

Elvira seemed stumped.

"The master is very busy," she said, as if that would be hard for a human like me to understand.

Elvira was definitely a newbie. Or maybe I was getting kind of arrogant. I was irritated with "Elvira." "Listen," I said, trying

CHARLAINE HARRIS

to sound pleasant. "You get Eric on the phone in two minutes or he'll be mighty unhappy with you."

"*Well*," Elvira said. "You don't have to be a bitch about it."

"Evidently I do."

"I'm putting you on hold," Elvira said viciously. I glanced at the employee door of the bar. I needed to hustle.

Click. "This is Eric," he said. "Is this my former lover?"

Okay, even that made things inside me thud and shiver in excitement. "Yeah, yeah, yeah," I said, proud of how unshaken I sounded. "Listen, Eric, for what it's worth, I had a visit today from a New Orleans bigwig named Copley Carmichael. He'd been involved with Sophie-Anne in some business negotiations about rebuilding the headquarters. He wants to establish a relationship with the new regime." I took a deep breath. "Are you okay?" I asked, negating in one plaintive question all my cultivated indifference.

"Yes," he said, his voice intensely personal. "Yes, I am . . . coping with this. We are very, very lucky we were in a position to . . . We're very lucky."

I let out my breath very softly so he wouldn't pick up on it. Of course, he would anyway. I can't say I'd been on pins and needles wondering how things were going with the vampires, but I hadn't been resting very easy, either. "Okay, very good," I said briskly. "Now, about Copley. Is there anyone around who'd like to hook up with him about the construction stuff?"

"Is he in the area?"

"I don't know. He was here this morning. I can ask."

"The vampire I am working with now would probably be the right woman for him to approach. She could meet him at your bar or here at Fangtasia."

"Okay. I'm sure he'd do either one."

"Let me know. He needs to call here to set up an appointment. He should ask for Sandy."

I laughed. "Sandy, huh?"

"Yes," he said, sounding grim enough to sober me in a hurry. "She is not a bit funny, Sookie."

"Okay, okay, I get it. Let me call his daughter, she'll call him, he'll call Fangtasia, it'll all get set up, and I've done my favor for him."

"This is Amelia's father?"

"Yes. He's a jerk," I said. "But he's her dad, and I guess he knows his building stuff."

"I lay in front of your fire and talked to you about your life," he said.

Okay, way out of left field. "Uh. Yeah. We did that."

"I remember our shower together."

"We did that, too."

"We did so many things."

"Ah . . . yeah. Okay."

"In fact, if I didn't have so much to do here in Shreveport, I would be tempted to visit you all by myself to remind you how much you enjoyed those things."

"If memory serves," I said sharply, "you kind of enjoyed them, too."

"Oh, yes."

"Eric, I really need to go. I got to get to work." Or sponta-neously combust, whichever came first.

"Good-bye." He could make even that sound sexy.

"Good-bye." I didn't.

It took me a second to gather my thoughts back together. I was remembering things I'd tried hard to forget. The days Eric had stayed with me—well, the nights—we'd done a lot of talking and a lot of sexing. And it had been wonderful. The companionship. The sex. The laughing. The sex. The conversa-tions. The . . . well.

Somehow going in to serve beers seemed drab, all of a sudden.

But that was my job, and I owed it to Sam to show up and work. I trudged in, stowed my purse, and nodded to Sam as I tapped Holly on the shoulder to tell her I was here to take over. We switched shifts for the change and convenience but mostly because the night tips were higher. Holly was glad to see me because she had a date that night with Hoyt. They were going to a movie and dinner in Shreveport. She'd gotten a teenager to babysit Cody. She was telling me this as I was getting it from her contented brain, and I had to work hard not to get confused. That showed me how rattled I'd been by my conversation with Eric.

I was really busy for about thirty minutes, making sure everyone was well-supplied with drinks and food. I caught a moment to call Amelia soon after that to relay Eric's message, and she told me that she'd call her dad the minute she hung up. "Thanks, Sook," she said. "Again, you're a great roomie."

I hoped she'd think of that when she and Octavia were devising a magical solution to my Tanya problem.

Claudine came into Merlotte's that evening, raising male pulses as she sauntered to the bar. She was wearing a green silk blouse, black pants, and black high-heeled boots. That made her at least six foot one, I estimated. To my amazement, her twin brother, Claude, trailed in after her. The racing pulses spread to the opposite sex with the speed of wildfire. Claude, whose hair was as black as Claudine's, though not as long, was as lovely a hunk as ever posed in a Calvin Klein ad. Claude was wearing a masculine version of Claudine's outfit, and he'd tied his hair back with a leather thong. He was also wearing very "guy" boots. Since he stripped at a club in Monroe on ladies' night, Claude knew exactly how to smile at women, though he wasn't interested in them. I take that back. He was interested in how much money they had in their purses.

The twins had never come in together; in fact, I didn't recall Claude setting foot in Merlotte's before. He had his own place to run, his own fish to fry.

Of course I went over to say hi, and I got a comprehensive hug from Claudine. To my amazement, Claude followed suit. I figured he was playing to the audience, which was pretty much the whole bar. Even Sam was goggling; together, the fairy twins were overwhelming.

We stood at the bar with me sandwiched between them, each with an arm around me, and I heard brains light up all around the room with little fantasies, some of which startled even me, and I've seen the most bizarre things people can imagine. Yep, it's all there for lucky me to see in living color.

"We bring you greetings from our grandfather," Claude

said. His voice was so quiet and liquid that I was sure no one else would be able to hear it. Possibly Sam could, but he was always good for discretion.

"He wonders why you haven't called," Claudine said, "especially considering the events of the other night, in Shreveport."

"Well, that was over with," I said, surprised. "Why tell him about something that had already turned out okay? You were there. But I did try to call him the other night."

"It rang once," Claudine murmured.

"However, a certain person broke my phone so I couldn't complete the call. He told me it was the wrong thing to do, that it would start a war. I lived through that, too. So that was okay."

"You need to talk to Niall, tell him the whole story," Claudine said. She smiled across the room at Catfish Hennessy, who put his beer mug down on the table so hard that it slopped over. "Now that Niall's made himself known to you, he wants you to confide in him."

"Why can't he pick up the phone like everyone else in the world?"

"He doesn't spend all his time in this world," Claude said. "There are still places for only our kind."

"Very small places," Claudine said longingly. "But very special."

I was glad to have kin, and I was always glad to see Claudine, who was literally my lifesaver. But the two sibs together were a little overpowering, overwhelming—and when they stood so close with me crowded between them (even Sam was having a visual from that), their sweet smell, the smell that made them so intoxicating to vampires, was drowning my poor nose.

"Look," Claude said, mildly amused. "I think we have company."

Arlene was sidling nearer, looking at Claude as if she'd spied a whole plate of barbecue and onion rings. "Who's your friend, Sookie?" she asked.

"This is Claude," I said. "He's my distant cousin."

"Well, Claude, nice to meet ya," Arlene said.

She had some nerve, considering the way she felt about me now and how she'd treated me since she'd started going to the Fellowship of the Sun services.

Claude looked massively uninterested. He nodded.

Arlene had expected more, and after a moment of silence, she pretended to hear someone from one of her tables calling her. "Gotta go get a pitcher!" she said brightly, and bustled off. I saw her bend over a table, talking very seriously to a couple of guys I didn't know.

"It's always good to see you two, but I *am* at work," I said. "So, did you just come to tell me my...that Niall wants to know why I called once and hung up?"

"And never called thereafter to explain," Claudine said. She bent down to kiss my cheek. "Please call him tonight when you get off work."

"Okay," I said. "I still wish he'd called me himself to ask." Messengers were all well and good, but the phone was quicker. And I'd like to hear his voice. No matter where my great-grandfather might be, he could wink back into this world to call if he really was that taxed about my safety.

I thought he could, anyway.

Of course, I didn't know what being a fairy prince entailed. Write that down under "problems I know I'll never face."

After another round of hugs and kisses, the twins sauntered out of the bar, and many wistful eyes followed them on their progress out the door.

"Hoo, Sookie, you got some hot friends!" Catfish Hennessy called, and there was a general tide of agreement.

"I've seen that guy at a club in Monroe. Doesn't he strip?" said a nurse named Debi Murray who worked at the hospital in nearby Clarice. She was sitting with a couple of other nurses.

"Yeah," I said. "He owns the club, too."

"Looks *and* loot," said one of the other nurses. Her name was Beverly something. "I'm taking my daughter next ladies' night. She just broke up with a real loser."

"Well..." I debated explaining that Claude wouldn't be interested in anyone's daughter, then decided that wasn't my responsibility. "Have a good time," I said instead.

Since I'd taken time out with my sort-of cousins, I had to hustle to sweeten everyone up. Though they hadn't had my attention during the visit, they had had the entertainment of the twins, so no one was really miffed.

Toward the end of my shift, Copley Carmichael walked in.

He looked funny alone. I assumed Marley was waiting in the car.

In his beautiful suit and with his expensive haircut, he didn't exactly fit in, but I got to give him credit: he acted like he came into places like Merlotte's all the time. I happened to be standing by Sam, who was mixing a bourbon and Coke for one of my tables. I explained to Sam who the stranger was.

I delivered the drink and nodded at an empty table. Mr. Carmichael took the hint and settled in.

"Hey! Can I get you a drink, Mr. Carmichael?" I said.

"Please get me a single malt scotch," he said. "Whatever you've got will be fine. I'm meeting someone here, Sookie, thanks to your phone call. You just tell me the next time you need anything, and I'll do everything in my power to make it happen."

"Not necessary, Mr. Carmichael."

"Please, call me Cope."

"Um-hmmm. Okay, let me get your scotch."

I didn't know a single malt scotch from a hole in the ground, but Sam did, of course, and he gave me a shining clean glass with a very respectable shot of it. I serve liquor, but I seldom drink it. Most folks around here drink the real obvious stuff: beer, bourbon and Coke, gin and tonic, Jack Daniel's.

I set the drink and cocktail napkin on the table in front of Mr. Carmichael, and I returned with a little bowl of snack mix.

Then I left him alone, because I had other people to tend to. But I kept track of him. I noticed Sam was keeping a careful eye on Amelia's dad, too. But everyone else was too involved in their own conversations and their own drinking to give much mind to the stranger, one not nearly as interesting as Claude and Claudine.

In a moment when I wasn't looking, a vampire joined Cope. I don't think anyone else knew what she was. She was a real recent vamp, by which I mean she'd died in the past fifty years, and she had prematurely silver hair that was cut in a modest chin-length style. She was small, maybe five foot two, and she was round and firm in all the right places. She was wearing little silver-rimmed glasses that were sheer affectation, because I'd never met a vampire whose eyesight wasn't absolutely perfect and in fact sharper than any human's.

"Can I get you some blood?" I asked.

Her eyes were like lasers. Once she was really giving you her attention, you were sorry.

"You're the woman Sookie," she said.

I didn't see any need to affirm what she was so sure of. I waited.

"A glass of TrueBlood, please," she said. "Quite warm. And I'd like to meet your boss, if you would fetch him."

Like Sam was a bone. Nonetheless, she was a customer and I was a barmaid. So I heated a TrueBlood for her and told Sam he was wanted.

"I'll be there in a minute," he said, because he was getting a tray of drinks ready for Arlene.

I nodded and took the blood over to the vampire.

"Thank you," she said civilly. "I'm Sandy Sechrest, the new area rep for the King of Louisiana."

I had no idea where Sandy had grown up, but it had been in the United States and had not been in the south. "Pleased to meet you," I said, but not with a whole lot of enthusiasm. Area rep? Wasn't that what sheriffs were, among their other functions? What did that mean for Eric?

At that moment Sam came to the table, and I left because I didn't want to look inquisitive. Besides, I could probably pick it up from his brain later if Sam chose not to tell me what the new vampire wanted. He was good at blocking, but he had to make a special effort to do it.

The three engaged in a conversation for a couple of minutes, then Sam excused himself to get back behind the bar.

I glanced at the vampire and the mogul from time to time in case they needed something more to drink, but neither of them indicated a thirst. They were talking very seriously, and both of them were adept at maintaining a poker face. I didn't care enough to try to latch onto Mr. Carmichael's thoughts, and of course Sandy Sechrest was a blank to me.

The rest of the night was the usual stuff. I didn't even notice when the new king's rep and Mr. Carmichael left. Then it was time to close everything out and get my tables ready for Terry Bellefleur to come in and clean early in the morning. By the time I really looked around me, everyone was gone but Sam and me.

"Hey, you through?" he said.

"Yeah," I said after another look around.

"You got a minute?"

I always had a minute for Sam.

Chapter 16

He sat in the chair behind his desk and tilted it back at the usual dangerous angle. I sat in one of the chairs in front of the desk, the one with the most padding in the seat. Most of the lights in the building were out except the one that stayed on over the bar area and the one in Sam's office. The building rang with silence after the cacophony of voices rising over the jukebox and the sounds of cooking, washing, footsteps.

"That Sandy Sechrest," he said. "She's got a whole new job."

"Yeah? What the king's rep supposed to do?"

"Well, as far as I can tell, she'll travel the state pretty much constantly, seeing if the citizens have problems with any vampires, seeing if the sheriffs have everything in order and under control in their own fiefs, and reporting in to the king. She's like an undead troubleshooter."

"Oh." I thought that over. I couldn't see that the job would detract from Eric's. If Eric was okay, his crew would be okay. Other than that, I didn't care what the vampires did. "So, she decided to meet you because . . . ?"

"She understood I had associations in the regional supernatural community," Sam said dryly. "She wanted me to know she was available to consult in the event 'problems arose.' I have her business card." He held it up. I don't know if I expected it to drip with blood or what, but it was only a regular business card.

"Okay." I shrugged.

"What did Claudine and her brother want?" Sam asked.

I was feeling very bad about concealing my new great-grandfather from Sam, but Niall had told me to keep him a secret. "She hadn't heard from me since the fight in Shreveport," I said. "She just wanted to check up, and she got Claude to come with her."

Sam looked at me a little sharply but he didn't comment. "Maybe," he said after a minute, "this will be a long era of peace. Maybe we can just work in the bar and nothing will happen in the supe community. I'm hoping so, because the time is coming closer and closer when the Weres are going to go public."

"You think it's soon?" I had no idea how America would react to the news that vampires were not the only things out there in the night. "You think all the other shifters will announce the same night?"

"We'll have to," Sam said. "We're talking on our website about it."

Sam did have a life that was unknown to me. That sparked

a thought. I hesitated, then plowed ahead. There were too many questions in my own life. I wanted to get at least some of them answered.

"How'd you come to settle here?" I asked.

"I'd passed through the area," he said. "I was in the army for four years."

"You were?" I couldn't believe I hadn't known that.

"Yeah," he said. "I didn't know what I wanted to do in my life, so I joined when I was eighteen. My mom cried and my dad swore since I'd been accepted to a college, but I'd made up my mind. I was about the stubbornest teenager on the planet."

"Where'd you grow up?"

"At least partly in Wright, Texas," he said. "Outside of Fort Worth. Way outside of Fort Worth. It wasn't any bigger than Bon Temps. We moved around all during my childhood, though, because my dad was in the service himself. He got out when I was about fourteen, and my mom's family was in Wright, so that's where we went."

"Was it hard settling down after moving so much?" I'd never lived anywhere but Bon Temps.

"It was great," he said. "I was so ready to stay in one place. I hadn't realized how hard it would be to find my own niche in a group of kids who'd grown up together, but I was able to take care of myself. I played baseball and basketball, so I found my place. Then I joined the army. Go figure."

I was fascinated. "Are your mom and dad still in Wright?" I asked. "It must have been hard for him in the military, with him being a shifter." Since Sam was a shapeshifter, I knew without him having to tell me that he was the first-born child of pure-blooded shapeshifters.

"Yeah, the full moons were a bitch. There was an herbal drink his Irish grandmother used to make. He learned how to make it himself. It was foul beyond belief, but he drank it on full moons when he had to be on duty and had to be seen all night, and that helped him maintain. . . . But you didn't want to be around him the next day. Dad passed away about six years ago, left me a chunk of money. I'd always liked this area, and this bar was up for sale. It seemed like a good way to invest the money."

"And your mom?"

"She's still in Wright. She married again about two years after Dad died. He's a good enough guy. He's regular." Not a shifter or any kind of supernatural. "So there's a limit to how close I can get to him," Sam said.

"Your mom's a full-blood. Surely he suspects."

"He's willfully blind, I think. She has to go out for her evening run, she says, or she's spending the night with her sister in Waco, or she's driving over to visit me, or some other excuse."

"Must be hard to maintain."

"I would never try to do that. I almost married a regular girl once, while I was in the service. But I just couldn't marry someone and keep that big a secret. It saves my sanity, having someone to talk to about it, Sookie." He smiled at me, and I appreciated the trust he was showing. "If the Weres announce, then we'll all go public. It'll be a great burden off me."

We both knew there would be new problems to face, but there wasn't any need to talk about future trouble. Trouble always came at its own pace.

"You got any sisters or brothers?" I asked.

"One of each. My sister is married with two kids, and my brother is still single. He's a great guy." Sam was smiling and his face looked more relaxed than I'd ever seen. "Craig's getting married in the spring, he says," Sam went on. "Maybe you can go to the wedding with me."

I was so astonished I didn't know what to say, and I was very flattered and pleased. "That sounds like fun. Tell me when you know the date," I said. Sam and I had gone out, once, and it had been very pleasant; but it was in the midst of my problems with Bill and the evening had never been repeated.

Sam nodded casually, and the little jolt of tension that had run through me evaporated. After all, this was *Sam*, my boss, and come to think of it, also one of my best friends. He'd clicked into that slot during the past year. I got up. I had my purse, and I pulled on my jacket.

"Did you get an invitation for the Fangtasia Halloween party this year?" he asked.

"No. After the last party they invited me to, they might not want me to come back," I said. "Besides, with all the recent losses, I don't know if Eric'll feel like celebrating."

"You think we ought to have a Halloween party at Merlotte's?" he asked.

"Maybe not with candy and stuff like that," I said, thinking

FROM DEAD TO WORSE

hard. "Maybe a goodie bag for each customer, with dry roasted peanuts? Or a bowl of orange popcorn on each table? And some decorations?"

Sam looked in the direction of the bar as if he could see through the walls. "That sounds good. Make a thing of it." Ordinarily we only decorated for Christmas, and that only after Thanksgiving, at Sam's insistence.

I waved good night and left the bar, leaving Sam to check that everything was locked tight.

The night had a cold bite to it. This would be one of the Halloweens that really felt like the Halloweens I'd seen in children's books.

In the center of the parking lot, his face turned up to the sliver of moon, his eyes closed, stood my great-grandfather. His pale hair hung down his back like a thick curtain. His myriad of fine creases were invisible in the moonlight, or else he'd divested himself of them. He was carrying his cane, and once again he was wearing a suit, a black suit. There was a heavy ring on his right hand, the hand gripping the cane.

He was the most beautiful being I'd ever seen.

He didn't look remotely like a human grandfather. Human grandfathers wore gimme caps from the John Deere place and overalls. They took you fishing. They let you ride on their trac- tors. They groused at you for being too pampered and then they bought you candy. As for human great-grandfathers, most of us hardly got to know ours.

I became aware of Sam standing by my side.

"Who is that?" he breathed.

"That's my, ah, my great-granddad," I said. He was right there in front of me. I had to explain.

"Oh," he said, his voice was full of amazement.

"I just found out," I said apologetically.

Niall stopped soaking up the moonlight and his eyes opened. "My great-granddaughter," he said, as if my presence in the Merlotte's parking lot was a pleasant surprise. "Who is your friend?"

"Niall, this is Sam Merlotte, who owns this bar," I said.

Sam extended his hand cautiously, and after a good look at it, Niall touched it with his own. I could feel Sam give a slight jerk, as if my great-grandfather had had a buzzer in his hand.

"Great-granddaughter," Niall said, "I hear you were in danger in the fracas between the werewolves."

"Yes, but Sam was with me, and then Claudine came," I said, feeling oddly defensive. "I didn't know there was going to be a fracas, as you put it, when I went. I was trying to be a peacemaker. We were ambushed."

"Yes, that's what Claudine reported," he said. "I understand the bitch is dead?"

By which he meant Priscilla. "Yes, sir," I said. "The bitch is dead."

"And then you were in danger again one night later?"

I was beginning to feel definitely guilty of something. "Well, that's not actually my norm," I said. "It just happened that the vampires of Louisiana got overrun by the vampires of Nevada."

Niall seemed only mildly interested. "But you went as far as dialing the number I left you."

"Ah, yes, sir, I was pretty scared. But then Eric knocked the phone out of my hand because he thought if you came into the equation, there'd be an out-and-out war. As it turned out, I guess that was for the best, because he surrendered to Victor Madden." I was still a little angry about it, though, even after Eric's gift of the replacement phone.

"Ahhh."

I couldn't make head nor tail of that noncommittal sound. This might be the downside of having a great-grandfather on site. I'd been called on the carpet. It was a feeling I hadn't had since I was a young teen and Gran had found out I'd skipped taking out the trash and folding the laundry. I didn't like the feeling now any more than I'd liked it then.

"I love your courage," Niall said unexpectedly. "But you are very frail—mortal, breakable, and short-lived. I don't want to lose you just when I finally became able to speak to you."

"I don't know what to say," I muttered.

"You don't want me to stop you from doing anything. You won't change. How can I protect you?"

"I don't think you can, not a hundred percent."

"Then what use am I to you?"

"You don't have to be of use to me," I said, surprised. He didn't seem to have the emotional set I had. I didn't know how to explain it to him. "It's enough for me—it's wonderful—just knowing you exist. That you care about me. That I have living family, no matter how distant and different. And you don't think I'm weird or crazy or embarrassing."

"Embarrassing?" He looked puzzled. "You're far more interesting than most humans."

"Thank you for not thinking I'm defective," I said.

"Other humans think you're *defective?*" Niall sounded genuinely outraged.

"They can't be comfortable sometimes," Sam said unexpectedly. "Knowing she can read their minds."

"But you, shapeshifter?"

"I think she's great," Sam said. And I could tell he was absolutely sincere.

My back straightened. I felt a flush of pride. In the emotional warmth of the moment, I almost told my great-grandfather about the big problem I'd uncovered today, to prove I could share. But I had a pretty good feeling that his solution to the Sandra Pelt–Tanya Grissom Axis of Evil would be to cause their deaths in a macabre way. My sort-of cousin Claudine might be trying to become an angel, a being I associated with Christianity, but Niall Brigant was definitely from another ethos entirely. I suspected his outlook was, "I'll take your eye ahead of time, just in case you want mine." Well, maybe not that preemptive, but close.

"There is nothing I can do for you?" He sounded almost plaintive.

"I'd really like it if you'd just come spend some time with me at the house, when you have some to spare. I'd like to cook you supper. If you want to do that?" It made me feel shy, offering him something I wasn't sure he'd value.

He looked at me with glowing eyes. I could not read his face, and though his body was shaped like a human body, he was not. He was a complete puzzle to me. Maybe he was exasperated or bored or repulsed by my suggestion.

Finally Niall said, "Yes. I'll do that. I'll tell you ahead of time, of course. In the meantime, if you need anything of me, call the number. Don't let anyone dissuade you if you think I can be of help. I will have words with Eric. He's been useful to me in the past, but he can't second-guess me with you."

"Has he known I was your kin for very long?" I held my breath, waiting for the answer.

Niall had turned to go. Now he turned back a little, so I saw his face in profile. "No," he said. "I had to know him better, first. I told him only before he brought you to meet me. He wouldn't help me until I told him why I wanted you."

And then he was gone. It was like he'd walked through a door we couldn't see, and for all I knew, that was exactly what he'd done.

"Okay," Sam said after a long moment. "Okay, that was really . . . different."

"Are you all right with all this?" I waved a hand toward the spot where Niall had been standing. Probably. Unless what we'd seen had been some astral projection or something.

"It's not my place to be okay with it. It's your thing," Sam said.

"I want to love him," I said. "He's so beautiful and he seems to care so much, but he's really, really . . ."

"Scary," Sam finished.

"Yeah."

"And he approached you through Eric?"

Since apparently my great-grandfather thought it was okay if Sam knew about him, I told Sam about my first meeting with Niall.

"Hmmm. Well, I don't know what to make of that. Vampires and fairies don't interact, because of the vampire tendency to eat fairies."

"Niall can mask his scent," I explained proudly.

Sam looked overloaded with information. "That's another thing I've never heard of. I hope Jason doesn't know about this?"

"Oh, God, no."

"You know he'd be jealous and that would make him mad at you."

"Since I know Niall and he doesn't?"

"Yep. Envy would just eat Jason up."

"I know Jason's not the world's most generous person," I began, to be cut off when Sam snorted. "Okay," I said, "he's selfish. But he's still my brother anyway, and I have to stick by him. But maybe it's better if I never tell him. Still, Niall didn't have any problem showing himself to *you*, after telling me to keep him a secret."

"I'm guessing he did some checking up," Sam said mildly. He hugged me, which was a welcome surprise. I felt like I needed a hug after Niall's drop-in. I hugged Sam back. He felt warm, and comforting, and human.

But neither of us was 100 percent human.

In the next instant, I thought, *We are, too.* We had more in common with humans than with the other part of us. We lived like humans; we would die like humans. Since I knew Sam pretty well, I knew he wanted a family and someone to love and a future that contained all the things plain humans want: prosperity, good health, descendants, laughter. Sam didn't want to be a leader of any pack, and I didn't want to be princess of anybody—not that any pureblood fairy would ever think I was anything other than a lowly by-product of their own wonderfulness. That was one of the big differences between Jason and me. Jason would spend his life wishing he was more supernatural than he was; I had spent mine wishing I was less, if my telepathy was indeed supernatural.

Sam kissed me on the cheek, and then after a moment's hesitation, he turned to go into his trailer, walking through the gate in the carefully trimmed hedge and up the steps to the little deck he'd built outside his door. When he'd inserted the key, he turned to smile at me.

"Some night, huh?"

"Yeah," I said. "Some night."

Sam watched while I got in my car, made a pressing gesture to remind me to lock my car doors, waited while I complied, and then went into his trailer. I drove home preoccupied with deep questions and shallow ones, and it was lucky there wasn't any traffic on the road.

Chapter 17

Amelia and Octavia were sitting at the kitchen table the next day when I shambled out. Amelia had used up all the coffee, but at least she'd washed the pot and it took only a few minutes to make myself a much-needed cup. Amelia and her mentor kept a tactful conversation going while I bumbled around getting some cereal, adding some sweetener, pouring milk over it. I hunched over the bowl because I didn't want to dribble milk down my tank top. And by the way, it was getting too cold to wear a tank top around the house. I pulled on a cheap jacket made of sweats material and was able to finish my coffee and cereal in comfort.

"What's up, you two?" I asked, signaling I was ready to interact with the rest of the world.

"Amelia told me about your problem," Octavia said. "And about your very kind offer."

Ah-oh. What offer?

I nodded wisely, as if I had a clue.

"I'll be so glad to be out of my niece's house, you have no idea," the older woman said earnestly. "Janesha has three little ones, including one toddler, and a boyfriend that comes and goes. I'm sleeping on the living room couch, and when the kids get up in the morning, they come in and turn on the cartoons. Whether or not I'm up. It's their house, of course, and I've been there for weeks, so they've lost the sense that I'm company."

I gathered that Octavia was going to be sleeping in the bedroom opposite me or in the extra one upstairs. I was voting for the one upstairs.

"And you know, now that I'm older, I need quicker access to a bathroom." She looked at me with that humorous deprecation people show when they're admitting to a passage-of-time condition. "So downstairs would be wonderful, especially since my knees are arthritic. Did I tell you Janesha's apartment is upstairs?"

"No," I said through numb lips. Geez, this had happened so fast.

"Now, about your problem. I'm not a black witch at all, but you need to get these young women out of your life, both Ms. Pelt's agent and Ms. Pelt herself."

I nodded vigorously.

"So," Amelia said, unable to keep quiet any longer, "we've come up with a plan."

"I'm all ears," I said, and poured myself a second cup of coffee. I needed it.

"The simplest way to get rid of Tanya, of course, is to tell your friend Calvin Norris what she's doing," Octavia said.

I gaped at her. "Ah, that seems likely to result in some pretty bad things happening to Tanya," I said.

"Isn't that what you want?" Octavia looked innocent in a real sly way.

"Well, yeah, but I don't want her to die. I mean, I don't want anything she can't get over to happen to her. I just want her away and not coming back."

Amelia said, "'Away and not coming back' sounds pretty final to me."

It sounded that way to me, too. "I'll rephrase. I want her to be off somewhere living her life but far away from me," I said. "Is that clear enough?" I wasn't trying to sound sharp; I just wanted to express myself.

"Yes, young lady, I think we can understand that," said Octavia with frost in her voice.

"I don't want there to be any misunderstanding here," I said. "There's a lot at stake. I think Calvin kind of likes Tanya. On the other hand, I bet he could scare her pretty effectively."

"Enough to get her to leave forever?"

"You'd have to demonstrate that you were telling the truth," Amelia said. "About her sabotaging you."

"What do you have in mind?" I asked.

"Okay, here's what we think," Amelia said, and just like that, Phase One was in place. It turned out to be something I could have thought of myself, but the witches' help made the planning run much more smoothly.

FROM DEAD TO WORSE

I called Calvin at home, and asked him to stop by when he had a minute to spare around lunchtime. He sounded surprised to hear from me, but he agreed to come.

He got a further surprise when he came into the kitchen and found Amelia and Octavia there. Calvin, the leader of the werepanthers who lived in the little community of Hotshot, had met Amelia several times before, but Octavia was new to him. He respected her immediately because he was able to sense her power. That was a big help.

Calvin was probably in his midforties, strong and solid, sure of himself. His hair was graying, but he was straight as an arrow in posture, and he possessed a huge calm that couldn't fail to impress. He'd been interested in me for a while, and I'd only been sorry I couldn't feel the same way. He was a good man.

"What's up, Sookie?" he said after he'd turned down the offer of cookies or tea or Coke.

I took a deep breath. "I don't like to be a tale-teller, Calvin, but we have a problem," I said.

"Tanya," he said immediately.

"Yeah," I said, not bothering to hide my relief.

"She's a sly one," he said, and I was sorry to hear an element of admiration in his voice.

"She's a spy," Amelia said. Amelia could cut right to the chase.

"Who for?" Calvin tilted his head to one side, unsurprised and curious.

I told him an edited version of the story, a story I was extremely sick of repeating. Calvin needed to know that the

Pelts had a big beef with me, that Sandra would hound me to my grave, that Tanya had been planted as a gadfly.

Calvin stretched out his legs while he listened, his arms crossed over his chest. He was wearing brand-new jeans and a plaid shirt. He smelled like fresh-cut trees.

"You want to put a spell on her?" he asked Amelia when I'd finished.

"We do," she said. "But we need you to get her here."

"What would the effect be? Would it hurt her?"

"She'd lose interest in doing harm to Sookie and all her family. She wouldn't want to obey Sandra Pelt anymore. It wouldn't hurt her physically at all."

"Would this change her mentally?"

"No," Octavia said. "But it's not as sure a spell as the one that would make her not want to be here anymore. If we cast that one, she'd leave here, and she wouldn't want to come back."

Calvin mulled this over. "I kind of like that ole girl," he said. "She's a live one. I've been pretty concerned over the trouble she's causing Crystal and Jason, though, and I've been wondering what steps to take about Crystal's crazy spending. I guess this kind of brings the issue front and center."

"You like her?" I said. I wanted all cards on the table.

"I said that."

"No, I mean, you *like* her."

"Well, her and me, we've had some good times now and then."

"You don't want her to go away," I said. "You want to try the other thing."

"That's about the size of it. You're right: she can't stay and keep on going like she is. She either changes her ways, or she leaves." He looked unhappy about that. "You working today, Sookie?"

I looked at the wall calendar. "No, it's my day off." I'd have two days in a row off.

"I'll get ahold of her and bring her by tonight. That give you ladies enough time?"

The two witches looked at each other and consulted silently.

"Yes, that will be fine," Octavia said.

"I'll get her here by seven," Calvin said.

This was moving with unexpected smoothness.

"Thanks, Calvin," I said. "This is really helpful."

"This'll kill a lot of birds with one stone, if it works," Calvin said. "Of course, if it don't work, you two ladies won't be my favorite people." His voice was completely matter-of-fact.

The two witches didn't look happy.

Calvin eyed Bob, who happened to stroll into the room. "Hello, brother," Calvin said to the cat. He gave Amelia a narrowed-eye look. "Seems to me like your magic don't work all the time."

Amelia looked guilty and offended simultaneously. "We'll get this to work," she said, tight-lipped. "You just see."

"I aim to."

I spent the rest of the day doing my laundry, redoing my nails, changing my sheets—all those tasks you save up for your day off. I went by the library to swap books and absolutely nothing happened. One of Barbara Beck's part-time assistants was on duty, which was good. I didn't want to experience the horror of the attack all over again, as I surely would in every encounter with Barbara for a long time to come. I noticed the stain was gone from the library floor.

After that, I went to the grocery store. No Weres attacked, no vampires rose. No one tried to kill me or anyone I knew. No secret relatives revealed themselves, and not a soul tried to involve me in his or her problems, marital or otherwise.

I was practically reeking with normality by the time I got home.

Tonight was my cooking night, and I'd decided to fix pork chops. I have a favorite homemade breading mix that I make in a huge batch, so I soaked the chops in milk and then dredged them with the mix so they were ready for the oven. I fixed baked apples stuffed with raisins and cinnamon and butter and popped them in to bake and I flavored some canned green beans and some canned corn and put them on low heat. After a while, I opened the oven to put in the meat. I thought about making biscuits, but there seemed to be more than enough calories on board.

While I cooked, the witches were doing stuff in the living room. They seemed to be having a good old time. I could hear Octavia's voice, which sounded very much like it was in teaching mode. Every now and then, Amelia would ask a question.

I did a lot of muttering to myself while I cooked. I hoped this magical procedure worked, and I was grateful to the witches for being so willing to help. But I was feeling a little sideswiped on the domestic front. My brief mention to Amelia that Octavia could stay with us for a little while had been a spur of the moment thing. (I could tell I was going to have to be more careful in conversations with my roomie from now on.) Octavia hadn't said she'd be in my house for a weekend, or a month, or any measure of time. That scared me.

I could have cornered Amelia and told her, "You didn't ask me if Octavia could stay *right now at this moment*, and it's my house," I supposed. But I *did* have a free room, and Octavia *did* need someplace to stay. It was a little late to discover that I wasn't entirely happy at having a third person in the house—a third person I barely knew.

Maybe I could find a job for Octavia, because regular earnings would allow the older woman her independence and she'd move out of here. I wondered about the state of her house in New Orleans. I assumed it was unlivable. For all the power she had, I guess even Octavia couldn't undo the damage a hurricane had done. After her references to stairs and increased bathroom needs, I'd revised her age upward, but she still didn't seem any older than, say, sixty-three. That was practically a spring chicken, these days.

I called Octavia and Amelia to the table at six o'clock. I had the table set and the iced tea poured, but I let them serve their own plates from the stove. Not elegant, but it did save on dishes.

We didn't talk a lot as we ate. All three of us were thinking about the evening to come. As much as I disliked her, I was a little worried about Tanya.

I felt funny about the idea of altering someone, but the bottom line was, I needed Tanya off my back and out of my life and the lives of those around me. Or I needed her to get a new attitude about what she was doing in Bon Temps. I couldn't see any way around those facts. In line with my new practicality, I'd realized that if I had to choose between continuing my life with Tanya's interference or continuing my life with Tanya altered, there was no contest.

I cleared the plates away. Normally, if one of us cooked, the other did the dishes, but the two women had magical preparations to make. It was just as well; I wanted to keep busy.

We heard the gravel crunching under the wheels of a truck at 7:05.

When we'd asked him to have her here at seven, I hadn't realized he'd bring her as a parcel.

Calvin carried Tanya in over his shoulder. Tanya was compact, but no featherweight. Calvin was definitely working, but his breathing was nice and even and he hadn't broken a sweat. Tanya's hands and ankles were bound, but I noticed he'd wrapped a scarf under the rope so she wouldn't get chafed. And (thank God) she was gagged, but with a jaunty red bandanna. Yes, the head werepanther definitely had a thing for Tanya.

Of course, she was mad as a disturbed rattler, wriggling and twisting and glaring. She tried to kick Calvin, and he slapped her on her butt. "You stop that now," he said, but not as if he was particularly upset. "You've done wrong; you got to take your medicine."

He'd come in the front door, and now he dumped Tanya on the couch.

The witches had drawn some things in chalk on the floor of the living room, a process that hadn't found much favor with me. Amelia had assured me she could clean it all up, and since she was a champion cleaner, I'd let them proceed.

There were various piles of things (I really didn't want to look too closely) set around in bowls. Octavia lit the material in one bowl and carried it over to Tanya. She wafted the smoke toward Tanya with her hand. I took an extra step back, and Calvin, who was standing behind the couch and holding Tanya by the shoulders, turned his head. Tanya held her breath as long as she could.

After breathing the smoke, she relaxed.

"She needs to be sitting there," Octavia said, pointing to an area circled by chalky symbols. Calvin plonked Tanya down on a straight-backed chair in the middle. She stayed put, thanks to the mysterious smoke.

Octavia started chanting in a language I didn't understand. Amelia's spells had always been in Latin, or at least a primitive form of it (she'd told me that), but I thought Octavia was more diverse. She was speaking something that sounded entirely different.

I'd been very nervous about this ritual, but it turned out to be pretty boring unless you were one of the participants. I wished I could open the windows to get the smell of the smoke out of the house, and I was glad Amelia had thought to take the batteries out of the smoke detectors. Tanya was clearly feeling something, but I wasn't sure it was the removal of the Pelt effect.

"Tanya Grissom," Octavia said, "yank the roots of evil out of your soul and remove yourself from the influence of those who would use you for evil ends." Octavia made several gestures over

Tanya while holding a curious item that looked awfully like a human bone wound around with a vine. I tried not to wonder where she'd gotten the bone.

Tanya squealed beneath her gag, and her back arched alarmingly. Then she relaxed.

Amelia made a gesture, and Calvin bent over to untie the red bandanna that had made Tanya look like a small bandit. He pulled another handkerchief, a clean white one, out of Tanya's mouth. She'd definitely been abducted with affection and consideration.

"I can't believe you're doing this to me!" Tanya shrieked the second her mouth would work. "I can't believe you kidnapped me like a caveman, you big jerk!" If her hands had been free, Calvin would have taken a pummeling. "And what the hell is up with this smoke? Sookie, are you trying to burn your house down? Hey, woman, would you get that crap out of my face?" Tanya batted at the vine-wrapped bone with her bound hands.

"I'm Octavia Fant."

"Well, goody, Octavia Fant. Get me out of these ropes!"

Octavia and Amelia exchanged glances.

Tanya appealed to me. "Sookie, tell these nuts to let me go! Calvin, I was halfway interested in you before you tied me up and dumped me here! What did you think you were doing?"

"Saving your life," Calvin said. "You ain't gonna run now, are you? We got some talking to do."

"Okay," Tanya said slowly, as she realized (I could hear her) that something serious was afoot. "What's all this about?"

"Sandra Pelt," I said.

"Yeah, I know Sandra. What about her?"

"What's your connection?" Amelia asked.

"What's your interest, Amy?" Tanya countered.

"Amelia," I corrected, sitting on the big ottoman in front of Tanya. "And you need to answer this question."

Tanya gave me a sharp look—she had a repertoire of them—and said, "I used to have a cousin who was adopted by the Pelts, and Sandra was my cousin's adopted sister."

"Do you have a close friendship with Sandra?" I said.

"No, not especially. I haven't seen her in a while."

"You didn't make a bargain with her recently?"

"No, Sandra and I don't see each other too much."

"What do you think of her?" Octavia asked.

"I think she's a double-barreled bitch. But I sort of admire her," Tanya said. "If Sandra wants something, she goes after it." She shrugged. "She's kind of extreme for my taste."

"So if she told you to ruin someone's life, you wouldn't do it?" Octavia was eyeing Tanya intently.

"I got better fish to fry than that," Tanya said. "She can go around ruining lives on her own, if she wants to do it so bad."

"You wouldn't be a part of that?"

"No," Tanya said. She was sincere, I could tell. In fact, she was beginning to get anxious at our line of questioning. "Ah, have I done something bad to somebody?"

"I think you got in a little over your head," Calvin said. "These nice ladies have intervened. Amelia and Miss Octavia are, ah, wise women. And you know Sookie already."

"Yeah, I know Sookie." Tanya gave me a sour look. "She won't make friends with me no matter what I do."

Well, yeah, I didn't want you close enough to stab me in the back, I thought, but I didn't say anything.

"Tanya, you've taken my sister-in-law shopping a little too much lately," I said.

Tanya burst into laughter. "Too much retail therapy for the pregnant bride?" she said. But then she looked puzzled. "Yeah, it does seem like we went to the mall in Monroe too many times for my checkbook. Where'd I get the money? I don't even like shopping that much. Why'd I do that?"

"You're not going to do it anymore," Calvin said.

"You don't tell me what I'm going to do, Calvin Norris!" Tanya shot back. "I won't go shopping because I don't want to go, not because you tell me not to."

Calvin looked relieved.

Amelia and Octavia looked relieved.

We all nodded simultaneously. This was Tanya, all right. And she seemed to be minus the destructive guidance of Sandra Pelt. I didn't know if Sandra had whipped up some witchcraft of her own, or if she'd just offered Tanya a lot of money and talked her into thinking Debbie's death was my fault, but the witches appeared to have been successful in excising the tainted Sandra portion of Tanya's character.

I felt oddly deflated at this easy—easy to me, that is—removal of a real thorn in my side. I found myself wishing we could abduct Sandra Pelt and reprogram her, too. I didn't think she'd be as easy to convert. There had been some big pathology going on in the Pelt family.

The witches were happy. Calvin was pleased. I was relieved. Calvin told Tanya he was going to take her back to Hotshot. The somewhat-puzzled Tanya made her departure with a lot more dignity than her entrance. She didn't understand why she'd been in my house and she didn't seem to remember what the witches had done. But she also didn't seem upset about that confusion in her memory.

The best of all possible worlds.

Maybe Jason and Crystal could work things out now that Tanya's pernicious influence was gone. After all, Crystal had really wanted to marry Jason, and she had seemed genuinely pleased that she was pregnant again. Why she was so discontented now ... I simply didn't get it.

I could add her to the long list of people I didn't understand.

While the witches cleaned up the living room with the windows open—though it was a chilly night, I wanted to get rid of the lingering smell of the herbs—I sprawled on my bed with a book. I found I wasn't focused enough to read. Finally, I decided to go outside, and I threw on a hoody and called to Amelia to let her know. I sat in one of the wooden chairs Amelia and I had bought at Wal-Mart at end-of-summer clearance-sale prices, and I admired the matching table with its umbrella all over again. I reminded myself to take the umbrella down and cover the furniture for the winter. Then I leaned back and let go of my thoughts.

For a while it was nice to simply be outside, smelling the

trees and the ground, hearing a whip-poor-will give its enig-matic call from the surrounding woods. The security light made me feel safe, though I knew that was an illusion. If there's light, you can just see what's coming for you a little more clearly.

Bill stepped out of the woods and strolled silently over to the yard set. He sat in one of the other chairs.

We didn't speak for several moments. I didn't feel the surge of anguish I'd felt over the past few months when he was around. He barely disturbed the fall night with his presence, he was so much a part of it.

"Selah has moved to Little Rock," he said.

"How come?"

"She got a position with a large firm," he said. "It was what she told me she wanted. They specialize in vampire properties."

"She hooked on vamps?"

"I believe so. Not my doing."

"Weren't you her first?" Maybe I sounded a little bitter. He'd been my first, in every way.

"Don't," he said, and turned his face toward me. It was radiantly pale. "No," he said finally. "I was not her first. And I always knew it was the vampire in me that attracted her, not the person who was a vampire."

I understood what he was saying. When I'd learned he'd been ordered to ingratiate himself with me, I'd felt it was the telepath in me that had gotten his attention, not the woman who was the telepath. "What goes around, comes around," I said.

"I never cared about her," he said. "Or very little." He shrugged. "There've been so many like her."

FROM DEAD TO WORSE

"I'm not sure how you think this is going to make me feel."

"I'm only telling you the truth. There has been only one you." And then he got up and walked back into the woods, human slow, letting me watch him leave.

Apparently Bill was conducting a kind of stealth campaign to win back my regard. I wondered if he dreamed I could love him again. I still felt pain when I thought of the night I'd learned the truth. I figured my regard would be the outer limits of what he could hope to earn. Trust, love? I couldn't see that happening.

I sat outside for a few more minutes, thinking about the evening I'd just had. One enemy agent down. The enemy herself to go. Then I thought of the police search for the missing people, all Weres, in Shreveport. I wondered when they'd give up.

Surely I wouldn't have to deal with Were politics again any time soon; the survivors would be absorbed in setting their house in order.

I hoped Alcide was enjoying being the leader, and I wondered if he'd succeeded in creating yet another little purebred Were the night of the takeover. I wondered who had taken the Furnan children.

As long as I was speculating, I wondered where Felipe de Castro had established his headquarters in Louisiana or if he'd stayed in Vegas. I wondered if anyone had told Bubba that Louisiana was under a new regime, and I wondered if I'd ever see him again. He had one of the most famous faces in the world, but his head had been sadly addled by being brought over at the last possible second by a vampire working in the morgue in Memphis. Bubba had not weathered Katrina well; he'd gotten cut off from the other New Orleans vampires and had had to subsist on rats and small animals (left-behind pet cats, I suspected) until he'd been rescued one night by a search party of Baton Rouge vamps. The last I'd heard, they'd had to send him out of state for rest and recuperation. Maybe he'd wind up in Vegas. He'd always done well in Vegas, when he was alive.

Suddenly, I realized I was stiff with sitting so long, and the night had grown uncomfortably cold. My jacket wasn't doing the job. It was time to go inside and go to bed. The rest of the house was dark, and I figured Octavia and Amelia were exhausted by their witch work.

I heaved myself up from the chair, let the umbrella down, and opened the toolshed door, leaning the umbrella against a bench where the man I'd thought was my grandfather had made repairs. I shut the toolshed door, feeling I was shutting summer inside.

Chapter 18

After a quiet and peaceful Monday off, I went in Tuesday to work the lunch shift. When I'd left home, Amelia had been painting a chest of drawers she'd found at the local junk store. Octavia had been trimming the dead heads off the roses. She'd said they needed pruning back for the winter, and I'd told her to have at it. My grandmother had been the rose person in our household, and she hadn't let me lay a finger on them unless they needed spraying for aphids. That had been one of my jobs.

Jason came into Merlotte's for lunch with a bunch of his coworkers. They put two tables together and formed a cluster of happy men. Cooler weather and no big storms made for happy parish road crews. Jason seemed almost overly animated, his brain a jumble of leaping thoughts. Maybe having the pernicious influence of Tanya erased had already made a difference.

But I made a real effort to stay out of his head, because after all, he was my brother.

When I carried a big tray of Cokes and tea over to the table, Jason said, "Crystal says hey."

"How's she feeling today?" I asked, to show proper concern, and Jason made a circle of his forefinger and thumb. I served the last mug of tea, careful to put it down evenly so it wouldn't spill, and I asked Dove Beck, a cousin of Alcee's, if he wanted any extra lemon.

"No, thanks," he said politely. Dove, who'd gotten married the day after graduation, was a whole different kettle of fish from Alcee. At thirty, he was younger, and as far as I could tell—and I could tell pretty far—he didn't have that inner core of anger that the detective did. I'd gone to school with one of Dove's sisters.

"How's Angela?" I asked him, and he smiled.

"She married Maurice Kershaw," he said. "They got a little boy, cutest kid in the world. Angela's a new woman—she don't smoke or drink, and she's in church when the doors open."

"I'm glad to hear that. Tell her I asked," I said, and began taking orders. I heard Jason telling his buddies about a fence he was going to build, but I didn't have time to pay attention.

Jason lingered after the other men were going out to their vehicles. "Sook, would you run by and check on Crystal when you get off?"

"Sure, but won't you be leaving work then?"

"I got to go over to Clarice and pick up some chain-link. Crystal wants us to fence in some of the backyard for the baby. So it'll have a safe place to play."

I was surprised that Crystal was showing that much foresight and maternal instinct. Maybe having the baby would change her. I thought about Angela Kershaw and her little boy.

I didn't want to count up how many girls younger than me had been married for years and had babies—or just had the babies. I told myself envy was a sin, and I worked hard, smiling and nodding to everyone. Luckily, it was a busy day. During the afternoon lull, Sam asked me to help him take inventory in the storeroom while Holly covered the bar and the floor. We only had our two resident alcoholics to serve, so Holly was not going to have to work very hard. Since I was very nervous with Sam's Blackberry, he entered the totals while I counted, and I had to climb up on a stepladder and then back down about fifty times, counting and dusting. We bought our cleaning supplies in bulk. We counted all those, too. Sam was just a counting fool today.

The storeroom doesn't have any windows, so it got pretty warm in there while we were working. I was glad to get out of its stuffy confines when Sam was finally satisfied. I pulled a spiderweb out of his hair as I went by on my way to the bathroom, where I scrubbed my hands and carefully wiped my face, checking my ponytail (as best I could) for any spiderwebs I might have picked up myself.

As I left the bar, I was so looking forward to getting in the shower that I almost turned left to go home. Just in time, I remembered I'd promised to look in on Crystal, so I turned right instead.

Jason lived in my parents' house, and he'd kept it up very nicely. My brother was a house-proud kind of guy. He didn't mind spending his free time on painting, mowing, and basic repairs, a side of him I always found a bit surprising. He'd recently painted the outside a buff color and the trim a glowing white, and the little house looked very spruce. There was a driveway that made a U shape in front. He'd added a branch that led to the porte cochere in back of the house, but I pulled up to the front steps. I stuffed my car keys in my pocket and crossed the porch. I turned the knob because I planned on sticking my head in the door and calling to Crystal, since I was family. The front door was unlocked, as most front doors were during the daytime. The family room was empty.

"Hey, Crystal, it's Sookie!" I called, though I tried to keep my voice subdued so I wouldn't startle her if she were napping.

I heard a muffled sound, a moan. It came from the biggest bedroom, the one my parents had used, which lay across the family room and to my right.

Oh, shit, she's miscarrying again, I thought, and dashed to the closed door. I flung it open so hard it bounced off the wall, but I didn't pay a bit of attention, because bouncing on the bed were Crystal and Dove Beck.

I was so shocked, so angry, and so distraught that as they stopped what they were doing and stared up at me, I said the worst thing I could think of. "No wonder you lose all your babies." I spun on my heel and marched out of the house. I was so outraged I couldn't even get in the car. It was really unfortunate that Calvin pulled up behind me and leaped from his truck almost before it stopped.

"My God, what's wrong?" he said. "Is Crystal okay?"

"Why don't you ask her that?" I said nastily, and climbed into my car only to sit there shaking. Calvin ran into the house as if he had to put out a fire, and I guess that was about the size of it.

"Jason, *dammit*," I yelled, thumping my fist on my steering wheel. I should have taken the time to listen to Jason's brain. He'd known good and well that since he had business in Clarice, Dove and Crystal would probably take the opportunity to have a tryst. He'd planned on me being dutiful and dropping by. It was just too big a coincidence that Calvin had shown up. He must have also told Calvin to check on Crystal. So there was no deniability, and no chance of hushing this up—not since Calvin and I both knew. I had been right to worry about the terms of the marriage, and now I had something entirely new to worry about.

Plus, I was ashamed. I was ashamed of the behavior of everyone involved. In my code of conduct, which doesn't really make me a very good Christian at all, what single people do in caring relationships is their own business. Even in a more casual relationship—well, if the people respect one another, okay. But a couple who's promised to be faithful, who's pledged that publicly, are governed by a whole different set of rules, in my world.

Not in Crystal's world, or Dove's world, apparently.

Calvin came back down the steps looking years older than he had when he'd bounded up them. He stopped by my car. He wore an expression twin to mine—disillusion, disappointment, disgust. Lots of *dis*es there.

"I'll be in touch," he said. "We got to have the ceremony now."

Crystal came out on the porch wrapped in a leopard-print bathrobe, and rather than endure her speaking to me I started the car and left as quickly as I could. I drove home in a daze. When I came in the back door, Amelia was chopping up something on the old cutting board, the one that had survived the fire with only scorch marks. She turned to speak to me and had opened her mouth when she saw my face. I shook my head at her, warning her not to talk, and I went straight into my room.

This would have been a good day for me to be living by myself again.

I sat in my room in the little chair in the corner, the one that had seated so many visitors lately. Bob was curled up in a ball on my bed, a place he was expressly forbidden to sleep. Someone had opened my door during the day. I thought about chewing Amelia out about that, then discarded the idea when I saw a pile of clean and folded underwear lying on top of my dresser.

"Bob," I said, and the cat unfolded and leaped to his feet in one fluid movement. He stood on my bed, staring at me with wide golden eyes. "Get the hell out of here," I said. With immense dignity Bob leaped down from the bed and stalked to the door. I opened it a few inches and he went out, managing to leave the impression that he was doing this of his own free will. I shut the door behind him.

I love cats. I just wanted to be by myself.

The phone rang, and I stood up to answer it.

"Tomorrow night," Calvin said. "Wear something comfortable. Seven o'clock." He sounded sad and tired.

"Okay," I said, and we both hung up. I sat there a while longer. Whatever this ceremony consisted of, did I have to be a participant? Yeah, I did. Unlike Crystal, I kept my promises. I'd had to stand up for Jason at his wedding, as his closest relative, as a surrogate to take his punishment if he was unfaithful to his new wife. Calvin had stood up for Crystal. And now look what we'd come to.

I didn't know what was going to happen, but I knew it was going to be awful. Though the werepanthers understood the necessity for breeding each available pure male panther to each available pure female panther (the only way to produce purebred baby panthers), they also believed once the breeding had been given a chance, any partnerships formed should be monogamous. If you didn't want to take that vow, you didn't form a partnership or marry. This was the way they ran their community. Crystal would have absorbed these rules from birth, and Jason had learned them from Calvin before the wedding.

Jason didn't call, and I was glad. I wondered what was happening at his house, but only in a dull kind of way. When had Crystal met Dove Beck? Did Dove's wife know about this? I wasn't surprised that Crystal had cheated on Jason, but I was a little astonished at her choice.

I decided that Crystal had wanted to make her betrayal as emphatic as it could possibly be. She was saying, "I'll have sex with someone else while I'm carrying your child. And he'll be older than you, and a different race from you, and he'll even work for you!" Twisting the knife in deeper with every layer.

If this was retaliation for the damn cheeseburger, I'd say she'd gotten a steak-size vengeance.

Because I didn't want to seem like I was sulking, I came out for supper, which was lowly and comforting tuna noodle casserole with peas and onions. After stacking the dishes for Octavia to take care of, I retreated back to my room. The two witches were practically tiptoeing up and down the hall because they were so anxious not to disturb me, though of course they were dying to ask me what the problem was.

But they didn't; God bless them. I really couldn't have explained. I was too mortified.

I said about a million prayers before I went to sleep that night, but none of them ended up making me feel any better.

I went to work the next day because I had to. Staying home wouldn't have made me feel any better. I was profoundly glad Jason didn't come into Merlotte's, because I would have thrown a mug at him if he had.

Sam eyed me carefully several times and finally he drew me behind the bar with him. "Tell me what's happening," he said.

Tears flooded my eyes, and I was within an ace of making a real scene. I squatted down hastily, as if I'd dropped something on the floor, and I said, "Sam, please don't ask me. I'm too upset to talk about it." Suddenly, I realized it would be a big comfort to tell Sam, but I just couldn't, not in the crowded bar.

"Hey, you know I'm here if you need me." His face was serious. He patted my shoulder.

I was so lucky to have him for a boss.

His gesture reminded me that I had lots of friends who would not dishonor themselves as Crystal had done. Jason had dishonored himself, too, by forcing Calvin and me to witness her cheap betrayal. I had so many friends who would not do such a thing! It was a trick of fate that the one who would was my own brother.

This thought made me feel better and stronger.

I actually had a backbone by the time I got home. No one else was there. I hesitated, wondering whether I could call Tara or beg Sam to take an hour off, or even call Bill to go with me to Hotshot . . . but that was just weakness talking. This was something I had to do by myself. Calvin had warned me to wear something comfortable and not to dress up, and my Merlotte's outfit was certainly both those things. But it seemed wrong to wear my work clothes to an event like this. There might be blood. I didn't know what to anticipate. I pulled on yoga pants and an old gray sweatshirt. I made sure my hair was pulled back. I looked like I was dressed to clean out my closets.

On the drive to Hotshot, I turned up the radio and sang at the top of my lungs to keep myself from thinking. I harmonized with Evanescence and agreed with the Dixie Chicks that I wasn't going to back down . . . a good spine-stiffening song to listen to.

I reached Hotshot well before seven. I'd last been out here at Jason and Crystal's wedding, where I'd danced with Quinn. That visit of Quinn's had been the only time he and I had been intimate. In hindsight, I regretted having taken that step. It had been a mistake. I'd been banking on a future that never came to pass. I'd jumped the gun. I hoped I'd never make that mistake again.

I parked, as I had the night of Jason's wedding, by the side of the road. There weren't nearly as many cars here tonight as there had been then, when many plain human people had been guests. But there were a few extra vehicles. I recognized Jason's truck. The others belonged to the few werepanthers who didn't live in Hotshot.

A little crowd had already assembled in the backyard of Calvin's house. People made way for me until I'd gotten to the center of the gathering and found Crystal, Jason, and Calvin. I saw some familiar faces. A middle-aged panther named Maryelizabeth nodded to me. I saw her daughter nearby. The girl, whose name I couldn't remember, was by no means the only underage observer. I got that creepy feeling that raised the hairs on my arms, the way I did every time I tried to picture everyday life in Hotshot.

Calvin was staring down at his boots, and he didn't look up. Jason didn't meet my eyes, either. Only Crystal was upright and defiant, her dark eyes catching mine, daring me to stare her down. I did dare, and after a moment she dropped her gaze to somewhere in the middle distance.

Maryelizabeth had a tattered old book in her hand, and she opened it to a page she'd marked with a torn piece of newspaper. The community seemed to still and settle. This was the purpose for which they'd assembled.

"We people of the fang and claw are here because one of us broke her vows," Maryelizabeth read. "At the marriage of

Crystal and Jason, werepanthers of this community, they each promised to remain true to their marriage vows, both in the way of the cat and the way of the human. Crystal's surrogate was her uncle Calvin, and Jason's was his sister, Sookie."

I was aware of the eyes of all the assembled community moving from Calvin to me. A lot of those eyes were golden yellow. Inbreeding in Hotshot had produced some slightly alarming results.

"Now that Crystal has broken her vows, a fact witnessed by the surrogates, her uncle has offered to take the punishment since Crystal is pregnant."

This was going to be even nastier than I'd suspected.

"Since Calvin takes Crystal's place, Sookie, do you choose to take Jason's place?"

Oh, *crap*. I looked at Calvin and I knew my whole face was asking him if there was any way out of this. And his whole face told me no. He actually looked sorry for me.

I would never forgive my brother—or Crystal—for this.

"Sookie," Maryelizabeth prompted.

"What would I have to do?" I said, and if I sounded sullen and grudging and angry, I thought I had a good reason.

Maryelizabeth opened the book again and read the answer. "We exist by our wits and our claws, and if faith is broken, a claw is broken," she said.

I stared at her, trying to make sense of that.

"Either you or Jason has to break Calvin's finger," she said simply. "In fact, since Crystal broke the faith completely, you have to break two, at least. More would be better. Jason gets to pick, I guess."

More would be better. Jesus Christ, Shepherd of Judea. I tried to be dispassionate. Who could cause the most damage to my friend Calvin? My brother, no doubt about it. If I was a true friend to Calvin, I would do this. Could I bring myself to? And then it was taken out of my hands.

Jason said, "I didn't think it would happen this way, Sookie." He sounded simultaneously angry, confused, and defensive. "If Calvin stands in for Crystal, I want Sookie to stand in for me," he told Maryelizabeth. I never thought I could hate my own brother, but at that moment I found out it was possible.

"So be it," said Maryelizabeth.

I tried to boost myself up mentally. After all, this wasn't maybe quite as bad as I'd anticipated. I'd pictured Calvin being whipped or having to whip Crystal. Or we might have had to do some awful thing involving knives; that would have been way worse.

I tried to believe this might not be so bad right up until the time two of the males carried out a pair of concrete blocks and put them on top of the picnic table.

And then Maryelizabeth produced a brick. She held it out to me.

I began to shake my head involuntarily because I felt a heavy twinge in my stomach. Nausea did flip-flops in my belly. Looking at the common red brick, I began to have an idea what this was going to cost me.

Calvin stepped forward and took my hand. He leaned over to talk very close to my ear. "Darlin'," he said, "you have to do this. I accepted this, when I stood up for her when she married.

And I knew what she was. And you know Jason. This might easily have been the other way 'round. I might be about to do this to you. And you don't heal as well. This is better. And it has to be. Our people require this." He straightened and looked me right in the eyes. His own were golden, utterly strange, and quite steady.

I pinched my lips together, and I made myself nod. Calvin gave me a bracing look and took his place by the table. He put his hand on the concrete blocks. With no further ado, Maryelizabeth handed me the brick. The rest of the panthers waited patiently for me to perform the punishment. The vampires would have dressed this all up with a special wardrobe and probably an extraspecial fancy brick from an old temple or something, but not the panthers. It was just a damn brick. I held it with both hands gripping one long side.

After I'd looked at it for a long minute, I said to Jason. "I don't want to talk to you again. Ever." I faced Crystal. "I hope you enjoyed it, bitch," I said, and I turned as quick as I could and brought the brick down on Calvin's hand.

Chapter 19

Amelia and Octavia hovered around for two days before they decided leaving me alone was the best policy. Reading their anxious thoughts just made me surlier, because I didn't want to accept comfort. I should suffer for what I'd done, and that meant I couldn't accept any easing of my misery. So I gloomed and sulked and brooded and rained my grim mood all over my house.

My brother came into the bar once, and I turned my back on him. Dove Beck didn't choose to drink at Merlotte's, which was a good thing, though he was the least guilty of the bunch as far as I was concerned—though that didn't make him any clean Gene. When Alcee Beck came in, it was clear his brother had confided in him, because Alcee looked even angrier than usual, and he met my eyes every chance he got, just to let me know he was my equal.

Thank God, Calvin didn't show. I couldn't have stood it. I heard enough talk around the bar from his coworkers at Norcross about the accident he'd had while he was working on his truck at home.

Most unexpectedly, on the third night Eric walked into Merlotte's. I took one look at him and suddenly my throat seemed to ease and I felt tears well up in my eyes. But Eric walked through as though he owned the place, and he went into the hall to Sam's office. Moments later Sam stuck his head out and beckoned to me.

After I walked in, I didn't expect Sam to shut the office door.

"What's wrong?" Sam asked me. He'd been trying to find out for days, and I'd been fending off his well-meant queries.

Eric was standing to one side, his arms crossed over his chest. He made a gesture with one hand that said, "Tell us; we're waiting." Despite his brusqueness, his presence relaxed the big knot inside me, the one that had kept the words locked in my stomach.

"I broke Calvin Norris's hand into bits," I said. "With a brick."

"Then he was . . . He stood up for your sister-in-law at the wedding," Sam said, figuring it out quickly. Eric looked blank. The vampires know something about the wereanimals—they have to—but the vamps think they are far superior, so they don't make an effort to learn specifics about the rituals and rhythms of being a were.

"She had to break his hand, which represents his claws in

panther form," Sam explained impatiently. "She stood up for Jason." And then Sam and Eric exchanged a look that scared me in its complete agreement. Neither of them liked Jason one little bit.

Sam looked from me to Eric as if he expected Eric to do something to make me feel better. "I don't belong to him," I said sharply, since all this was making me feel handled in a major way. "Did you think Eric coming would make me all happy and carefree?"

"No," Sam said, sounding a little angry himself. "But I hoped it would help you talk about whatever was wrong."

"What's wrong," I said very quietly. "Okay, what's wrong is that my brother arranged for Calvin and me to check on Crystal, who's about four months pregnant, and he fixed it so we'd get there at about the same time. And when we checked, we found Crystal in bed with Dove Beck. As Jason knew we would."

Eric said, "And for this, you had to break the werepanther's fingers." He might have been asking if I'd had to wear chicken bones and turn around three times, it was so obvious he was inquiring into the quaint customs of a primitive tribe.

"Yes, Eric, that's what I had to do," I said grimly. "I had to break my friend's fingers with a brick in front of a crowd."

For the first time Eric seemed to realize that he'd taken the wrong approach. Sam was looking at him in total exasperation. "And I thought you'd be such a big help," he said.

"I have a few things going in Shreveport," Eric answered with a shade of defensiveness. "Including hosting the new king."

Sam muttered something that sounded suspiciously like, "Fucking vampires."

This was totally unfair. I'd expected tons of sympathy when I finally confessed the reason for my bad mood. But now Sam and Eric were so wrapped up in being irritated with each other that neither one of them was giving me a moment's thought. "Well, thanks, guys," I said. "This has been a lot of fun. Eric, big help there—I appreciate the kind words." And I left in what my grandmother called high dudgeon. I stomped back out into the bar and waited on tables so grimly that some people were scared to call me over to order more drinks.

I decided to clean the surfaces behind the bar, because Sam was still in his office with Eric . . . though possibly Eric had left out the back door. I scrubbed and polished and pulled some beers for Holly, and I straightened everything so meticulously that Sam might have a wee problem finding things. Just for a week or two.

Then Sam came out to take his place, looked at the counter in mute displeasure, and jerked his head to indicate I should get the hell out from behind the bar. My bad mood was catching.

You know how it is sometimes, when someone really tries to cheer you up? When you just decide that by golly, nothing in the world is going to make you feel better? Sam had thrown Eric at me like he was throwing a happy pill, yet he was aggravated that I hadn't swallowed it. Instead of being grateful that Sam was fond enough of me to call Eric, I was mad at him for his assumption.

I was in a totally black mood.

Quinn was gone. I'd banished him. Stupid mistake or wise decision? Verdict still out.

Lots of Weres were dead in Shreveport because of Priscilla, and I'd watched some of them die. Believe me, that sticks with you.

More than a few vampires were dead, too, including some I'd known fairly well.

My brother was a devious manipulative bastard.

My great-grandfather wasn't ever going to take me fishing.

Okay, now I was getting silly. Suddenly, I smiled, because I was picturing the prince of the fairies in old denim overalls and a Bon Temps Hawks baseball cap, carrying a can of worms and a couple of fishing poles.

I caught Sam's eye as I cleared a table of plates. I winked at him.

He turned away, shaking his head, but I caught a hint of a smile at the corners of his mouth.

And just like that, my bad mood was officially over. My common sense kicked in. There was no point in lashing myself over the Hotshot incident any longer. I'd had to do what I'd had to do. Calvin understood that better than I did. My brother was an asshole, and Crystal was a whore. These were facts I had to deal with. Granted, they were both unhappy people who were acting out because they were married to the wrong spouse, but they were also both chronologically adults, and I couldn't fix their marriage any more than I'd been able to prevent it.

The Weres had dealt with their own problems in their own way, and I'd done my best to help them. Vampires, ditto... sort of.

Okay. Not *all* better, but enough better.

When I got off work, I wasn't completely annoyed to find Eric waiting by my car. He seemed to be enjoying the night, standing all by himself in the cold. I was shivering myself because I hadn't brought a heavy jacket. My Windbreaker wasn't enough.

"It's been nice to be by myself for a while," Eric said unexpectedly.

"I guess at Fangtasia you're always surrounded," I said.

"Always surrounded by people wanting things," he said.

"But you enjoy that, right? Being the big kahuna?"

Eric looked like he was mulling that over. "Yes, I like that. I like being the boss. I don't like being...overseen. Is that a word? I'll be glad when Felipe de Castro and his minion Sandy take their departure. Victor will stay to take over New Orleans."

Eric was *sharing.* This was almost unprecedented. This was like a normal give-and-take between equals.

"What's the new king like?" Cold as I was, I couldn't resist keeping the conversation going.

"He's handsome, ruthless, and clever," Eric said.

"Like you." I could have slapped myself.

Eric nodded after a moment. "But more so," Eric said grimly. "I'll have to keep very alert to stay ahead of him."

"How gratifying to hear you say so," said an accented voice.

This was definitely an *Oh, shit!* moment. (An OSM, as I called them to myself.) A gorgeous man stepped out from the trees, and I blinked as I took him in. As Eric bowed, I scanned

Felipe de Castro from his gleaming shoes to his bold face. As I bowed, too, belatedly, I realized that Eric hadn't been exaggerating when he said the new king was handsome. Felipe de Castro was a Latin male who threw Jimmy Smits into the shade, and I am a big admirer of Mr. Smits. Though perhaps five foot ten or so, Castro carried himself with such importance and straight posture that you couldn't think of him as short—rather, he made other men look too tall. His dark thick hair was clipped close to his head, and he had a mustache and chin strip. He had caramel skin and dark eyes, strong arched eyebrows, a bold nose. The king wore a cape—no kidding, a real full-length black cape. I'll tell you how impressive he was; I didn't even think of giggling. Other than the cape, he seemed dressed for a night that might include flamenco dancing, with a white shirt, black vest, and black dress slacks. One of Castro's ears was pierced, and there was a dark stone in it. The overhead security light didn't let me get a better idea of what it might be. Ruby? Emerald?

I'd straightened up and I was staring again. But when I glanced at Eric, I saw he was still bowing. Ah-oh. Well, I wasn't one of his subjects and I wasn't going to do that again. It had gone against my Americanness to do it once.

"Hi, I'm Sookie Stackhouse," I said, since the silence was getting awkward. I automatically held out my hand, remembered vamps didn't shake, and snatched it back. "Excuse me," I said.

The king inclined his head. "Miss Stackhouse," he said, his accent strumming my name delightfully. ("Meees Stekhuss.")

"Yes, sir. I'm sorry to meet you and run, but it's really cold out here and I need to get home." I beamed at him, my lunatic beam I give when I'm really nervous. "Good-bye, Eric," I babbled, and stood on tiptoe to kiss him on the cheek. "Give me a call when you have a minute. Unless you need me to stay, for some crazy reason?"

"No, lover, you need to go home and get into the warmth," Eric said, clasping both my hands in his. "I'll call you when my work permits."

When he let go of me, I did an awkward sort of dip in the king's direction (American! Not used to bowing!) and hopped into my car before either vampire could change his mind about my departure. I felt like a coward—a very relieved coward—as I backed out of my space and drove out of the parking lot. But I was already debating the wisdom of my departure as I turned onto Hummingbird Road.

I was worried about Eric. This was a fairly new phenomenon, one that made me very uneasy, and it had started the night of the coup. Worrying about Eric was like worrying about the well-being of a rock or a tornado. When had I ever had to worry about him before? He was one of the most powerful vampires I'd ever met. But Sophie-Anne had been even more powerful and protected by the huge warrior Sigebert, and look what had happened to her. I felt abruptly, acutely miserable. What was wrong with me?

I had a terrible idea. Maybe I was worried simply because Eric was worried? Miserable because Eric was miserable? Could I receive his emotions this strongly and from this great a distance? Should I turn around and find out what was happening? If the king was being cruel to Eric, I couldn't possibly be of any assistance. I had to pull over to the side of the road. I couldn't drive anymore.

I'd never had a panic attack, but I thought I was having one now. I was paralyzed with indecision; again, not one of my usual characteristics. Struggling with myself, trying to think clearly, I realized I had to turn back whether I wanted to or not. It was an obligation I couldn't ignore, not because I was bonded to Eric, but because I liked him.

I turned the wheel and did a U-turn in the middle of Hummingbird Road. Since I'd seen only two cars since I'd left the bar, the maneuver was no big traffic violation. I drove back a lot faster than I'd left, and when I got to Merlotte's, I found that the customer parking lot was completely empty. I parked in front and pulled my old softball bat out from under the seat. My grandmother had given it to me for my sixteenth birthday. It was a very good bat, though it had seen better days. I crept around the building, taking advantage of the bushes that grew at the foundation for cover. Nandinas. I hate nandinas. They're straggly and ugly and leggy, and I'm allergic to them. Though I was covered with a Windbreaker, pants, and socks, the minute I began threading my way among the plants, my nose began to run.

I peeked around the corner very cautiously.

I was so shocked I couldn't believe what I was seeing.

Sigebert, the queen's bodyguard, had *not* been killed in the coup. No, sirree, he was still among the undead. And he was here in the Merlotte's parking lot, and he was having a lot of fun with the new king, Felipe de Castro, and with Eric, and with Sam, who had been swept up in the net probably by simply leaving his bar to walk to his trailer.

I took a deep breath—a deep but *silent* breath—and made myself analyze what I was seeing. Sigebert was a mountain of a man, and he'd been the queen's muscle for centuries. His brother, Wybert, had died in the queen's service, and I was sure Sigebert had been a target of the Nevada vamps; they'd left their mark on him. Vampires heal fast, but Sigebert had been wounded badly enough that even days after he'd fought, he was still visibly damaged. There was a huge cut across his forehead and a horrible-looking mark just above where I thought his heart would be. His clothes were ripped and stained and filthy. Maybe the Nevada vamps thought he'd disintegrated when in fact he'd managed to get away and hide. *Not important,* I told myself.

The important part was that he'd succeeded in binding both Eric and Felipe de Castro with silver chains. How? *Not important,* I told myself again. Maybe this tendency to mentally wander was coming from Eric, who was looking much more battered than the king. Of course, Sigebert would see Eric as a traitor.

Eric was bleeding from the head and his arm was clearly broken. Castro was bleeding sluggishly from the mouth, so Sigebert had maybe stomped on him. Eric and Castro were both lying on the ground, and in the harsh security light they both looked whiter than snow. Sam had been tied to the bumper of his own truck somehow, and he wasn't damaged at all, at least so far. Thank God.

I tried to figure out how I could conquer Sigebert with my aluminum softball bat, but I didn't come up with any good ideas. If I rushed him, he'd just laugh. Even as grievously wounded as he was, he was still a vampire and I was no match for him unless I had a great idea. So I watched, and I waited, but in the end I couldn't stand to see him hurting Eric anymore; believe me, when a vampire kicks you, you get plenty hurt. Plus, Sigebert was having a great time with the big knife he had brought.

The biggest weapon at my disposal? Okay, that would be my car. I felt a little pang of regret, because it was the best car I'd ever had, and Tara had sold it to me for a dollar when she'd gotten a newer one. But it was the only thing I could think of that would make a dent in Sigebert.

So back I crept, praying that Sigebert would be so absorbed in his torture that he wouldn't notice the sound of the car door. I laid my head on the steering wheel and thought as hard as I've ever thought. I considered the parking lot and its topography, and I thought about the location of the bound vampires, and I took a deep breath and turned the key. I started around the building, wishing my car could creep through the damn nandina bushes like I had, and I swung wide to allow room to charge, and my lights caught Sigebert, and I hit the accelerator and went straight at him. He tried to get out of the way, but he was none too bright and I'd caught him with his pants down (literally—I really didn't like to think about his next torture plan) and I hit him very hard, and up he bounced, to land on the roof of the car with a huge thud.

I screamed and braked, because this was as far as my plan had gone. He slid down the back of the car, leaving a horrible sheet of dark blood, and disappeared from view. Scared he'd pop up in the rearview mirror, I threw the car into reverse and hit the pedal again. *Bump. Bump.* I yanked the gear stick into park and leaped out, bat in hand, to find Sigebert's legs and most of his torso were wedged under the car. I dashed over to Eric and began fumbling with the silver chain, while he stared at me with his eyes wide. Castro was cursing in Spanish, fluently and fluidly, and Sam was saying, "Hurry, Sookie, hurry!" which really didn't help my powers of concentration.

I gave up on the damn chains and got the big knife and cut Sam free so he could help. The knife came close enough to his skin to make him yelp a time or two, but I was really doing the best I could, and he didn't bleed. To give him credit, he made it over to Castro in record time and began freeing him while I ran back to Eric, laying the knife on the ground beside us as I worked. Now that I had at least one ally who had the use of his hands and legs, I was able to concentrate, and I got Eric's legs unbound (at least now he could run away—I guess that was my thinking) and then, more slowly, his arms and hands. The silver had been wound around him many times, and Sigebert had made sure it touched Eric's hands. They looked ghastly. Castro had suffered even more from the chains because Sigebert had divested him of his beautiful cape and most of his shirt.

I was unwinding the last strand when Eric shoved me as hard as he could, grabbed the knife, and leaped to his feet so swiftly I saw only a blur. Then he was on Sigebert, who had actually lifted the car to release his own trapped legs. He'd begun dragging himself out from under, and in another minute he would have been ambulatory.

Did I mention it was a big knife? And it must have been sharp, too, because Eric landed by Sigebert, said, "Go to your maker," and cut off the warrior vampire's head.

"Oh," I said shakily, and sat down abruptly on the cold parking lot gravel. "Oh, wow." We all remained where we were, panting, for a good five minutes. Then Sam straightened up from the side of Felipe de Castro and offered him a hand. The vampire took it, and when he was upright, he introduced himself to Sam, who automatically introduced himself right back.

"Miss Stackhouse," the king said, "I am in your debt."

Damn straight.

"It's okay," I said in a voice that wasn't nearly as level as it should be.

"Thank you," he said. "If your car is too damaged to repair, I will be very glad to buy you another one."

"Oh, thanks," I said with absolute sincerity, as I stood up. "I'll try to drive it home tonight. I don't know how I can explain the damage. Do you think the body shop would believe I ran over an alligator?" That did happen occasionally. Was it weird that I was worried about the car insurance?

"Dawson would look at it for you," Sam said. His voice was as odd as mine. He, too, had thought he was going to die. "I know he's a motorcycle repairman, but I bet he could fix your car. He works on his own all the time."

"Do what is necessary," said Castro grandly. "I will pay.

Eric, would you care to explain what just happened?" His voice was considerably more acerbic.

"You should ask your crew to explain," Eric retorted, with some justification. "Didn't they tell you Sigebert, the queen's bodyguard, was dead? Yet here he is."

"An excellent point." Castro looked down at the crumbling body. "So that was the legendary Sigebert. He's gone to join his brother, Wybert." He sounded quite pleased.

I hadn't known the brothers were famous among the vampires, but they'd certainly been unique. Their mountainous physiques, their broken and primitive English, their utter devotion to the woman who'd turned them centuries before—sure, any right-minded vampire would love that story. I sagged where I stood, and Eric, moving faster than I could see, picked me up. It was a very Scarlett and Rhett moment, spoiled only by the fact that there were two other guys there, we were in a humdrum parking lot, and I was unhappy about the damage to my car. Plus not a little shocked.

"How'd he get the jump on three strong guys like you-all?" I asked. I didn't worry about Eric holding me. It made me feel tiny, not a feeling I got to enjoy all that often.

There was a moment of general embarrassment.

"I was standing with my back to the woods," Castro explained. "He had the chains arranged for throwing. . . . Your word is almost the same. *Lazo.*"

"Lasso," Sam said.

"Ah, lasso. The first one, he threw around me, and of course, the shock was great. Before Eric could land on him, he had

Eric as well. The pain from the silver...very quickly we were bound. When this one"—he nodded toward Sam—"came to our aid, Sigebert knocked him unconscious and got rope from the back of Sam's truck and tied him up."

"We were too involved in our discussion to be wary," Eric said. He sounded pretty grim, and I didn't blame him. But I decided to keep my mouth shut.

"Ironic, eh, that we needed a human girl to rescue us," the king said blithely, the very idea that I'd decided not to voice.

"Yes, very amusing," Eric said in a dreadfully unamused voice. "Why did you return, Sookie?"

"I felt your, ah, anger at being attacked." For "anger" read "despair."

The new king looked very interested. "A blood bond. How interesting."

"No, not really," I said. "Sam, I wonder if you'd mind driving me home. I don't know where you gentlemen left your cars, or if you flew. I *do* wonder how Sigebert knew where to find you."

Felipe de Castro and Eric shared almost identical expressions of deep thought.

"We'll find out," Eric said, and set me down. "And then heads are going to roll." Eric was good at setting heads to rolling. It was one of his favorite things. I was willing to put my money on Castro sharing that predilection, because the king was looking positively gleeful in anticipation.

Sam fished his keys out of his pocket without a word, and I climbed into the truck with him. We left the two vampires involved in a deep conversation. Sigebert's corpse, still partially under my poor car, was almost gone, leaving a dark greasy residue on the gravel of the parking lot. The good thing about vampires—no corpse disposal.

"I'll call Dawson tonight," Sam said unexpectedly.

"Oh, Sam, thank you," I said. "I'm so glad you were there."

"It's the parking lot of my *bar*," he said, and it might have been my own guilty reaction, but I thought I detected some reproach. I suddenly came to the full realization that Sam had walked into a situation in his own backyard, a situation he had no stake or interest in, and that he'd almost died as a result. And why had Eric been in the parking lot back of Merlotte's? To talk to me. And then Felipe de Castro had followed to talk to Eric . . . though I wasn't sure why. But the point was, them being there at all was my fault.

"Oh, Sam," I said, almost in tears, "I'm so sorry. I didn't know Eric would wait for me, and I sure didn't know the king would follow him. I still don't know why he was there. I'm so sorry," I said again. I would say it a hundred times if it would take that tone out of Sam's voice.

"It's not your fault," he said. "I asked Eric to come here in the first place. It's their fault. I don't know how we can pry you loose from them."

"This was bad, but somehow you're not taking it like I thought you would."

"I just want to be left in peace," he said unexpectedly. "I don't want to get involved in supernatural politics. I don't want to have to take sides in Were shit. I'm not a Were. I'm a shapeshifter, and shifters don't organize. We're too different. I hate vampire politics even more than Were politics."

"You're mad at me."

"No!" He seemed to be struggling with what he wanted to say. "I don't want that for you, either! Weren't you happier before?"

"You mean before I knew any vampires; before I knew about the rest of the world that lies outside the boundaries?"

Sam nodded.

"In some ways. It was nice to have a clear path before me," I said. "I do get really sick of the politics and the battles. But my life wasn't any prize, Sam. Every day was a struggle just to act like I was a regular human, like I didn't know all the things I know about other humans. The cheating and infidelity, the little acts of dishonesty, the unkindness. The really severe judgments people pass on each other. Their lack of charity. When you know all that, it's hard to keep going sometimes. Knowing about the supernatural world puts all that in a different perspective. I don't know why. People aren't any better or worse than the supernaturals, but they're not all there is, either."

"I guess I understand," Sam said, though he sounded a little doubtful.

"Plus," I said very quietly, "it's nice to be valued for the very thing that makes regular people think I'm just a crazy girl."

"Definitely understand that," Sam said. "But there's a price."

"Oh, no doubt about it."

"You willing to pay?"

"So far."

We chugged up my driveway. No lights on. The witchy duo had gone to bed, or else they were out partying or casting spells.

"In the morning, I'll call Dawson," Sam said. "He'll check out your car, make sure you can drive it, or he'll get it towed to his place. Think you can get a ride to work?"

"I'm sure I can," I said. "Amelia can bring me in."

Sam walked me to the back door like he was bringing me home from a date. The porch light was on, which was thoughtful of Amelia. Sam put his arms around me, which was a surprise, and then he just snugged his head in close to mine, and we stood there enjoying each other's warmth for a long moment.

"We survived the Were war," he said. "You made it through the vampire coup. Now we lived through the attack of the berserk bodyguard. I hope we keep up our record."

"Now you're scaring me," I said as I remembered all the other things I'd survived. I should be dead, no doubt about it.

His warm lips brushed my cheek. "Maybe that's a good thing," he said, and turned to go back to his truck.

I watched him climb in and reverse, and then I unlocked the back door and went to my room. After all the adrenaline and the fear and the accelerated pace of life (and death) in the parking lot of Merlotte's, my own room seemed very quiet and clean and secure. I'd done my best to kill someone tonight. It was only by chance Sigebert had survived my attempt at vehicular homicide. Twice. I couldn't help but notice that I wasn't feeling remorseful. This was surely a flaw, but at the moment I just didn't care. There were definitely parts of my character I didn't approve of, and maybe from time to time I had moments when I didn't like myself much. But I got through each day as it came to me, and so far I'd survived everything life had thrown at me. I could only hope that the survival was worth the price I'd paid.

Chapter 20

To my relief, I woke up in an empty house. Neither Amelia's nor Octavia's throbbing heads were under my roof. I lay in bed and reveled in the knowledge. Maybe the next time I had a whole day off, I could spend it completely alone. That didn't seem a likely occurrence, but a girl can dream. After I planned my day (call Sam to find out about my car, pay some bills, go to work), I got into the shower and really scrubbed. I used as much hot water as I wanted. I painted my toenails and my fingernails, and I pulled on a pair of sweatpants and a T-shirt and went in to make some coffee. The kitchen was spanking clean; God bless Amelia.

The coffee was great, the toast delicious spread with blueberry jam. Even my taste buds were happy. After I cleaned up from breakfast, I was practically singing with the pleasure of solitude. I went back to my room to make my bed and put on my makeup.

Of course, that was when the knock came at the back door, nearly making me jump out of my skin. I stepped into some shoes and went to answer it.

Tray Dawson was there, and he was smiling. "Sookie, your car is doing fine," he said. "I had to do a little replacing here and there, and it's the first time I ever had to scrape vampire ash off an undercarriage, but you're good to go."

"Oh, thanks! Can you come in?"

"Just for a minute," he said. "You got a Coke in the refrigerator?"

"I sure do." I brought him a Coke, asked if he wanted some cookies or a peanut butter sandwich to go with it, and when he'd turned that down, I excused myself to finish my makeup. I'd figured Dawson would run me to the car, but he'd driven it over to my place, as it turned out, so I'd need to give him a ride instead.

I had my checkbook out and my pen in hand when I sat at the table opposite the big man and asked him how much I owed him.

"Not a dime," Dawson said. "The new guy paid for it."

"The new king?"

"Yeah, he called me in the middle of the night last night. Told me the story, more or less, and asked me if I could look at the car first thing in the morning. I was awake when he called, so it didn't make me no nevermind. I got over to Merlotte's this morning, told Sam he wasted a phone call since I already knew all about it. I followed him while he drove the car out to my place, and we put it up on the rack and had a good look."

This was a long speech for Dawson. I put my checkbook back in my purse and listened, silently asking him if he wanted more Coke by pointing at his glass. He shook his head, letting me know he was satisfied. "We had to tighten up a few things, replace your windshield fluid reservoir. I knew just where another car like yours was at Rusty's Salvage, and it didn't take no time to do the job."

I could only thank him again. I drove Dawson out to his repair shop. Since the last time I'd driven by, he'd trimmed up the front yard of his home, a modest but tidy frame house that stood next door to the big shop. Dawson had also put all the bits and pieces of motorcycles under cover somewhere, instead of having them strewn around in a handy but unattractive spread. And his pickup was clean.

As Dawson slid out of the car, I said, "I'm so grateful. I know cars aren't your specialty and I do appreciate your working on mine." Repairman to the underworld, that was Tray Dawson.

"Well, I did it because I wanted to," Dawson said, and then he paused. "But if you could see your way to it, I'd sure like it if you'd put in a word for me with your friend Amelia."

"I don't have much influence over Amelia," I said. "But I'll be glad to tell her what a sterling character you are."

He smiled very broadly: no suppression there. I didn't think I'd ever seen Dawson crack such a grin. "She sure looks healthy," he said, and since I had no idea what Dawson's criteria for admiration were, that was a big clue.

"You call her up, I'll give a reference," I said.

"It's a deal."

We parted happy, and he loped across the newly neat yard to his shop. I didn't know if Dawson would be to Amelia's taste or not, but I'd do my best to persuade her to give him a chance.

As I drove home, I listened to the car for any strange noise. It purred away.

Amelia and Octavia came in as I was leaving for work.

"How are you feeling?" Amelia said with a knowing air.

"Fine," I said automatically. Then I understood she thought I hadn't come home the night before. She thought I'd been having a good time with someone. "Hey, you remember Tray Dawson, right? You met him at Maria-Star's apartment."

"Sure."

"He's going to call you. Be sweet."

I left her grinning after me as I got into my car.

For once, work was boring and normal. Terry was substituting since Sam hated to work on Sunday afternoons. Merlotte's was having a calm day. We opened late on Sunday and we closed early, so I was ready to start home by seven. No one showed up in the parking lot, and I was able to walk directly to my car without being accosted for a long, weird conversation or being attacked.

The next morning I had errands to run in town. I was short on cash, so I drove to the ATM, waving at Tara Thornton du Rone. Tara smiled and waved back. Marriage was suiting her, and I hoped she and JB were having a happier time of it than my brother and his wife. As I drove away from the bank, to my astonishment I spotted Alcide Herveaux coming out of the offices of Sid Matt Lancaster, an ancient and renowned lawyer. I pulled into Sid Matt's parking lot, and Alcide came over to talk to me.

I should have driven on, hoping he hadn't noticed me.

The conversation was awkward. Alcide had had a lot to deal with, in all fairness. His girlfriend was dead, brutally murdered. Several other members of his pack were also dead. He'd had a huge cover-up to arrange. But he was now the leader of the pack, and he had gotten to celebrate his victory in the traditional way. In hindsight, I suspect he was fairly embarrassed at having sex with a young woman in public, especially so soon after his girlfriend's death. This was quite a bundle of emotions I was reading in his head, and he was flushed when he came to my car window.

"Sookie, I haven't had a chance to thank you for all your help that night. It's lucky for us your boss decided to come with you."

Yeah, since you wouldn't have saved my life and he did, I'm glad, too. "No problem, Alcide," I said, my voice wonderfully even and calm. I was going to have a good day, dammit. "Have things settled down in Shreveport?"

"The police don't seem to have a clue," he said, glancing around to make sure no one else was within hearing distance. "They haven't found the site yet, and there's been a lot of rain. We're hoping sooner rather than later they'll cut back on their investigation."

"You-all still planning the big announcement?"

"It'll have to be soon. The heads of other packs in the area have been in contact with me. We don't have a meeting of all the leaders like the vampires do, mostly because they have one leader for each state and we have a hell of a lot of packleaders. Looks like we'll all elect a representative from the packleaders, one from each state, and those representatives will go to a national meeting."

"That sounds like a step in the right direction."

"Also, we might ask other wereanimals if they want to come in with us. Like, Sam could belong to my pack in an auxiliary way, though he's not a Were. And it would be good if the lone wolves, like Dawson, came to some of the pack parties . . . came out howling with us or something."

"Dawson seems to like his life the way it is," I said. "And you'll have to talk to Sam, not me, about whether he wants to associate with you-all formally."

"Sure. You seem to have a lot of influence with him. Just thought I'd mention it."

I didn't see it that way. Sam had a lot of influence over me, but whether I had any over him . . . I was dubious. Alcide began making the little shifts in stance that told me as clearly as his brain had that he was about to go his way on whatever business had brought him to Bon Temps.

"Alcide," I said, seized by an impulse, "I do have a question."

He said, "Sure."

"Who's taking care of the Furnan children?"

He looked at me, then away. "Libby's sister. She's got three of her own, but she said she was glad to take them in. There's enough money for their upbringing. When it comes time for them to go to college, we'll see what we can do for the boy."

"For the boy?"

"He's pack."

If I'd had a brick in my hand, I wouldn't have minded using it on Alcide. Good God almighty. I took a deep breath. To give him credit, the sex of the child wasn't the issue at all. It was his pure blood.

"There may be enough insurance money for the girl to go, too," Alcide said, since he was no fool. "The aunt wasn't too clear about that, but she knows we'll help."

"And she knows who 'we' is?"

He shook his head. "We told her it was a secret society, like the Masons, that Furnan belonged to."

There didn't seem to be anything left to say.

"Good luck," I said. He'd already had a fair share of that, no matter what you thought about the two dead women that had been his girlfriends. After all, he himself had survived to achieve his father's goal.

"Thank you, and thanks again for your part in that luck. You're still a friend of the pack," he said very seriously. His beautiful green eyes lingered on my face. "And you're one of my favorite women in the world," he added unexpectedly.

"That's a real nice compliment, Alcide," I said, and drove away. I was glad I'd talked to him. Alcide had grown up a lot in the past few weeks. All in all, he was changing into a man I admired much more than I had the old one.

I'd never forget the blood and the screaming of the horrific night in the abandoned office park in Shreveport, but I began to feel that some good had come out of it.

When I returned home, I found that Octavia and Amelia were in the front yard, raking. This was a delightful discovery. I hated raking worse than anything in the world, but if I didn't go over the yard once or twice during the fall, the pine needle buildup was dreadful.

I had been thanking people all day long. I parked in the back and came out the front.

"Do you bag these up or burn them?" Amelia called.

"Oh, I burn 'em when there's not a burn ban on," I said. "It's so nice of you both to think of doing this." I wasn't aiming to gush—but having your very least favorite chore done for you was really quite a treat.

"I need the exercise," Octavia said. "We went to the mall in Monroe yesterday, so I did get some walking in."

I thought Amelia treated Octavia more like a grandmother than a teacher.

"Did Tray call?" I asked.

"He sure did." Amelia smiled broadly.

"He thought you were fine-looking."

Octavia laughed. "Amelia, you're a femme fatale."

She looked happy and said, "I think he's an interesting guy."

"A bit older than you," I said, just so she'd know.

Amelia shrugged. "I don't care. I'm ready to date. I think Pam and I are more buddies than honeys. And since I found that litter of kittens, I'm open for guy business."

"You really think Bob made a choice? Wouldn't that have been, like, instinct?" I said.

Just then, the cat in question wandered across the yard, curious to see why we were all standing out in the open when there was a perfectly good couch and a few beds in the house.

Octavia gave a gusty sigh. "Oh, hell," she muttered. She straightened and held her hands out. *"Potestas mea te in formam veram tuam commutabit natura ips reaffirmet Incantationes praeviae deletae sunt,"* she said.

The cat blinked up at Octavia. Then it made a peculiar noise, a kind of cry I'd never heard come out of a cat's throat before. Suddenly the air around him was thick and dense and cloudy and full of sparks. The cat shrieked again. Amelia was staring at the animal with her mouth wide open. Octavia looked resigned and a little sad.

The cat writhed on the fading grass, and suddenly it had a human leg.

"God almighty!" I said, and clapped a hand over my mouth.

Now it had two legs, two hairy legs, and then it had a penis, and then it began to be a man all over, shrieking all the while. After a horrible two minutes, the witch Bob Jessup lay on the lawn, shaking all over but entirely human again. After another minute, he stopped shrieking and just twitched. Not an improvement, really, but easier on the eardrums.

Then he lunged to his feet, leaped onto Amelia, and made a determined effort to choke her to death.

I grabbed his shoulders to pull him off of her, and Octavia said, "You don't want me to use magic on you again, right?"

That proved a very effective threat. Bob let go of Amelia and stood panting in the cold air. "I can't believe you did that to me!" he said. "I can't believe I spent the last few months as a cat!"

"How do you feel?" I asked. "Are you weak? Do you need help into the house? Would you like some clothes?"

He looked down at himself vaguely. He hadn't worn clothes in a while, but suddenly he turned red, very nearly all over. "Yes," he said stiffly. "Yes, I would like some clothes."

"Come with me," I said. The dusk was coming on as I led Bob into the house. Bob was a smallish guy, and I thought a pair of my sweats might fit him. No, Amelia was a little taller, and a clothes donation from her would be only fair. I spotted the basket full of folded clothes on the stairs where Amelia had left it to carry up the next time she went to her room. Lo and behold, there was an old blue sweatshirt and a pair of black sweat pants. I handed the clothes to Bob wordlessly, and he pulled them on with trembling fingers. I flipped through the stack and found a pair of socks that were plain white. He sat down on the couch to pull them on. That was as far as I could go toward clothing him. His feet were larger than mine or Amelia's, so shoes were out.

Bob wrapped his arms around himself like he feared he was going to disappear. His dark hair was clinging to his skull. He blinked, and I wondered what had happened to his glasses. I hoped Amelia had stored them somewhere.

"Bob, can I get you a drink?" I asked.

"Yes, please," he said. He seemed to be having a bit of trouble getting his mouth to form the words. His hand moved up to his mouth in a curious gesture, and I realized it was just like my cat Tina's movement when she had raised her paw to lick it before she used it to groom herself. Bob realized what he was doing and lowered his hand abruptly.

I thought about bringing him milk in a bowl but decided that would be insulting. I brought him some iced tea instead. He gulped it but made a face.

"Sorry," I said. "I should have asked if you like tea."

"I do like tea," he said, and stared at the glass as if he'd just connected tea with the liquid he'd had in his mouth. "I'm just not used to it anymore."

Okay, I know this is really awful, but I actually opened my mouth to ask him if he wanted some kibble. Amelia had a bag of 9Lives on the back porch shelf. I bit the inside of my mouth, hard. "What about a sandwich?" I asked. I had no idea what to talk to Bob about. Mice?

"Sure," he said. He didn't seem to know what he wanted to do next.

So I made him a peanut butter and jelly, and a ham and pickle on whole wheat with mustard. He ate them both, chewing very slowly and carefully. Then he said, "Excuse me," and got up to find the bathroom. He shut the door behind him, and stayed in there for a long time.

Amelia and Octavia had come in by the time Bob emerged.

"I'm so sorry," Amelia said.

"Me, too," Octavia said. She looked older and smaller.

"You knew all along how to change him?" I tried to keep my voice level and nonjudgmental. "Your failed attempt was a fraud?"

Octavia nodded. "I was scared if you didn't need me, I wouldn't get to visit anymore. I'd have to go stay all day at my niece's. It's so much nicer here. I would have said something soon, because my conscience was bothering me something awful, especially since I'm living here." She shook her gray head from side to side. "I'm a bad woman for letting Bob be a cat for extra days."

Amelia was shocked. Obviously, her teacher's fall from grace was an amazing development to Amelia, clearly overshadowing her own guilt about what she'd done to Bob in the first place. Amelia was definitely a live-in-the-moment kind of person.

Bob came out of the bathroom. He marched up to us. "I want to go back to my place in New Orleans," Bob said. "Where the hell are we? How did I get here?"

Amelia's face lost all its animation. Octavia looked grim. I quietly left the room. It was going to be very unpleasant, the two women telling Bob about Katrina. I didn't want to be around while he tried to process that terrible news on top of everything else he was trying to handle.

I wondered where Bob had lived, if his house or apartment was still standing, if his possessions were somehow intact. If his family was alive. I heard Octavia's voice rising and falling, and then I heard a terrible silence.

Chapter 21

The next day I took Bob to Wal-Mart to purchase some clothes.
Amelia had pressed some money into Bob's hand, and the young
man had accepted it because he had no choice. He could hardly
wait to get away from Amelia. And I couldn't say as how I
blamed him.

As we drove to town, Bob kept blinking around him in
a stunned way. When we entered the store, he went to the
nearest aisle and rubbed his head against the corner. I smiled
brightly at Marcia Albanese, a wealthy older woman who was
on the school board. I hadn't seen her since she'd given Halleigh a wedding shower.

"Who's your friend?" Marcia asked. She was both naturally social and curious. She didn't ask about the head rubbing,
which endeared her to me forever.

"Marcia, this is Bob Jessup, a visitor from out of town," I said, and wished I'd prepared a story. Bob nodded at Marcia with wide eyes and held out his hand. At least he didn't poke her with his head and demand to have his ears scratched. Marcia shook hands and told Bob she was pleased to meet him.

"Thanks, nice to meet you, too," Bob said. Oh, good, he sounded really normal.

"Are you going to be in Bon Temps long, Bob?" Marcia said.

"Oh, God, no," he said. "Excuse me, I have to buy some shoes." And he walked off (very smoothly and sinuously) to the men's shoe aisles. He was wearing a pair of flip-flops Amelia had donated, bright green ones that weren't quite big enough.

Marcia was clearly taken aback, but I really couldn't think of a good explanation. "See you later," I said, and followed in his wake. Bob got some sneakers, some socks, two pairs of pants, two T-shirts, and a jacket, plus some underwear. I asked Bob what he'd like to eat, and he asked me if I could make salmon croquettes.

"I sure can," I said, relieved he'd asked for something so easy, and got the cans of salmon I'd need. He also wanted chocolate pudding, and that was easy enough, too. He left the other menu selections up to me.

We had an early supper that night before I had to leave for work, and Bob seemed really pleased with the croquettes and the pudding. He looked much better, too, since he'd showered and put on his new clothes. He was even speaking to Amelia. I gathered from their conversation that she'd taken him through the websites about Katrina and its survivors, and he'd been in

FROM DEAD TO WORSE

contact with the Red Cross. The family he'd grown up in, his aunt's, had lived in Bay Saint Louis, in southern Mississippi, and we all knew what had happened there.

"What will you do now?" I asked, since I figured he'd had a while to think about it now.

"I've got to go see," he said. "I want to try to find out what happened to my apartment in New Orleans, but my family is more important. And I've got to think of something to tell them, to explain where I've been and why I haven't been in touch."

We were all silent, because that was a puzzler.

"You could tell 'em you were enchanted by an evil witch," Amelia said glumly.

Bob snorted. "They might believe it," he said. "They know I'm not a normal person. But I don't think they'd be able to swallow that it lasted so long. Maybe I'll tell them that I lost my memory. Or that I went to Vegas and got married."

"You contacted them regularly, before Katrina?" I said.

He shrugged. "Every couple of weeks," he said. "I didn't think of us as close. But I would definitely have tried after Katrina. I love them." He looked away for a minute.

We kicked around ideas for a while, but there really wasn't a credible reason he would have been out of touch for so long. Amelia said she was going to buy Bob a bus ticket to Hattiesburg and he would try to find a ride from there into the most affected area so he could track down his people.

Amelia was clearing her conscience by spending money on Bob. I had no issue with that. She should be doing so; and I hoped Bob would find his folks, or at least discover what had happened to them, where they were living now.

Before I left for work, I stood in the doorway of the kitchen for a minute or two, looking at the three of them. I tried to see in Bob what Amelia had seen, the element that had attracted her so powerfully. Bob was thin and not particularly tall, and his inky hair naturally lay flat to his skull. Amelia had unearthed his glasses, and they were black-rimmed and thick. I'd seen every inch of Bob, and I realized Mother Nature had been generous to him in the man-bits department, but surely that wasn't enough to explain Amelia's ardent sexcapades with this guy.

Then Bob laughed, the first time he'd laughed since he'd become human again, and I got it. Bob had white, even teeth and great lips, and when he smiled, there was a kind of sardonic, intellectual sexiness about him.

Mystery solved.

When I got home, he would be gone, so I said good-bye to Bob, thinking I'd never see him again, unless he decided to return to Bon Temps to get revenge on Amelia.

As I drove into town, I wondered if we could get a real cat. After all, we had the litter box and the cat food. I'd ask Amelia and Octavia in a couple of days. That would surely give them time to stop being so antsy about Bob's cat-dom.

Alcide Herveaux was sitting at the bar talking with Sam when I came into the main room ready for work. Odd, him turning up again. I stopped for a second, and then made my feet move again. I managed a nod, and waved to Holly to tell her I was taking over. She held up a finger, indicating she was taking care of one customer's bill, and then she'd be out of there. I got a hello from one woman and a howdy from another man, and I felt instantly comfortable. This was my place, my home away from home.

Jasper Voss wanted another rum and Coke, Catfish wanted a pitcher of beer for himself and his wife and another couple, and one of our alcoholics, Jane Bodehouse, was ready to eat something. She said she didn't care what it was, so I got her the chicken tender basket. Getting Jane to eat at all was a real problem, and I hoped she'd down at least half of the basket. Jane was sitting at the other end of the bar from Alcide, and Sam jerked his head sideways to indicate I should join them. I turned Jane's order in and then I reluctantly went over to them. I leaned on the end of the bar.

"Sookie," Alcide said, nodding to me. "I came to say thank you to Sam."

"Good," I said bluntly.

Alcide nodded, not meeting my eyes.

After a moment the new packleader said, "Now no one will dare to try to encroach. If Priscilla hadn't attacked at the moment she picked, with us all together and aware of the danger we faced as a group, she could have kept us divided and kept picking us off until we'd killed each other."

"So she went crazy and you got lucky," I said.

"We came together because of your talent," Alcide said. "And you'll always be a friend of the pack. So is Sam. Ask us to do a service for you, any time, any place, and we'll be there." He nodded to Sam, put some money on the bar, and left.

Sam said, "Nice to have a favor stashed in the bank, huh?"

I had to smile back. "Yeah, that's a good feeling." In fact, I felt full of good cheer all of a sudden. When I looked at the door, I found out why. Eric was coming in, with Pam beside him. They sat at one of my tables, and I went over, consumed with curiosity. Also exasperation. Couldn't they stay away?

They both ordered TrueBlood, and after I served Jane Bodehouse her chicken basket and Sam warmed up the bottles, I was headed back to their table. Their presence wouldn't have rocked any boats if Arlene and her buddies hadn't been in the bar that night.

They were sneering together in an unmistakable way as I put the bottles in front of Eric and Pam, and I had a hard time maintaining my waitress calm as I asked the two if they wanted mugs with that.

"The bottle will be fine," Eric said. "I may need it to smash some skulls."

If I had been feeling Eric's good cheer, Eric was feeling my anxiety.

"No, no, no," I said almost in a whisper. I knew they could hear me. "Let's have peace. We've had enough war and killing."

"Yes," Pam agreed. "We can save the killing for later."

"I'm happy to see both of you, but I'm having a busy evening," I said. "Are you-all just out barhopping to get new ideas for Fangtasia, or can I do something for you?"

"We can do something for you," Pam said. She smiled at the two guys in the Fellowship of the Sun T-shirts, and since she was a wee bit angry, her fangs were showing. I hoped the sight would subdue them, but since they were assholes without a lick of sense, it inflamed their zeal. Pam downed the blood and licked her lips.

"Pam," I said between my teeth. "For goodness' sake, stop making it worse."

Pam gave me a flirty smile, simply so she'd hit all the buttons.

Eric said, "Pam," and immediately all the provocation disappeared, though Pam looked a little disappointed. But she sat up straighter, put her hands in her lap, and crossed her legs at the ankle. No one could have looked more innocent or demure.

"Thank you," Eric said. "Dear one—that's you, Sookie—you so impressed Felipe de Castro that he has given us permission to offer you our formal protection. This is a decision only made by the king, you understand, and it's a binding contract. You rendered him such service that he felt this was the only way to repay you."

"So, this is a big deal?"

"Yes, my lover, it is a very big deal. That means when you call us for help, we are obliged to come and risk our lives for yours. This is not a promise vampires make very often, since we grow more and more jealous of our lives the longer we live. You'd think it would be the other way around."

"Every now and then you'll find someone who wants to meet the sun after a long life," Pam said, as if she wanted to set the record straight.

"Yes," Eric said, frowning. "Every now and then. But he offers you a real honor, Sookie."

"I'm real obliged to you for bringing the news, Eric, Pam."

"Of course, I'd hoped your beautiful roommate would come in," Pam said. She leered at me. So maybe her hanging around Amelia hadn't been entirely Eric's idea.

I laughed out loud. "Well, she's got a lot to think about tonight," I said.

I'd been thinking so hard about the vampire protection that I hadn't noticed the approach of the shorter of the FotS adherants. Now he pushed past me in such a way that he rammed my shoulder, deliberately knocking me to the side. I staggered before I managed to regain my balance. Not everyone noticed, but a few of the bar patrons did. Sam had started around the bar and Eric was already on his feet when I turned and brought my tray down on the asshole's head with all the strength I could muster.

He did a little bit of staggering himself.

Those that had noticed the bit of aggravation began applauding. "Good for you, Sookie," Catfish called. "Hey, jerkoff, leave the waitresses alone."

Arlene was flushed and angry, and she almost exploded then and there. Sam stepped up to her and murmured something in her ear. She flushed even redder and glared at him, but she kept her mouth shut. The taller FotS guy came to his pal's aid and they left the bar. Neither of them spoke (I wasn't sure Shorty *could* speak), but they might as well have had "You haven't seen the last of us" tattooed on their foreheads.

I could see where the vampires' protection and my friend of the pack status might come in handy.

Eric and Pam finished their drinks and sat long enough to prove they weren't skedaddling because they felt unwelcome and weren't leaving in pursuit of the Fellowship fans. Eric tipped me a twenty and blew me a kiss as he went out the door—so did Pam—earning me an extra-special glare from my former BFF Arlene.

I worked too hard the rest of the night to think about any of the interesting things that had happened that day. After the patrons all left, even Jane Bodehouse (her son came to get her), we put out the Halloween decorations. Sam had gotten a little pumpkin for each table and painted a face on each one. I was filled with admiration, because the faces were really clever, and some of them looked like bar patrons. In fact, one looked a lot like my dear brother.

"I had no idea you could do this," I said, and he looked pleased.

"It was fun," he said, and hung a long strand of fall leaves—of course, they were actually made of cloth—around the bar mirror and among some of the bottles. I tacked up a life-size cardboard skeleton with little rivets at the joints so it could be positioned. I arranged this one so it was clearly dancing. We couldn't have any depressing skeletons at the bar. We had to have happy ones.

Even Arlene unbent a little because this was something different and fun to do, though we had to stay a bit later to do it.

I was ready to go home and go to bed when I said good night to Sam and Arlene. Arlene didn't answer, but she didn't throw me the look of disgust she usually awarded me, either.

Naturally, my day wasn't over.

My great-grandfather was sitting on my front porch when

I got to the house. It was very strange to see him in the front porch swing, in the odd combination of night and light that the security lamp and the dark hour combined to create. I wished for one moment that I was as beautiful as he was, and then I had to smile at myself.

I parked my car in the front and got out. Tried to walk quietly going up the steps so I wouldn't wake Amelia, whose bedroom overlooked the front. The house was dark, so I was sure they were in bed, unless they'd been delayed at the bus station when they delivered Bob.

"Great-grandfather," I said. "I'm glad to see you."

"You're tired, Sookie."

"Well, I just got off work." I wondered if he ever got tired himself. I couldn't imagine a fairy prince splitting wood or trying to find a leak in his water line.

"I wanted to see you," he said. "Have you thought of anything I can do for you?" He sounded mighty hopeful.

What a night this was for people giving me positive feedback. Why didn't I have more nights like this?

I thought for a minute. The Weres had made peace, in their own way. Quinn had been found. The vampires had settled into a new regime. The Fellowship fanatics had left the bar with a minimum of trouble. Bob was a man again. I didn't suppose Niall wanted to offer Octavia a room in his own house, wherever that might be. For all I knew, he had a house in a babbling brook or under a live oak somewhere deep in the woods.

"There is something I want," I said, surprised I hadn't thought of it before.

"What is it?" he asked, sounding quite pleased.

"I want to know the whereabouts of a man named Remy Savoy. He may have left New Orleans during Katrina. He may have a little child with him." I gave my great-grandfather Savoy's last known address.

Niall looked confident. "I'll find him for you, Sookie."

"I'd sure appreciate it."

"Nothing else? Nothing more?"

"I have to say...this sounds mighty ungracious...but I can't help but wonder why you seem to want to do something for me so badly."

"Why would I not? You are my only living kin."

"But you seem to have been content without me for the first twenty-seven years of my life."

"My son would not let me come near you."

"You told me that, but I don't get it. Why? He didn't make an appearance to let me know he cared anything about me. He never showed himself to me, or..." Played Scrabble with me, sent me a graduation present, rented a limousine for me to go to the prom, bought me a pretty dress, took me in his arms on the many occasions when I'd cried (growing up isn't easy for a telepath). He hadn't saved me from being molested by my great-uncle, or rescued my parents, one of whom was his son, when they drowned in a flash flood, or stopped a vampire from setting my house on fire while I was sleeping inside. All this guarding and watching my alleged grandfather Fintan had allegedly done had not paid off in any tangible way for me; and if it had paid off intangibly, I didn't know about it.

Would even worse things have happened? Hard to imagine.

I supposed my grandfather could have been fighting off hordes of slavering demons outside my bedroom window every night, but I couldn't feel grateful if I didn't know about it.

Niall looked upset, which was an expression I'd never seen him wear before. "There are things I can't tell you," he finally said. "When I can make myself speak of them, I will."

"Okay," I said dryly. "But this isn't exactly the give-and-take thing I wanted to have with my great-grandfather, I got to say. This is me telling you everything, and you telling me nothing."

"This may not be what you wanted, but it's what I can give," Niall said with some stiffness. "I do love you, and I had hoped that would be what mattered."

"I'm glad to hear you love me," I said very slowly, because I didn't want to risk seeing him walk away from Demanding Sookie. "But acting like it would be even better."

"I don't act as though I love you?"

"You vanish and reappear when it suits you. All your offers of help aren't help of the practical kind, like the stuff most grandfathers—or great-grandfathers—do. They fix their granddaughter's car with their own hands, or they offer to help with her college tuition, or they mow her lawn so she doesn't have to. Or they take her hunting. You're not going to do that."

"No," he said. "I'm not." A ghost of a smile crossed his face. "You wouldn't want to go hunting with me."

Okay, I wasn't going to think about that too closely. "So, I don't have any idea of how we're supposed to be together. You're outside my frame of reference."

"I understand," he said seriously. "All the great-grandfathers you know are human, and that I am not. You're not what I expected, either."

"Yeah, I got that." Did I even know any other great-grandfathers? Among friends my own age, even grandfathers were not a sure thing, much less great-grandfathers. But the ones I'd met were all 100 percent human. "I hope I'm not a disappointment," I said.

"No," he said slowly. "A surprise. Not a disappointment. I'm as poor at predicting your actions and reactions as you are at predicting mine. We'll have to work through this slowly." I found myself wondering again why he wasn't more interested in Jason, whose name activated an ache deep inside me. Someday soon I was going to have to talk to my brother, but I couldn't face the idea now. I almost asked Niall to check on Jason, but then I changed my mind and kept silent. Niall eyed my face.

"You don't want to tell me something, Sookie. I worry when you do that. But my love is sincere and deep, and I'll find Remy Savoy for you." He kissed me on the cheek. "You smell like my kin," he said approvingly.

And he poofed.

So, another mysterious conversation with my mysterious great-grandfather had been concluded by him on his own terms. Again. I sighed, fished my keys out of my purse, and unlocked the front door. The house was quiet and dark, and I made my way through the living room and into the hall with as little noise as I could make. I turned on my bedside lamp and performed my nightly routine, curtains closed against the morning sun that would try to wake me in a few short hours.

Had I been an ungrateful bitch to my great-grandfather? When I reviewed what I'd said, I wondered if I'd sounded demanding and whiney. In a more optimistic interpretation, I thought I might have sounded like a stand-up woman, the kind people shouldn't mess with, the kind of woman who speaks her mind.

I turned on the heat before I got into bed. Octavia and Amelia hadn't complained, but it had definitely been chilly the past few mornings. The stale smell that always comes when the heat is used the first time filled the air, and I wrinkled my nose as I snuggled under the sheet and the blanket. Then the *whoosh* noise lulled me into sleep.

I'd been hearing voices for some time before I realized they were outside my door. I blinked, saw it was day, and shut my eyes again. Back to sleep. The voices continued, and I could tell they were arguing. I cracked open one eye to peer at the digital clock on the bedside table. It was nine thirty. Gack. Since the voices wouldn't shut up or go away, I reluctantly opened both eyes at one time, absorbed the fact that the day was not bright, and sat up, pushing the covers back. I moved to the window to the left of the bed and looked out. Gray and rainy. As I stood there, drops began to hit the glass; it was going to be that kind of day.

I went to the bathroom and heard the voices outside hush

now that I was clearly up and stirring. I threw open the door to find my two housemates standing right outside, which was no big surprise.

"We didn't know if we should wake you," Octavia said. She looked anxious.

"But I thought we ought to, because a message from a magical source is clearly important," Amelia said. She appeared to have said it many times in the past few minutes, from the expression on Octavia's face.

"What message?" I asked, deciding to ignore the argument part of this conversation.

"This one," Octavia said, handing me a large buff envelope. It was made of heavy paper, like a super-fancy wedding invitation. My name was on the outside. No address, just my name. Furthermore, it was sealed with wax. The imprint in the wax was the head of a unicorn.

"Okey-dokey," I said. This was going to be an unusual letter.

I walked into the kitchen to get a cup of coffee and a knife, in that order, both the witches trailing behind me like a Greek chorus. Having poured the coffee and pulled out a chair to sit at the table, I slid the knife under the seal and detached it gently. I opened the flap and pulled out a card. On the card was a handwritten address: 1245 Bienville, Red Ditch, Louisiana. That was all.

"What does it mean?" Octavia said. She and Amelia were naturally standing right behind me so they could get a good view.

"It's the location of someone I've been searching for," I said, which was not exactly the truth but close enough.

"Where's Red Ditch?" Octavia said. "I've never heard of it." Amelia was already fetching the Louisiana map from the drawer under the telephone. She looked up the town, running her finger down the columns of names.

"It's not too far," she said. "See?" She put her finger on a tiny dot about an hour and a half's drive southeast of Bon Temps.

I drank my coffee as fast as I could and scrambled into some jeans. I slapped a little makeup on and brushed my hair and headed out the front door to my car, map in hand.

Octavia and Amelia followed me out, dying to know what I was going to do and what significance the message had for me. But they were just going to have to wonder, at least for right now. I wondered why I was in such a hurry to do this. It wasn't like he was going to vanish, unless Remy Savoy was a fairy, too. I thought that highly unlikely.

I had to be back for the evening shift, but I had plenty of time.

I drove with the radio on, and this morning I was in a country-and-western kind of mood. Travis Tritt and Carrie Underwood accompanied me, and by the time I drove into Red Ditch, I was feeling my roots. There was even less to Red Ditch than there was to Bon Temps, and that's saying something.

I figured it would be easy to find Bienville Street, and I was right. It was the kind of street you can find anywhere in America. The houses were small, neat, boxy, with room for one car in the carport and a small yard. In the case of 1245, the backyard was fenced in and I could see a lively little black dog running around. There wasn't a doghouse, so the pooch was an indoor-outdoor animal. Everything was neat, but not obsessively so. The bushes around the house were trimmed and the yard was raked. I drove by a couple of times, and then I wondered what I was going to do. How would I find out what I wanted to know?

There was a pickup truck parked in the garage, so Savoy was probably at home. I took a deep breath, parked across from the house, and tried to send my extra ability hunting. But in a neighborhood full of the thoughts of the living people in these houses, it was hard. I thought I was getting two brain signatures from the house I was watching, but it was hard to be absolutely sure.

"Fuck it," I said, and got out of the car. I popped my keys in my jacket pocket and went up the sidewalk to the front door. I knocked.

"Hold on, son," said a man's voice inside, and I heard a child's voice say, "Daddy, me! I get it!"

"No, Hunter," the man said, and the door opened. He was looking at me through a screen door. He unhooked it and pushed it open when he saw I was a woman. "Hi," he said. "Can I help you?"

I looked down at the child who wiggled past him to look up at me. He was maybe four years old. He had dark hair and eyes. He was the spitting image of Hadley. Then I looked at the man again. Something in his face had changed during my protracted silence.

"Who are you?" he said in an entirely different voice.

"I'm Sookie Stackhouse," I said. I couldn't think of any artful way to do this. "I'm Hadley's cousin. I just found out where you were."

"You can't have any claim on him," said the man, keeping a very tight rein on his voice.

"Of course not," I said, surprised. "I just want to meet him. I don't have much family."

There was another significant pause. He was weighing my words and my demeanor and he was deciding whether to slam the door or let me in.

"Daddy, she's pretty," said the boy, and that seemed to tip the balance in my favor.

"Come on in," Hadley's ex-husband said.

I looked around the small living room, which had a couch and a recliner, a television and a bookcase full of DVDs and children's books, and a scattering of toys.

"I worked Saturday, so I have today off," he said, in case I imagined he was unemployed. "Oh, I'm Remy Savoy. I guess you knew that."

I nodded.

"This is Hunter," he said, and the child got a case of the shys. He hid behind his father's legs and peeked around at me. "Please sit down," Remy added.

I shoved a newspaper to one end of the couch and sat, trying not to stare at the man or the child. My cousin Hadley had been very striking, and she'd married a good-looking man. It was hard to peg down what left that impression. His nose was big, his jaw stuck out a little, and his eyes were a little wide-spaced. But the sum of all this was a man most women would look at twice. His hair was that medium shade between blond and brown, and it was thick and layered, the back hanging over his collar. He was wearing a flannel shirt unbuttoned over a white Hanes T-shirt. Jeans. No shoes. A dimple in his chin.

Hunter was wearing corduroy pants and a sweatshirt with a big football on the front. His clothes were brand-new, unlike his dad's.

I'd finished looking at them before Remy'd finished looking at me. He didn't think I had any trace of Hadley in my face. My body was plumper and my coloring was lighter and I wasn't as hard. He thought I looked like I didn't have a lot of money. He thought I was pretty, like his son did. But he didn't trust me.

"How long has it been since you heard from her?" I asked.

"I haven't heard from Hadley since a few months after he was born," Remy said. He was used to that, but there was sadness in his thoughts, too.

Hunter was sitting on the floor, playing with some trucks. He loaded some Duplos into the back of a dump truck, which backed up to a fire engine very slowly, guided by Hunter's small hands. To the astonishment of the Duplo man sitting in the cab of the fire engines, the dump truck let go of its load all over the fire engine. Hunter got a big kick out of this, and he said, "Daddy, look!"

"I see it, son." Remy looked at me intently. "Why are you here?" he asked, deciding to get right to the point.

"I only found out there might be a baby a couple of weeks ago," I said. "Wasn't any point in tracking you down until I heard that."

"I never met her family," he said. "How'd you know she was married? Did she tell you?" Then, reluctantly, he said, "Is she okay?"

"No," I said very quietly. I didn't want Hunter to become interested. The boy was loading all the Duplos back into the dump truck. "She's been dead since before Katrina."

I could hear the shock detonate like a little bomb in his head. "She was already a vamp, I heard," he said uncertainly, his voice wavering. "That kind of dead?"

"No. I mean really, finally."

"What happened?"

"She was attacked by another vampire," I said. "He was jealous of Hadley's relationship with her, ah, her . . ."

"Girlfriend?" No mistaking the bitterness in her ex-husband's voice and in his head.

"Yeah."

"That was a shocker," he said, but in his head all the shock had worn off. There was only a grim resignation, a loss of pride.

"I didn't know about any of this until after she passed."

"You're her cousin? I remember her telling me she had two. . . . You got a brother, right?"

"Yes," I said.

"You knew she had been married to me?"

"I found out when I cleaned out her safe-deposit box a few weeks ago. I didn't know there had been a son. I apologize for that." I wasn't sure why I was apologizing or how I could have known, but I was sorry I hadn't even considered the fact that Hadley and her husband might have had a child. Hadley had been a little older than me, and I guessed Remy was probably thirty or thereabouts.

"You look fine," he said suddenly, and I flushed, understanding him instantly.

"Hadley told you I had a disability." I looked away from him, at the boy, who jumped to his feet, announced he had to go to the bathroom, and dashed out of the room. I couldn't help but smile.

"Yeah, she said something. . . . She said you had a hard time of it in school," he said tactfully. Hadley had told him I was crazy as hell. He was seeing no signs of it, and he wondered why Hadley had thought so. But he glanced in the direction the child had gone, and I knew he was thinking he had to be careful since Hunter was in the house, he had to be alert for any signs of this instability—though Hadley had never specified what form of craziness I had.

"That's true," I said. "I had a hard time of it. Hadley wasn't any big help. But her mom, my aunt Linda, was a great woman before the cancer got her. She was real kind to me, always. And we had some good moments now and then."

"I could say the same. We did have some good moments," Remy said. His forearms were braced on his knees and his big hands, scarred and battered, hung down. He was a man who knew what hard work was.

There was a sound at the front door and a woman came in without bothering to knock. "Hey, baby," she said, smiling at Remy. When she noticed me, her smile faltered and faded away.

"Kristen, this is a relative of my ex-wife's," Remy said, and there wasn't any haste or apology in his voice.

Kristen had long brown hair and big brown eyes and she was maybe twenty-five. She was wearing khakis and a polo shirt with a logo on the chest, a laughing duck. The legend above the duck read, "Jerry's Detailing." "Nice to meet you," Kristen said insincerely. "I'm Kristen Duchesne, Remy's girlfriend."

"Pleased to meet you," I said, more honestly. "Sookie Stackhouse."

"You didn't offer this woman a drink, Remy! Sookie, can I get you a Coke or a Sprite?"

She knew what was in the refrigerator. I wondered if she lived here. Well, none of my business, as long as she was good to Hadley's son.

"No, thanks," I said. "I've got to be going in a minute." I made a little production out of looking at my watch. "I got to go to work this evening."

"Oh, where is that?" Kristen asked. She was a little more relaxed.

"Merlotte's. It's a bar in Bon Temps," I said. "About eighty miles from here."

"Sure, that's where your wife was from," Kristen said, glancing at Remy.

Remy said, "Sookie came with some news, I'm afraid." His hands twisted together, though his voice was steady. "Hadley is dead."

Kristen inhaled sharply but she had to keep her comment

to herself because Hunter dashed back into the room. "Daddy, I washed my hands!" he shouted, and his father smiled at him.

"Good for you, son," he said, and ruffled the boy's dark hair. "Say hello to Kristen."

"Hey, Kristen," Hunter said without much interest.

I stood. I wished I had a business card to leave. This seemed odd and wrong, to just walk out. But Kristen's presence was oddly inhibiting. She picked up Hunter and slung him on her hip. He was quite a load for her, but she made a point of making it look easy and habitual, though it wasn't. But she did like the little boy; I could see it in her head.

"Kristen likes me," Hunter said, and I looked at him sharply.

"Sure I do," Kristen said, and laughed.

Remy was looking from Hunter to me with a troubled face, a face that was just beginning to look worried.

I wondered how to explain our relationship to Hunter. I was pretty close to being his aunt, as we reckon things here. Kids don't care about second cousins.

"Aunt Sookie," Hunter said, testing the words. "I got an aunt?"

I took a deep breath. *Yes, you do, Hunter,* I thought.

"I never had one before."

"You got one now," I told him, and I looked into Remy's eyes. They were frightened. He hadn't spelled it out to himself yet, but he knew.

There was something I had to say to him, regardless of Kristen's presence. I could feel her confusion and her sense that something was going on without her knowledge. But I didn't have the space on my agenda to worry about Kristen, too. Hunter was the important person.

"You're gonna need me," I told Remy. "When he gets a little older, you're gonna need to talk. My number's in the book, and I'm not going anywhere. You understand?"

Kristen said, "What's going on? Why are we getting so serious?"

"Don't worry, Kris," Remy said gently. "Just family stuff."

Kristen lowered a wriggling Hunter to the floor. "Uh-huh," she said, in the tone of someone who knows full well she's having the wool pulled over her eyes.

"Stackhouse," I reminded Remy. "Don't put it off till too late, when he's already miserable."

"I understand," he said. He looked miserable himself, and I didn't blame him.

"I've got to go," I said again, to reassure Kristen.

"Aunt Sookie, you going?" Hunter asked. He wasn't quite ready to hug me yet, but he thought about it. He liked me. "You coming back?"

"Sometime, Hunter," I said. "Maybe your dad will bring you to visit me someday."

I shook Kristen's hand, shook Remy's, which they both thought was odd, and opened the door. As I put one foot on the steps, Hunter said silently, *Bye, Aunt Sookie.*

Bye, Hunter, I said right back.